"So

"I'm … oing to phra… e a wild anim… ? To make him look like a city slicker? "I'm here to make sure he has everything he needs to fit back in."

"Clothes?"

"Yes."

"Haircut? Manicure, that kind of thing?"

"Yes, of course." Perry felt suddenly rather embarrassed at his own perfectly manicured hands.

"But nae makeup?" Lisa asked.

"Well, yes if it's needed. At least for the cameras—"

But Perry never got the chance to finish his explanation. Lisa looked at Bridie, and they both burst into laughter.

"And if he doesnae want all that?"

For the first time, Perry felt in a truly alien setting. "It's quite usual in the media world."

"I'm sure it is," Bridie said. "But this is Greg Ventura we're talking about. The man who hasn't bought new clothes for a year, who doesn't have a decent mirror in his house. The man who thinks he's barely one step up in looks from Willie Aitken's pigs."

Welcome to

Dreamspun Desires

Dear Reader,

Love is the dream. It dazzles us, makes us stronger, and brings us to our knees. Dreamspun Desires tell stories of love featuring your favorite heartwarming heroes, captivating plots, and exotic locations. Stories that make your breath catch and your imagination soar.

In the pages of these wonderful love stories, readers can escape to a world where love conquers all, the tenderness of a first kiss sweeps you away, and your heart pounds at the sight of the one you love.

When you put it all together, you find romance in its truest form.

Love always finds a way.

Elizabeth North

Executive Director
Dreamspinner Press

Clare London

Romancing the Ugly Duckling

Dreamspun Desires

Published by

Dreamspinner Press

Published by
DREAMSPINNER PRESS

5032 Capital Circle SW, Suite 2, PMB# 279,
Tallahassee, FL 32305-7886 USA
www.dreamspinnerpress.com

ISBN: 978-1-63533-386-2
Digital ISBN: 978-1-63533-387-9
Library of Congress Control Number: 2016915797
Published June 2017
v. 1.0

Printed in the United States of America
∞
This paper meets the requirements of
ANSI/NISO Z39.48-1992 (Permanence of Paper).

CLARE LONDON took her pen name from the city where she lives, loves, and writes. A lone, brave female in a frenetic, testosterone-fueled family home, she juggles her writing with her other day job as an accountant.

She's written in many genres and across many settings, with award-winning novels and short stories published both online and in print. She says she likes variety in her writing while friends say she's just fickle, but as long as both theories spawn good fiction, she's happy. Most of her work features male/male romance and drama with a healthy serving of physical passion, as she enjoys both reading and writing about strong, sympathetic, and sexy characters.

Clare currently has several novels sulking at that tricky chapter-three stage and plenty of other projects in mind… she just has to find out where she left them in that frenetic, testosterone-fueled family home.

Clare loves to hear from readers, and you can contact her here:

Website: www.clarelondon.com
E-mail: clarelondon11@yahoo.co.uk
Blog: www.clarelondon.com/blog
Facebook: www.facebook.com/clarelondon
Twitter: @clare_london
Goodreads: www.goodreads.com/clarelondon
Amazon: www.amazon.com/author/clarelondon

By Clare London

Romancing the Wrong Twin
Romancing the Ugly Duckling

Published by **DREAMSPINNER PRESS**
www.dreamspinnerpress.com

Chapter One

SOMEWHERE along the line, at some distant, unremembered stage of a previous life, Perry Goodwood must have done something *really* good. His too small but tastefully decorated office in the Latham Agency, London, was currently full of men. Tall, dark-haired, dancing-eyed, perfectly groomed, shirt-straining-torso'd men. Four of them. *Brothers*, no less.

He hadn't seen such a fine selection of male gorgeousness since he was a young gay teenager with copies of *Men's Health* secreted under his mattress. And even then, the gorgeousness had been static, easily creased, and with eyes only for the camera. Today's exhibition was nothing remotely like that titillating but ultimately unsatisfying experience of his youth. This was, quite honestly, a lusty heaven come to life—and it was all happening in *his* office! Perry Goodwood, lowly assistant fashion designer, occasional actor/model, and makeover consultant to several TV stars. Well, B-list ones, at least. Admittedly, Perry's personal client portfolio—and any further plans for developing worldwide domination—was still a work in progress.

But someone, somewhere, had recommended his services to this astonishing group of Adonises. If Perry hadn't known that person was his rather creepy boss, Eddy Latham, he'd have offered to love them forever.

"So, Mr. Goodwood, can you help us?"

Perry blinked hard. Someone was talking to him. One of the gorgeous *brothers* was talking to him. The one who seemed older and in charge of the group. He was staring at Perry with earnest dark eyes. An errant curl teased his forehead, and the beautifully trimmed beard brushed his strong, manly jaw like a caress.

Perry's lower lip wobbled with excitement.

"It's a matter of total discretion, of course," the man continued. "My family can trust you on that, I'm sure."

Perry hadn't matched all the other names to the faces, partly because they all began with the initial G, and partly because his brain had shorted out after the third firm, warm, crushing handshake. But he recognized this hero at least. Geoffrey Ventura, Premier League footballer for the last ten years, with a hallowed place in the England squad for the last five, though Perry would've been hard-pressed to name the tournaments as he never watched football, just the footballers. But Geoff Ventura was also a darling of the press, one of the wittiest and most quoted sports celebrities in the media, and eldest sibling of a family notable for its testosterone-fueled sportsmen and their glamorous social partners.

Perry had suffered crushes on many a straight man in his time, but he didn't dare admit that, in his teens, he'd had a picture of rising star Geoff Ventura under his bed. And now the man himself was here. In Perry's office.

Heavens, you already know all this. Get a grip, Perry!

"Of course you can trust me," Perry said. "We pride ourselves at the Latham Agency in delivering what our client wants in a professional and discreet way." God, he sounded like he was reading from the glossy brochure.

"Mr. Latham told us we could rely on you," Geoff said. "I'm so reassured."

That was amazing in itself. Perry couldn't remember the last time Eddy Latham, the owner of the PR agency, had been that positive about Perry's career prospects. Eddy wasn't the world's best at staff motivation. But for the moment, Perry's cynicism was squashed by the glow from Greg Ventura's praise. "I'll certainly do my best for you. What is it exactly you need?"

"It's not us who needs it," said another brother at Geoff's shoulder.

Perry had placed all the other Venturas by now. This slightly more scowly one was Gerry, ex-university rower and now something Big in City Finance. He'd married a supermodel who was purportedly related to the ill-fated Russian royal family, if *Who's Doing Who?* was to be believed. It was the magazine of choice in the agency staff room, bought and pored over religiously every week by Perry's friend and colleague, Antony.

"Gerry's right," Geoff said. He looked slightly uncomfortable. "We need your help for our brother Greg."

Perry didn't remember a fifth brother in any of the celebrity interviews. "There's another one like you?"

Gerry Ventura snorted.

"Gerry, please," Geoff said warningly.

"Greg didn't want to be part of the family, Geoff. He's the one who scarpered off as soon as he was old enough, didn't he? Don't see why we're chasing after him now."

"He ran off?" Perry was having trouble keeping up, let alone understanding what it had to do with him.

"Greg lives elsewhere," Geoff said smoothly.

"Fucking middle of nowhere," Gerry muttered.

"But he's still family," contributed one of the remaining two brothers. They looked a few years younger than the others, just as well-dressed but considerably livelier, and more alike in the flesh than in photos, which was to be expected as they were the twins, George and Gareth. They'd both had short-lived but controversial careers in movies, and now had investments in a long list of London nightclubs. Lived most of their lives in those establishments too, as Perry recalled from media gossip.

"And that's the point, isn't it?" said the other twin. The two of them rocked back on their heels, crossing their arms and presenting a brace of smug, mirror-image grins.

Perry looked to Geoff for guidance. "The point…?" He only had two seats in his office, which he'd offered to Geoff and Gerry at the start, then taken Gerry's seat himself because Gerry hadn't seemed to want to settle. He now stood with the twins, all of them ranged behind Geoff like an imperial guard protecting their emperor.

Geoff leaned forward in his chair, reaching out a beautifully manicured hand to grasp Perry's, as if they were the only people in the world. The one thing that saved Perry's head from being turned by this personal attention—and it threatened to set him spinning more than that poor girl in *The Exorcist*—was that he remembered seeing Geoff use this tactic before in a TV interview.

"You see, Perry," Geoff said in his smooth, very persuasive way, "we have a commitment. A media contract."

"A potential contract," Gerry snapped.

Geoff's shoulders tensed but otherwise he ignored his brother, his gaze still fixed on Perry. "Yes, it's still potential at this delicate stage of the negotiations. And it's contingent on the whole family being involved—all the brothers. We all need to be available, and together."

Perry nodded slowly. Things were becoming clearer. "And your brother Greg isn't with you?"

Gerry snorted again. "Not in any bloody way."

Geoff bit his lip as if restraining his temper with difficulty. "Certainly not in terms of location. And not… well, not in his lifestyle choices either. That's why we've come to Latham's Agency. Greg needs to be back here in London with us—and looking his very best—by the end of next month to sign the deal."

"It's all or nothing," said Twin #1.

"All for one and one for all!" added Twin #2 gleefully. He turned to Twin #1, and they high-fived each other.

"Bloody kids," Gerry muttered.

Perry was still floundering a bit, but before he could ask any more questions, his boss stuck his head around the door. "Everything going well?" he asked with loud, blustering, and rather insincere jollity.

Perry resisted rolling his eyes. At times like this, Eddy Latham was the worst kind of boss, in that he wanted to be in on all the projects but was never prepared to do any of the work. "Everything's fine, Mr. Latham."

Unfortunately that wasn't enough incentive for Eddy to withdraw. Instead he eased himself into the room with the other five men, taking up a position beside Perry's chair. Eddy was only five foot six, but about the same measurements around the middle. As the Venturas took several steps to the side to accommodate him, Perry couldn't help comparing it to a rush-hour commuter jumping onto the train just as it pulled away and squeezing everyone else along inside the carriage.

"As I suggested, Peregrine's your man," Eddy said confidently. He was the only person who ever used Perry's full name. "He launched Mandy Price, the glamor model turned TV presenter. And Professor Ignatius Froome, that academic who never brushed his hair or cleaned his teeth before Peregrine took him in hand. I'm sure you remember them both? The makeovers were impressive. My agency's credentials speak for themselves."

Unfortunately, Perry remembered both of those obstreperous clients with nothing less than horror. He'd long suspected Eddy passed all the lost causes to Perry so that if Perry succeeded, the agency would benefit, but if he failed to deliver the makeover—well, it'd be Perry's fault alone. This wasn't going to be one of *those* jobs, was it?

Geoff Ventura glanced at Perry. "This is far more than a cosmetic job."

"I can do far more than a cosmetic job," Perry said smartly.

A small smile twitched at the edge of Geoff's lips. "Yes, I'm sure you can."

"Geoff, you're not serious?" Gerry snapped. "This can't work."

Geoff frowned at his brother. "We have no other choice."

"Rubbish! I say we negotiate without Greg."

Geoff shook his head. "They won't agree to that. I've tried. It's all or none of us."

"No fucking way." Gerry's face grew darker. "They won't go with the Howells instead of us. They wouldn't be that stupid. A bunch of ponced-up shop boys and girls without an ounce of genuine talent between them? With us, they have real celebrity. We've all succeeded in our own field. We have true credibility. The public loves us."

Perry's ears pricked up. The Howells were another celebrity family from south London, and always in the popular media. They consisted of three wannabe supermodels, a loud-mouthed matriarch, and several young men with impossibly white teeth, and Perry followed their exploits avidly. Well, he *was* gay. And only human. In fact, it had been his mischief that renamed them in the office as the Howlers.

Geoff shrugged, but his expression had hardened. "The public loves them too. It's what the media does, Gerry. Chooses what makes the best TV, regardless of merit."

Perry leaned surreptitiously toward the twins, speaking half under his breath. "Are we talking about a TV deal here?"

Twin#1—possibly George—nodded vigorously. "A reality show series. You know, like the Kardashians? It'd be really big. The production company wants to feature a London family."

Gareth joined in. "They approached both us and the Howells, and they're filming simultaneous pilot episodes next month."

"A day in the life," George said breathlessly.

"Warts and all!" Gareth followed with a deep chuckle, though only he and George seemed to be finding this whole thing funny.

In fact, Gerry's face was like thunder as he leaned over to hiss at Geoff. "We need this show, you hear me?"

"Things not so rosy in the financial garden? I hear you've been overtrading in some of your more bullish deals," Geoff said snidely.

"Don't get high and mighty with me. *I* hear you haven't been chosen for the first team squad this season, so you'll be needing another income as well."

"For God's sake—!"

"Gentlemen, please!" Eddy cried, flapping his hands as if to cool them all down.

"I'm just saying that this is an opportunity we don't want to miss," Gerry growled, still glaring at Geoff. "And it's critical we all look good—that we all look *civilized*. We've got a reputation to maintain."

"Even Greg?" Geoff said tightly.

"Especially Greg," Gerry snapped.

The room fell silent for a moment. Geoff looked weary, Gerry still glared, and the twins tried, unsuccessfully in Perry's opinion, to look innocent of everything.

Perry asked tentatively, "About your brother Greg. Can you give me any idea what I'd be working with?"

"Go on," Gerry said to Geoff. "Show him."

With a low sigh, Geoff pulled out a photo from his jacket's inner pocket and handed it to Perry.

The first surprise was that the photo was of a teenage boy rather than a man. Wasn't Greg Ventura an adult like his brothers? It looked like an old photograph too: something about the fuzzy quality of the print. The boy was in the foreground, leaning back against a wooden fence in a field, scowling at the camera as if he wanted to attack it with the heavy spade he gripped in one hand. Perry could see his resemblance to the other Ventura brothers in his square jaw and smoldering eyes, but the similarity ended there. He had none of their rugged, elegantly styled good looks. He was tall and broad, but his limbs looked too large for his body, obvious in the clumsy way he slouched against the fence. His dark hair was all over the place, badly cut with lank tangles brushing his shoulders and hanging over his forehead. The clothes didn't do much to help either. His jeans were patched in several places, and worn and stained over the knees. And in Perry's opinion, a faded flannel shirt was rarely a good look on such a young man. Was that dirt on the rolled-up sleeve, or something worse? Perry gave a private shudder.

The worst thing was the acne. Poor kid was covered with it, from chin to forehead, what Perry could see of his skin under the thatch of hair. No wonder he tried to hide his face. His nose was big in proportion to his cheeks, his eyes very widely spaced. That generous mouth might have been attractive in a smile, but instead it was twisted in a weirdly uneven and unpleasant scowl.

"Um. What is he… twelve? Thirteen?" Perry asked.

"Twenty-five at the moment," George said with a grin.

"Nearly twenty-six," Gareth added. "His birthday is in two months' time."

"But this photo—"

"It's the only one I could find," Geoff said shortly. For a brief moment, he looked pained. "That's him at our uncle's farm in Hampshire. We used to spend school holidays there."

"Ghastly place," Gerry muttered. "Wild animals and filth everywhere."

"Greg loved it!" George retorted.

"You're a snob, Gerry," Gareth added. The twins didn't seem to have any shame in insulting their elders.

"He never liked having his photo taken," Geoff said, his gaze on the image.

"Not bloody surprised." That was Gerry again. "Look at the state of him! A grubby, lopsided, goblin-faced lump. I always said he was some kind of throwback. Nothing like the rest of us. No wonder we called him the Ventura Ugly Duckling."

"You mean *you* did," Geoff said quietly.

"No one ever contradicted me," Gerry said smugly, as if this was a familiar argument.

Geoff and the twins all flushed.

Perry took another look at the photo. He'd rarely seen a man's looks he couldn't improve with careful dressing and a good hairstylist, but he was struggling to decide where to start with Greg Ventura.

"Peregrine?" Eddy was giving Perry what he called a *pointed look*. "What's your plan of action?"

My—what the hell? Perry drew a deep breath. "Where is Greg now?"

"The Western Isles," Geoff said.

Perry had no idea where that was. He'd never been anywhere but London in his whole life.

Geoff continued, "We'll pay for everything, of course."

Perry could imagine Eddy's eyes lighting up with pound signs. The deal was already done, he could see, insurmountable challenge or not. "Okay. Well, if you'd like to bring him in to the agency, I can assess what needs to be done."

Gerry laughed. "Oh, he won't come here."

"I'm sorry?"

Geoff bit back what looked like a long-suffering sigh. "I've rung him several times, but his phone never seems to be charged up."

"Or he's ignoring you," George muttered, then winked at Gareth.

"I sent him a letter in the end," Geoff said carefully, as if he was afraid of angrier words spilling out against his will, "explaining it all, and that it was time he came back to London. His reply was… well, brusque in the extreme."

"One creased postcard," Gareth said, with some glee. "Didn't even put enough postage on it. Geoff had to pay the excess on delivery."

"It said—" George added.

"I'm here to stay!" the twins chorused together.

Geoff sighed and stood, straightening his cuffs as if preparing to leave. "It appears he won't leave the Isles. At least, not at the moment. You'll have to go to him."

Perry blinked hard, scrambling to his feet in Geoff Ventura's wake. "Go where?"

Geoff peered at him as if he were mentally challenged. "To Scotland. We'll make the arrangements. Then you can do your magic with Greg right there, and bring him back in good time for the filming."

"Remember," Gerry added darkly. "He has to come willingly. He has to take part in the show with us all. And he has to look as *good* as us all. He can't show us up. The media will rip us to shreds if he appears in his ugly duckling mode."

"Go to Scotland?" Perry's attention was still fixed on that shocking nugget of news. He swung around to face Eddy, but Eddy wasn't meeting his gaze. "I can't do that!"

"Peregrine. It's only for a week or so. We'll talk about it later. Not now, please."

"I mean," Perry gabbled on, aware that the Venturas were looking at him with varying degrees of sympathy, amusement, and vindictiveness. "I have other clients. I have a flat, a social life. Weekly lunch with my mother."

Eddy turned to the Venturas and gestured to the door with his plump hand, albeit the space only allowed for single-file exit from the room. “It’ll be fine,” he said pointedly.

Perry stood, watching them all walk across the office floor on their way out, where all he could hear was the floating thread of Eddy’s voice, declaring gaily, “We’ll be in touch!”

Chapter Two

GREG Ventura knew things weren't going his way when he sank into mud so deep it seeped in over the top of his Wellington boots.

Fuck.

Greg lifted his feet out of the ditch, one after the other. The squelch inside the boots was revolting. Trust him to find a patch of peat bog that hadn't dried out since the last rain. With a sigh, he used his stick to scope out firmer ground and adjusted his route down the hillside back to his croft. The evening was moving in fast, as it did on the small Scottish island of North Uist, and he wanted to get back home before nightfall. Not that he wasn't prepared to walk the hills at night, but it wasn't his preferred option. By now, he knew the terrain as well as any local around here, but it was never a sensible option to scramble in the dark.

A wet nose nudged at his hand, and he instinctively reached for his dog's head. "Yes, Rory," he murmured. "We're going back now. Warm blankets, food, and a beer, right? Well, maybe not the beer for you. Last time you insisted on a taste, you threw up on my bedroom rug."

The dog snuffled. Rory, a wise and trusty Border collie, obviously didn't see any need for a verbal reply when humans usually answered their own questions. Instead, he crouched down as if at the starting line, then raced away ahead of his master toward home.

Greg strode after him, grinning. As he reached the border of the croft, the ground was more secure, the peaty marshland now far behind him. The weather had been bright and dry for several days, but Greg could tell by now when storms were on their way. Moisture hung in the air like a thin, ragged blanket, dampening his hair and catching in his throat when he called to Rory. It had been a very wet winter on the Scottish Isles, and despite the first signs of spring appearing with the heather and the return of birds wheeling and foraging over the bog, the sky on the horizon was still tinged gray and bleak with clouds.

And Greg loved it.

To him, the change of weather was part of the wild, browbeaten beauty of this place. For as far as he could see, the scenery rolled away, flat and often dark, broken not by trees but by low scrub. He knew that after a few hundred yards either way he'd find one of the many small inland lochs, the clear water glittering in any weather, fish darting and twisting under the surface. Off the northwest coast of Scotland, North Uist was the country's tenth largest island. That didn't give a real sense of it, though, because it was still only three hundred-odd square kilometers in size, with only a thousand inhabitants, excluding the birds, of course, which numbered far more thousands. It was a bird watcher's paradise, or so Greg had been told by the natives. He wasn't personally interested in watching wildlife, not even the basking sharks and seals that were seen off the coast.

He craved the solitude.

On the outskirts of Lochmaddy, the largest town on the island, Greg's rented croft was in a set of three. Each had a small cottage at the end of a long stretch of land. His place only measured six acres, yet they were all far enough apart that when he reached home, he could believe he was the only inhabitant for miles. To the left was Alasdair Campbell, a middle-aged sheep farmer who was happy to coexist with his neighbor with the minimum of conversation, but a grudging but friendly nod of the head when they met. On the other side was the Mackie family, fierce old Cameron and his wife, Aileen. The adults all lived alone at present. The children of North Uist often left for the bright lights or a career on mainland Scotland, but they just as often came back, either to settle or for temporary respite.

Greg understood the situation perfectly. He'd been living in and around Scotland for almost five years, and two years ago had landed up in North Uist. He hadn't wanted to move again since: it had been the best decision he'd ever made in his life. Maybe it had started out for him as a refuge as well—though he wasn't going to dwell on those early days now—but it had grown into his home. He might not have been drawn by the lure of family: in fact, it was the complete opposite. But he loved the wild, bleak beauty of the landscape and the forced simplicity of lifestyle. Each day was about basic essentials, reliance on the community, and blessed, hassle-free peace. He had enough money to live on, a part-time job, and the time to paint. He didn't need any more in his life, did he?

Reaching his back door several minutes after Rory, he let them both in. He stamped his feet on the mat and slid out of the boots. Mud had seeped into his thick woolen socks, so he rolled them off as well. The cool air inside the cottage tickled his sweaty toes.

A hot bath was what he needed. He'd been restless all day, and the long walk hadn't eased it. He also needed to paint; he knew that. It had been a hobby of his since he was a boy, and he'd returned to it here on the island. There was one particular view of the shore that he wanted to work on, and his fingers itched to revisit the canvas. He hadn't found time over the last couple of days, between chopping firewood, doing repairs around the house, and looking after Rory when the dog picked up a thorn in his paw. There was still more work to do in the cottage before he could truly relax, and he and Rory also needed supper.

He pottered around downstairs, peeling off his clothes as he went. He didn't bother turning on either the small TV or the radio. The croft was rarely silent in itself—tonight the wind whistled through a split in the kitchen window frame that was on his list to fix, and Alasdair's sheep gave the occasional soft bleat. Greg didn't have sheep of his own, although it was expected of crofters in this part of the world. But he'd made his compromise with the community by renting his land out to Alasdair, who let his flock wander over both crofts.

A quiet *beep* from the living room interrupted his thoughts. It was his mobile, pleading for a fresh charge. Greg constantly forgot where he'd left it.

Rory gave another snuffle and stared up at him.

"Dammit." Greg frowned. That reminded him—though he couldn't have explained to anyone how he and

Rory conversed so instinctively—that Greg had agreed to meet his mate Dougie at the pub that evening. He didn't feel particularly sociable, but there were few enough occasions to get together, and friends were to be treasured. They might even get to play a few hands of cribbage.

"What a wild social life I have, eh?" He laughed and scratched Rory's ears. "No one would believe it back in London."

That was odd. He hadn't thought much about London for a long time. The nostalgia was strangely disturbing. But he wouldn't waste time on introspection; that wasn't his way. He flipped on the boiler switch to heat up more water for his bath, scooped up his dirty clothes to go in the machine, and made his way upstairs.

IT wasn't even really a pub, just a back room at Angus McMillan's farm, where Angus's entrepreneurial sons had put in a few beer taps and set up tables and chairs around the hearth. Most of the time they arranged regular deliveries of beer and spirits from the mainland, but on the odd occasion it all ran out—like after every ceilidh night they ever catered for—customers had to make do with the sons' home brew. Greg had found it an acquired taste. When he mentioned that tactfully to Dougie, Dougie had roared with laughter.

"You're too good t' them, man!" he said, his lilting Scottish burr much more pronounced when he drank. "It's muck, nae fit for sheep dip. But there's enough alcohol in it not t' notice after a wee while."

Tonight, Greg saw Dougie at a table by the window, already halfway down his pint. It probably wasn't his first either. Greg ambled over to join him.

"Mine's a pint," Dougie said, and he grinned at Greg. He never much bothered with proper greetings. He was a short but strong young man, a few years older than Greg, who'd run the local store ever since his parents retired back to Edinburgh. This enterprise consisted of converting his hallway and living room with shelving and cupboards, and opening up to customers needing everything from general groceries to boat repairs, including a postal service back and forth from the mainland. The fact his sister Bridie also sold clothing, books, chocolate, and provided an endless supply of free tea, cake, and island gossip meant they were always busy.

Greg grinned back and fetched him a fresh pint without question. They sat together at the small table in comfortable companionship.

"Bridie says are you coming t' the ceilidh next Saturday?"

"I doubt it. I'm not exactly built for dancing." Greg didn't need to look at his long arms and legs to know how he towered over most of his peers. The ceilidhs were the main source of entertainment for the community. Small though the area was, almost everyone came out to dance, sing, and drink themselves even happier, once a month and on special occasions. The village hall was decorated with streamers that luckily didn't look their age when the lights were turned down low, the musicians on North Uist put on a show as good as any professional band, and Angus's sons ordered in extra supplies of everything drinkable.

"Aye. Wayne Sleep you're not," said Dougie. He drained the rest of his glass, then belched loudly. "None of us can dance, man. We're a disgrace t' our kilts. But it's always a bloody fine evening."

"I'll see. May have work to do around the house." Greg wanted to change the subject. He'd never attended any of the ceilidhs since he arrived, but no one was ever interested or bold enough to challenge him on his antisocial behavior, apart from Dougie.

"You thinking of a good new excuse right now?" Dougie raised his eyebrows.

"What do you mean?"

"I know you cannae face the ceilidhs. But why not? It's just a dance and a few drams."

Greg didn't know what to say. Well, he *did*, but he couldn't lay all his burdens on Dougie's shoulders.

"All the time you've been here—you won't be seen at a social, and you won't be drawn out," Dougie continued, though in a quieter tone. His expression was sympathetic. "You have nae contact with the mainland either."

"I don't need it," Greg said. "Just… drop it."

Dougie nodded slowly, though his expression was still quizzical. "Bridie would take you in a turn around the floor, y'know. If you're scared of a wee bit o' dancing."

Greg smiled and took another sip of beer, refusing to be baited. Bridie was in her twenties and still single, a pretty and friendly girl but with probably far too few choices on Uist. "She needs someone more handsome than me. She shouldn't have to settle for an ugly duckling."

Dougie's eyes narrowed. "Now why the hell d'you say that?"

Greg's heart started beating faster, and he made an effort to keep his voice steady. "It's just a phrase."

Dougie made a snorting noise. "A stupid scunner, you are. She thinks you're bonny, and she'd tell you you're talking baws."

Greg chuckled at the Scottish slang. It enchanted him, even after years of hearing it. "I most certainly am not talking balls. I'm flattered, believe me, but I'm not right for Bridie."

"That's damn right," Dougie muttered into his beer.

"What?"

"Ach, it's nae to do with your looks," Dougie said quickly. "I mean, it's because you're a fan o' the rainbow tartan." And he burst into raucous laughter at his own joke.

Greg blinked hard. He'd never openly discussed his sexuality with anyone on the island. The attitude in Scotland's cities toward gay people was largely welcoming and even proud, but the isles were a much smaller and tighter community. He knew there were still B&Bs that wouldn't rent to a gay couple, and parts of the church that wouldn't perform ceremonies. It hadn't been a problem so far, in that he'd kept a low profile with the croft's landlord, Mary McMullen, and he definitely didn't have any plans for marriage. That said, he didn't like bigotry, but he'd come to understand that this was a small world of its own, and things moved more slowly. Besides all that, he wasn't going to expose his private life to anyone indiscriminately.

But it seemed he'd been outed without even knowing.

"Yes," he said slowly. "That's why. You're right. Is that a problem for anyone?"

Dougie grinned. "As long as ye keep it in your own breeks, no skin off my nose."

At the table a few feet away, a couple of middle-aged men shifted on their seats—had they heard? Were they worried Greg would start talking about gay sex in Technicolor detail?—but then settled to arguing loudly about the football instead.

Dougie clapped his hand on Greg's shoulder. His eyes twinkled. "Bridie'd still have you, man, if you could see your way t' swinging either way."

At that point, Greg laughed too and surrendered to Dougie's insistence that it was Greg's round again. Up at the bar, while he was waiting patiently for service, Dougie appeared at his side. He stood there silently at first, and although Greg knew he didn't need Dougie's help with a couple of glasses of beer, he waited just as quietly. He'd done a lot of that over the years. He'd learned when Dougie had something more to say and was preparing it first in his mind.

"Got another message from your brother," Dougie finally said. "Came in today's post."

Greg nodded slowly. *Another one.*

Dougie made one of his many, expressive snorting noises. "So, you going t' ask?"

"About the message?" Greg sighed. "Why? It'll be the same as the last one."

"Aye." Dougie nodded. "'Twas."

Greg raised his eyebrows. Not that he wouldn't share the contents with Dougie after reading it, but the shopkeepers mysteriously seemed to know the contents of everyone's post regardless.

Dougie snorted again. "I'm nae opening your mail, man. It was just a card."

Not even a letter this time, just a postcard. Though considering how he'd replied to the last message, Greg would have expected anything further to be terse. But it was another example of how the lure of family—or lack of, in his case—refused to lie low. "It's simple, Dougie. He wants me back in London, and I have no intention of going."

"Why's he so interested now?"

"I don't know. Something about a TV appearance by the family. They need all of us there or it can't go ahead."

"Jesus God, man." Dougie looked as disgusted as if Greg had suggested they sacrifice a baby to demons. "Why on earth would they do that?"

Greg grimaced. "Money, I expect." His family had always worshiped that particular god.

Dougie grimaced too. Greg wondered if the pair of them looked like goblin bookends.

"It's bad news, man." Dougie shook his head mournfully. "What you gonnae do?"

Angus's younger son plunked a glass full of rich beer on the countertop, and Dougie took another gulp.

"Do about what, gentlemen?" came a feminine voice behind them.

Greg, startled halfway to lifting his own pint, just managed to catch the glass before it tipped off the edge of the counter.

"Bridie," Dougie crowed. "Just in time t' pay for the drinks."

"No," said Angus's son hastily. He'd gone very red, and his gaze was fixed on the table rather than Bridie, but everyone already knew he had a huge crush on her. "On the house." Then he rushed away to another part of the room.

Dougie shook his head and laughed, then hugged Bridie welcome. She was also short, and shared a broad face and dark auburn hair with her brother, but the freckles on her nose were cute and her full figure drew every eye in the place. She'd been a good friend to Greg, especially when he'd first arrived and found her accent was a lot easier to understand than most.

"Greg." Bridie's cheeks were pink from the cold air outside—she would have walked from their shop to Angus's, only a matter of a couple of miles. "Good to see you out of that cottage. You're looking bonny."

"You see?" Dougie said to Greg, eyebrows raised again. "You're nae ugly duckling there."

"Leave it." Greg had no illusions about his shortcomings. But even if he wasn't good-looking, he was male and single, and he supposed that made him a person of interest in such a small place.

"They want him back in t' smoke," Dougie told Bridie.

Bridie frowned. "Those brothers of yours? The ones who never come to see you? Who don't even bother to send you a proper letter?"

Greg winced. "There's no love lost between us, Bridie, we all know that."

"But that's *all* we know, love, isn't it? You don't share the whole story." She placed her hand on his shoulder and gave a comforting squeeze, so he didn't feel it was a criticism of his lack of friendship. Her more delicate palm didn't make much impact on Greg's solid muscles, but he appreciated the thought behind it. "It's your decision when you feel ready to talk about your family—"

Which would be never.

"—but we're here when you need us. And if you do wanna go back to London…?"

Greg shook his head. "No," he said abruptly. Talking had never done him any good; neither had fighting. The only thing that had brought him peace and self-respect was escape from London. The Western Isles were a bloody fine place to come to terms with yourself and what gifts you *did* have, and he wouldn't put that at risk after all these years. Return to London, and all its noise and filth and speed? Return to be poked and posed and presented as a mockery of the man he really was, just to satisfy his family's greed?

"No," he repeated firmly. "That won't be happening."

Chapter Three

"**BUT** what the hell do I pack?" Perry was on the verge of panic. His bed was covered with several neat piles of clothing and footwear, but his suitcase was still empty. It wasn't as if he had a massive wardrobe to start with—he understood the sense of owning just a few good quality, well-matched items, although his decision was influenced more by his pathetic salary than fashion maths—but he was still reeling from this latest career development.

Scotland.

Scotland!

"Isn't it always raining there?" Antony, thin and nervy, even on a calm day, was perched on the edge of Perry's bed. He'd crossed his legs, and he swung his foot back and forth, up and down. The jittery movement was starting to annoy Perry. "Or snowing? Aren't there hurricanes?"

"Bloody hell, you're a total Philistine!" Perry's other friend, Candace, shared Reception duties with Antony at the Latham Agency, where the pair of them seemed to spend most of their time miming through ABBA hits, surfing the latest fashion trends online, and bickering. She sat beside him now on Perry's bed, shoulder to shoulder, partners in crime. They'd even dyed a streak of their hair the same blue, though friendship didn't stop her snorting with scorn right now. "You've never been north of Watford, have you? I bet you think they're all still wearing woad and charging into battle with bloody Mel Gibson."

"What's woad? Some kind of mascara?"

"You're joking, right?"

"You'd notice, *right*?"

Perry bit back a sigh. Antony and Candace were good friends of his—weren't they?—but he wondered at the wisdom of calling them over to help him get ready for the trip.

"Seriously," Candace said, turning back to Perry. "It's a beautiful country, you'll love it."

"Have you been there?" Antony said to her, pierced eyebrow raised.

"I googled it," Candace muttered back with a glare. She turned a gleaming smile back to Perry. "Fresh, clean air, gorgeous heather, friendly people. No local council roadworks outside your flat all week, no struggling for a seat on the bus with hordes of commuters, no pigeons shitting on your windowsill, and no gangs fighting over drugs in the back alley."

"Darling, you gotta move from that part of London," Antony murmured.

Candace ignored him pointedly. "Scotland will be an adventure!"

Perry wasn't sure how he felt about adventure, but didn't dare say so.

"There are animals." Antony gave a gentle but obvious shudder. "In the wild." Up, down, up, down, his foot went.

Candace slapped him on the arm. "Jesus. What a wuss you are! Just a few sheep and dogs."

Antony turned a soulful gaze on Perry. "Perry's allergic to dogs."

"Well," Perry said, in the interests of full disclosure, "I'm not exactly allergic, they just make me nervous—"

Antony had continued regardless. "Oh God. Are any of these clothes any use, anyway? Will you have to wear a kilt?"

"What?" Perry felt increasingly like he was in a West End sitcom.

"Of course not," Candace replied confidently. "He's a visitor, that's all." She glanced at Perry. "I mean, you won't. Or will you? There are some fabulous leather ones in the sample room, though I'm not sure they're your size—"

"No," Perry said firmly.

"Of course not," Candace agreed, in the kind of patronizing tone that was no agreement at all. "And this guy you're going to make over isn't Scottish either, is he?"

Perry shook his head firmly. He had no idea, really, but none of the other Ventura brothers had spoken with any kind of an accent. He wished he had time to do more online searches on the family, but apparently he was booked to leave the next morning.

"See? It'll be like a bloody holiday," Candace crowed.

Perry was still uncertain, and Antony looked totally unconvinced. When he flounced off to the kitchen to get them all a beer from Perry's small supply in the fridge, Perry turned to Candace.

"You're just saying that to cheer me up, aren't you? All that stuff about a holiday, and how wonderful it'll be?"

"No, of course not!" Candace winced. "Well, yes, okay, I am. My older sister went to Scotland once, but she drank a shitload of single malt on the first night and doesn't remember much of the rest of the trip. Except that, yes, it rained. All the bloody time."

Perry sat down heavily on the bed. "Oh God. You're no help at all. I'm traveling to some kind of wilderness I've never heard of, where I'm expected to transform a total stranger into a glamorous, twenty-first century New Man—and then I have to persuade him to return happily to the place he ran away from years ago. How am I going to do all that?"

"You've done it before, haven't you? Transformed people."

"Only in London itself. In a studio, in a salon, with full wardrobe and makeup close by. And that's when they *wanted* to be transformed."

Candace hugged him. "You won't be on your own, will you? Eddy always sends a whole team to support a makeover." She sniggered and clapped Perry on the shoulder with just a little too much force. "Perry, you really need to man up. They're not sending you to the Amazon jungle."

Man up. Right. That had been a common insult thrown at Perry through much of his life, from his parents, bosses, and friends. He wasn't as fey as Antony, and he didn't particularly want to be as forceful as

Candace could be. But he couldn't help being naturally cautious, could he? University had been three years of huge challenge, mixing with so many people for the first time, needing to handle his own living expenses, learning to juggle academic work and partying, and then looking for a job. He was quietly proud of what he'd done at the agency, even if the promotion prospects weren't as good as he'd been promised. He seemed to have a knack for making clients look their best and finding what suited them. Some of them had even complimented his work in front of Eddy. It had certainly helped bolster his self-esteem—it had also kept him in place through the last round of redundancies.

And he desperately needed this job, not only for his own self-respect, but for salvaging what he could from the bloody awful mistake that was Henry, his ex. A whole year wasted with that tosser, a whole year of emotional upheaval and anguished breakup, and *then* to find that Henry had betrayed him in the worst way possible—

Antony placed a cold supermarket beer in his hand and chinked a tentative cheers. "Just go as you are," he said kindly. "You're cute just like that. And wardrobe will bring so much stuff, they'll have outfits for you too, won't they? Just in case you're, oh I don't know, wearing something that clashes with the heather."

Candace rolled her eyes and chugged her beer.

"You wanna borrow some things, Perry, love?" Antony said softly.

Perry stood up to let Antony collapse back down on the bed beside his bestie, and he looked at his friends' outfits. Antony was wearing skinny jeans and one of his usual neon-yellow tee shirts, which looked fabulous against his dark skin but was a color that made Perry look like a ghost with jaundice. Candace was wearing four layers on her top, rose-patterned leggings, and a stretchy skirt that barely covered her crotch. Perry knew he didn't have the legs for that look either.

"No, I'm fine. Thanks." He'd have to pack what he had and hope it was appropriate. After all, Antony was right, the agency's wardrobe department would bring clothing on the trip, accounts would authorize expenses if he needed to pay for dry cleaning, and makeup would have plenty of hair product he could beg the use of if need be.

"Perry?" Candace was peering at him. Both she and Antony looked more worried now. "Have they paid directly for your flight and hotel? You don't want the hassle of… you know, claiming that back and everything."

How embarrassing. They were good friends, and both knew the dire straits he was in since Henry left. He loved them for their concern, even if he blushed at their clumsy attempt at tact. But then, without their help, he wouldn't even be here today.

"Things are fine," he reassured them. At least, he assumed they were. He'd been e-mailed the air tickets to Glasgow and then on to Skye. Apparently he could get transport from there to Greg Ventura's location, and he was sure the agency team would have booked accommodation. He couldn't worry about all those extras right now: that was someone else's responsibility.

He was saved from having to give further details by his phone ringing.

"Perry darling!" The voice across the tinny line was loud enough for everyone to hear, and not just because you could barely swing a cat in Perry's bedroom.

He blinked hard. A headache was threatening. "Hello, Mother."

"The grapevine tells me you're on course for a promotion!" She sounded far more gleeful than he did. And where did she get her intelligence from? Not Perry, who rang her the absolute minimum times his duty required. A quick glance at Candace and Antony showed no sign of guilt. Mind you, he'd learned they were great actors, if their ABBA impressions were anything to go by.

"Well, not exactly. I mean, it may happen. If I do well. If I help out with this… um… sensitive project."

"Who?" she almost squealed.

"What do you mean?"

"Who is it you're working on? Tell me at once! I promise I'll keep it secret."

Perry rolled his eyes. *Like that's ever happened.* His mother leaked secrets like a sieve on the Titanic. "I can't say, Mother. It's confidential. And it's early days yet. I won't really know how things are going to go until I get to the Western Isles—"

"The where?"

"Scotland, Mother."

There was a small but pregnant silence. "Scotland? You mean…?"

"The country, yes." Good grief, Perry was almost looking forward to going there so the place could prove everyone's horror wrong. If, in fact, it could. "It's a beautiful country, you know. Fresh, clean air, gorgeous heather, friendly people." Over on the bed, Candace smirked at him. Perry flipped her off. "And it's not the end of the world. I fully expect to be back in a week or so."

"They said a month," Candace mouthed at him and rolled her eyes again. "I listened in. Up to a month."

There was silence again, but he could hear his mother breathing heavily. "But what about our lunch date?"

"We'll have to reschedule. Or maybe miss this month." *You know, Mother. Show some spontaneity for the first time in years.*

"That's going to be very inconvenient."

"For God's sake!" he burst out. "This is my job. It's very important to me to do well. This is going to be a great opportunity, and I'm going to take it, whatever else has to give way."

Antony's eyes were wide. Candace mouthed, "Wow!" and gave him an enthusiastic thumbs-up.

"There's no need to take that tone with me, Perry."

Perry knew, with the inevitability of fat molecules settling on his thighs after a bag of chocolate buttons, that he'd pay for this for months to come.

LONDON City Airport was a large and confusing building. Perry hadn't flown before, it was tremendously early in the morning, and he hadn't had time for his breakfast camomile tea. He was sure Eddy had said they'd all meet up by the departure gates, but so far Perry hadn't recognized anyone he knew from the agency. He waited as long as he could, and his flight was being called to board when he finally lost his nerve.

He rang Eddy Latham direct: none of the staff would be in the agency at this time. "Eddy, where are the others?"

"Peregrine, is that you? What time is it? The reception here is very poor." Eddy cleared his throat. Maybe it was because Perry had woken him, or maybe he was playing for time. Perry knew which he believed. "Others, love?"

"The team coming with me." Dread was creeping slowly through Perry's gut. "There's wardrobe, and hair, and usually someone to run about with coffees and things. And what about one of your promotions managers?" Eddy never let any of his design assistants loose without supervision.

There was a moment of utter silence from Eddy's end. Then, "Let me get back to you on that. I can't possibly call everything to mind right here and now. I'll call you back when I've checked into it."

Perry knew he'd be on the plane by then. He wasn't letting go of this that easily, though he was startled by his own assertiveness. "Surely you can tell me now how many will be coming? Are they on a later flight?"

Eddy coughed again. Perry knew it was a sure sign of truth avoidance. "Eddy? Tell me!"

"To be honest with you, Peregrine, there's been some kind of monumental cock-up. No one thought to tell me before last night, and believe me, I'll have something to say to promotions later. But when I checked the diary, it seems like everyone was booked out elsewhere."

"What do you mean—everyone?"

"Well, apart from you, Peregrine. And that's lucky, isn't it?"

The dread had settled as a roiling ache by now. "I don't understand." But he did. Oh *God*, he did. He was setting out for a foreign place without any support at all.

"I'll sort it out later, Peregrine. But you'll have to manage on your own for the time being. It's a great opportunity for you." It was a weird echo of what Perry had said to his mother only yesterday. "I'm sure you can hold the fort for a while."

For how long? "These are the Venturas, Eddy. They're famous! They're expecting us to send a team to meet Greg, to explain to him what's needed, and style him appropriately. To bring him back over to England in time for the pilot."

"…hold the fort…. Didn't I say…?" There was some kind of interference on the line. At least, that's probably what Eddy would claim. However, Perry had seen Eddy in his office far too often, speaking in garbled vowel sounds and claiming a "bad line" when he didn't want to continue a phone conversation.

"What about the travel plans? The hotel? I don't even know where I'm staying!"

"I'll get someone to text you. Just do your best." Eddy's voice rang clearly for long enough to deliver this coup de grâce. "I'll send others when I can, of course I will. All you have to do…. It's easy…. Even you can…." The line was drifting again. "…just make him look good, and…."

"Eddy?" In the background, Perry could hear his flight being announced again. They were chasing the final few passengers.

"…then back to London…."

"Eddy!" *For fuck's sake!* Perry was not going to let the agency get away with this, he definitely wasn't, they had no right to abandon him like this, to send him off on his own without the full client service package—

"…be no trouble for you, right?" Eddy finished with a chuckle and the line chose that moment to drop out completely.

"Mr. Goodwood to the departure gate," droned the overhead announcement. "Two minutes before the departure gate closes."

Perry stood frozen for ten seconds, staring at his silent phone. Then he picked up his messenger bag, turned toward the gates, and started running.

Chapter Four

GREG finished the final brushstrokes on the background of a view over the loch, and stepped back to take a more leisurely look at the overall effect. At the last minute, he avoided putting his foot on his spare palette, full of wet paint. He'd learned over the months of living here to keep all his possessions well out of reach until he needed them specifically. Otherwise he'd stumble into them, drop them, or trample them underfoot. That was just how it was with him.

He scratched absentmindedly at his beard and smiled to himself: he was really pleased with this painting. It was a commission for a gallery in Edinburgh. God knew how they'd come across his work, but he'd been astonished and flattered to be asked to contribute to a new exhibition of the art of the Highlands. He didn't fool himself he'd sell it for thousands—though he'd been making a modest living on his art for over a year now—and he was dreading the day they asked him to attend an exhibition in person. But for the time being, it certainly satisfied his soul. Funnily enough, he wasn't clumsy with actual painting: that always flowed well.

He'd converted the dining room in the cottage into a studio and workshop. The light was good during the day, and at night he could leave his current projects up on the easel until he had free time to work on them again. Tonight, the rain outside was getting much heavier. Predicted storms were on the way. Glancing at his watch, he decided to start cleaning up. Then he'd settle in his armchair in front of the living room fire with the latest Lee Child and a couple of glasses of whiskey, in the anticipation of a quiet hour or two before bed, with just his own and Rory's company.

Then the call came. Well, not so much a call as an insistent hammering on the door. Rory stirred in his basket by the fire, but surprisingly didn't leap to his feet or bark, so Greg had to assume it was someone they already knew and trusted. But *Christ*. What was the crisis? Was the pub on fire? Had aliens landed in the chapel? He couldn't imagine who'd be lunatic enough to come out in this weather at this time of night for anything less.

He hurried to the hallway and struggled momentarily with his front door, as the wind chose just that minute to blow against the cottage. When he finally wrenched it open, the rain blasted into his face and he couldn't focus until he blinked it away.

Two men stumbled through his doorway, personification of the cold and the wet. Their clothes steamed and glistened in the light of Greg's hallway, and their faces were gray, their features grimacing against the weather. Puddles of water started gathering on the mat almost immediately.

"Thank fuck you were in!" one blustered. He was swaddled in a full-length, waterproof coat and trousers, with heavy Wellington boots and a scarf wrapped around the lower half of his face. Despite the disguise, Greg recognized Dougie, and not just because of the cursing. Dougie always knew how to dress appropriately for the weather.

The other man hadn't moved an inch since they staggered into the hallway. He stood at least seven inches shorter than Greg's six foot three, dripping into a growing puddle of water around his feet, and he was shivering. It was obvious that *he* most certainly wasn't dressed for the downpour. He had no waterproof clothing, no headwear for protection, just a lightweight jacket that had probably been very stylish before it got drenched. Now it looked as elegant as a used dishcloth. At least he was wearing a sweater, in concession to the chillier evening, but his jeans were oddly ripped at the knees and completely sodden. Greg could see the skin beneath the rips turning red with the cold. And his footwear…. Greg swallowed heavily, not sure whether to laugh or cry. His visitor wore a pair of suede boots with a stacked heel and a neon logo on the side. Greg couldn't tell what they'd looked like originally—or read the logo—because they were now stained the color of sheep shit.

"What the hell, Dougie? Who's the sprat?"

Water was running down the sodden creature's face and into its white-lipped mouth. The gargled noise that came from its throat may have been a greeting or an attempt to avoid drowning.

Dougie snorted. "It's your London guest, man. Had ye forgotten he was coming?"

Oh my fucking God. Had that gone ahead? Greg hadn't given the project a thought after his last testy postcard to Geoff. He was sure he'd made it clear that hell would freeze over before he had any bloody interest in their daft schemes, and there was no point in them sending any tomfool design team over to talk to him.

Hadn't he?

Dougie shook his head angrily, spraying the hall afresh with raindrops. "Have you let your fucking phone run flat again? Poor wee thing couldn't get through t' you, and there's nae answer at his posh London agency. Lucky I was out at the ferry collecting supplies for the shop. Found him standing around, nae more than a drowned rat."

Greg stared at the newcomer, aghast. "But I told them not to bother. I wasn't going back to London, I wasn't taking part in any bloody stupid TV program, and I definitely didn't want an even more bloody stupid stylist coming here!"

The young man spluttered again. His face had gained some color now he was indoors. Or—Greg winced belatedly—perhaps that was fury at the insults.

"Looks like he didn't get the memo," Dougie muttered.

"What's his name?"

Dougie rolled his eyes. "Christ, man, we haven't had time t' share birth histories! Poor bastard said he was coming t' meet you, so I brought him right here." He peered at the visitor as if he'd unearthed the Loch Ness monster and found it less than impressive.

Greg felt much the same. Uncertainly, he asked again, "What's your name?"

"Peregrine Goodwood," the man said. "From the Latham Agency." His voice was surprisingly clear, and he looked older than Greg had first thought, when he'd been nothing but a streak of damp clothing. But he was still a skinny little thing, with no fat reserves on his body. He looked slight enough to be blown away in the gales around here. Apart from that, Greg couldn't tell what he properly looked like because his face was scrunched up from cold and distress, and his hair could've been anywhere between blond and black. The relentless Highlands rain painted everything the same muddy hue.

"Peregrine? What kinda joke is that?" Dougie whooped with laughter. He shucked back his hood and shook the excess water off his hair like Rory did when he'd been swimming in the loch. He wasn't remotely concerned about waterlogging Greg's furnishings, though Greg didn't have much time for the *Ideal Home Show* himself.

"Call me Perry," the man said defensively. Like Dougie, he gave himself a shake, shifting his hair off his forehead. "Look, are we just going to stand here taking the piss out of my name? Or can I dry off somewhere? Otherwise I'm likely to develop hypothermia."

Greg was taken aback at the kid's assertiveness and, to be honest, a little impressed. He thought this slim, effete little thing would've talked and walked like all the airheaded media types he saw last time he was in the English capital. Instead, Perry looked ready to give as much lip back to Dougie as he got.

"Come to the fire, for God's sake. Dougie, bring in his case and fetch some towels from the airing cupboard."

Dougie raised his eyebrows but dragged a once-smart, now sopping wet suitcase into the hall, then marched off toward the kitchen in his boots, trailing water as he went.

When the young man seemed too cold and distressed to move briskly enough on his own, Greg prodded him forward into the living room. Rory had vanished from his basket, probably resettling somewhere else in the cottage to continue his restful sleep. Greg had plenty of sympathy with that, having had his own peaceful evening so rudely interrupted. He guided Perry to stand on a spot on the rug in front of the fire.

"They told me it'd be like this," Perry said resentfully.

"What?"

"Scotland. They said it always rained."

Greg felt his hackles rise. "It was perfectly bonny last week. Looks like you brought the bloody rain with you. This blew up in only the last few hours."

Dougie marched into the room in his jeans and sweater, having presumably abandoned his waterproofs and boots in the kitchen, and with an armful of towels. Greg picked up the first one, a thick, pale-colored quality bath sheet. His mother had never been to visit him here but had considered her duty discharged with a gift set of linens. Greg had never bothered using them for himself.

Dougie whipped the towel out of his hands and started rubbing at the young man's hair. But Perry snatched it from Dougie in turn.

"I can manage on my own, thank you very much." Clutching the towel in one hand, he peeled off his jacket with the other, then held it out at arm's length.

Greg frowned. "What d'you want us to do with that?"

"Do you have a hanger for it? It'll need to dry out in its shape. A padded one would be best."

Dougie stared at him and laughed.

Greg cleared his throat. This guy was the limit. "I don't have any padded anything, apart from a quilt. I may be able to find a wooden hanger." He'd inherited a wardrobe from Mary McMullen's granny when he took on the croft, and there had been a few fittings left in there. He kept his own clothes in a drawer, although he did fold things neatly. He wasn't a complete savage.

Perry handed over the jacket with a much less confident air, then glanced down at his other damp clothing. His shirt clung snugly to his chest.

To his surprise, Greg found he was looking too. Perry was slender, but he had a nicely shaped torso and enough muscle tone for his build. Something glinted under the material, on his left nipple.

Piercing?

Greg's mouth went dry. He glanced across at Dougie, to find his friend grinning at him.

"Is there somewhere I can dry off?" Perry asked, his voice tight.

"Yes. I mean, yes, there's a small utility area off the kitchen." Greg used it sometimes to wash up and change after he'd been out on the peat bog. He also hung up his washing there to dry when the weather was too bad to air it in the garden. "Here, I'll show you." He turned awkwardly, bumping into the sofa and tumbling the remaining pile of towels onto the floor.

"I'll find it, thanks." Perry didn't actually sound very grateful at all. He turned and shuffled out of the room and down the hall to the kitchen. His boots squelched with every step, and a trail of water dripped behind him from the hem of his jeans.

When he was out of sight, Dougie chuckled. "If we're talking about rainbow tartan, he's your perfect candidate. How come ye never grew up a fairy like that?"

Greg scowled. Anyone could tell Perry was gay, but he wasn't sure he liked Dougie laughing at the kid like that. "We're not all the same, man."

Dougie held his hands up in supplication. "Didn't mean t' offend. We're all different, I know, rainbow or not. We okay?"

"Yes, we're okay." Greg smiled ruefully. "I'm just not in a very good mood. This whole thing caught me unprepared."

"Hello?" Perry called from the kitchen.

Greg moved nearer the door. "Everything all right?"

"I… my shirt's ruined. Do you have anything I could wear while it dries out?"

Greg chased away the unbidden and worrying vision of Perry bare chested. "There are clean clothes in the laundry basket behind the door. Probably a sweatshirt and some tracksuit bottoms."

"Thanks." Perry's voice wobbled. For God's sake, he wasn't crying, was he? "I didn't want to come here tonight, you know. But every step has taken so long, the whole day was gone before I knew it. And the ferry journey… I wasn't remotely prepared for *that*." He sounded like he gulped air in quickly at the memory.

Dougie grinned and winked at Greg, waving his hand up and down to approximate the choppy seas that afternoon.

"Then they never sent me any information about where I'm staying, so I thought I'd go into town and check the hotels."

"Does he mean in Lochmaddy?" Dougie muttered. "Wouldn't have taken him very long."

"But I couldn't find a taxi rank anywhere either."

"Dunderheed thinks he's back in the city," Dougie growled, his Scottish accent broadening.

Greg shushed him with a gesture of his own. "There's a bus," he answered Perry. "Though not frequent. And it's best to book a taxi in advance."

"I thought...." Perry's voice broke a little more. "I expected that had been done already."

Greg bit his lip. Sounded like the poor sod had just been dumped here.

"Do you have the number of a local B&B?" Perry asked. "I'll make do with that until...." His sigh was audible even through the kitchen walls. He sounded like he'd run out of viable options.

"Ach," Dougie butted in. "It's a trek back into Lochmaddy, even if I had the time t' take you. Out here, the only place is Fergus and Mary's, where they rent out rooms t' bird watchers in season. But you can't go there."

"What do you mean?"

"Their youngest is having her bairn early, so they've shut up for weeks."

"But I need somewhere to stay!"

"Babies take precedence, man," Dougie said gleefully.

Perry fell silent again.

Greg shifted restlessly. Bit difficult to chat through two doors. Then Dougie nudged him fiercely in the ribs.

"You going t' put some breeks on?"

"What?" Greg looked down and realized he was dressed in nothing but an undervest, a pair of woolly socks, and his boxers. The pair with purple thistles on that Dougie had bought him for a joke birthday present.

"Oh, shit!"

He dashed back into the living room and grabbed the jeans he'd thrown over the back of the sofa. *Bloody hell.* One of the great joys of living on his own was being able to throw off his clothes at the end of the day and pad around the cottage in his underwear. He often painted in next to nothing, at least when the cottage was warm enough. Now this uninvited guest had put paid to that. He scooped up an Aran cardigan he'd draped over the armchair and shrugged it on, then rejoined Dougie in the hallway. Perry still hadn't emerged from the kitchen.

"So what are you going t' do with him tonight?" Dougie said in a stage whisper.

"What?"

"I have t' go now. You'll have t' put the kid up here."

"Here? Oh, no way. There'll be somewhere he can stay in the village."

"Man, he's been travelin' all day. He's exhausted. The B&B is closed, everyone else with sense is in their bed. And no, before you ask, I've nae room either. Bridie's friend Lisa is over from Glasgow for a few days, and it's bad enough having t' share a bathroom with the two o' them. You have a spare room here, Greg."

"Christ. I don't want anyone staying."

"Wrap him in a blanket and you'll barely know he's here." Dougie's eyes twinkled. "A willowy little thing like tha'? You could share *your* room. He'd take nae space in that big bed o' yours."

What the hell was Dougie implying? "Now wait a bloody minute—"

"Ach, no, of course, you might roll over in the night and crush the wee thing." Dougie laughed heartily again.

"You said you were going?" Greg said pointedly. He knew he was blushing. Damn Dougie and his mischief making, thinking every gay man leaped on any other available gay man, whether they were seriously attracted or not. Not that Perry wasn't attractive, though Greg wasn't entirely sure how he'd come to that conclusion when he'd only seen brief, wet moments of him—

Dougie was laughing again, pulling his waterproofs back on. "I'll call in t'morrow, see how things have gone."

"What things?"

Dougie tilted his head toward the kitchen. "Your midnight snack."

"Go!" Greg snapped.

THE kitchen door finally creaked open and Perry stood there. He looked swamped in a blue fleece hoodie of Greg's and a pair of sweatpants that pooled around his ankles.

"Yes, I know," he said testily, although Greg hadn't asked a question. "Blue isn't really my color."

Greg thought Perry actually looked pretty sweet in plainer clothes, but he wasn't going to say so. He only just resisted rolling his eyes. "Needs must. You can't put yours back on yet. And it looks like you'll have to stay over tonight." Could he sound any less hospitable? "I have a spare room. You can take a bath if you want—there's hot water left in the tank. And I can find you a tee shirt to sleep in. Tomorrow your clothes will dry out, or we'll get you kitted out in something more… suitable."

Perry ran his hand through his hair. Greg could see it was blond, now he'd toweled it dry, and it fell in a mess of wild little curls. Aye. *Sweet.*

"And then you'll send me back to Glasgow?"

"Aye. Send you back." Greg stared at Perry's pale hands that had emerged from under the heavy cuffs of the hoodie. Long, slim fingers. Graceful. Probably manicured. Without thinking, he shoved his own calloused, dirty-finger-nailed hands behind his back.

Perry sighed again. His voice was firmer now he was dry and dressed. "Couldn't you have called me direct and told me not to come? It would have saved me that horror. The sea… the lurching…." He looked paler at the mere memory.

Greg felt a small twinge of guilt. It had never even crossed his mind. "Aye, I suppose so. I'm sorry."

Perry looked startled. Hadn't he expected an apology? "Well, we can discuss it all tomorrow after a calm night's sleep."

Discuss what? In Greg's mind, his decision had been made a long time ago. He wasn't up for renegotiation.

"Please show me to your spare room." And Perry—though he tried to hide it behind his hand—gave a large yawn.

Greg led the way up the narrow stairs, Perry tripping delicately behind him. It made Greg feel even more of a clodhopper. A whine came from behind one of the doors on the first floor.

Perry started. "What was that?"

So that was where Rory had got to. "It's Rory, my dog. He'll be fine with you staying. He'll have heard my voice with yours."

"I…. Dog?" Perry looked slightly nauseated.

Jesus. That'd be all Greg needed, a city type who was allergic to pets. "Here we are." He pushed open the door of his small spare room. Thankfully, the bed was made and the floor clean. Dougie had stayed over a couple of weeks ago, after a late-night drinking session, and Greg had changed the bed after his visit.

Perry sidled in past him, as if afraid of touching any part of Greg. Greg watched him take nimble footsteps over to the bed in Greg's borrowed socks and surreptitiously test the mattress. His narrow shoulders relaxed a little.

"You'll be okay?" Greg thought he ought to ask.

"I'll have to be, won't I?" There was that spark of spirit again, the one that both intrigued and startled Greg. Perry hitched up the sweatpants and wrinkled his nose as if sniffing the air in the room. "I know I'll feel a lot more civilized when I can get all the rain out of my ears. And I hope to God you have a decent dry cleaners on the island, because those were some of my best clothes."

Ah. Greg barely hid his scowl as he turned and left, pulling the bedroom door closed behind him with more of a slam than he'd planned. There was the London arrogance he'd been expecting.

It had just been temporarily underwater.

Chapter Five

PERRY woke up to a blinding beam of light in his eyes and a hot, suffocating panic.

Fuck!

He barely bit back a scream before realizing the light was crack-of-dawn sunlight. He lay in a strange room, in an unfamiliar bed, wrapped in a thick, freshly laundered duvet—and there were no curtains at the window.

But the suffocation was something else. A weight lay on his chest, pressing on his heart, warm, solid, and—alive? It moved gently but rhythmically, up and down. Steamy, rich-smelling breath gusted against his cheek. *Keep calm!* He tensed, his heart thumping hard. *Where the hell am I? What's happening?* The events of the previous day rushed back into the forefront of his memory. The nightmare journey to the Western Isles: the brutal rain, the mocking Dougie, and the hostile Greg Ventura. Tentatively he wriggled, but the heavy weight barely shifted.

It growled instead.

“Help!” With a loud shriek, Perry wrenched himself free and rolled out of the bed, hitting the floor with a painful thump. He was dressed only in a long, oversized tee shirt, originally black, he guessed, but now worn gray from many washes. His bare white limbs sprawled from underneath the hem and sleeves like the splayed appendages of an alien sea creature. This morning look was truly shocking. And, oh God, but he *hated* gray.

There was no time to wallow in fashion distress. The monster launched itself off the bed after him, a blur of hair, teeth, and panting breath. Perry shrieked again and threw his hands over his head. On the other side of the room, he heard the bedroom door burst open and heavy footsteps cross to where Perry lay on the floor.

“What the fuck’s going on?” Greg shouted over Perry’s yells.

“I’ve been attacked!”

Greg grabbed the dog—for Perry now saw the monster for what it really was—by its collar and held it to his side. He was wearing pajamas this morning, the top unmatched to the bottom, and his hair was squashed flat on one side of his head. “You stupid arse, it’s only Rory. He lives here. It’s his room when he’s not sleeping with me.”

“His room? He’s a dog!”

“Aye. Well spotted.” Rory strained in Greg’s grip to get back to Perry, his tongue hanging out of his mouth, his eyes bright, and ears pricked up. “He just wants to play. You have to appreciate that, if you’re sharing with him.”

“*Sharing* with him?”

Greg gave a loud, pained sigh. “I have him safe.”

Perry peered hard, checking the dog was held tightly. "Yes, I can see that."

Greg bit his lip. Was he trying not to laugh? "So… um. You can get back up now."

To his horror, Perry realized he was still lying on the floor with his legs akimbo, showing everything from his ankles to his upper thighs, and probably all the private bits in between. He hadn't asked for the loan of a pair of briefs when he went to bed, thinking his own trunks would be dry by morning. He couldn't wear another man's underwear, could he? But now he dearly wished he had. Tugging the tee shirt between his legs, he scrambled up to his feet, hot with embarrassment.

Rory finally wriggled out of Greg's grasp and bounded up to Perry, tail wagging. Perry stood his ground as best he could. He even managed to reach down and pet the dog gingerly on his furry head. Rory gave a doggy gasp of pure bliss.

Greg shook his head. "He likes you. Fuck knows why."

"Charmed, I'm sure."

Greg gave a short, mirthless laugh. He called Rory back to his side, and the dog spun happily on his back legs, torn between the two people he wanted to engage with.

Perry braced himself for more of his host's brusqueness, but Greg was silent now. His gaze settled somewhere around Perry's bare knees, drifted slowly up over his hips and belly, then darted back up to Perry's face. Greg Ventura looked flushed, and something more than angry.

What's the matter with him now? Perry resisted pulling the tee shirt down farther. After all, he was decent enough now. If he offended his reluctant landlord, that was Greg's hard luck. But he took the opportunity of a return look at the man in the flesh. There hadn't been much time for an appraisal the previous night.

Greg was tall, broad, and ungainly. That much was obvious from first impressions. His steps had been heavy up the stairs, his movements clumsy as he grabbed the dog. Last night he'd been parading about in his underwear, and this morning he was dressed in mismatched pajamas, barefooted, and with his hair uncombed. He had a scrappy beard and an appalling haircut—did he do it himself with kitchen scissors?—a laborer's hands, and the dress sense of a scarecrow. And even though he was the same age as Perry, he was *huge*, or so it seemed in comparison to Perry's compact five foot eight.

But Perry was an honest man, and he realized with some surprise that Greg Ventura was far from—what had Gerry Ventura called his brother?—an ugly duckling. His eyes were beautifully shaped and his slightly crooked nose striking. The lopsided twist to his mouth when he smiled—which admittedly hadn't been much in evidence—was quirky. And where had that teenage acne gone? His skin, though weather-beaten, was wonderfully unmarked.

And his body… well, it may have been huge, but he was *built*, no one could deny that. Even hidden by the pajamas, Perry could imagine strength in those muscles and a well-defined six-pack. Perry felt surprisingly warm, considering this cottage didn't appear to have any bloody central heating. Surely he couldn't be attracted to Greg Ventura? He wasn't usually drawn to such a muscular bear type. He preferred more elegant men with smooth manners and careful grooming.

Like Henry?

Yes, indeed. There'd never been two men less alike than Greg and Perry's ex, Henry Mortimer, at least as far as looks. If he'd been asked, Perry would have protested he didn't judge people purely on their looks, but he couldn't deny his bias up to date. His ex had been a handsome, slick, highly fashion-conscious salesman, who turned heads when they were out together.

And a thief. Well, yes, there was that.

Whereas Greg Ventura…? Greg was a raw, ill-mannered, big hulk of a man, with little to no cultivation, and fuck-off-ness radiating from every pore. But underneath all that show, he had the potential to look gorgeous, though in a very different way from his brothers. They had designer suits and a social charm that was prized in the city—but Perry had to admit men like that were plentiful in media. In contrast, Greg was far out of the ordinary.

It was something about his direct and uncompromising gaze. *Honesty.* Perry was sure wit and intelligence must also lurk beneath the frowns. And despite his clumsy size, Greg seemed comfortable in his body in a totally instinctive way, toned and buffed by manual labor and coping with nature's elements.

Perry's fingertips itched. He wanted to cut that hair away from Greg's face to showcase the wide jaw and strong features. He wanted to rip away those shabby pajamas and dress him in a shirt that would skim his abs and flat belly, tailored trousers that molded to his thighs, and a jacket that would sit perfectly on those magnificent shoulders….

Perry's head swam. He seemed to have got derailed at the "rip away" thought, and what Greg would look like without any clothes at all. *Good grief.* Perry blamed yesterday's traumatic journey for his sudden and bizarre fixation on a straight man. Which Greg was. Wasn't he? Perry's gaydar was obviously one of the things still waterlogged. Antony would be ashamed of him.

Greg cleared his throat. He was looking down now at the wriggling Rory as if he didn't dare look up at Perry again. "The kettle's on. You better come downstairs to the kitchen for some breakfast."

He dragged Rory out of the room, catching his hip on the door handle and cursing under his breath. And the bedroom door slammed shut behind the man and his dog.

Chapter Six

PERRY was on his second mug of tea and third round of thickly cut toast and marmalade when a loud knocking at the front door roused them both. Greg scowled. Perry didn't make any comment, but he reckoned Greg Ventura scowled so often, he'd end up with permanent furrows that no amount of moisturizer would redeem.

"I haven't had this much harassment for weeks," Greg muttered, pushing back his chair.

Perry jumped up from his own chair and followed him out of the kitchen. Before coming to breakfast, he'd thrown on the clothes Greg lent him the night before, and now he had to remember not to trip over the too-long trousers. Despite his embarrassment at how badly things were going so far, he needed to stay in touch with his mission as best he could. He'd received at least ten text messages already from Candace and Antony, asking what was happening. It was a relief that the mobile coverage was good out here, and the Wi-Fi appeared strong. He didn't want to miss any contact from Eddy with details of the makeover team's arrival.

Two girls stood on Greg's doorstep—one dark-haired, outdoorsy type, and a curvier girl with bleached blonde hair. As Perry watched curiously, they marched past Greg and into the cottage.

"Don't bother asking to come in, Bridie," Greg said to the dark-haired girl. "My house is your house. Oh, but wait a minute—it's not, is it?"

"Shut up, you miserable old git." She walked over to Perry and held out her hand. "Bridie McKennagh, I'm Dougie's sister. And this is my friend Lisa."

Lisa grunted and nodded. Perry suspected Bridie did the talking for all her friends. She reminded him of Candace.

"We thought you'd need some guidance in your new place," Bridie continued gleefully. "Where to go, what to see, what to do. Oh, and the right clothes to wear. Especially walking boots." She brandished two large laundry bags like she'd won an Oscar. Lisa had a messenger bag slung over her arm, presumably bulging with other goodies. "We've got the whole morning to spare."

"No," Greg said. It was almost a growl. "You're not staying. Say what you have to say and leave me in peace."

Perry bridled. What a rude arse he was! Bridie was obviously used to Greg's antisocial ways because she just ignored him. But Perry made a point of shaking Bridie's hand politely. He could understand and appreciate proper manners. "It's a pleasure to meet you."

"What a bonny young man you are!" Bridie's gaze roamed over him appreciatively. "You'll be such a treat to dress."

Perry felt his spirits lift. A woman after his own heart! He could only hope her ideas of style matched his own, because she seemed like a breath of fresh air among her canvas-draped menfolk. He plucked apologetically at the sagging hem of the blue fleece. "I have to admit this is far from my usual look—"

"He's not a bloody doll, Bridie," Greg interrupted sharply. "It won't be long before his own clothes are dry. He doesn't want a useless set of country clobber cluttering up his city wardrobe. He'll only have to carry it all back when he leaves."

"Which—" Perry started to say.

"—won't be for a while," Bridie finished.

"—is any time now!" Greg announced at the same time.

Greg and Bridie glared at each other. Lisa plucked at Perry's sleeve. "You gotta room tae change'n?" she asked.

Her Scottish accent was much stronger than Bridie's, and Perry struggled to understand it. At least he recognized the word "room." "I'm in the bedroom at the back," he said.

"Rory's room?" Bridie poked her finger in Greg's chest. "Was that your or Dougie's idea? Rory won't have been pleased."

"He wasn't." Perry interrupted before Greg's next protest got going. "He sat on my chest this morning and scared the shit out of me."

Bridie's eyes grew wide, and then she laughed. To Perry's surprise, he found himself laughing with her. And, even more amazing, Greg joined in. He had a loud, hearty laugh that rang out in the small cottage. He sounded genuinely happy, as if he'd expelled all his troubles with his laughter.

It was enchanting and another astonishing side to the man.

Lisa tugged Perry's sleeve again. "Gae oopstairs?" he thought she said, and he nodded back.

"We'll keep you posted," Bridie said to Greg. There was apparently no room for maneuver.

Greg sighed heavily and turned away. As Perry made his way back up the stairs in Bridie and Lisa's wake, he couldn't resist looking over his shoulder to watch Greg's lumbering stride back into the kitchen.

PERRY was disappointed there was no fine linen in the selection of clothes the girls had brought him, and no bright colors. It was all in a palette that could only be called *country lifestyle*. But he had to admit he felt more comfortable—and warmer—in the moleskin trousers and casual shirt and sweater they'd found. He gave a mini catwalk show in the spare bedroom, while the girls sat on the bed and clapped happily. It made them all smile, and for the first time since he left London, he felt relaxed.

"We weren't sure of your size," Bridie explained. "Because Dougie's about as sensitive as a peat bog to that kind o' thing, but he described you in a vague way, in relation to Greg." She glanced at Lisa, and they definitely smirked at each other. "And we're very limited on what we carry at the shop. This was the best we could do at short notice."

"I'll pay you back for them, of course."

"Ach, no trouble. Mebbe you can advise me on stocking up the styles for summer. You obviously wear only the best, a rich city man like yourself."

Perry needed to shift that topic of conversation quickly, but Bridie's next comment was a startling choice.

"You're gay, aren't you, Perry?"

"Um. Yes." Where was this conversation going? Perry knew it wasn't much of an issue in London, but here in these odd rural lands… wasn't this one of the areas of the United Kingdom that still refused to marry same-sex couples? Heavens, he'd heard they still closed shops on Sundays!

"Good," she continued. "You can tell Greg all about it."

"I… sorry?" Perry caught Lisa's gaze. She rolled her eyes ruefully in Bridie's direction, as if very used to Bridie's boldness. "I'm not sure what you mean, Bridie," he said. He didn't run training courses in it, for God's sake.

"He hides away here on the island, and he doesn't get out enough. He needs to see that gay men can have fun as well."

"Um." Perry felt a bit like Alice must have done, falling down the rabbit hole. "Greg is gay?"

"Ach, yes, though you'd never know it. He never acts it."

What does she expect? Perry wondered if gay islanders were meant to wear pink wellies.

"He never goes out with a man, though of course there are precious few options on this island. Never orders gay porn movies from the shop. He won't even join a dating site. He needs to be more like men on the mainland, like you."

Lisa coughed exaggeratedly. "Bridie, ma love—"

Bridie flushed bright red. "Oh my good God, I'm so sorry! I've only just met you and I'm making all these assumptions. You'll hate me."

Perry had to laugh. “It’s okay. Lots of gay men have a full social life, it’s true. But there’s absolutely no similarity between my and Greg’s lifestyle, so if all we have in common is being gay, I don’t think comparisons are valuable. And how do you know he hasn’t joined a dating site?”

Bridie turned even deeper red. “Dougie does laptop repairs at the shop as well. He made some joke last time he repaired Greg’s that he didn’t find any porn or chat rooms.”

Or Greg knew enough to clear his browser history, Perry thought. For a brief moment, he felt affinity with the man.

“Ignore ma gal,” Lisa said, but she was smiling at Bridie all the time.

“I’m not a clever talker, I know.” Bridie was still flushed but spoke with determination. “But there’s nothing wrong with wanting him to be happy. He kept it secret for a long time—well, he thought he did, but of course we knew straight away.”

“I can imagine,” Perry said drily.

“Because he wouldnae take ye to the ceilidh,” Lisa murmured in Bridie’s ear.

“I don’t have much time for those stupid dances, Lisa, and you know that. But I’m always happy to go with Greg for company. I reckon he needs to let his hair down. Needs to feel free to be himself.”

“Aye. We all need tha’,” Lisa said.

Perry couldn’t help noticing a strange edge to her tone. And privately, he thought if Greg Ventura let his hair down any further, he’d resemble an Old English sheepdog, but he deemed it wise to keep that to himself. “So you say he’s hiding out here? Is that what he says?”

"Ach, he doesn't say anything about it." Bridie frowned. "Never has done, since he arrived. It took us a long time to bring him out of his shell, and all he'll say is that he likes to paint here and will never go back to London. And he has no love for that family o' his. His brothers treated him badly as a bairn, and mebbe they're still doing it."

"He doesnae think much o' hisel'," Lisa said quietly.

What did she mean? As far as Perry was concerned, Greg had been an opinionated, rude, aggressive arse so far. That wasn't the behavior of a shrinking violet. Perry sat on the end of the bed between the pair of them. Lisa had a thick bar of chocolate she was encouraging him to share, and he reckoned he deserved a couple of squares after the ordeal he'd suffered.

Bridie nudged him boisterously with her shoulder. "So tell us about the TV program."

"What program?" Perry said cautiously, through a mouthful of chocolate.

"Ach, is it meant to be a secret? Greg's already told Dougie enough for us all to know Greg's family want him back in London for a TV show. They've been writing to him. Begging him to come back."

"And what does he think about that?"

Startlingly, both girls snorted, one in each of his ears.

"Greg says he'd rather drown in a loch," Bridie said. Lisa nodded vigorously in agreement.

"It's a wonderful opportunity," Perry said recklessly. Promotion wasn't his usual area, but his loyalty to the agency—and need for success—obliged him to try and cover that role as well. "It could run to a long series, and TV's well paid. He'd be a household name."

"Aye. Like he said." Bridie winced. "He'd rather drown."

"So how d'ye think ye'll get him tae the mainland if he doesnae want tae go?" Lisa asked.

"Well, I'm not really in charge of the logistics. That'll be up to his family, I suppose."

"So what *are* ye here for?"

Perry supposed if he was ever stuck for more than a couple of weeks in this godforsaken place, he'd get used to the blunt way they communicated. "I'm a stylist. I'm here…." How was he going to phrase it? To make Greg Ventura look less like a wild animal and more like his handsome brothers? To make him look like a city slicker? "I'm here to make sure he has everything he needs to fit back in."

"Clothes?"

"Yes."

"Haircut? Manicure, that kind of thing?"

"Yes, of course." Perry felt suddenly rather embarrassed at his own perfectly manicured hands. Bridie in particular needed some help with her own nails.

"But nae makeup?" Lisa asked.

"Well, yes if it's needed. At least for the cameras—"

But Perry never got the chance to finish his explanation. Lisa looked at Bridie, and they both burst into laughter.

"And if he doesnae want all that?"

For the first time, Perry felt in a truly alien setting. "It's quite usual in the media world."

"I'm sure it is," Bridie said. "But this is Greg Ventura we're talking about. The man who hasn't bought new clothes for a year, who doesn't have a decent mirror in his house. The man who thinks he's barely one step up in looks from Willie Aitken's pigs."

"Willie Aitken?"

Bridie and Lisa just looked at each other and shook their heads sadly.

Perry was shocked. "That's outrageous! He's different from his brothers, I can see that. But he's a very good-looking man in his own way."

"Aye." Bridie looked at him curiously. "We agree with you. But *he* won't."

"Never," Lisa agreed.

"So how do you plan on getting around that?"

Well. And that was Perry's own personal million-dollar question, wasn't it?

Chapter Seven

GREG had to admit he was startled—and admiring, to be honest—when Perry Goodwood came back downstairs in new clothes. Of course, it was just a selection of country separates from the shop—although why Bridie called them "separates," when it only made sense to wear them together, Greg had no bloody idea—but Perry had a way of standing that made the outfit look different. Made it look good. Not that Greg ever took any notice of clothes, but… still. The way Perry held himself, the way the fabric followed the lines of his slender body….

Good. Yes, that was definitely the word.

"What do you think?" Bridie was hopping about behind Perry like a silly girl. Anyone would think she'd been dressing a pop star.

Greg cleared his throat. "That's a damn sight more suitable." Perry now wore sensible trousers with full knees to them, a pair of hiking boots, a polo shirt, and a close-fitting red sweater. Very close-fitting. He had a nicely shaped torso.

"And?"

"And what?" Greg stared at them all—Lisa was lurking in the background too—without any idea what Bridie meant.

"He looks very handsome, don't you think?"

"Well. I mean…." What *did* he mean? He scowled at being backed into some kind of a corner. "It's not for me to say, is it?"

Perry looked embarrassed, which he well might, with this stupid scenario going on. He ran his hand through the outrageously wild, blond curls Greg had noticed last night, and said apologetically, "Things will be much better when I can get some hair gel and smooth this mess down—"

"No, leave it!" Who said that? With a shock, Greg realized it had been him. The thought of ruining the way those cute curls fell over Perry's forehead, the way they just asked for fingers to run through them…. Dammit, was he going mad?

Everyone had swiveled to stare at him. *Fuck.*

"It looks okay to me," he muttered. "Don't know why people use all that stupid product."

Bridie lifted her eyebrows.

Lisa glanced between Perry and Greg. "Time tae go," she said to Bridie.

"Aye. I'll show you out," Greg growled.

"Thanks again, Bridie," Perry called, waving to the girls.

At the front door, Bridie lingered until Greg was the only one in earshot. "Greg, you'll be all right with the bonny lad?"

"Of course I will. He's on his way home shortly, anyway."

Bridie nodded as if she knew something Greg didn't. It was a familiar gesture he'd learned to expect over the years he'd known her and Dougie. "Give him a chance," she whispered. "Let him tell you about the show."

"I'm not doing it, Bridie. I'm not going back to London, and definitely not for *them*."

"Your brothers? Your anger toward them…." She sighed. "You know, it's hard for me to understand."

Greg's heart sank. He really didn't want any more of this, not right now. But he knew Bridie only meant well. "You're close to Dougie, I know. You've always had a good relationship with your family, and I envy that. But it was never like that with my brothers, and it's never going to be."

"Bad feeling eats away at you, Greg. Maybe the show is a way to mend those bridges—"

"It was their choice, Bridie," he said abruptly. The sudden pain in his chest startled and scared him. He'd thought he was immune by now. "I didn't come here to spite them. I came here to save my sanity." Her eyes widened, and he realized he'd said far more than he'd wanted to.

Still, she wouldn't let go. "Then give Perry a chance, just for him. He needs this job."

"Did he say something?"

"Ach, no. I suspect he's as stubbornly proud as you are. But you saw the state o' his clothes—the ones he arrived in. They may have been designer in the first place, but he's had more than his fair wear out o' them.

The shoes are worn through on the sides, and the jacket seams are threadbare. I think old Willie Aitken is more comfortably dressed, and you know *he* sleeps in his mother's pig barn."

Greg didn't know whether to laugh, cry, or demand to know exactly what Bridie was trying to say.

"Just go easy on him," she whispered again as she slipped through the door to join Lisa. "And yourself."

GREG loped back into his living room. Perry sat on the edge of the sofa, staring at the door into Greg's studio. Greg had left it slightly ajar and the midday sun spun a pale brightness through the gap.

"Is that where you work? Bridie says you paint."

Greg ignored him, walked over to the door, and closed it decisively.

Perry sighed quietly. "Can I offer to make some lunch? I can cook pretty well. Or should I go out and buy something?"

"What you should do is go home," Greg said. The shock on Perry's face was surprisingly hard to bear. But Greg hadn't had to think before speaking for a long time now, and why should he start for an uninvited stranger?

"I could stay for a while," Perry said slowly. "I'm dressed for the part now."

Perhaps he meant it as a joke, but Greg didn't feel humorous. "They're just clothes. Pity you won't get the wear out of them."

"You're still against working with me?"

"Of course I am. I'm sorry you've wasted your time—"

"No, you're not," Perry interrupted, with spirit.

Greg was tempted to laugh, but surely now was not the time. He was meant to be chasing this pest out of his life, not enjoying the banter. "No, I'm not, you're right. I didn't ask for anyone to come, and I don't have time or manners to deal with you."

"Good God, you're a rude bastard!"

"Maybe." Greg didn't feel offended. He never had, and plenty had called him the same. "But it's my life."

There was a long moment of silence. Greg had expected Perry to rant, not stare at Greg as if examining a new species of being. Perhaps that's what he was to Perry.

"Believe me," Perry said finally. "I want to leave. But I can't."

"Of course you bloody can." Greg threw himself down in the armchair by the hearth. He needed to set the fire soon for the evening, but damned if he was going to do that without sorting out the Perry problem first. He often ended up a sooty mess, and he didn't want to look a fool in front of anyone else.

Perry's jaw tightened. "You're a master class in confrontation, you know? I've got a job to do. I can't go back until it's finished."

"And that job is?"

"To get Greg Ventura back to London, to present him to the TV producers in the same style and fashion as the other Ventura brothers. That means dressed in something other than jumble and looking as good as they do."

"On your own?" Greg heard the scorn in his voice.

Perry flushed. "The rest of the team is following soon," he said bravely. "And I have excellent credentials."

"I know." Suddenly, Greg couldn't resist the mischief. "I saw them in their full glory this morning."

Perry went even redder, and his hands instinctively darted toward his groin as if prepared to cover it up. "That's not what I meant, and you know it. I'm a good stylist, even without the rest of the department's resources."

"For God's sake." Greg groaned, and he leaned back in the armchair. He knew he wasn't being fair to Perry, but then who was being fair to *him*? "I'm not casting aspersions on you. I have no idea what makes a good stylist—it's far down my want-to-know list—but I'm sure you're good enough. It's more the fact that the job is an impossible one."

"You've made it clear that you don't welcome coming back to London."

"Not just that. The makeover thing, as well." Greg hated feeling uncomfortable and angry, all at the same time. "I'm a lost cause. Didn't they tell you that, those perfect brothers of mine? Didn't they tell you I broke the Ventura mold when I was born? I never had their looks or their physical grace, let alone the manners. I'm a clumsy, odd-looking reject, and it'll take far more than a single stylist to make a silk purse out of this sow's ear. They should've told you what a crap hand they were dealing you."

"They showed me a picture of you—"

"There you are, then."

"You were only twelve!" Perry snapped. "No one would judge a man on the basis of that. We all go through that unattrac—awkward stage as a child. You're well past it now, so what's your problem?"

And wasn't that the point? It was Greg's problem, and he had to live with it. Alone. "I don't want to talk about it anymore."

"Do you know how childish that sounds?"

"Do you know how little I care?"

They glared at each other. Greg noticed Perry's eyes had beautiful little glimmers of azure in them when he was angry. Yes, it was official: he *was* going mad. He rose from the armchair. "I'll call Dougie to come and fetch you to the hotel. They can tell you there about the boat times back to the mainland. I have to get some work done or today's completely wasted."

"Work? You mean painting?"

"That's only part of it. I have other work." No, he wasn't going into it now. He wasn't going to waste any more daylight hours in idle chat, not even when Perry looked so eager and concentrated on him. There were calls to make to the mainland, bills to invoice. He started to pass Perry, to leave the room.

"Greg. Mr. Ventura. Please." Perry put his hand on Greg's arm.

Greg stopped dead. It took a huge effort not to wrench away. Perry was far too close. Greg wasn't used to people living with him in his house, and the personal-space invasion was almost shocking. It felt like a very long time since anyone touched him at all. *Nonsense!* He was just tired, annoyed, and frustrated. Perry was so slight, but so very *obvious*, though Greg wasn't sure why he thought that way. Was it because Perry looked good and smelled gorgeous—how come Greg's own shower gel smelled so delicious on someone else?—and he wanted to be close to Greg, and he'd looked so lost in Greg's huge tee shirt that morning, but his long, lean, bare legs had looked so sexy as he sprawled on the floor of the spare bedroom…?

Greg growled instead. That was his usual defense, and it had always worked before. "You think you can seduce me to go along with this stupid project? Think I'm so hard up I'll go for any gay man who comes my way?"

Perry winced and snatched his hand back. "God no! Nothing was further from my mind. Despite Bridie's bizarre plots."

"Plots?"

Perry laughed nervously. "She thinks you need to get out more. Find a social life. Enjoy yourself. Date some men."

"And she thinks I should date *you*?" It was only when Perry flushed that Greg realized how harsh that sounded. But what the hell was Bridie thinking? Even if Greg had been interested—which he wasn't, of course he wasn't—what chance would he have with a bright little button like Perry Goodwood?

"Like I said." Perry's voice was calm, but it seemed to take him an effort. "There's nothing further from my mind."

There was another awkward silence between them.

Then Perry took a deep breath. "So, what do we do now? You don't want me here. To be brutally honest, I don't want to be here either. But can't we make some kind of a deal? At least for a few days."

"What do you mean?"

"Give me some time to talk to you. To make their case. *My* case."

Greg was already shaking his head before Perry had finished his sentence. "I don't have that time."

Perry frowned. "Yes, I know. You work, you told me. So in return, I'll help you in your work. Then you can make time."

Greg stared. Perry hadn't even asked him what work he did! Didn't he realize there wasn't much of a call for personal lifestyle jobs in this part of Uist? He imagined Perry Goodwood—slender, wiry, almost pretty—his delicate hands hauling slabs of peat for the smokehouse. He imagined Perry hauling the sheep in for Alasdair to shear; imagined him dressed for fishing in the middle of the loch; imagined him in full scuba gear on the island coast, diving for scallops.

"Why are you laughing?" Perry asked. "Was it that bloody funny?"

"Yes," Greg said bluntly. "But I appreciate the offer."

"So that's what we'll do?"

Good God. This must be how they trained them nowadays in London. Like Rottweilers. "You're persistent, aren't you? Annoyingly so."

Perry's eyes glinted. "Yes. And yes."

Greg couldn't help himself—he grinned. "Okay. You help me out for the next couple of days, then I promise I'll sit down with you and you can explain about the show. But no promises. You already know how I feel."

"But I don't understand why."

"That's my business."

Perry nodded. "You may not always feel like that."

"I will. What makes you think you can change that?" He'd had a lifetime with his family, either in person or in mind. Nothing or no one could erase that.

Perry smiled, just a soft twist of his mouth that maybe Greg wasn't even meant to see. "Let's see, shall we? And in the meantime…."

What now?

"If it's just for a couple of days, is there any point in ferrying me off to a hotel? Especially if we'll be working together. Discussing things. Exploring ideas."

Oh, for fuck's sake. Greg gave a huge, exaggerated sigh. "I suppose not. You can stay here. But keep out of my way at other times. And you'll have to share the chores."

"No problem!" Perry looked animated again, and inexplicably excited. "I'll go and rustle up something for lunch, shall I?"

Chapter Eight

WHAT the hell had possessed him to say he'd stay at the croft?

Perry seemed to have spent most of his first day as unpaid kitchen help. A lunch of ham sandwiches had been easy to provide, but afterward, when Greg had locked himself away in his studio, Perry had tried to prepare for supper as well.

And that went… not so well.

He spent the whole afternoon trying to sort out Greg's kitchen so he could cook them a supper that was nutritionally balanced, only to give up and substitute almost every nuanced spice he had at home with Greg's single pot of chili powder. There were plenty of fresh vegetables and pasta in the fridge, but a horrible lack of anything out of the ordinary. Perry had eventually made Moroccan lamb with couscous, but with parsley and chili instead of coriander, and brown rice instead of the couscous. He prided himself on improvisation, but he was sorely tested. The only good result was that Greg ate heartily and very appreciatively, and he fetched a fabulous, fresh loaf of bread from a small cupboard in the utility room to accompany it, followed by some raspberries. Perry had a strong suspicion Greg had baked the bread, judging by its weird shape, but he couldn't fault the taste. And the raspberries were bigger and sweeter than anything he'd ever seen in the supermarket at home.

After the meal, they settled in the living room again. Greg poured himself a glass of what he introduced as his homemade wine, but Perry politely declined a glass for himself. He couldn't recall any decent wine he'd ever drunk being that particular shade of purple. He was definitely making a mental shopping list for when he could find somewhere civilized, and gin and tonic would come several steps above couscous on that.

Greg picked up a book and started reading. Perry waited awhile—after deciding against asking what they could watch on the miniscule TV in the corner of the living room, with obvious dust settling on the controls—then coughed to get Greg's attention. "Where do you need me tomorrow?"

Greg peered at him over the book. "What are you talking about?"

"Working together, remember? Um. What exactly do you do, apart from painting?"

Greg's look was possibly sly, but that could have been due to the waning light outside the cottage.

"Sometimes I work in the Sea Bird restaurant."

Perry thought he remembered seeing a sign to that place on his journey here in Dougie's car. The building itself had been very small, more like a tea room, with a single light on in the front porch, and it didn't look very open for business. But he'd go with the flow. "Are you a chef?"

Greg laughed. He seemed more relaxed tonight. "No, I think you've realized my cooking skills aren't the best. And it's not really big enough for a chef and full kitchen staff. I mean, it wouldn't meet your London standards."

"That has nothing to do with anything."

"What?"

"My London… standards, experience, whatever you want to call it. I'm in Uist now, and I want to know what you do here."

Greg was looking at him oddly. Was he, Perry, coming across as too bossy? God, this man was impossible to gauge properly.

"It's more of a large dining room where friends can hang out." Greg still sounded reasonably relaxed. "It's owned by a couple of elderly sisters who are marvelous cooks, and we sometimes hire it out for a celebration. We're not big on dinner parties here, you can imagine. I help out with serving when it's busy. But mainly I provide the fish dishes, especially scallops."

"You're a fisherman?"

Greg nodded slowly, his gaze still on Perry. "Yes, you could say that. I'm a diver. I dive for scallops."

"Can't you just… I don't know." *Buy them in a shop?* "Don't they have official suppliers?"

Greg frowned. "Hand-collected scallops are better. The sweeter ones are chosen, and the dish is more precious. Haven't you ever tasted the difference?"

It pained Perry to admit weakness, but he did. "I've never had scallops in my life."

Greg's eyes narrowed. "I thought you lived in the center of the sophisticated city?"

"We can't all afford posh restaurants," Perry snapped back, then blushed at—yet again—having to admit a shortcoming.

"Oh." Greg blinked. "Well, you'll see them in the raw when you come out in the boat tomorrow with me."

"When I…? Tomorrow…? Boat?"

Greg smiled slowly. "Yes. The weather should be fine, so I'm driving west past Lochmaddy to one of my favorite coastal seawater lochs. I'll pack some provisions so we can eat lunch there. You can help carry the equipment, then collect the scallops into boxes and keep watch for me."

"We… I…." Perry was struggling for words. Worse, Greg seemed to realize it and find it highly amusing. "I've never been in one."

"One what?"

"Boat. I've never been in a boat. Well, until the ferry two days ago."

Greg nodded, also slowly. "That's fine. You can stay here if you want."

"No!" Perry's cry was instinctive. Did this brute of a bloke think he, Perry, was a lightweight? "I will not! We made a deal."

"Okay. Well, I hope Bridie brought a selection of decent waterproofs as well as your day clothes, because you'll need them."

"You said the weather should be fine…."

"Just in case," Greg said ominously. He concentrated back on his book.

Perry sat silently for a long moment. In fact, everything was silent, inside the cottage and out, apart from the occasional call from a bird, and Greg turning a page. Perry wasn't used to such quiet. Nor was he used to living in close quarters with a man who barely tolerated him, and actually wanted him to get lost. There was a small pile of paperbacks on the table beside Greg's armchair, and Perry picked one up. He also wasn't used to reading anthologies of horror stories, his preference being for romantic comedies and the occasional biography—but he supposed there was always a first time. Opening it to the first chapter, he bit back a sigh. At least he'd won this stage of the battle with Greg Ventura, and he had more time to convince him about the TV project.

But thinking about the trip out onto a likely freezing Scottish loch tomorrow, he wasn't sure whether the price would be too much to pay.

Chapter Nine

THE next day dawned bright and clear, though the morning air was cold. Perry knew this, because he was out in it from an early hour—a *very* early hour. Rory had woken him, his doggy nose sniffling at Perry's ear until he was rewarded with Perry's groan and a ruffle of his head. Then a crash in the kitchen downstairs had alerted Perry to the fact Greg was up and getting ready for a day's work and he, Perry, was expected to join him. A snatched cup of tea, some toast, and then a ride in Greg's old Jeep out to a deserted stretch of beach. Greg parked in front of a small wooden hut beside a lake and started unpacking his diving equipment. Perry stood helplessly, clapping his hands to keep warm, and wondering where the nearest coffee franchise was.

The lake was small, and framed on almost all sides by steeper banks, but he could hear the waves from the nearby sea and smell the salty tang. A bird wheeled overhead, swooped, and then was gone. The air was so fresh, it almost hurt to breathe.

"Don't stand dawdling!" Greg called from the other side of the Jeep. "Help me with this, if you want to be useful."

The following half hour passed in a bit of a blur for Perry. They lifted the boat down from the roof, carried it down a small wooden jetty, and lowered it into the water. Greg added a couple of bags of assorted equipment, nothing of which was recognizable to Perry, then Perry was left to wait, yawning and stamping his booted feet against the cold, while Greg changed into his wet suit inside the ramshackle hut. When he strode back out, Perry found himself admiring the way the rubberized suit clung to every line of Greg's body, from his broad shoulders to strong, muscular thighs, past a really well-shaped arse—

"Carry this," Greg said, landing an air tank in Perry's arms. He turned away and shimmied down into the boat. It rocked underneath him, then settled. Looking up at Perry on the deck, he held out a hand. "Come on, then!"

Perry realized very quickly he'd stepped out of a frying pan into a fire—or rather, a watery nightmare. The boat was more like a dinghy—small, cramped, and so light it bumped alarmingly over the waves at speed. Perry clung on with one hand to the side, the other hand on his life jacket, and prayed for his breakfast tea and toast to stay down. He could swim, he'd assured Greg, but in truth he rarely did. Candace was a strong and keen swimmer, visiting the local pool before work several days a week.

She regularly asked Perry if he wanted to come along, but Perry always refused. The chlorine made such a mess of his hair.

But maybe he saw the sense of it now—now, when it was probably too late.

They came to a halt in the middle of the loch, or as near the middle as Perry could imagine, and Greg dropped the anchor. Rocking the boat again, he pulled on his hood and wriggled the air tank onto his back. When the webbing got stuck on his left shoulder, Perry reached over and helped out. His hand looked very small and very white against the wide expanse of Greg's back. Nodding thanks, Greg grabbed a long sleeve of netting, shaped like a narrow basket, and attached it to the line and buoy in the bottom of the boat.

"What's that?" Perry asked.

"It's a net to put the scallops in. I'll bring it up when it's full enough, and you can add them to the box we brought." Greg's voice was slightly muffled behind his collar. He threw the buoy out into the water, where it disturbed the surface for only a moment, then settled like an odd-shaped olive in a martini glass. Greg turned at the last minute to face Perry. "Okay?"

Perry nodded dumbly. What else was there to say?

"If you see any problems on the loch or on shore, just tug the rope three times, and I'll surface again." Before Perry could make any response, Greg attached his mouthpiece and rolled backward over the edge of the boat.

***HE'S** gone.*

Perry was surprisingly shocked. One minute they'd been together in the boat, and now… he was alone. He didn't know whether to stand up or stay sitting in the bow. Should he help with the rope? Perry watched for a while as it fed out into the loch. Greg had explained this end of it remained well secured in the boat, and he would use it as a guide when he wanted to resurface. Perry peered over the edge of the boat. *You'd never know anyone had dived in at all.* His reflection rippled in the surface of the water as the boat bobbed. But otherwise things were still. A few seagulls wailed in the sky, and flocks of birds he didn't recognize swooped overhead. They were fascinating in the patterns they made against the clouds and the innate way they moved as one. The wind brushed his face and swept on by.

He sat there for what seemed like a long time. Partly because he didn't know what else to do, and partly because he was terrified of rocking the boat. How long did it take to dive for scallops? An hour? All day? How many scallops would Greg collect? Ten or a hundred? Perry didn't even know what they looked like in the wild, if that's what you called life on the loch bed. Where the water was clear, he could see fish darting past the boat, but in places it was cloudy and he couldn't see far beneath the surface. Maybe that was where Greg was diving and disturbing the sandy bottom. How did he see where he was going?

Slowly, Perry felt his muscles relaxing. The smell of the sea was unfamiliar but pleasant, the sound of the waves very soothing. Thank God it wasn't choppy like his ferry journey had been. The tension eased out of him with the breeze. He couldn't remember the last time he'd genuinely had nothing to do except sit and wait. At least, not without a head full of worry and anticipation and plans, always looking ahead to the next job, the next bill that had to be paid. Always concerned at who was watching him, who would be judging him, where he might take a misstep. *How odd.* He'd never realized what stress he was living with, until he stepped outside it. And when did he ever do that? He worked long hours, his best friends worked with him so their conversation was always peppered with office tales, his mother pressed him constantly about his progress on the corporate ladder, and sometimes it felt like Eddy stood at his shoulder waiting for him to fail. He was so rarely alone except for his sleeping hours, and never *really* alone like here, where no one was within miles of him.

This is a good place. Perry couldn't deny it—and suddenly he didn't want to. *Ha!* Nobody was there to argue with him. The air was startlingly clean, and now he had the right clothes, he was at a comfortable temperature despite the chill. The smells had been weird to start with, but he was getting used to the lack of smoke and diesel and enjoying the fragrant heather and the tang of the sea instead. The waves lapped at the boat with soft, gentle slaps. Birds continued to wheel overhead, and the seat in the side of the boat wasn't too uncomfortable under his bum if he stretched out his legs in front of him.

His eyes felt deliciously heavy. He'd just close them for a moment. He had been woken disgustingly early, after all.

Chapter Ten

WHEN Greg's head appeared suddenly over the side of the boat, Perry jolted up on the seat. "My God!" Had he fallen asleep? How embarrassing!

As Greg hauled himself over the side, Perry rushed to grab the strap of his tank, helping to pull him in. The net basket thingy was full of shells that Perry recognized. He'd used them at his primary school to mix paint in—empty ones, that was. These were bigger than his palm and muddy with sand, but the smell of sea water on them had its own special flavor.

Greg landed with a wet slap on the seat beside him. "It's a good haul."

"Yes? Great."

Greg glanced at him, his eyes scrunched up behind his mask. "Going back in for another batch."

“Sure.” Perry nodded. “I’ll just get the rest of these out, then your net’s ready for round two.” He tipped the shells into a box Greg had lodged under the seat, then handed the net back to him with a flourish. “There we are, ready to go!”

Greg blinked hard. It looked like he wanted to say something but couldn’t articulate it for a moment. He gave a bemused smile, then put back the mouthpiece and slid over into the loch again.

The process repeated several times more, and Perry watched Greg as he dove beneath the water each time. For such a large man, he was very graceful. There was no sign of his clumsiness on land. He kicked smoothly, powerfully, as he guided himself deeper and out of Perry’s sight. And when he reappeared, he swung himself back into the boat with ease, steadying himself with strong arms and a firm grip on the side of the craft.

Finally, Greg told Perry he had enough scallops and didn’t want to disturb the loch bed any more. He peeled off his mask and hood and sat with Perry on the seat, his suit drying off. When he opened a bag with sandwiches and fruit in it, Perry found he was alarmingly hungry. It wasn’t as if he’d done any exercise to merit it, but the fresh air obviously had that effect. They ate the food and drank from water bottles in companionable silence.

“We’ll set off back to the shore now?” Perry asked. Dammit, had he sounded whiney? He didn’t mean to, but Greg was so bloody touchy….

Greg nodded, not noticeably irritated by him. “You did well.”

“Me? I’m not sure I did anything useful at all.” Perry laughed softly. “But you didn’t think I would?”

Greg smiled ruefully. "No, I didn't."

Despite the implied criticism, Perry found the honesty refreshing. He broke off half a bar of chocolate and handed it to Greg as his share. "What's next to do?"

Greg shook his head. "Not much. This is enough for today. The dive went well. I'll deliver these to Marty Calvin on Harris—" Catching Perry's eye, he added, "It's the island north of us. Marty will salt them today for preserving, and they'll go in for smoking tomorrow."

"Smoking?" Perry was beginning to think this was a whole new language.

Greg laughed and leaned over to pull the anchor back up. "You've never tasted a smoked, hand-caught scallop? Wait, I remember. You told me you haven't." He sighed, almost theatrically. "It's magnificent." Greg's eyes were shining, and his face glowed from the fresh air and the success of the dive. His smile was wide and genuine, and utterly charming.

Perry's heart missed a beat.

In that instant, he saw exactly what magic Greg had inherited from the Ventura family. It wasn't the standard, chiseled good looks of his brothers: it was the charisma of a man doing what he loved, in a place he loved, without interference or the restrictions of duty. Greg came alive that day, at least to Perry.

He was *definitely* no ugly duckling.

"Perry?" Greg was staring at him, puzzled. "You look weird."

Oh crap, I didn't say anything aloud, did I? Perry cleared his throat, knowing he'd blushed. "I'm fine. Are you really a diver? As a job, I mean?"

Greg blinked at the abrupt question, but grinned. "Busted! Aye, I've been teasing you, I admit it. Yes, I do dive, and yes, I do help out at the Sea Bird. But that would never pay enough to keep me in bread and whiskey."

"So how do you manage?"

"Well, there's money from my grandmother's inheritance. We all had a bequest."

"All your brothers?"

"Aye. As soon as we reached eighteen. I was third in line by age. Gerry likes cars, fast and expensive ones, so that's where his share went. And Geoff… well, he spent his on a new wardrobe or three. I wonder how much one of his suits costs him nowadays?"

"You don't want to know."

"No, you're right." Greg shrugged. "I left home not long after that, and I've no idea how they handle their money nowadays. I suspect Gareth gambled most of his bequest, but that's his problem. Even George, as his twin, can't keep him out of the casinos, and he probably lost *his* share in loans to Gareth. Anyway, Gran's money keeps me going when I haven't sold any paintings."

"Wait a minute. Paintings? You're a *professional* artist?"

For the first time, Greg looked embarrassed. "Just a few landscapes. Nothing special."

"But you sell them? In galleries?"

Greg shifted on his seat. "We should get going now. The chill settles deep as the afternoon travels in."

"Tell me." Perry frowned.

"Oh, for God's sake. Occasionally I sell one or two. There are small galleries in Stornoway and sometimes one of my works finds its way to the mainland."

Perry was amazed and thrilled. Somehow that suited Greg so well—the isolated and creative artist wedded to the stark, striking landscape around him. "Are they of the island? Of the sea? It's magnificent inspiration! If I had talent, I'd be painting this all day, every day."

Greg stared at him. He looked equally amazed. "Um. Yes, they are of the island. You didn't seem so keen on this place when you arrived."

Perry flushed. "I'll admit it's very different from the city, and I'm appalled by the weather, and the boggy peat fields, and the lack of public transport, and the godforsaken isolation—"

"And the water?"

"Oh God yes, *that*. There is *so much* water here! Bloody place is obsessed with it. Over eight hundred lochs, apparently, just on this island—"

"And so you've been googling this godforsaken place?" Greg asked drily.

My turn to get busted. Perry fell silent, embarrassed at being caught out in his growing fascination with North Uist. The salty air must be stronger than he'd imagined.

"That's what I mainly paint," Greg said quietly. "The sea. The shore. The morning light over the dunes. I don't really do it for the money."

Perry watched Greg's eyes as they shifted out of focus, as if he was looking inside rather than at Perry. Yet Perry wasn't insulted. Greg's gaze was responding to something much deeper and more beautiful.

"The TV show will pay really well," Perry said tentatively. Greg frowned, and Perry immediately regretted bringing it up.

"This is my day, remember? You're not allowed to pimp your agenda."

Perry smiled. "Sorry." *Smile again. Please!* "So what else do you paint? Any city scenes? Portraits?"

Greg snorted. "Hardly, when other things are much more rewarding. I paint the sea and the lochs, and the wildlife it cherishes. There are plenty of seals and birds to admire. Maybe the odd selkie too. This country's full of legend about them."

"Selkies?" Was Greg teasing him again? "What are they?"

"Sea sprites. Mermen and women. Legend has it if they come to land, they can be caught and kept as lovers, if you hide their pelt."

Perry started to laugh, then bit it back at the look in Greg's eyes. "You believe all that? Fairy tales?"

Greg stared back at him coolly. "Don't mock it, Perry. There are a lot of things in life that aren't explained by science." And while Perry cast around for a suitable answer, Greg started up the engine and directed the boat on its way back to the jetty.

They moored up and Greg left Perry on the jetty again while he went to change back into his clothes. Perry wriggled out of his life jacket and put the box of scallops down beside him.

His phone buzzed in his pocket to alert him to a text, and he tugged it out, wondering who was calling. Candace had already texted him the night before, and Antony had promised to call him soon for a proper chat. And Perry's mother had never bothered learning how to text in the first place.

It was from the agency! Perry had been waiting so long for this, to hear when the cavalry was turning up. Candace had been vague on the timetable, but Perry knew Eddy would have played this project close to his chest. And now he recognized Eddy's personal number. *At last!* He called up the message immediately.

Team can't make it after all. Sorry. Know you can manage. Take another week. Report in when you can. Eddy

"Team can't make it?" Perry stared at his phone in horror. *I'm completely on my own?* He didn't have anything with him to help—no wardrobe, no hair stylist, no photo equipment, no simulation app to show Greg how his new look would be. And what was with "take another week"? One minute there was a major crisis with the TV filming approaching, now Eddy—not known for his laissez-faire approach—was telling Perry to stay in Scotland. Wasn't he needed back in London ASAP? These were definitely mixed messages.

Worst of all was the lack of moral support. It felt like a betrayal. In fact, it *was* a betrayal! His fury bubbled up, making his head swim and his eyes smart.

He'd thought he was doing so well! He was bonding with Greg, learning what made the guy tick, observing him for guidance on how to present him for TV. Ignoring any personal agenda as completely unprofessional—*okay, so some of my "bonding" may have strayed into fawning territory*—he knew he hadn't mistaken the way Greg had opened up today, had laughed, had nudged and teased Perry, had been glad to share the day and his love of the island, had been keen to… well, to enjoy real life.

But who was Perry to know what real life was? He looked up at the glimmering sky, listening to the high-pitched cries of birds and the lapping water of the loch against the jetty. *How beautiful it all is.* He'd only been here a couple of days, but for one astonishing moment, he'd felt as if this was the perfect place to be.

It was the peace that attracted him, that was it. After all, he'd suffered a lot in the last few days, hadn't he? Damn Eddy and his bloody shitty agency! Perry had uprooted himself from his comfy, if rather too-bijou flat in London, traveled out to the wilds of nowhere, exposed himself and his delicate skin to nature and all her brutal elements, eaten loads of calorificly wrong foods, and now ventured out into the middle of a loch, for God's sake, all in the name of this job! He was just glad he'd managed the whole of today's trip without throwing up or getting in the way.

And that, of course, was when he fell in.

He was so engrossed in gazing at the sky and trying to assimilate the cruel text from London, he took a step backward without looking. His foot tangled in a coil of rope, and he toppled. His phone flew out of his hand in one direction and clattered to the deck, while his body lurched the opposite way. He had time for only one loud yelp. The last thing he saw before he plunged off the edge of the jetty was Greg spinning back around to look, eyes wide and mouth even wider.

Probably shouting at me for being a city idiot was Perry's last, aggrieved thought. Then he hit the cold, dark water with a *thwack* and thought no more.

Chapter Eleven

GREG had shrugged his shoulders out of his wet suit and was halfway to the hut to change when he heard the yell.

Perry?

He spun around just in time to see Perry tilted dangerously on the edge of the jetty. Greg opened his mouth to shout a warning—their eyes met, Perry's face contorted in shock and fear. Then he fell sideways into the water.

The splash was loud, and bursts of water sprayed up onto the wooden slats.

He's not wearing a life jacket!

Greg didn't even think—he just reacted. He raced back down the jetty, wriggling into his wet suit again, zipping it sharply up to his neck. Even before the bubbles had dispersed from where Perry fell, he dived in after him.

Perry had sunk like a stone, though luckily he hadn't drifted far from the jetty. But he was flailing around and bloody difficult to grab. Greg dodged a swinging fist too late, and it smacked him on his unprotected cheek. He let himself sink deeper, below Perry, making sure to keep away from Perry's thrashing feet. Then he kicked back upward and grabbed him around the waist. Pushing hard with his legs, he dragged them together up to the surface.

Perry spluttered, gasping in air, his eyes closed tight, his face deathly white. Water ran down his face, and his hair was a stringy, sodden mess. He fought with surprising strength.

"Perry!" Greg spoke fiercely, sharply in his ear. "Calm down! I have you. You're safe. You hear me?" He couldn't get Perry out of the loch while he was struggling. Perry had to cooperate.

"Greg?"

"Hush." Greg held him tight, treading water for them both. "Hush." He didn't know what else to do or say. He'd been trained in life saving, but that was usually on an unconscious body, not a lithe adult one that was very much alive, and writhing like a desperate fish. Finally, Perry stilled. Maybe he'd heard Greg at last, or maybe he was just exhausted. It was probably only a minute or so since they surfaced, but it had felt like ages.

Greg guided Perry's hands onto the jetty, levered him up, then lifted himself up beside him. He sat there for a long moment, gathering his breath and cradling a soaked Perry in his arms.

"Greg?"

"Hm?"

Perry's voice was very shaky. "Thanks for saving my sorry arse."

Greg chuckled. They needed to get somewhere dry and warm, but he wanted Perry's heart rate to slow down a bit first. So if Perry wanted to joke, Greg could do that too. "You're going to need more new clothes. You keep ruining your stuff."

Perry groaned. "I said this place had too much water, didn't I?"

"Perhaps you were trying to be some kind of selkie."

"I'm opening a London branch?"

Greg laughed. Perry was slender and water-slicked, smelling of the loch. Give him a tail and fins, and he could be one of the graceful seals Greg often saw, but transformed into a man. A sea sprite.

My sea sprite.

Where had that thought come from?

"I think they're better used to life in the sea." Perry sighed. "It doesn't seem to be my forte." His laugh was weak and soft, but his smile was brave.

"Come on. We need to get you back to the house," Greg said.

Perry went almost limp in Greg's arms. "Please," he whispered.

Greg bundled Perry into the Jeep, fumbled his way back into his clothes—not an easy job, when the wet suit still clung—and then drove as fast as he dared back to the croft. He just left the boat where it was, fairly sure it'd be safe for a few hours until he could fetch it back in a separate trip, though Perry had insisted they bring the box of scallops back with them. By the time they arrived, Perry had dried off a lot, but he was shivering. Greg all but frog-marched him into the living room. He'd never learned the niceties of nursing, but efficiency was more important in a crisis, right? He grabbed a pair of his own pajamas from the clean laundry pile in the kitchen and pushed them into Perry's arms. "Put these on quickly. I'll get this room heated."

Perry paused, looking confused.

"Perry?" Greg took his arm and sat him down on the sofa. "Change out of those clothes." Was he too shy or something? "I'll turn my back."

He heard the rustle of clothes behind him as he crouched down to light a fire. When he turned back, the flames catching well and the heat already springing up, Perry was dressed in the too-large pajamas and huddled in a corner of the sofa. "The loch was really cold," he whispered.

Greg nodded absently. "Always is, even with a wet suit. Fabulous, though. Bracing. Fierce."

"Yes. I'm sure." Perry didn't sound convinced.

Greg caught Perry's wide-eyed gaze, and his chest clenched in startling and inexplicable pain. Perry looked so bloody miserable. *It's all my fault!* Greg knew he should never have taken the poor sod out in the boat. He'd just been showing off, challenging Perry's city life with his own outdoor choices. How stupidly childish he'd been, and at Perry's expense. It was a sobering thought. It had been a long while since he'd been so ashamed of his behavior.

Perry could have drowned....

Perry coughed. "Greg, I—"

"Wait!" Without bothering to explain, Greg ran upstairs and hauled Perry's duvet off the bed. He carried it down to the living room, wrapped it around Perry's shoulders, and sat down on the sofa beside him. His arm reached all the way around Perry's body, even with the duvet tucked in. He paused a moment—a strange shiver of emotion ran through him—then he tightened his grip and drew Perry in close.

"*Oh*. That's better." Perry's sigh was a delicious sound that sprang goose bumps down Greg's spine. "So much better."

"I'll run you a bath later. For the moment, just rest." Perry was pliant in Greg's arms, and he rested his head against Greg's cheek. "Ouch." Greg bit back the wince of pain from the bruise underneath.

"What is it?" Perry lifted his head to peer at Greg's face. He placed his fingers against Greg's cheekbone, and his eyes widened. "Shit. Did I kick you when I was under?"

"Socked me on the face. It's fine." Greg didn't want him to pull away. He *really* didn't. And what's more, he knew it wasn't just because he wanted to keep Perry warm. "You were drowning at the time, so I forgive you. I thought you said you could swim?"

Perry laughed shakily. "I can. Honest. It was just the shock."

"Aye?" He felt the heat from Perry's blush against his neck.

"No. Actually… no, I can't swim, at least not very well. I got my ten yards certificate at school, but that was the absolute minimum."

Greg rolled his eyes. "It's bloody good exercise. And there are all those pretentious gyms in the city you could use."

Perry's nose wrinkled and he dropped his head into the folds of the duvet. "All that hassle changing clothes, and getting wet then dry again, and the chlorine in my hair? Ugh, no."

Greg laughed. For some reason, Perry's fancy ways were amusing right now, rather than downright pathetic.

Perry's skinny little body felt much warmer. His arms had curled around Greg's waist in return, and his messy curls were soft against Greg's chin. Greg would have liked to see his face again, but he wasn't going to disturb this current cessation of hostilities. It felt too good.

"Thank you," Perry said softly, his words a gentle breath on Greg's throat.

"You already said that." But Greg kept his tone light.

"I mean… I'm sorry I spoiled the day."

"What the hell does that mean?"

"It was a wonderful time. Well, up until I fell in. You were a different man out there today. So much in your element. I loved watching you dive."

"I…? You did?"

"You were marvelous," Perry said, on a yawn. Somehow it pushed him in even closer to Greg's chest. "So graceful. Really strong." There was a smile in his voice. "You're the selkie, really. You were beautiful in the water."

Greg was stunned. Was Perry taking the piss? No one had ever accused Greg of being graceful *or* beautiful. But Perry sounded thoughtful, not sarcastic.

"I was the clumsy idiot who brought it all to an end," Perry continued. "I'd never be the kind of selkie you'd keep, eh? Way too much trouble."

Greg cleared his throat. It was painfully tight. "Oh, I don't know about that."

"Mm?" Perry lifted his head again. His lips were millimeters from Greg's, their breath mingling. Their faces were so close, Perry's features were just a blur. *Don't think about it, just do it.* Greg leaned forward that tiny, insignificant yet totally consuming distance and kissed Perry.

It wasn't much of a kiss—it was less than passionate, yet somehow much more touching. Greg felt a shiver of delight almost immediately. Perry's mouth opened slightly to let loose a soft sigh, and Greg took it into his own mouth, following the shape of Perry's lips with his own, brushing his tongue against the tip of Perry's.

Perry didn't pull away. Instead, he melded closer to Greg and darted his tongue into Greg's mouth. Desire shot through Greg like a bolt from the blue. He couldn't remember feeling such a pure, strong emotion for a long time. He tightened his grip on Perry, sliding a hand under the bulky duvet to find Perry's body. His palm landed on a slender, muscular thigh.

Oh God. Suddenly he was terrified of doing the wrong thing. But how could he bear to let go?

Perry seemed just as eager to stay close. His breath hitched, and he pressed his mouth onto Greg's more fiercely. With an awkward shake, he threw off the duvet and climbed into Greg's lap, pushing Greg back against the sofa cushions. Still touching, still kissing all the time, neither of them breaking hold. Greg clung to him, tangling his tongue against Perry's, breathing in Perry's smell of cold loch and warm desire. It was something like a miracle, and his head swam with excitement and shock. His hips were twisted awkwardly on the sofa cushion, but he couldn't mistake the pressure of his swelling cock inside his briefs. His jeans were way too tight for this. Not that he had any special "making out" style of clothing put aside for the ludicrously unlikely event of a gorgeous London man letting him run his hands down his back, feeling every gorgeous knob of his spine, and then cup gently over the equally ludicrously gorgeous globes of his gorgeous arse—

"Well!" Perry said and pulled away, though only a little way. His voice was shaky and his eyes were very,

very bright. Greg prayed that wasn't because he was running a fever.

"Good or bad 'well'?" Greg asked bluntly. His head swam with confusion now. If Perry told him he was way out of order, he'd be mortified—

"Oh, definitely good." Perry gave a small but sweet little smile, like he was nursing an internal secret. Then he bent over Greg again, his eyes twinkling with humor as if he were sharing that secret very happily and quite openly. "Very good. Can we do it again?"

Chapter Twelve

PERRY was wondering how long he could survive on the sofa, perched on Greg's lap, without having to get up for annoying bodily habits like food and the toilet. He could live this way for hours. Days. As long as his lips could cope with it.

Greg laughed, a wonderful sound with a soft, purring edge to it. He was a greedy but very sensuous kisser. Perry couldn't believe how exciting it was. He ran his fingertips along Greg's chin, ruffling his beard. Greg almost winced, as if he wasn't used to being touched that way—so intimately—at all. But then he relaxed into it, nuzzling against Perry's touch, while Perry kept his fingers gentle.

And *oh*… but it felt good.

They kissed for a long, leisurely time. Greg had started out quite tentative—it had been unexpected and very disarming—but his hands grew bolder the longer he kept hold of Perry. Perry felt like a rare bird captured by a hunter, yet one who was a bit bemused by his luck. Perry wriggled and moaned, almost in song, against the possessive cage that Greg's body had created. Greg gripped tighter, and his mouth claimed Perry even more fiercely.

And oh, but it felt *wonderfully* good!

They broke for air at last, with a deep groan from Greg and a heartfelt sigh from Perry that took him almost by surprise. He was so hard he could match one of the logs in the fireplace, and from the way Greg was shifting beneath him—ah *yes*, that was it—he was in the same state of arousal.

Easy does it. Perry was in no rush. This was something special.

He settled back against Greg's chest. His breathing rose and fell faster than Greg's, but Greg's deeper rhythm was stimulating. For several minutes they just lay on the sofa together, arms wrapped around each other. Perry allowed himself to savor the bliss that was still thrumming through his veins.

"So," Greg said at last. His voice was hoarse.

"Hm?"

"So now it's your turn."

"Sorry?"

"It was the deal, remember? You sat in my boat all that time and suffered that disgracefully fresh sea air. For God's sake, you took a freezing cold dip."

Perry chuckled and was glad when Greg joined in. Perry didn't often bear grudges.

"But now it's time for your pitch."

"My…?"

Greg gave an exaggerated sigh, though he was still smiling. "To tell me about this London business. The makeover. Your *mission*, remember?"

"I suppose so." Perry was surprised how reluctant he was to relinquish his current position. But Greg was right, they had a deal. "If you're sure."

"God, you're a bad bargainer, aren't you?"

Perry snuffled a laugh and sat up. He felt colder the minute he pulled away from Greg's chest. "Okay, you're right. Let me get my files." He clambered off the sofa and padded out of the room. A quick run upstairs, and a few minutes later he returned with his small, stylish briefcase. Greg glanced at the case and his eyes widened.

Oh well. Perry sighed to himself, but bravely. He knew the large, salt-rimmed water stain on the back of his luggage meant it would never recover from his arrival in the Scottish rain. But it could be replaced, couldn't it? It wasn't as important as… other things. He settled back on the sofa but a distance away from Greg so he could reach the low table beside it.

"You're up for this?" Greg said suddenly. "After the water? Maybe tomorrow—"

"Hey. I'm not letting you go that easy." Perry chuckled, his banter restored. "I'm dry now, and I wasn't that long in the loch, was I? I'll have a hot bath before bed and make sure to keep wrapped up warmly."

"Okay. But I know you're waiting for the rest of your team—" Greg started.

"Oh, they're not coming."

"What?"

Perry grimaced. "They've aband—I mean, I'm their sole representative for the project." He couldn't look Greg in the eye any longer. Greg's gaze was soft, his expression tender. Perry didn't want to humiliate himself in front of his man.

My man?

The sound from Greg was like a growl. "So how come it was the most important thing on the bloody planet to drag me off to London, and now—it's not?"

"It's still important." Perry bristled in defense. "Of course it is! It's just that… people are busy elsewhere."

Greg snorted. "Sounds like you've been dumped on, in my opinion."

"It's fine. I can cope. I know all the details." Perry cleared his throat. "Well, most of them. And I can check out the rest later."

An unfamiliar expression twisted Greg's face. Perry might even have mistaken it for sympathy. "You tell me about it, Perry. Just you. That's fine by me."

"Yes?" Perry tried not to blush at the unexpected support. He pulled a bundle of photos out of the case. "It will be a big budget show. It'll follow the family's progress over the course of several months, with professional editing, of course, to produce hour-long episodes. You know how those programs go."

"No I don't. I don't watch TV."

"You—what?" Perry was momentarily stunned at the concept of someone who didn't watch popular culture. Whether you loved or despised it, it was part of everyone's life. Wasn't it?

"Well, the odd sporting event at Dougie's." Greg shrugged. "That's not to say I can't guess what relation 'professional editing' bears to real life. But they want my family?"

"They're big news back in London, Greg. The Venturas are well-known in sport and business. And now the twins are dating oligarchs or something equally glamorous."

"Even George?"

Perry caught Greg's eye. His smile was of a fellow conspirator. "Yes, I gathered he's gay as well. Or maybe bisexual, because he's been dating men and women. Let's say he's generous in his fluidity."

Greg laughed. "George was always generous with favors, fluid or not. He never had any money, was always having his heart broken. But the bisexual thing… that's okay with the media?"

"It's hardly scandal any longer. Maybe some people disapprove, but it's still—"

"Newsworthy?"

"Yes. I'm afraid so. But that's the way it'll become fully acceptable, isn't it? With familiarity." Perry could hear his voice tighten.

"Have you been discriminated against?" Greg asked bluntly.

"Sometimes." Perry bit his lower lip. "I've been passed over for a couple of jobs I know I could have done well. And my mother's not much of a support, I must say. She still thinks I'm going through a teenage phase. But I've never let those things stop me."

Greg's eyes had darted down to where Perry's lip eased out between his teeth, but his tone was enthusiastic. "Good for you."

Perry felt even more flushed. "I'm good at my job. I love it! My talent is making the best of people, especially when they don't recognize it in themselves."

"They're bloody lucky to have you," Greg said firmly.

"Um. I haven't even made the pitch yet," Perry said with a small laugh. He tilted his head to one side, considering the mystery that was Greg Ventura. "May I ask, is that why you came here? Because you're gay and you suffered discrimination…?"

Greg's scorn came out as another snort. "God, no. There was always so much drama going on in my family, being gay was probably the least interesting thing. Not compared to the time Gerry crashed a demonstration sports car into a shopping center when he hadn't even passed his test, the time a dozen naked female fans streaked onto the pitch when Geoff was taking a trial for Arsenal, the time the twins took a train—on their own, aged six—to find the real Middle Earth. Jesus, it was one spotlight thing after another, but it was *never* the gay thing."

Perry stared at him, wide-eyed.

"The pitch," Greg said firmly. "I haven't talked about any of this for years, and I'm not about to start now. Off you go."

Chapter Thirteen

AT first, Greg felt quite sanguine about it all. Perry smiled as he spread a selection of photos on Greg's small wooden side table with a flourish that looked faintly ridiculous from a pale young man with tousled hair, dressed in pajamas that fell in folds around his ankles. But Greg didn't find it ridiculous at all. He just wanted to smile back. He'd never imagined he could be so sentimental about a man, let alone one he'd only just met….

"Here's the look I'm going for, you see?" Perry said brightly. "It doesn't have to be a suit like that"—he pointed at a group shot of Geoff, Gerry, and a couple of other men in elegant suits—"because I'm not sure the cut would suit your shoulders. You'd look better in a single-breasted, and it's really fashionable at the moment. Straight leg trousers and ankle boots would look perfect."

Greg couldn't take his eyes off the photo. "I haven't worn a suit since my graduation."

"Well, I think it's expected for the interview at the beginning of the pilot episode. But then it'll be casual clothes, I'm sure. I know just the designer to use for your jeans and a whole range of shirts. To be honest, you'll wear it better than your brothers, you know? You have a wonderfully natural way of walking tall that they don't have, at least not without working at it." Perry cleared his throat and blushed. "I mean, it's obviously a result of the outdoor life here."

Greg wasn't listening properly. The photo held his attention as if by emotional glue. He'd had no idea he would feel like this, seeing pictures of his brothers after all these years. Spreading out another half-dozen, he slid his gaze from one to another. *Here they all are.* There was Geoff in his football kit, worn in this shot for effect rather than for a game. His hair was perfectly groomed and his skin shone with good, clean, unsweaty health. God, he looked like a movie star. The twins' picture had been taken at some kind of premiere, because Greg could see the red carpet stretching away behind them. They'd slung an arm around each other's shoulders, their heads close together, accentuating their similarity. Luxury fabric suits; big grins on their faces; provocative amusement in their eyes. Greg ran his fingers slowly over the photos, following the shape of his brothers' faces. A picture of Gerry in another setting again—he was at a club, surrounded by well-dressed older businessmen. Maybe they were even politicians. Whatever the situation was, Gerry looked comfortable and confident.

Greg hadn't seen his brothers in the flesh since he left home at twenty-one. *Five years ago. A fucking* age *ago.* For a moment, he didn't know what the emotions of that memory meant to him. Was he sad? Nostalgic? Bitter? Lonely? He'd made his choice—or rather, he'd always reckoned they made it for him. He'd started to tell Perry about the dramas in the Ventura family from when he was growing up. It had all been true. His brothers were atrocious attention-seekers, desperate always for the limelight. He knew now, with the hindsight of maturity, that was where the bullying started.

In his early years, when they were all small kids together, there had been good times. There was only six years in age between all the Ventura boys, and they'd been left to their own devices for a lot of the time: their high-flying parents weren't often available for play. The games had been fun, the camaraderie reassuring.

But things had swiftly changed.

Greg was different from the very beginning—much bigger in build, much slower to banter, more serious about life. He stood out from the others, and for all the wrong reasons. The teasing had started mildly at first, just something that brothers "do," just a way for the tumble of boys to differentiate themselves—all from the same family, all in each other's pockets. And then it grew more malicious. Gerry Ventura may have initiated that edge, but it became such an integral part of Greg's life, he couldn't have said for certain who started it or where it began. Just that it did—and it consumed his life. Obviously he couldn't do anything about his looks—that was just the way he was, with odd features and ungainly limbs—but the teasing also exacerbated his clumsiness. He was bright enough, but a gangly child often falling over his own feet and stuttering for words was a gift to jokes at his expense. And that, of course, meant he did it all the more. He was pointed at and laughed at, an anomaly in among his athletic and more graceful siblings. They were succeeding at sports, in popular clubs, with girls. How could Greg be part of the same glorious family? The nickname Ugly Duckling was coined at around age fourteen, when school groups became cliques, and girls—even though Greg knew by then he wasn't interested in them sexually—became the judges of whether a boy was good-looking or a loser.

Greg Ventura didn't meet the grade.

His school life was a misery, even when he grew older and could recoup some ground with good academic results and minor success in basketball. But as soon as he had his degree in Art and his inheritance, he left home. And never looked back.

Why should he? Did they have any idea how they'd hurt him? How painful his childhood and teenage years had been? Maybe not. But he'd be damned if he'd remain a victim for the rest of his life, so he took himself away from the temptation. Better for all of them that he led his life elsewhere. And he'd always reckoned that strategy was successful.

But here was Perry, today, with no idea of the real story behind these photos; no idea of the real reason for keeping the Ventura brothers divided. Earnest, naive Perry, who probably had an army of happy, loving family members and friends. Who just wanted to do his job well. Stirring things up, poking his nose in where it wasn't wanted. Disturbing this particular lochful of Greg's miserable baggage.

It isn't Perry's fault.

Of course it bloody wasn't. But who else was with Greg at that moment?

He sat up abruptly, refocusing on the living room with some difficulty. "I can't do this."

"What?" Perry was startled. "Did I say something wrong? I haven't been through the whole process with you yet."

"Not today. Sorry." Greg wanted to leave the room, wanted to hit something, wanted to do anything but talk further about his family. He stood, swaying slightly on his feet. It was Perry who'd had the physical shock today, wasn't it? But Greg felt worse, both exhausted and horribly, resentfully restless.

"This isn't fair—" Perry started.

"*Fair*?" Greg nearly spat the word, and Perry recoiled. Greg dragged himself back under control and stood. "We'll… you can tell me later. Tomorrow." *Maybe never.*

Perry looked like he was struggling with his words too. "I… okay. If that's what you want."

Perry had said that earlier, hadn't he? When Greg had insisted they do this—insisted that Perry had his chance to put his case. *This is all my doing… all my fault.* Unfortunately, that didn't stop him acting like a shit. He stumbled past Perry toward the door.

"Greg? Wait—"

But Greg didn't. He passed over the bottle of homemade wine on the windowsill and grabbed a nearby bottle of whiskey instead. And he left the room in a rush.

Chapter Fourteen

GREG slept badly. *Really* badly.

When he woke, the light stabbed his eyes, the duvet was strangling him in a bizarre tangle around his neck, and his head felt like a battle reenactment society was practicing inside. With cannon. Fighting his way out of bed, he dragged himself into the bathroom and splashed cold water over his face, trying to wake up his piggy little eyes and ease his horribly parched lips. He crawled into an old, comfortable pair of sweats and a clean but unironed tee shirt, pulled on his boots, then stumped clumsily down the stairs. He should have been up hours ago. Rory needed feeding and a walk, and Greg vaguely remembered offering to help Alasdair with the sheep this morning. And the scallops should have been taken down to Marty's yesterday; they'd be spoiled by now. Life just kept getting better. Not.

He paused in the hallway. The morning light from the open kitchen door still seemed way too bright, but maybe it'd improve after a mug of strong tea. He could actually smell a pot brewing, hear the pop of the toaster. Oh, if only life were that easy, that he could just wish for tea and the pot would warm itself!

Shuffling into the kitchen, he discovered it wasn't the power of his mind that had conjured up breakfast, but Perry.

Perry had his back to him, whipping up what looked like scrambled eggs in a bowl on the counter. Greg's mouth watered immediately in anticipation. It was one of his favorite breakfasts, not that Perry would have known that. Greg peered suspiciously at Perry, wondering for a minute if he was a hallucination, and Greg was still in a drunken sleep. *It's what I deserve for my shitty behavior last night. Perry so pissed off he's avoiding me, and me having to make my own damned breakfast—*

"Morning," Perry said cheerily, though he didn't turn around. "I won't say good, right?"

Greg gave a mumble that could have been taken as any word from "no" to "Nebuchadnezzar," and slumped down in one of the kitchen chairs. The wooden table rattled at the impact and a fork fell on the floor.

Perry whipped a little faster. Rory sat a few inches away, eyes lifted up to Perry in the hope some food would escape and launch itself his way. "Eggs okay for you?" Perry continued. "I still haven't got to any shops to stock up on anything more interesting. But you ought to eat something."

"Fine."

Perry poured them into the pan and started stirring. Greg opened his mouth to say he liked a lot of pepper, but before he could speak, Perry reached for the pepper mill and ground a healthy amount of seasoning into the mix.

Magic. Greg sat silently, nursing his headache and coveting the eggs, watching Perry at work. It was odd to have someone else in his kitchen. Perry popped more bread in the toaster and started buttering the slices already laid out on a plate. Greg didn't recognize the plate: probably another gift from his parents he'd never really acknowledged. He rarely went to the back of his kitchen cupboards. He ate most things—apart from his evening meal—off the kitchen counter or on the way to his work.

"A man called Marty came around early about the scallops," Perry said, his voice as brisk as his stirring. "Before I went to bed last night, I moved them into that cold area off the kitchen, and so they were still chilled this morning. He said they'd be fine, and he'll smoke them today."

He turned at last, but didn't meet Greg's gaze. Placing the toast and eggs and a large mug of hot tea in front of Greg, he sat in the chair opposite him. Rory skittered across the floor and resettled at Perry's feet. The cleared plate in front of Perry showed his breakfast was already eaten, and his mug of tea was half-finished. Greg wondered just how long Perry had been up.

The toast smelled rich and buttery, the eggs fragrant and heaped on top, just as Greg liked it. It tasted even better. Even so, he felt strange, and it wasn't nausea from the hangover. He had a sneaking suspicion this was what shame felt like.

Perry reached down to rub Rory behind the ears. Rory's eyes drifted shut like the sluttiest boyfriend ever.

Greg wondered ruefully how he was going to recapture the bloody dog's loyalty when Perry went back to London.

Perry's going back to London....

I kissed Perry....

Perry tasted so bloody good....

"Look here—" Greg began, spraying a few toast crumbs over the table.

"The agency called me," Perry said at the same time. "I'm needed back there."

They both paused and stared at each other.

Something made Greg wonder if Perry was telling the truth. He looked shifty in some weird way. "So. Okay. I mean." Christ, couldn't he even get a sentence out clearly? "You mean today?"

"Soon as I can sort out a ferry crossing." Perry buried his attention in the top of his mug.

Greg didn't think any cup of tea could be *that* interesting, even if his tasted like a welcome slurp of heaven. But Perry obviously didn't want to face him. With an even worse stab of nausea, Greg wondered if this was all about the kiss?

Dammit. He was amazed how distressed he felt if that was the case.

Perry was talking again. "I mean, I think it's pretty obvious there's no mileage in this project for me, is there? You made that clear… um. Well, yesterday. After… when you saw the photos."

"Aye." Greg couldn't seem to make his head match up with his mouth. He wished Perry would keep quiet, just until Greg's head stopped thumping, and he could get things straight enough to make a sensible reply—

"What's up?" Perry had looked up suddenly and caught Greg with his eyes all goggling. "You're staring at me like a lunatic."

"Of course I'm bloody not."

"Ha-ha. That's better. More like the Greg Ventura we all know and… well, know." Perry cleared his throat, collected up his and Greg's empty plates, and took them to the sink. He started to run the hot water.

"You don't have to do the chores," Greg grumbled.

"I want to help out."

"It won't make any difference to my decision, you know."

The back of Perry's neck went pink and his shoulders tightened. "I know that. Good grief, can't you accept some help without thinking everyone's out to trade?"

"You're the media man. You should know."

"Oh, fuck you!" And Perry pushed past him, out of the kitchen.

Well, that went well. Greg stared morosely at his now empty tea mug and would have kicked himself if he had the energy to move.

Rory barked at him, just once. It was definitely an accusation.

THERE was a knock at the door, but by the time Greg stomped to open it, Bridie had already let herself in. No one locked their doors on the island, Greg had learned that in the first week he arrived, and he'd never had cause to regret it. Though maybe, judging by the serious frown on Bridie's usually pretty face, he'd rethink that now.

"What's up with Perry? I could hear your voices from down the path."

Bloody village life. "Why the hell would I know?"

"Because you're probably the one who pissed him off."

"Oh for God's sake. Why is everyone having a go at me?"

She frowned. "So perhaps I should ask, what's up with *you*? Have you been drinking?"

Greg let loose of the whole damned mess, his temper along with it. "It's my fucking house, my fucking time! Maybe drinking's the only way to cope with life around here at the moment."

Bridie blinked hard but, as expected, didn't retreat. "It's not Perry's fault you've got a stinking hangover."

"No? Why the hell not?" Greg knew he was being childish and cruel, but that wasn't going to stop him right now, was it? His head ached, his mouth was dry, he really *had* pissed off Perry, and now Bridie was standing there with her holier-than-thou face on, when all he wanted to do was to be left alone to wallow in his resentment and self-pity. "He comes into my house uninvited, with his ridiculous London gloss and the wrong clothes. He tries to drag me back to that filthy, smoke-ridden city, to tart myself up like some prostitute, to take part in an obscenely tacky TV show. And you know what's the worst?"

"Greg. Wait—" Bridie's eyes were wide.

Greg ignored her. He was on a roll. "He's even bewitched my bloody dog! What's that all about?"

"Shut up, you blithering idiot," she hissed.

At the last minute, Greg paused, sensing something from her expression. He twisted around slowly, and even his blurry hangover vision couldn't miss what she'd seen seconds before he had.

Fuck.

Perry was standing in the doorway of the living room, his face white. He'd heard every word.

Chapter Fifteen

PERRY stood in Greg Ventura's spare bedroom, his suitcase open on the bed, his small wardrobe of London clothes tumbled in any old how. He was usually such a careful packer. If you rolled shirts carefully, they'd emerge needing minimal pressing. Pack underwear into your boots, or around the edges of the case to prevent your toiletries from rolling about. Finally, place towels on top of everything, to keep the clothes even further protected. Perry usually followed this method religiously, because he didn't have enough outfits to play spares. Every item was precious and wholly necessary for his professional London image.

The state of his case today reflected the state of his mind.

Rory sat at his feet, eyes gazing up at him, ears pricked. He was probably waiting for someone to take him for his morning walk. Perry and Greg had been too busy arguing to look after the dog. *Shameful*, Rory's expression said, though maybe there was a flicker of sympathy in his big brown eyes.

Perry let himself down onto the edge of the mattress and sank his head in his hands. "Sorry, guy," he said. Yes, now he was talking to the animals. Another reason this place was way too disturbing. "I'm out of here. You're stuck with the grumpy old git from now on."

He knew he had to leave the croft now. No other choice, right? But he didn't want to go. And he especially didn't want to go with those harsh words of Greg's ringing in his ears.

Ridiculous. Filthy. Obscenely tacky.

Okay, so they hadn't all been used to describe Perry himself. But to Greg, Perry was London, and vice versa. Perry was the walking proof of everything Greg hated and despised. This visit had been marked for failure from the very start. Greg had never hidden the fact he was hostile and dismissive, but Perry had continued regardless, and he'd made a complete fool of himself.

At the doorway, someone cleared their throat.

Perry nearly jumped off the bed. "What the hell?"

"Sorry." Greg stood there, looking like death that hadn't even bothered warming up.

"Creeping up on me like that—!"

"No. I mean, sorry for what I said."

"You mean, I wasn't meant to hear?"

"No. I mean, I shouldn't have said it in the first place."

"Oh." Perry took a deep breath. It was a pretty fine apology, as far as they went. And there was no point in getting overexcited about things, was there? "You were right, of course. Possibly a tad rude about it, but the facts are there for all to see."

"A tad rude?" Greg snorted. "I was a bloody pig."

Perry also snorted, half disgust, half laughter. *Are mannerisms contagious?* "Sit down," he said, gesturing to a space on the bed beside him. "You're intimidating, standing up there."

"Not just standing up here," Greg said, but he sat down regardless.

"Has Bridie gone home?"

"Aye. She just left, after bending my ear about what a shit I am."

Perry wanted to laugh, partly at Greg's brutal honesty and partly at his miserable expression. "She speaks her mind, I must say."

"She actually came over to remind me about the ceilidh."

"What's a kaylee? I heard the word before, like it's something special."

"A *ceilidh.*" Greg repeated it as if the spelling would appear magically on the wall in front of them. It still sounded the same nonsense to Perry. "It's a dance. A knees-up, in your language."

Perry was tempted to stick out his tongue. "No need for the translation, I know what you mean. So what about it? Is that the height of your social excitement around here?" To Perry's surprise Greg didn't lash back out at him, though Perry knew he was straying into the rude camp himself.

"I'm afraid so. This community's pretty small to start with, just one pub, one village hall, and a couple of musicians. You'd have to travel to Benbecula or Stornoway if you wanted anything like a proper club."

"I'm not here for the social life," Perry said tightly.

"Pity," Greg said. He seemed very interested in playing with Rory's floppy ears. "I thought you might want to come along."

"To the ceilidh?"

Greg shrugged but his expression was far from casual. "It's on Saturday. Everyone can take a guest."

"I won't still be here, will I?"

"Won't you?" Greg shook his head in frustration, then winced as if it hurt. He turned his mournful eyes up to Perry's face. "I'll say it again, I'm sorry. Seriously, I am."

Perry was silent for a moment. Greg sounded genuine.

Whereas Greg obviously thought Perry was unconvinced, because he continued, "You don't have to leave, Perry. I didn't mean all that shit. I was just lashing out because I'm a crappy morning-after drunk. You're still entitled to your half of the deal, right? A chance to tell your side of the story. Explain what it's all about. A fair hearing."

"There's not much point, is there?" Perry raised his eyebrows. "Let's be real here, Greg. Your kind of hostile audience doesn't change its spots."

"God. You're right." Greg gave a rueful chuckle. "But I was still a shit. I'm sorry. I said that already, didn't I?"

"Yes. Several times." Despite himself, Perry felt a smile twitch at the edge of his mouth. Greg might behave like a truculent toddler sometimes, but he was just as honest and full-on with his apologies. Perry could almost say it was charming.

"Don't go." Was that a wheedle in Greg's tone? "Stay a few days. Could you manage that? I mean, I know they need you back there straight away—"

"No, they don't."

"Huh?"

Secretly, Perry doubted Eddy would pay his expenses for two days, let alone ten, but why the hell not? He sighed. "Actually, they said I was to take another week. So I guess I could stay. But the cost of the hotel—"

"Stay here," Greg said quickly. "That's what I meant."

Perry sneaked a look at him out of the corner of his eye. Greg was quite flushed. "Okay. Thanks."

"Perry? About the kissing…."

Perry bit his lip to stop the urge to butt in. *I want him to be honest about this too.*

Greg gave a quiet groan. "It was really great."

"Yes, it was." Perry found he was smiling. "So, whose guest will I be at the ceilidh? Bridie's?"

"Bridie's taking Lisa."

It wasn't a proper answer, nor was it the one Perry hoped for. Suppose he'd have to take what little encouragement he was given—

"Mine," Greg added awkwardly. "You'd be my guest."

Perry remembered something Bridie had said about Greg. "You don't go to these events, do you? Not usually, anyway."

"No," Greg said in a clipped tone. "I don't, usually."

Perry smiled again, but this time to himself. Ridiculous how excited he felt at the thought of a night out in a drafty bar with homegrown music and some clodhopping line dancing.

Or was it the thought of a night out with Greg Ventura?

"That'd be fine," he said brightly, good humor restored. "I'll look forward to it!"

Chapter Sixteen

GREG was sort of disturbed at how quickly he got used to having Perry around. He'd always considered the cottage barely big enough for him on his own, but it seemed Perry wasn't large or noisy enough to cramp Greg's style. He moved quickly and gracefully, a slender creature who smiled and chatted, but not too excessively, and seemed to know what was happening in the croft's schedule at any time, inside and outside the house. And by God, the man made brilliant scrambled eggs!

Over the next couple of days, they ate all their meals together, which Perry usually cooked. At least, he did on condition that Greg took him to Dougie's shop first, where he could stock up on ingredients. Greg's fridge had never had so much stuff in it, most of which he had no idea what to do with. Luckily, Perry did. And

Perry tidied up too. At first it had irritated Greg, not being able to find things in the same place as usual. But then favorite items he'd lost months ago started turning up. He also crashed into things less often—the small size of the cottage combined with his untidiness had been a stumble waiting to happen. Now the place was cleaner, and despite his natural clumsiness, he could stride confidently from one end of the house to another without breaking a single thing.

During the days, Greg went diving or closeted himself in his studio, painting. He didn't take Perry diving with him anymore, but they went together to deliver boxes of scallops to Marty, who showed Perry around his smokehouse with righteous pride. Perry looked impressed by it all, especially when Marty hauled the huge blocks of dried peat in for fuel, and Perry said all the right things about the facilities to make Marty smile wider than he ever did for Greg. In fact, Perry seemed to have that effect on most people. Greg had been prepared for villagers to find a London upstart pretentious and unsympathetic, but of course Perry wasn't naturally like that, was he? At first, he still carried on like a Londoner, but his eyes were bright and curious, and he had genuine interest in learning what was going on. Plus, he seemed to be developing a fondness for the island that Greg had never anticipated—he wondered if it had taken Perry by surprise as well. Even Perry's clothes were starting to look like an islander's, albeit his borrowed fleece hoodie now had a couple of rainbow badges on it, and his hiking boots had neon-colored laces.

Otherwise, Greg wasn't entirely sure what Perry did with his time. Sometimes he heard cars draw up, some laughter, and the front door slamming as Perry "popped out for a bit!" Shopping bags would appear in the hallway, full of kitchen utensils or bathroom accessories, or random things with no visible use that also looked way too frilly and bright to fit with Greg's austere décor. Needless to say, most of the items stayed, finding a sneaky place somewhere in the cottage. Perry also took Rory for walks and generally spoiled the animal with too much attention. But whatever he did during the day, he was usually around when Greg returned from a diving trip or emerged from the studio with hands covered in paint and a blinding thirst for tea. And he was always there at mealtimes. He even appeared to look forward to the time spent together.

It was weird.

Greg wasn't sure what he was meant to make of it all. Another disturbing effect was that Greg was conscious of Perry's presence all the time, even when Perry was being his most unassuming. They shared the bathroom amicably—well, Perry diplomatically let Greg go first in the mornings—and did laundry and chores together. Perry put his shaver on the bathroom shelf next to Greg's; Greg moved his boots aside in the hall so Perry could put his new footwear beside them. Though Greg wasn't sure about the blue-and-white-striped Wellington boots settled jauntily next to his plain khaki pair.

Perry was certainly trying not to disrupt things too much, Greg could tell. And he was good company to have around. He even seemed to be adapting to Greg's routines, though why the hell would anyone be bothered with that? Suspicious still, Greg wondered if Perry was creeping around him, still trying to persuade Greg back to London. Though Perry hadn't mentioned the TV program again, and Greg didn't remind him. Let sleeping dogs lie, right?

More disappointingly, in Greg's opinion, there hadn't been any further intimacy. No more snogging. They shared the evenings sitting in the living room, where Greg read his thrillers and Perry had appropriated the end of the sofa by the table, where he kept a sketch pad and a pile of magazines he liked to flick through. Greg had never seen any of them in the shop, so maybe Bridie had ordered them in specially. Greg drank his homemade wine after dinner and sometimes whiskey, but Perry stuck to water and the occasional gin and tonic. Greg knew Bridie had ordered *that* in especially for Perry.

But no more kisses.

On Friday evening, Greg cast a rueful glance over at the sofa, where Perry was engrossed in a magazine. He'd bought another load of chocolate at the shop that morning—almost as if he'd been starved of it before now—and was absently chewing on a square of it right now. For a few moments, Greg watched the movement of Perry's mouth like his own personal movie. Then he bit back a sigh, and levered himself up out of the armchair. "Just gonna finish up in the studio," he murmured. It felt odd: he wasn't used to reporting in to anyone on his comings and goings.

Perry looked up, his eyes wide, the blue color surprisingly clear. "May I see?"

"See what?"

Perry had developed this habit of raising one eyebrow when Greg barked at him. It seemed to represent a mixture of "get over yourself" and "moderate your language" and, much to Greg's chagrin, had that very result.

"Your work," Perry said gently but firmly. "I've only seen the one in my—in the spare bedroom."

Greg frowned. "Didn't tell you that was one of mine, did I?"

"Maybe I'm psychic where art's concerned," Perry said with a small smile. "Or maybe it's because you signed it at the bottom."

Greg rolled his eyes. “Oh, aye.” He didn’t keep many of his pictures—after all, if he had a market, he needed to sell them while he was still in fashion—but he’d kept a small study of the loch he’d taken Perry to that time, a scene from the very early morning. It was one of his personal favorites.

“So, can I come in?”

Greg couldn’t really say no, could he? Well, he could, but he knew Perry’s look would tell him how bloody churlish that was. Perry followed him into the studio, his gaze taking in the large window Greg had built into the seaward wall, which let in so much fabulous light in the mornings.

“This is great! No wonder you love being in here.”

“Aye.” Greg looked around as well, although the place was already familiar to him. But he turned as Perry did, slowly and appreciatively. It *was* great, wasn’t it? A burst of unfamiliar pride washed over him. The conversion had been all his own work.

“Is this your latest picture?” Perry paused by Greg’s easel.

Greg never thought to cover his canvas when he stopped work. Why should he, when he was always on his own? But now he felt stupidly scared of Perry looking at it. Perry would judge its immaturity: he’d have seen real art, London gallery stuff, not broad-brush, generic sea scenes from an island where there were no trees and nothing but sheep and sea birds for foreground interest—

“It’s fabulous,” Perry breathed, transfixed.

It was of the loch again. These were the scenes Greg was asked for most often, and the ones that sold well. Buyers seemed to like the pathways sweeping through the peat bogs to the dunes and overhead the terns swooping low for pickings from the sea. They liked the wide, clear stretches of sea water, with the occasional boat bobbing in the distance and fronds of grass at the shore. Their imagination was piqued by the mist of the early morning over the heather and the purple indigo skies of the evening.

"You're very talented," Perry said softly.

Was he trying deliberately to embarrass Greg? "Dunno about that."

"You've drawn the beauty of the loch so well. Awesome, but in perfect, mutual balance with the land."

Greg blinked. Perry had a way of expressing exactly what he, Greg, was thinking himself… how could that be?

"I can smell the air," Perry said more softly. "Dammit, I can feel the cold of the water!"

Greg smiled. "Bring back happy memories?"

Perry chuckled. "God, no, thanks. The reminder of my one dip is enough for me."

He leaned slightly toward Greg, and for a shocked, marvelous moment, Greg was tempted to draw him in and kiss him again. There was a hint in Perry's body language that encouraged Greg to think he wouldn't mind: he might even welcome it. *Do it. Do it!* And then Perry took a step in the other direction, tilting his head to concentrate further on the painting, and Greg… well, he lost his bloody nerve.

"You've captured it wonderfully. You have a real empathy with beauty."

Greg shrugged, angry with himself, with frustration, with embarrassment. "Well, even an ugly painter can recognize beauty in such a scene."

Perry's head snapped around to face him. "Why the hell did you say that?"

"Hey. Forget it." Greg frowned and shook his head. It had been a stupid comment, he knew, though it was genuinely thought. But Perry's anger startled him.

Perry turned back to the painting. He'd been relaxed, smiling at Greg, but now he looked hurt for some inexplicable reason. "Well, I'm off for a bath and bed."

"Um. Okay." Greg picked up his palette, unsure whether to continue. "Thanks for making supper. That chicken pie was great."

"No problem." Perry shrugged off the gratitude. "Thank *you* for the viewing. I appreciate it." He glanced again at Greg and seemed about to speak. Then he shook his head rather sadly, took one last, long gaze at the painting, and backed almost apologetically out of the studio.

Chapter Seventeen

SATURDAY night would be Perry's first proper introduction to other villagers. Or so Greg had explained to him, when they turned up at the village hall for the ceilidh. Perry had nodded, wisely keeping his mouth shut. Greg was in a half-bad mood already, obviously irritated at having been tricked into coming to this at all, conveniently forgetting it'd been his own idea. He'd also had to iron a shirt—Perry had insisted—and find clean jeans to wear.

Perry himself had chosen to wear a deep purple, fitted shirt and smart black trousers. It was one of the outfits that he'd brought with him, and he momentarily wondered if he'd look too weird among these country folk, but he felt good in it. He felt right: he felt like *Perry*. He was also relieved to be proved wrong, to find most people in the village hall had dressed smartly. They obviously used the event as an excuse to show off the slightest bit of finery. Maybe it wasn't London fashion, but the selection of kilts, blouses, and flowing skirts was a splash of fabulous color against the drab walls.

The room was filled with people of all ages, though he understood the younger children were taken home before the heavy drinking started. Greg homed straight in on the bar and forged a clumsy path for them both across the room. Perry decided not to make a fuss and followed meekly in his wake. He was surprised at how many people nodded to them as they passed. When he realized they were actually greeting *him*, he glowed from inside.

Greg, however, looked more irritated than glowing. "You've been in and out of Bridie and Dougie's shop all week," he hissed. "You said it was to stock up on food for the cottage."

"It was," Perry murmured back. *Amongst other things.* He'd learned swiftly where the fount of all knowledge settled on this part of the island.

Greg's eyes narrowed. "Not just to nose around and gossip?"

"What on earth do you think I'm like?" But Perry couldn't help a small smile. "The people here are charming, Greg, and very welcoming." *Unlike some I could mention*, he was about to add, but to be honest, things had moved on since then, hadn't they? Greg was no longer the totally aggressive, rude bear he'd been when Perry arrived.

What a difference a few days made! As they reached the bar, Perry sneaked a quick look at Greg in his smartly pressed clothes and his hair combed into some kind of style, his tall frame imposing at Perry's side, his eyes bright, his scowl unable to hide the fullness of his lips—

"What d'ye want?" Greg asked abruptly. The gathering obviously accentuated his adopted Scottish accent.

"A beer, if ye will," Perry bantered back, making sure to roll his *R*s in the country burr he'd heard all around him tonight.

Greg blinked twice. Maybe he wanted to laugh, but was still wedded to his irritation. The bartender rapped on the makeshift counter to get Greg's attention. As usual, where drink was concerned, one of Angus's sons was on duty. They'd just moved the pub from their back room to the village hall. Greg rummaged in his pocket for his wallet.

"It looks lovely," Perry said.

"What? The beer?"

Perry rolled his eyes. "The hall, I mean. The lights up at the windows, and the pots of heather along the sills. It makes it very sociable, almost festive."

Greg stared at him, while Angus's son waited none too patiently for Greg's payment.

"You didn't notice, did you?" Perry sighed. "I know you were keen for your beer but I think you should pay more attention to village events. I know this isn't exactly Stringfellows, but someone's made an effort to make it fun."

"And that, my wee bairn, will be me!" cried Bridie gleefully, appearing beside them. She was wearing a gloriously vivid red dress with a plunging neckline and, Perry assessed, a bra that was two sizes too small. She looked a little drunk already, and Lisa—in dungarees, no less, but at least they were in patterned fabric—hovered at her shoulder as if they were attached by a short chain. When she caught Bridie's eye, they beamed at each other.

Well, well, well.

"It's great," Perry said and clinked his glass against Bridie's in cheers. After he poked Greg in the ribs, Greg grudgingly did the same.

"You've got a busy dance card," Bridie said with a smirk to Perry.

"I'm sorry?"

"Old Mally wants to tell you another war story he just remembered—"

"Which I suspect is the same as the one he told me on Tuesday," Perry said with a smile.

"Louisa says you've promised her a drink, though she shouldn't drink anything too strong on her medication—"

Perry lifted a hand in greeting to an elderly lady in a vibrant lilac skirt suit on the other side of the bar. She started waddling over to them, hobbled by her presumably unfamiliar strappy shoes.

"—and *all* the McAllister children say you promised to dance with them."

"Good God," Greg muttered, and took another slurp of his beer. "Where and when did you meet all these people?"

"Just round and about," Perry said airily.

"Come and meet Alasdair's grandson," Bridie continued, pointedly ignoring Greg. "He's only over from Inverness for the weekend. I think he'd like to meet *you*!"

Perry didn't have time to wonder what that meant, because Greg caught his wrist and brought him up short.

"Don't be long," Greg said abruptly, then flushed. "I mean, it's your round next."

Perry considered him for a moment, his smile growing wider. "A thirsty man waits for no one," he said to Bridie with a rueful shrug.

"A Scottish proverb of your own?" She smirked back.

"I wouldnae dare," he said in his best "Scottish" and grinned back. "But men are the same in London or Scotland, ye ken?"

She broke out into loud, dirty laughter and started to tug him away across the room. When Perry glanced back to the bar, he saw Greg staring after him, shaking his head in some despair.

Chapter Eighteen

BY the time Perry managed to grab another drink and a quiet moment, Greg had moved to a free spot on the perimeter of the hall where a man could put his beer glasses on the windowsill and then watch everyone else moving around. Perry sidled up and took the spot beside him, leaning back against the wall. He met Greg's gaze and smiled in greeting. Greg just nodded, then turned his attention back to the room. He'd seemed to take a breath of relief, but Perry convinced himself he'd imagined it.

Against the opposite wall, a group of musicians were tuning up. There was an old man on the drums, two teenagers on acoustic guitars, a woman on a cello, and a child who looked no older than six with a violin. A man sat a couple of feet away from them with what Perry recognized as bagpipes. *Heavens.* The Brit Awards it was not. But as they launched into a light, lively tune, he felt his spirits rise. He even started tapping his foot.

"Finished with the fan club?" Greg said.

Perry bristled. "They're friends, Greg. I like talking to everyone, there's always something interesting to—"

Greg's hand landed on his wrist. "Sorry," he said gruffly. "I like them too. I didn't mean it to sound like that. It was just a joke."

Perry smiled and nodded. The hand on his wrist stayed in place. Greg's palm was warm, and Perry's heartbeat was faster than usual. He gestured at a group of men in Highland dress at the bar. "Are they wearing the kilts for a bet?"

"Of course not. They're entitled to wear one. They like to show it off at social events."

Perry admired the way the skirt settled on a man's hips, and the selection of long socks highlighted several fine pairs of calves. "Do you have one?" he asked Greg.

Greg gave a scornful bark. "No, my family's not Scottish. Well, not for many generations."

Another tantalizing clue to Greg's background, Perry thought, filing it away mentally. "So you could be entitled to one?"

"Hell. I don't know. I haven't bothered looking."

Good grief. Greg really was an uphill battle sometimes. "Aren't there guest ones you can wear? Just for dressing up?"

Greg laughed at last. "Are you always on fashion duty?"

Perry allowed himself to lean closer to Greg. The smell of Greg's body wash was very clear to him, despite the perfumes and other smells that filled the hall. It was reassuring in a very deep, and perhaps worrying way. "You'd look so good. Your legs are perfect for a kilt."

"What the hell?" Greg stared at him, his face suddenly red.

"For God's sake." Perry didn't think Greg was so easy to embarrass. "I saw you in the wet suit, remember? And in your boxers, that first night I arrived. And you're not exactly discreet when you wander back and forth to the bathroom in the mornings."

Greg had now gone a strange shade of purple somewhere between scarlet and lavender. Perry liked it. After all, it was satisfying to get payback for all the times he'd embarrassed Perry, intentionally or not. Perry took another gulp of his latest gin and tonic and nearly choked. Angus's boys were heavy-handed on the spirits, he'd say that for them. Braced for it now, he took another drink. The dancing was just starting in the middle of the floor, and he was getting into the swing.

Over by the bar, a young man laughed too loudly, surrounded by a small group of young women. He looked in his early twenties, stocky and handsome, and as fit as a professional sportsman.

Greg looked between the young man and Perry. "You met him?"

Perry nodded. "Alasdair's grandson? Yes. I saw the resemblance, of course."

Greg shook his head ruefully. "Yes, of course you did. I mean, you must have met the reclusive Alasdair at least *once* since you arrived, and now you can immediately recognize all his relatives."

Perry wrinkled his nose at Greg. "You're just jealous."

"Of what?"

"Of me meeting the gorgeous, gay grandson." Pleased with his witty alliteration, he took another slurp of drink and leaned against the wall again. He almost misjudged it but covered up his stumble by guiding his hand behind him.

Greg's drink seemed to catch in his throat. "Gay?"

"You didn't know?"

"Yes, I did, but I didn't think anyone else did."

Perry looked at the way the young man moved, the way he put his arm on one girl's shoulder, the way he chinked his glass of wine against another young man's. "Oh definitely, I'd say." At that very moment, the grandson's eyes lifted and caught Perry's gaze. And he winked.

Greg must have caught the wink too, because he snorted. "He's been slavering over you ever since Bridie introduced you."

"Slavering? You make him sound like Rory."

They both laughed. Greg was silent for another moment, then said, "You could go and chat to him. Have a drink. Dammit, you could probably dance with him."

Perry wasn't sure where this conversation was going, but the gin had souped up his courage, and he really liked standing here close to Greg, bantering away. "Dance? Here?"

"We're not completely medieval, you know. Some of the old guys wouldn't cope well, but no one's going to burn you at the stake for gay practices nowadays." Greg took a quick look at the other end of the bar where some of the elder statesmen of the village were frowning over at the grandson. "Well. Maybe some of them would."

Perry peered at Greg over the top of his glass. "They know *you're* gay? In the village, I mean?"

"I don't advertise it. Bridie and Dougie know, of course."

Perry suspected that meant that everyone on North Uist now did, but he wisely kept his counsel. "So the grandson… he's not your type?"

Greg laughed, spraying a little beer into his beard. "God, no."

"What is your type, then?" Perry asked mischievously.

Greg paused for a significant moment, then said, "I'm not talking about that now."

"Seriously. I don't mean to embarrass you, I just want to know. I mean, where do you go?"

"Go?"

"For God's sake, Greg Ventura, talking to you is like trying to get blood out of a stone. I mean, when you want male company. Gay male company." Perry lowered his voice and hissed, "Sex!" Beside him, a young married couple and their teenage daughter shifted a few feet farther away, the daughter wide-eyed. Perry ignored them and continued. "I can't believe you've gone without all these years. You're a very passionate man. So what do you do?"

"Oh Christ," Greg muttered. "If you must know, I go into Stornaway. Or over to the mainland now and then." Greg was blinking really hard as if he didn't want to tell Perry. He couldn't be *shy*, could he? "Not that I have much more choice there. I suspect it's similar to the London clubs, even if it's a smaller community. They're all looking for the young and the handsome."

"Like you," Perry said with spirit. And drank some more of the spirit in his hand.

Greg laughed, rather too loudly because the family beside them tried to move even farther away. An old man at a small table on the edge of the dance area turned around and glared at them both.

"Keep y'r sassenach ways t' y'self, lad," he grumbled. "We old 'uns wannae hear the music, not y'r guffawing."

Guffawing? Perry had an irresistible desire to laugh, but knew that'd be the very worst thing to do.

Instead, he jabbed Greg in the ribs. "See?" he hissed, half under his breath so, hopefully, only Greg would hear. "You're a *lad* around here, not some old codger who can't pull a twink to save his life."

Greg's lavender face was back on show. "I don't…. Perry, things are very different here. We don't have any twinks."

"Nonsense! You have Alasdair's grandson." More gin gave him more courage; it was fascinating how that worked. "You have *me*. Let's dance, then."

"Perry!"

Perry didn't listen to Greg's protests, just grabbed his hand and dragged him out onto the dance floor.

Chapter Nineteen

FOR a few minutes, they were lost in the melee of other dancers, swinging off others' arms and tapping boots in time with the music. Perry had been right—Scottish dancing was like a line-dancing session, though less regimented, and much more fun. He slid a hand around Greg's waist and concentrated on one of the more tricky bobbing step sequences.

It was another moment before he realized, one, Greg wasn't following in step any longer, and two, people were staring at them. Greg stopped, stock-still, in the middle of the whirling dancers.

"What's the matter?" Perry flipped an unruly lock of hair off his sweaty forehead. It was growing out of its usual, fiercely clipped style: he should have it cut sometime soon. "Why have you stopped?"

"Perry. I… haven't done this before."

"Dancing? But you're very light on your feet. I think the music helps you keep the rhythm." It was true. Greg may have been clumsy in other things, but for that brief while, he'd bobbed at Perry's side and tripped along in tandem, without any upset.

"No! I don't mean…."

Perry suddenly realized Greg didn't mean dancing per se, but dancing with a man. But no, he wasn't going to apologize for dragging Greg Ventura out of his comfort zone. He stopped too, his hands on his hips.

"You feel safe here, don't you?"

Greg stared at Perry as if his very soul were being flayed. "Y-yes," he stammered.

"I don't mean to upset that. But how much do you care, Greg? How much do you want to hide?" He knew he was throwing down a challenge. He knew Greg lived and was respected in this community and wouldn't want to be judged badly. But Greg was gay, wasn't he? There was no denying it. If he preferred to dance with men rather than women, he was only living his own life. He wasn't bringing on the end of the world.

Was Greg thinking the same? He seemed to hang on the edge of a mental precipice, his hand still outstretched but not touching Perry's. The music shifted in the background, the tone dropping, the beat slowing as another dance started up.

Please, Greg. Perry would cope with being laughed at, but he didn't want that for Greg. However, he did want Greg to be true to himself. And he knew suddenly how much he wanted to share that moment of truth with Greg.

Something touched his fingertips: a hand grasped his.

Greg swung him around but didn't hand him over to another dancer. Instead he grasped Perry around the waist and brought them face-to-face.

"Oh!" It was all Perry could manage.

They were close, like when the kiss had started. The Kiss, Perry thought, giving it its deserved capitals. He'd wanted more ever since, hadn't he? And wasn't this the first time he'd found Greg in a relaxed, happy mood, and maybe open to some more making out…?

"Not now," Greg whispered against his left ear.

Not…? Had he said that aloud? Then Perry realized he was gripping Greg's hip, his fingers squeezing the beginnings of Greg's buttock. *In public! Oh my God.* He immediately let go.

"So let's dance," Greg said softly. And swept them both into the reel that was currently marching across the floor.

GREG danced off the floor about twenty minutes later, and Perry followed blithely. The dipping and skipping had made him quite dizzy. Or that may have been the gin. Everyone seemed to know the steps of every dance, but he reckoned he'd put up a good enough show as a beginner. The tiptoeing and swirling certainly beat his usual twerking for a full-body workout. His hips would feel the ache tomorrow morning.

Greg paused near their original place by the wall. He was breathing faster than usual and there was a thin sheen of sweat on his forehead. He looked really, truly alive, like when he was diving, or lost in his painting, or playing catch with Rory and the dog's favorite old, chewed ball….

Perry tried to pull himself together. He was spending way too much time watching Greg Ventura.

"That's enough dancing for me," Greg said. He grabbed the pint he'd left on the windowsill before they'd taken to the floor, and took a long, grateful draft.

"Has someone said something to you?" Perry was ready to fight on their behalf—

"No. I'm just knackered."

Perry laughed, happily reassured. "No way. You're the one who's so fit. I'm the one with sea water still in his lungs from falling in the loch. There's way too much water in this place, and it's all out to get me."

Greg didn't take his eyes from Perry's face. They were heavy-lidded, as if sleepy. "So am I," he said, his voice low and throaty. "All out to get you. Can we go home now?"

Perry's heart blipped, threw a cheer, and settled again. "I guess so. Do you want to say good-bye to anyone? I said I'd catch up soon with Lisa—she wants me to go through a wholesaler's catalog with her, to order some hairdressing equipment. Did you know she's a fully trained stylist? You probably do. And Marty wants to talk to you about your scallops. I think I persuaded him to take another delivery a month—"

"Perry." Greg's voice was ragged. His hand tightened on Perry's. "I need you."

"I.... Of course." Perry's breath hitched. He wondered how fast he could race back to Greg's croft with such painfully tight briefs. The look in Greg's eyes was hotter and more raw than anything he'd ever imagined turned in his direction.

Alasdair's grandson caught Perry's eye as he crossed the floor, hand in Greg's.

The expression on his face was definitely disappointment.

Chapter Twenty

IT seemed far too many miles back to Greg's place. Perry had worn proper shoes at the ceilidh but wisely brought his "very useful but never to be seen back in London" hiking boots for the journey to and from the croft. He still struggled to keep up with Greg's long stride. He'd never done much exercise before now, just darting back and forth across the city with his work. Presumably two thousand steps in London's gritty air or up and down the steps of the Tube station didn't equate to two thousand steps in the bracingly fresh air of the Scottish Highlands. He certainly felt much fitter and more alert after only a few days here. Taking Rory for walks helped, of course. Or did Rory actually take *him* for the walk? It felt like it sometimes, when the dog bounded ahead, leaving Perry stepping more gingerly over the peat bog until he got a proper footing. But Rory always graciously returned when Perry called and had often alerted Perry to bad weather on its way, by diverting their path to lead more directly back to the croft. Not that Perry had any bloody idea where he was at any time anyway. Thank God the dog did. He could have done with Rory tonight, as there were no damned streetlights, and the roads were uneven, and if he lost sight of Greg he'd be lost in the middle of nowhere—

And then Greg turned right at a low stone wall and Perry could see the cottage ahead. Greg had left a small lamp on in the window of the living room, a very welcome sight. Perry stumbled after Greg through the gate and up the garden, and fetched up behind him at the front door, giving a small *whoof* sound as he tried to catch his breath.

Greg looked back over his shoulder. His eyes were shaded by the door's overhang, hiding part of his face and creating a rather sinister look. "You okay? Did I go too fast?"

"Never," Perry said bravely. "I'm totally fine."

"Yes." Greg smiled and cupped Perry's cheek. "That ye are. Damned fine."

Perry sucked in what breath he had left and savored the touch of Greg's palm on his skin. When Greg put his other hand to Perry's other cheek, Perry let himself be cradled and pulled closer in. Greg's lips were cold from the walk, but his pulse ran warmly through his kiss. Perry opened his mouth quickly, flicking his tongue against Greg's, encouraging him in with every stroke.

"Inside," Greg murmured. "The nights here get cold enough to freeze off anyone's balls, not just a brass monkey's." He fumbled a little with the door key but it eventually unlocked and let them into the cool, quiet cottage. They paused in the hallway.

"You want something to drink? Eat?" Greg was obviously struggling to be a good host, but his hands were all over Perry. As Perry shrugged out of his coat, Greg was there to take it and trail his fingers over Perry's shoulders. When Perry kicked off his boots, Greg hunkered down to help out but apparently got distracted running his hand along Perry's thighs.

"Greg?" When Greg looked up, his cheeks pink from the cold night air, his eyes slightly unfocused and his lips damp, Perry reckoned he'd never seen such a beautiful sight. "I'm not hungry. Not for food, anyway."

"Jesus," Greg muttered, straightening up. "What am I saying? I'm a clumsy arse, I'm way out of practice with this—"

"Shut up." And Perry kissed him hard, quickly, to make the point stick. "This isn't about saying or doing the right thing. We just do what we want, right?"

"Right," Greg said dumbly. He'd rested his hands back on Perry's hips and was reaching for more kisses as if Perry was a magnet he couldn't resist. "You're gorgeous."

Perry flushed. He'd never been so… he searched for the right word. *Appreciated.* That was it. No one had ever looked at him like Greg did—without artifice, without calculation, without one eye on how they were looking themselves. There was just desire, and need, and that very sincere appreciation. Perry was too used to men who schemed, manipulated, and generally fucked you over. Greg was an honest bloke, without pretension, without manners too, unfortunately, but Perry could work on that….

Greg kissed him, hot and wet with lots of tongue, and Perry stopped worrying about working on anything except that.

They stumbled up the stairs to Greg's bedroom, acting like schoolboys, giggling and peeling off their clothes until they were in their briefs, flicking balled-up socks at each other and grabbing for any hold they could get. Perry couldn't remember having such fun with a lover! Then, in the quiet, dim room, they both dropped their underwear, and business grew more serious.

"Lights on?" Perry whispered.

Greg only grunted in reply, but it was definitely a no. The moonlight through the curtains gave a silvery aura to the bedroom furniture rather than full illumination, but the atmosphere it cast was magical. Greg's kisses now pushed more than caressed, and his breath shortened. Perry felt an equivalent tension, his arms aching to hold Greg, his legs ready to part around Greg's hips. *Mustn't rush things—*

But it was impossible not to. They tumbled down onto the bed together, kissing hard and greedily. Perry shivered with delight at the feel of Greg's hardened cock thrusting against his hip. Greg's skin was hot, yet the hair on his torso was slightly damp after the walk home, creating a delicious tickle against Perry's nipples. He could barely move, trapped inside Greg's embrace, could do nothing but arch with pleasure under the fierce kisses, thrusting his own erection against Greg's belly, begging wordlessly for relief.

"Oh. *Oh.*" Greg groaned in his ear. "Jesus. *Clumsy.* Sorry—!"

"Uh? No. Don't be." Perry was startled to hear his own voice so hoarse. "It's good. It's *great.*"

Greg chuckled, which morphed into another groan. "All the time, dancing, holding on to you…."

"What? What about it?"

"Wanted *this*," Greg hissed. His voice sounded so broken, Perry didn't feel bad about his own hoarseness. "Wanted to kiss you again. Touch *this*." He dipped his head and tongued the small bar threaded through Perry's left nipple.

Perry yelped loudly, and every nerve he had clenched up. "Fuck!"

"That sensitive, eh? I always wondered."

"Not… always," Perry ground out. Greg held him very tightly, that was why playing with his piercing was so arousing. Wasn't it? And the way Greg's beard scratched over the tip of his nipple…. *Oh!* Greg bit gently at him, drawing the nipple and the bar in and out between his lips. *Oh, hell's bells!* Perry's cock was so hard it must have been stabbing Greg in the belly.

"I just wanna touch all of you." Greg sounded almost shocked at the idea. "It's all so good, you're so good—" He slid his hands down and cupped Perry's arse. He dug his fingers into the flesh, tugging the cheeks slightly apart.

"Oh, God, please." Perry panted into Greg's neck. His skin itched with the need to be touched like *that*, that was no problem! "Will you fuck me? Have you got condoms?"

Greg stilled, his hands on Perry's bum.

Shit. "I'm sorry!" It was Perry's turn to sound broken. "Too fast, I know, I know, I just really like doing it, and I really like *you*, I want you to—"

Greg's chest rumbled like an incoming storm over Perry's splayed body. Was he *laughing*?

"No. Don't… apologize. Never! Not for that. Jesus." Greg shifted so that he still held on to Perry, but they could look each other properly in the face. Greg was very flushed and his eyes twinkled, but his mouth was twisted in a grimace. "It's just… I don't."

Perry blinked. "Don't have any condoms?"

Greg flushed even more. "Um. I… get some if I'm traveling. You know? Like I said, going to the mainland. But here…."

"Why bother? I see." Perry rolled his eyes. The relief that Greg wasn't rejecting him was immense.

"Apart from the humiliation I'd suffer from Dougie and Bridie if I bought at the shop," Greg muttered.

Perry started to laugh.

"Way to kill the mood," Greg said, a little poutily.

"Stupid arse," Perry said fondly. "That's not likely, is it? But I have some in my case. Let me up and I'll grab them from my room." He wriggled off the bed but paused for one moment to gaze happily at Greg, who had rolled onto his back on top of the duvet. There was a faint sheen of sweat on his skin, glinting in the half-light. Perry's gaze followed the trail of hair from Greg's broad chest down to his belly, then to the nest of pubic hair around his jutting cock. "It's good to laugh," Perry said softly. "Sex should be fun, not a chore. Not boring. Not unimaginative."

"Get back here fast," Greg growled. He fisted a hand around his cock and began to stroke it, almost lazily. "I'll show you imagination."

Perry all but ran to the spare bedroom and scrabbled in the bottom of his wash bag for lube and a condom. Then, having paused for a millisecond, he scrabbled again and pulled out another handful. Wishful thinking or wise anticipation? He'd let Greg be the judge of that.

He padded back into Greg's room. He registered quickly—and with a shock—that Greg was no longer on the bed. Then a hard, hot body pressed up against him from behind and hissed in his ear, "Gotcha!"

Perry gasped, laughed, and leaned back into Greg's grasp.

"I only went to the bathroom," Greg murmured into his ear. "Did you think I'd run away?"

"You can try," Perry said smartly. "But you wouldn't get far. I can probably run faster than you."

"Aye?"

"Yes. You wanna try it?"

"Not right now." Greg's hips nudged at Perry's arse. "Did you mean that about wanting me to fuck you?"

"You better believe it," Perry quipped. Oh, this was fun! He grabbed Greg's hand and pulled him back to the bed. They had a moment's scramble with the lube, and then Greg snatched the condom out of Perry's hand. He paused for the slightest of heartbeats.

"Just start slow," Perry whispered. He wondered if Greg was nervous, or maybe less experienced than Perry imagined. Neither was a problem, of course. Nothing was, right at this moment. He wished he could implant that in Greg's psyche too.

Greg didn't reply, but the grin he lifted Perry's way was wide and wicked. He pushed Perry onto his back and ran his lubed fingers up the inside of Perry's thigh. When they pressed gently inside, Perry yelped.

"Too much?" Greg asked, pausing.

"Hell, no!" Perry stretched back, lifting himself up toward Greg to encourage him. "Come on, keep going."

"You were right," Greg said, firmly caressing and stretching Perry in preparation, with laughter and some amazement in his tone. "When you said you liked it."

Perry would have laughed too in agreement, but just about then, Greg's cock nudged against his entrance. Perry wanted to concentrate on this: he didn't want to miss a second. He reached up a hand to grip Greg's shoulder.

"Okay?" Greg whispered.

He needed reassurance, Perry realized, almost too late. "Please," he whispered back, nodding. "I want to feel you there."

Greg pressed in more firmly, all the way, slowly and steadily, until his groin jutted against Perry's. Perry bent his legs farther, making a harbor around Greg's hips. His eyes half closed as he savored the delicious pressure. His laughter calmed and he pursed his lips, concentrating fully on Greg rocking back and forth, shifting Perry on the mattress beneath him.

It was marvelous: so very splendid. Perry *did* like sex, but this time he felt something more than just the physical effect of hitting his hot button. Greg's lips brushed his shoulder now and then, and Perry remembered the chilled heat of their kiss after the fall in the loch. When Greg gripped a hand on Perry's arm, Perry remembered being guided across the dance floor that night. When Greg groaned above him, he glanced up and caught the glint of Greg's deep, dark gaze on him. Perry's heart soared.

Oh fuck. I've got it bad.

Then he shut his eyes completely and surrendered to the utter joy.

Chapter Twenty-One

GREG woke slowly and languorously.

This was the kind of morning after he dreamed of: no hangover, no grumpiness, no effort required to face another bleak or troubling day. On some days, especially when he'd first moved here, he'd suffered his choice of all of those.

This morning was delightfully different. The second he woke he could hear Perry's breath beside him, tickling his nape. Perry was spooned up to his back, his slim thighs against Greg's legs. One of Perry's hands hung limply over Greg's waist, the fingertips brushing his belly.

It's all about Perry.

Greg felt a satisfaction and relief he hadn't felt for years. Such pleasure too. They'd played for much of the night, it seemed. When he was tired, Perry had soothed him to sleep for a while. When he stirred, horny again, Perry had chuckled and met his passion with equal enthusiasm. And when he'd felt oddly sentimental, Perry had drawn him close under the covers and just hugged him. Greg hadn't experienced such uninhibited comfort with emotions… well, ever, as far as he could remember. Tension and defensiveness had ruled his life for as long as he could recall. But last night, he realized suddenly, at no time had he worried about how he looked, good or bad. He'd stripped off and bounced about on his bloody bed and let Perry see everything he had. Happily, and—dammit—proudly.

Perry made a snuffling noise into Greg's neck.

Sudden, vivid excitement washed over Greg, tugging at his morning wood, which was already raring to go. He reached blindly behind him, wanting to grab Perry's hip but managing a handful of thigh instead. Perry obviously slept higher on the pillow than Greg did. Which gave him a new and mischievous inspiration. He eased his way out from under Perry and inched farther down the bed. Perry's smooth chest was warm, the skin soft with sleep, and the piercing rolled gently in his nipple as Greg slid down over it. Perry's navel dipped as his stomach muscles clenched: there was a tiny, stray white feather from the duvet caught in his pubic hair.

Greg sighed with what he suspected was true, unalloyed happiness. He didn't actually know, because the closest he'd ever come was on days when he was out on the loch or on a solitary walk with Rory. One day he'd like to share that comparison with Perry, if only to see Perry's grin and rolling eyes in return….

Perry snuffled again and Greg anchored a gentle hand on his hip to keep him still. Then he slid his mouth over Perry's limp, soft dick and licked. No response. Smiling to himself, he thought it was a treat for him to suck Perry off regardless of Perry's attention. The skin was smooth and the sheath creased up on his tongue as he moved slowly up and down its length. It tasted of.... Perry, of course. What did he expect? Honey and strawberries? That made him chuckle, and the vibration obviously alerted Perry, who suddenly went unnaturally still.

Greg took another long, lascivious lick. His beard brushed against Perry's balls on the up stroke. They shifted inside the sac, coming alive with the stimulus. Perry's cock began to swell. Soon Greg wouldn't be able to take it all in his mouth: he'd never mastered that deep-throat thing. He wondered briefly if Perry had. He was slightly startled at Perry's knowledge and experience of these things, judging by last night. Such a delicate little chap he was, but with such a huge sexual appetite, and a cheeky, filthy mouth when he was properly distracted....

Perry groaned and kicked the duvet off his feet.

Greg pushed it fully off the side of the bed so they both lay uncovered. "Good morning," he mumbled around his mouthful.

"Already?" Perry sighed, his voice still thick with sleep but with a thread of laughter awakening in it. "Are you sure?"

Greg chuckled again, so that Perry sucked in a breath and moaned with pleasure at the sensation. Then he began sucking Perry off in earnest.

Perry arched above Greg like a beautiful sea creature. For a man who professed such a love/hate relationship with the sea, he moved with all its grace and sensuousness. The climax built gradually but strongly—Greg could feel

Perry's leg muscles tense up either side of Greg's head—and then Perry reached down and snatched a handful of Greg's hair.

"*Oh*" was all he said, half a word, half a blissful sigh.

Yes. Greg didn't even speak it aloud. The way he and Perry were rocking together in rhythm, it was as if they communicated without words. His own cock was thrusting against the sheet below, seeking attention but, in a perverse way, enjoying the suspense.

Perry came at last—though Greg could have continued for hours, whether or not his jaw would have locked in protest in the end—and Greg swallowed him down gratefully. They didn't speak, but the relief and pleasure seeped through both their bodies. Perry collapsed on the mattress, and Greg climbed back up the bed to lie beside him. He slung an arm around Perry's shoulders and kissed him firmly. He wasn't letting Perry either go back to sleep or get out of bed just yet. Not least because he still had a hard-on to rival a tentpole.

Then Perry snuffled—though how could he, when Greg had his mouth on him, kissing his breath away? Realization struck like a pair of sheep shears dropped on his toe, and Greg groaned aloud. "Oh Jesus!"

Perry's mouth opened but now in surprise. "What? What's happened?"

Greg flung himself across the foot of the bed and hung his head over the edge. Perry followed him. They both stared down at the floor where two bright eyes looked up at them, twinkling in the pale morning light.

"Rory," Greg said weakly. "I forgot to put his basket out."

"He usually sleeps with me," Perry said thoughtfully. "I mean, in the spare room. It was his room before mine, right?"

"That's true." Greg looked across at Perry. "Did you move him in here last night?"

Perry raised his eyebrows. "Did I…? When do you think I had time to do that? You were manhandling me from the minute we reached the front door."

Greg started grinning. He liked that word: *manhandling*. It was a perfect description. Actually, it was something he ought to spend more time practicing. He trailed a hand absently along Perry's bare side.

"So how did he—and his basket—get in here?" Perry looked bemused. "Did he drag it in himself?"

"He could if he wanted. He's strong and canny." Bemusement was a good look on Perry, Greg thought, though any look would be good on him. The best one of all, of course, was the twist of shocked ecstasy on his face when he came—

Rory barked and wagged his tail, eyes on Greg.

"He's a dirty voyeur," Greg said, glaring back. "Bad dog!"

"You think he wanted to watch?" Perry didn't seem upset. In fact his eyes were alight with mischief. "Wow. What a pervert."

Greg started laughing, loudly and carelessly. He rolled back onto the bed, splayed out. Seconds later, Perry slid over his body, also laughing, reaching to kiss Greg's mouth, his cock brushing a damp trail all the way up Greg's naked thigh.

"Looks like you'll soon be ready for the next showing," Greg murmured, missing Perry's mouth because of laughing too much, but not missing the chance to grab a handful of Perry's gorgeous arse.

Perry arched against him, his piercing catching the tip of Greg's nipple with a cool, metallic flip. "Maybe just some messing about. Your last blowjob pulled me inside out, and I need some recovery time." He shuddered happily and wriggled his hips. "Maybe it's your turn to suffer."

Greg sucked in a sharp breath, and his cock hardened even more against his thigh.

"But we'd better make it good," Perry whispered against Greg's ear, reaching down to cup Greg's balls. "Now we've got an audience!"

Chapter Twenty-Two

PERRY'S trips to the village shop were always a treasure trove of who he'd meet, who he'd confuse, and who would confuse him in return. Greg had been very perceptive when he accused Perry of staying to gossip, which he did more often than not. But Perry assumed the morning after the ceilidh—that was, the morning after the *night after* the ceilidh—was going to be an extra special challenge. So he was pleasantly surprised when, after breakfast, Greg insisted on coming with him.

"I can get the shopping on my own, you know," Perry said. "Or phone it in. Dougie will box it up and bring it along to the croft later today." He couldn't miss the big grin on Greg's face. "What's so funny?"

"You. Getting comfortable with the village routine."

Greg's grin didn't ease up. He seemed a different, much happier person this morning. He'd gazed at Perry all during breakfast and nearly fell over Rory, trying to fetch Perry's coffee for him so Perry didn't have to get up from his chair in the middle of eating his muesli. The more cynical London Perry would have written it off as the amazing effect of a good shag on a man's mood. But then Greg caught hold of Perry as he ambled across the kitchen to fetch more shopping bags and pulled him onto his lap for a deep, long, and heartfelt kiss.

Perry abandoned his cynicism, along with his inhibitions, and just enjoyed it.

"We could go back to bed," Greg murmured. He wriggled his hands sneakily down the back of Perry's trousers.

"No fishing there," Perry said, laughing. His groin was keen, but his slightly fragile arse needed time to recover. "Let's get the shopping done and prepare lunch, and then—"

"Then?" Greg waggled his eyebrows like he was a cartoon voyeur on a seaside postcard.

Perry's laughter increased. "Then… we'll see."

"Okay. But the sooner we go, the sooner we can come back." Greg leaped up from his chair. "Where did I leave the car keys?"

"You sure you don't want to stay here? I can walk to the shop. After all, you don't much like shopping."

"I want to go with you," Greg said, with a daft look in his eye that implied he'd probably follow blindly even if Perry suggested a ramble up Ben Nevis before lunch.

And guess what? Despite embracing what he knew was an alarmingly seductive risk—after all, when had a holiday romance ever worked out well?—Perry felt entirely the same. He'd make the most of this, for as long as he had with Greg. Why wouldn't he? He hadn't felt this happy and relaxed for a long, long time.

He watched the man of the moment moving confidently around the kitchen, gathering up bags and the list of shopping necessities that Perry now encouraged him to keep, and even whistling under his breath….

Greg. Wonderful, honest, argumentative, antisocial, sexy Greg.

Perry's heart constricted. So maybe he was seeing things through the Good Shag Goggles as well, but he doubted that was the sole reason for the leap in his chest when he saw Greg, or the happiness always bubbling under his banter, or the shiver of pleasure he felt when Greg touched him, even in passing. A seductive risk, eh? Just a holiday romance? Perry hid his sigh and the nausea churning in his gut, knowing it was already too late.

I've really *got it bad.* It was what he'd said to himself last night.

It was totally, increasingly true.

THE shop wasn't busy, but Bridie waved to Perry as he entered, her eyes dancing with an enthusiastic mix of "good morning," "tell me the damn news before I explode with curiosity," and "wait a minute, I'm at work here."

"I'll just serve young Fiona," she called, "and then I'll be with you, Perry."

"No rush," he said. Greg drifted off to look at a selection of fishing gear, while Perry stood patiently by the counter, browsing through the new selection of style magazines Bridie had ordered in this week. From Bridie's comment, he assumed that young Fiona was the little girl skipping between the aisles, headed for the counter. She looked about seven years old. The basket over her arm was too big for her to carry comfortably, but she seemed proud to be in charge of it. It was currently filled with some packets of porridge oats, a chocolate bar, and a plastic bag of knitting yarn. On top of them was a long, thin, cloth doll in a well-worn and probably well-loved knitted dress.

Bridie sold yarn from a large basket over in one corner of the shop, with a selection of knitting patterns and needles. Perry glanced over Fiona's dark curly head and saw a tall, angular woman sorting through the bags of wool, obviously looking for something in particular. She was in her sixties, at least, and with strong, striking looks. Her gray hair was styled well, and as far as Perry could see from this distance—and without peering rudely—her skin was healthily freckled around the natural wrinkles. She wore trousers and a sensible pair of walking boots, but the design of her sweater was an astonishingly bright blend of turquoise and lilac diamond shapes.

As Perry hovered longingly over the display of chocolate—he reckoned all this fresh air counteracted calories, didn't it?—Fiona wriggled past him. He smiled at her. "That's a wonderful yarn in your basket. Is it for an Argyll sweater?"

Fiona nodded. She looked Perry up and down, her eyes growing so large they looked like they'd pop out of her head. "Grannie will knit it for Grampy. Grannie knitted Emily's dress too. See?" She waved her doll under Perry's nose. "Grannie knits the best in the village."

"I should think so," Perry said with another smile. "Intarsia isn't a technique everyone can master."

Out of the corner of his eye, he registered the older woman by the yarn basket lifting her head, but she didn't turn around. "Is this one of Grannie's?" Perry placed a reverent finger on the shoulder of Fiona's sweater cardigan. It was a marvelously complex design on a relatively small garment: a mix of heather-colored diamonds with pale pink threads running through them. "I love the traditional Argyll pattern," Perry said softly and admiringly. "This one has a wonderfully childlike style."

"Are ye calling me a child?"

He jumped. The old woman's voice was surprisingly robust. She'd crept up on Perry without him even noticing. Greg appeared at his other shoulder, also rather suddenly, clutching a bait box like a shield to his chest.

"Perry?" Greg said warningly. "You haven't yet met—"

Perry ignored him. He wasn't intimidated: not this morning and—the way he currently felt—possibly not ever again. "Certainly not," he said to the woman. "I meant your design has a unique charm to it that I haven't seen anywhere in the fuddy-duddy old men's sweaters and socks they wear around here."

"Oh my God" came Greg's mutter. Perry knew that despairing tone. Greg had probably closed his eyes too.

"That'll be right, will it?" the woman said drily. "They're all my designs as well."

Perry winced a little. But he lived on this planet too, didn't he? He had a right to his opinions and his advice. Maybe the "in crowd" in Uist wasn't the same as in London, but in his opinion, everyone wanted to look good. *Always.* Wherever they lived, whatever money they had, whatever their personal style. Though when someone cleared his throat in the background, Perry wondered whether Greg Ventura would prove the exception to that rule.

"Everyone's entitled to their own taste," he said soothingly. "I'm sure many wouldn't like my choice of clothing either"—he ignored Fiona's spontaneous giggle—"but the important thing is we all feel good in ourselves, right?"

The woman blinked as if trying to translate a foreign language. Her accent was strong, but Perry had heard worse. He was sure she'd understood him in return.

"Grannie!" Fiona plucked at her elbow. "Bridie's packed up all the shopping for me and Emily. Can we go?"

The woman smiled at Fiona absentmindedly. She never took her eyes off Perry. "You ken knitting?" she asked him.

"I…?"

"You have enough opinions on it, wee lad. I'd expect ye t' be more than passing the time o' day."

Oh good God. He thought he knew what she meant. "Yes, I know all about it. In fact, I do a fair bit of knitting myself at home. In London, that is." The woman's nose wrinkled at the mention of the city, as if it were a bad smell she didn't have time to clean up. "I've run a few designs through Camden Market, hoping to get noticed by a fashion buyer."

The woman raised her eyebrows in query. Fiona giggled again.

"No, nothing sold yet," Perry said grudgingly. "But nothing ventured, eh?" He felt warmth behind him and knew Greg had moved closer. He was startled at how good that felt.

"He's a designer, Aileen," Greg said. "He works for a prestigious London media firm."

His breath brushed past Perry's ear, and Perry had to swallow his instinctive moan.

"If 'twere that prestigious, Greg, lad, he'd have shown a clean pair o' heels back t' the mainland before now. He has his reasons for stayin', I guess."

What did she guess? Perry was torn between turning around to catch Greg's expression and staying fixed on the woman's. He didn't think he should show weakness at this critical stage of the confrontation.

"But mebbe it's not the prestige ye both find attractive," she said, more gently. Perry may have been mistaken, but that certainly looked like a twinkle in her eye, despite now fixing her steely gaze on Greg.

"Aileen," Greg said. His voice sounded breathless. "It was good to see you, but isn't Cameron waiting for you in the car?"

"Grampy!" Fiona squealed and dashed out of the shop.

"Wait!" Perry cried, panicking for her safety, but at the last minute he spotted a large off-road vehicle parked outside. As he watched, Fiona ran to it with obvious familiarity. When he looked back, Aileen whoever-she-was was peering at him with an odd expression on her face.

"She's a lively one, isn't she?" Perry said cheerily. He was damn sure that sigh behind him meant Greg had closed his eyes again.

"Aye," Aileen said. "A real handful." She glanced over Perry's shoulder at Greg, then back to Perry. "Her Grampy spoils her, I'm afraid t' say."

She laid her yarn choices on the counter, waiting for Bridie to parcel them up. The shop door chimed again, and Perry turned to see an old man swagger in. He wore a kilt, the proper socks—Perry couldn't remember what they were called, though several people at the ceilidh had spent time trying to explain the Highland dress to him—and a smart overcoat.

Greg stepped out from behind Perry and faced the new customer.

How interesting. Perry wondered who the old man was, to merit this acknowledgment.

"Greg." The man's voice was gravelly but firm.

"Cameron." Greg nodded back. He looked a little pale.

"I'll be a moment," Aileen said to the man who was presumably… her husband? Perry found with delight they were the perfect example of when a married couple ends up looking like each other. The same gray hair, broad shoulders, and tight mouth. The steely glint was common too.

The old man turned to Greg. "Saw you with that young London fellow last night. Cut a fine figure on the dance floor."

That young fellow? Like I'm not even here! Perry tensed up, but Greg just nodded. "Yes. I saw you there too, Cameron. And how's your Mairi these days? Is she visiting with Fiona?"

"Nay. She sent the bairn alone t' us for a holiday. They won't let her take time off herself. I'm nae keen on her staying in that place."

That place? Perry raised his eyebrows in question.

"Mairi is Cameron's daughter, Fiona's mother," Greg murmured in explanation. "Mairi's a widow, and working as a theater sister at a mainland hospital."

Cameron gave a cheerful hack and spit into his hankie. "Not sure of 'em over there, lad. They're nae like us."

"No, indeed," Perry agreed, though he wasn't exactly sure who the statement had been directed to. Greg's hand, resting almost on the small of Perry's back, tapped him once, quickly, as if he was warning Perry against too much sarcasm. *You have no idea*, Perry thought, remembering the vicious banter he survived in the London office. Right now, he was just being polite.

"Boy," Cameron said sharply. It took Perry several moments to realize Cameron *was* talking to him now. "Here's my Mairi. You'll want t' see her." Cameron reached into the inside pocket of his old coat and brought out a surprisingly glossy photo. It looked like one of the makeover sessions that were offered on the Internet. Perry was prepared to forego any professional critique, but it was actually well done. Of course, that was mainly because Mairi was a very pretty girl.

"She's lovely," he said with warmth. "You must be very proud of her."

"Aye. She's very pretty," Cameron said, his voice warm.

"Well, not just that," Perry said quietly. "I actually meant, because she's got a responsible and prestigious job."

There was a sudden silence in the room. Aileen stared at him openly now. Bridie was obviously trying not to laugh, and Greg looked torn between running for cover and protecting the poor young outlander he'd thrown to the Scottish wolves.

Cameron frowned. "So. Are ye one o' those hom'sexuals?"

Perry had no problem being asked, even that bluntly. He just hoped the man's gruff words expressed interest rather than insult. Maybe Greg was nervous too—he'd gone as motionless as stone. "Yes, I'm gay."

Aileen just blinked, still staring at him.

"Cannae say I understand it," Cameron continued. "Not when ye got the ladies t' look at. Take my Mairi, for instance."

Perry tried to imagine old Cameron in the same family as the lovely nurse in the photo but totally failed. And he'd always thought he had such a vivid imagination.

"Grampy!" came a wail from the car outside.

"The bairn!" Cameron turned swiftly and left the shop without so much as a good-bye.

Aileen, however, paused a moment longer, her parcel now under her arm. "Come t' afternoon tea, boy," she said to Perry, her eyes twinkling again. "We're neighbors, y'know."

The Mackies? So that's who they were. Perry had never yet bumped into anyone from that croft. "I'd love to," he said politely. "But I'm not here on North Uist for long."

Aileen nodded, her gaze flickering between him and Greg. "We'll see," she said, then turned to follow her husband and granddaughter. "We'll see," drifted back as the door closed behind her.

Chapter Twenty-Three

BACK at the cottage, Greg made straight for the wine. Perry settled on the sofa with a hot coffee instead. It was only lunchtime, after all, though neither of them took much interest in the sandwiches Perry had made.

"Cameron Mackie is like an unofficial laird of the village," Greg said, having taken a large gulp of his drink. He sounded awed. "He's been here for as long as anyone can remember. His word is law. Dougie's terrified of his temper."

"He seemed a perfectly pleasant man to me." Though Perry had quickly identified the gleam in the old man's eye, showing his mind was as sharp as a man forty years his junior. But it amused Perry to see Greg out of sorts.

"How did you dare?" Greg asked.

"You mean, answer him back? They're just people, Greg." Perry spoke bravely, but actually he was worrying now he'd been too cheeky. Would this make trouble for Bridie and her shop? Or perhaps for Greg himself? Perry felt a strange twist inside at the thought of that.

"It was bloody good entertainment," Greg said and suddenly grinned. "You're a bold young man, Perry Goodwood."

"Is that a good thing?"

"What do you think?" Greg winked at him. That look was creeping back into his eyes, the one that broadcast how much he wanted to tumble Perry to the rug right now and get him naked, then slide his mouth right over Perry's dick and—

"Do you really knit?" Greg said instead.

Perry shook himself out of his lustful dream. "Of course I do. Why would I lie about it?"

Greg's expression was more thoughtful. "No, you don't, do you?"

"Knit? I just said—"

"No, I mean lie. You don't lie."

The way Greg said it, it sounded like an insult. "I've been known to stretch the truth. I believe in the occasional, compassionate white lie."

"Like telling someone they look good when they don't?"

"No." A shiver ran down Perry's spine. The warning this time was more than just watching his tongue with powerful old men. Where was Greg going with this?

"What happens when you come up against someone who's just too ugly to find anything complimentary?" Greg had turned his head so he was ostensibly looking at something out of the living room window.

"I never have," Perry said firmly.

"Perry, don't be stupid—"

"And don't call me stupid!" he snapped back. "I have as much right to my opinion as you have. And I have never, ever, seen someone ugly. It's a cruel and unnecessary word."

"What the hell does that mean?"

"No one's ugly, Greg. Everyone has attraction, good features, a personality that can sparkle and charm."

"Now you're talking like one of those bloody magazines."

"No, I'm talking from my heart."

"You're fooling yourself."

Were they arguing again? Perry was suddenly scared—scared of what Greg was exposing, scared of saying the wrong thing, now they were… what? Not yet dating, yet definitely intimate. Where did that really leave him?

"No, I'm not," he said carefully. "Everyone can look good, Greg. It's not about clothes or makeup or a good haircut. Though, good grief, that can really help. It's about the personality showing through, the confidence, the reaching out. Then a connection can be made, and it's no longer just a two-dimensional photo in your hand but a real person, face-to-face."

Greg still hid his face from Perry, but his shoulders were shaking.

"Tell me," Perry said sharply, then toned it down to repeat, "Tell me what the problem is. Please, Greg. Tell me why you think this way."

"I can't."

"Don't you think I deserve to know?"

Greg shook his head vehemently. "It's not that. Of course you bloody do! But I… can't relive that now."

Perry took a deep breath. "Looks to me like you never stopped living it in the first place. Come here."

Greg peered back over his shoulder at Perry. His eyes were red around the edges. "Don't fucking patronize me, Perry."

"Wouldn't dream of it," Perry said smartly. "Come here or there's definitely no more sex, before or after lunch."

Greg's eyes widened, then his mouth twitched. He shambled over and sat next to Perry on the sofa, but his back was rigid, his hands clenched on his lap. Perry didn't try to unknot him yet. He just put a hand over Greg's and squeezed gently in solidarity.

"It's because of your brothers, right? The guys I met in London?"

Greg scowled. "You thought they were great, didn't you?"

"Well." Perry knew he should be honest. "Geoff seemed pleasant enough. And he's pretty buff. I confess I had a crush on him when he was player of the year. Hey, I was young, right?" Greg was half smiling: that was a good sign. "Gerry seemed—excuse me—a bit of a prat. Too fond of talking over everyone, getting his own way. The twins were fun, though I think they'd be exhausting over a period of time."

"God, yes." Greg's expression twisted with pain. "And so you've seen and learned more about my family than I have in the last five years."

"You kept in touch, surely? They said you left home when you were old enough, but I can't imagine—"

"Nothing. Not a word between us, apart from the occasional Christmas card, when I let people know where I was. Believe me, though, it was mutual. We don't come from a history of closeness. My parents live in Switzerland and have more or less cast us all adrift. They sent me news of the family for a while after I left."

"But…?"

"It felt alien. It was all about football tournaments and rowing challenges and London promotions, parties, girlfriends and wives. Sometimes several times over."

"From what I've read about your brothers, I wonder where they find the time," Perry suggested. Greg's smile back at him was genuine at last. "How did it get so bad between you all, Greg?"

"I've always been the butt of the jokes," Greg said. "My looks, you know?" He rushed on, as if he knew Perry would challenge that. "And I'm slower and clumsier than them all. Pretty crap at sports, no lover of partying, and useless with girls."

"I'm not complaining about that," Perry said softly, and squeezed Greg's hand again.

Greg's expression was sad. "Well, me neither, really. But that's how we were all judged—how we appeared in public. Even George, when people knew he was gay, found cute pop stars to date. The media was part of our family from a young age."

"And you?"

"I didn't play the game, deliberately or naturally. It was best I got out of the way and left them to it."

"But now they need you back?"

"Aye. Finally, someone wants *all* the Venturas, not just the pretty ones."

"Stop that!" Perry was angry and pained, all at the same time.

"Perry. I'm talking about years of being told I was shit. All through school, and not just my brothers, but their cronies too. You don't shake that off overnight, if ever. However, intellectually I try to tell myself it was just their game." He gave one of his lopsided smiles. "Oh, there were happier times, when we were children. But as soon as Geoff started his football career and photographers began hanging around… well, my life turned miserable and stayed there."

"You were a kid, that's all, these things even out over time—"

"Look at me, Perry!" Greg's voice rose. "My nose is *still* too big, my mouth crooked, my eyes too wide. I can't cross a room without falling over something."

"Heavens, you're hardly Quasimodo."

"But that's not the point." Greg sounded weary and irritated. "The point is that my brothers—"

"—were perfect. I see." Perry took a deep breath and clasped both of Greg's hands. "But they *weren't* perfect, were they? They bullied you, Greg. They picked on you because you have a unique look, because you didn't fit the mold. And…." It had to be said. "Because you let them."

Greg stiffened. For a second, it looked as if he'd pull away.

Perry hurried on, "You're so much more than looks, don't you see? Look how you stood up for me!"

"Huh? When?"

God, Greg could be so… so *obtuse* sometimes. "When we were in the shop and Aileen Mackie fixed on me like a knitting needle spearing a bug."

Greg chuckled. "I suppose so. The Mackies scared the shit out of me when I arrived. Thank God I don't meet them often." His expression softened again. "Perry. Thank you for listening. Well, you bloody well pushed me into talking, but you know what I mean. Sorry I'm nothing but a whiner."

For God's sake! "No, you're not." His own harsh, personal memories made Perry's mouth go dry. "Self-esteem isn't something you buy more of in Tesco's. You hear me? When it's been worn down, it takes a hell of a lot to build it up again."

Greg peered at him, puzzled, perhaps, by something in Perry's tone. "Perry? Are you okay?"

"I'm fine. And so are you." Perry rubbed his palms together. "And I'll make you see that, Greg Ventura. We're gonna work on it."

"I'd prefer to work on something else," Greg murmured. "You know. Right now, anyway. You said, after the shopping…?"

Perry frowned, pretending to be reluctant. Really, he just wanted to ask—no, beg!—Greg to take him to bed and roger the life out of him, at least until supper. There hadn't been many stretches of time today when he hadn't been thinking about Greg, and last night, and how good Greg had looked and been and said and *done*….

"Hm." Greg's expression gave a strange twist. "I see."

Ah crap, he's changed his mind….

But Greg slid a hand around Perry's neck, grasped the hair at his nape, and tugged. "Don't cut this," he said, his voice low and rough. "Not while I have the chance to take you like this."

Oh fuck! Perry's whole body shuddered with delight, and he stretched his head back, leaning into Greg's palm and baring his throat. "I certainly hope so."

Greg licked his lips, his eyes almost too bright for comfort. "Good. We're on the same page."

When he let Perry go, Perry scrambled off the sofa and skittered to the stairs. His legs felt shaky and his belly ached, but no way did it have anything to do with indigestion from a rushed lunch. He turned, breathless, to see Greg at the living room doorway, smiling smugly at Perry's eagerness. "Are you coming?" Perry said.

"What was it you said just now?" Greg's expression was mischievous. "I certainly hope so!"

Chapter Twenty-Four

PERRY was turning out to be a surprise in so many ways. At least, he was surprising Greg.

Over the next few days, Perry accompanied Greg on his daily walks with Rory, where the dog still flirted disgustingly with his new friend, nipping around Perry's heels with near ecstasy as they walked, when he'd usually race away from Greg. In the afternoons, if Greg wasn't working, they'd visit a loch or Marty's smokehouse or just stroll along the beach. In other spare hours, Perry would clean the house or help Greg dig vegetables in his small garden, and had even shamelessly tricked Greg with a vegetable pasta dish for supper. Greg never even realized it had no meat until he'd cleaned two platefuls of it. Perry was also picking up a slight Scottish accent, referring to Dougie as Doogie, and rolling the *R* in

Bridie. The London edges were being rubbed right off him. What was more, the villagers had all taken to him in a ridiculously short time.

Perry was very charming, of course. That smile of his would lure sea birds off the loch. It made a mischievous dimple in his left cheek. And he seemed to be able to talk to anyone, even the awe-inspiring Mackies. Admittedly, some of the villagers didn't understand Perry's London accent—or pretended not to—and his clothes continued to cause high humor in the pub, even when Greg persuaded him to put that fleece sweater on top of his colorful shirts.

Most of all he seemed happy to be with Greg. It was stupid to find that so weird, of course—Greg wasn't a complete loser; he had friends, didn't he?—but Greg kept waiting for the other shoe to drop. Meanwhile, Perry continued to boost Greg's ego at every opportunity. Funny, it seemed genuine too. Perry teased him when he messed up, just like any good mate would—the banter between them was sharp and full of amusement. But when Greg did something well, Perry was quick with praise and admiration. It felt surprisingly good.

Perry took up his knitting again. The day after they'd met the Mackies in the shop, Bridie sent over some needles and patterns and a note from Aileen about the diamond design Greg had never known was called Argyll. Perry seemed fascinated by it and began knitting endless squares of the stuff, all in different—and Greg had to admit, very beautiful—color blends.

"What are you gonna make from them, though?" he asked Perry one morning. "Join 'em all up and make one of those granny blankets?"

Perry looked up from the craft niche he was creating around him on the living room sofa and frowned, but with a smile that took the sting out of it. "I'd like to create my own version of the design," he said. "Something modern yet stylish."

Greg peered at the large square of knitting Perry had already done that morning. He worked really fast. "Is that a rainbow?"

"Yes." Perry nodded, obviously pleased with his efforts. He pushed the hair back off his forehead—he still hadn't cut it, thank God. "I thought it'd look good on children's sweaters. The colors are muted because of the type of wool, but that emphasizes the fact it's handmade." He held up the sample, musing, "I could adapt this onto fabric too, you know."

"You think we should all wear rainbows?"

Perry raised an eyebrow. "Not this boldly, no. I know that won't go down so well. But these shades could be woven into something more subtle, without losing the overall cheer."

Greg just smiled. He didn't feel like heaping scorn on the idea of his community sporting rainbow tartan or something equivalently daft. He just felt like… smiling.

It was good having Perry around.

BRIDIE called on Perry the next lunchtime to mind the shop. Dougie was away in Glasgow and Bridie had to take Lisa to the dentist. Apparently, Lisa was a complete baby and had to be nursed through root canal work. Greg had no idea what that was, but privately thought she was a wuss. At least until Perry returned and explained the procedure in graphic detail, and with a certain amount of glee at turning Greg's stomach over afternoon tea and cake.

"Is Lisa still around?" Greg said grumpily. "I don't know what she finds so interesting here. Glasgow's a city full of action and plenty of opportunity for a good hairdresser, I'd think. Whereas here...."

"You have Maggie Shaw hacking away at people's hair with sheep shears," Perry said drily with a quick glance at Greg's own hair. "Yes, no comparison there."

"Maggie's been good enough for the villagers in the past."

"Greg, the world moves on, even here. You can't possibly think you can stop it." When Greg didn't immediately reply, Perry laughed. "You do, don't you?"

"Believe me, if anyone wants to move away from the past, it's me."

"But you're not moving on, stuck out here. You're trying to freeze time. To hide."

It made Greg pause.

"And Lisa," Perry continued, bustling about with an armful of his clean washing and, Greg noticed, more than a few of his items too. "She's not here for the career prospects. Haven't you realized?"

"What?"

"She's here for Bridie."

"Aye. They've been friends since school days."

"Greg." Perry sighed. The look in his eyes was a strange mixture of fondness and pity. "They're adult women now. Lisa and Bridie want to be more to each other than schoolgirl friends."

Greg stared at him. "What? Do you mean they're...?"

"Yes."

"I see." Greg took a careful breath. "Do you think Dougie knows?"

"He's been sharing a house with the pair of them for ages—I assume Lisa comes to stay regularly? Well, you'll probably find he's noticed something. He's not much of a brother if he hasn't."

Greg darted a look at Perry. Was that some kind of barbed comment about Greg as a brother? Maybe about Greg's brothers, in relation to him—

"And no, that comment had no hidden agenda," Perry said quietly.

How does he do that? Know what I'm thinking?

"I reckon," Greg said quickly, and with no care as to whether it'd make any sense in the current conversation at all, "I'll teach you to swim."

Perry stared at him, eyes wide. Then he smiled. "Okay. In the loch?"

"Aye. We'll borrow you a wet suit. Alasdair has a couple of adult ones he keeps for when his grandson comes to visit."

"You'll let me wear something that's touched the skin of the gorgeous gay grandson?" Perry murmured mischievously.

Greg growled, grabbed for him, and missed. Perry tripped away like that sea creature he could resemble when he was at his most slippery. When Greg finally caught him, almost breathless with laughter and mischief, the first swimming lesson had to be postponed—at least until after Perry had rolled Greg onto the sofa and sucked him off.

It took a while before Greg could get his limbs to work to order again.

Chapter Twenty-Five

PERRY saw what he reckoned was the best of Greg Ventura over the days following their get-together at the ceilidh. And no, that didn't just mean the man's fabulous body—and fun appetite—in bed. Greg was relaxed and as confident as Perry had ever seen him.

Why did Greg let those damn brothers of his get to him so much? He should have moved on. *Like I know how easy—or not—that is!* Perry ignored the inner voice that reminded him things were rarely that simple. Instead, he started devising little ways to support and strengthen Greg's self-esteem. He complimented Greg on how he looked; encouraged him when he smiled; approved when he shrugged into the tee shirts Perry thought suited him best. If Greg grew morose at his clumsiness or made some disparaging remark about his looks, Perry was there to kiss and distract him, and tell him just how bloody stupid—and untrue—that was. The one situation where Greg never seemed to worry about himself was in bed during sex.

Perry didn't mind however many distractions they had like that!

Greg actually began to overcome his natural clumsiness. Maybe that started because Perry kept the house in much better order, but as the days went by, Greg strode around more confidently, his head held high so he could see obstacles in his way. He was far more likely to notice his surroundings.

Perry loved the swimming lessons best. He still hesitated to jump voluntarily into the depths, but once Greg had gone in and held out his arms to catch him, he grew more willing. The sea water lochs were the best for practice, where the water itself supported him, but he found himself looking forward to swimming in the fresh water lochs, which had a peace and beauty of their own. He had the basics already, so it was just a matter of Greg teaching him better strokes and building up his confidence. While he was in the water, Greg swam beside him, a hand under his torso at all times to hold him up if needed and words of encouragement in his ear to help develop his style. At those times, Greg was the sea creature and Perry his splash-about sidekick. And best of all was at the end of the sessions, when Greg would grasp him around the waist and lift him up onto the jetty. Perry could just about manage to pull himself up out of the loch, but it seemed both of them enjoyed this little ritual.

"Can't believe you never tried one of those posh city gyms," Greg said one afternoon as they sat on the jetty after Perry's lesson and ate thick-sliced cheese and homemade pickle sandwiches. The air around the loch was warm and still, apart from a clutch of midges buzzing around. It was so beautiful, Perry could just sit there absorbing the wild, stark beauty for hours. "They have pools, don't they?"

"Some of them," Perry said. If he kept his head down, maybe Greg would move the subject on.

"Well, you can join up when you go back. Keep up this good work."

A strange silence fell, as if both of them realized at the same time what all that meant.

"I'll… um. Fetch the towels from the car," Greg said gruffly.

Perry didn't answer. The specter of London had landed yet again, hadn't it? And it was taking on a whole new horror.

PERRY turned over in bed—in Greg's bed—and slammed the Off button on his phone. *Bloody texts!* He'd been ignoring Candace's calls for two days—now they'd sicced Antony on him as well. Perry had been cowardly keeping his phone turned off as often as possible, but as soon as he turned it back on, it beeped furiously with messages. It was 6:00 a.m. and he had ten missed calls.

It was like the worst kind of wake-up call.

"London again?" Greg yawned behind him. The duvet jerked away from Perry as Greg stretched his arms.

"I have to go back," Perry said. "As soon as possible."

Greg snorted. He rolled over and slid an arm around Perry's shoulders. "They've crapped on you, why do you care about them? You're a good-looking man, you could do anything, work anywhere—"

Things snapped. Perry had no idea why he lost control so quickly—well, he bloody well did, but he couldn't admit to that right now—but he was tired, so *tired*, of his daily battles. Just for one short period of time here on Uist he'd escaped them, but now everything would settle back on his shoulders again.

He twisted his head sharply to glare at Greg. "What the hell do you know about it? You think I don't struggle to look good every single bloody day? You think I get out of bed fully groomed?"

"I know you don't," Greg said, obviously without thinking first. He blushed bright red.

"Yes, well. You think this is easy to manage"—Perry tugged painfully at his hair and the uneven curls that fell any which way now he'd stopped using product—"and I keep this shape by eating all the meat we cook?" Though, actually, he reckoned he'd toned up rather than put on weight since he'd been here, but he wasn't going to admit to that either.

Greg was staring at him like he'd suddenly grown two heads.

"And my career. What *about* my career? You think I can just flit from job to job and not get a reputation as unreliable? This is my chance to make something of myself, Greg! I've never had a client this important, a project this big."

"Okay…."

"That's another thing you've assumed," Perry rushed on, ignoring the look of shock dawning on Greg's face. He swung his legs out of bed and stood up. And stayed there, totally naked and shaking, because he just didn't know what else to do. "That all I've ever wanted is to make celebrities look prettier, and to get my name on a TV team list. I never wanted this fucking job in the first place!" He knew his voice was too shrill, too loud. "I was all set to be a designer in my own right, but do you know how fucking difficult it is to get anywhere in London without knowing the right people?"

"No," Greg said quietly. He didn't move at all. It looked like he was trying really hard not to.

"Well, it's hugely fucking difficult, and I just don't know anyone influential enough. So I thought a job in media would be a route toward the job I really want. A chance to network with the right people."

"I'm sure…." Greg swallowed heavily. He looked nervous. "Well, I mean, yes, you'll surely…."

"No, I bloody well won't!" Perry snapped. "I'm no further forward than I was a year ago. I'm too good at getting the job done and doing what I'm told. Why the hell would they promote me out of a job they sorely need doing, and well?"

He realized what he'd said the minute it spilled out of his mouth. He'd effectively shut the door on his own ambitions. But what else was he meant to do? He ached sometimes to work on the designs on the shoots. He anguished at the mistakes they were making in style and setting; he dreamed painfully, night after night, of the collections he could be planning for the new season.

But still they yelled for him to get the coffee—and to charm reluctant TV celebrities like Greg bloody Ventura.

"I never realized," Greg said. Slowly, he swung his legs out from under the duvet. "But why are you letting it get to you? Tell them to get lost. You can stay here as long as you bloody well like."

Perry felt as if the breath had been knocked out of him. Not that he could imagine anything he could do on North Uist that didn't involve water or sheep—but he was blown away by the fact that Greg had just said that, without any second thought. "That can't happen."

"You don't have to—"

"Greg, I do. I have to go back. I have to do a lot of things I probably don't want to." Of course, Greg could do what he liked, couldn't he? He had no ties, no commitments. He'd truly escaped it all. So he'd given up his family as a result, but that hadn't been a hardship at the time. In fact, it sounded like it had been a good coping strategy. But that wasn't Perry's situation, was it?

"No, you don't," Greg said mulishly. "You shouldn't have to lead a miserable life."

"You don't know anything about it!"

"You won't tell me!"

They'd both raised their voices. Perry sighed and tried to rein in his anger. "Okay, so you might as well know. I have to go back to my tiny little flat and my disgracefully ill-paid, overladen job, and the panic I feel every time I get a call at home out of the usual—"

"What do you mean—?"

"I have to go back," he almost yelled, tears pricking his eyes at last, "because I can't afford not to!"

Chapter Twenty-Six

GREG stared at him, uncomprehending. "Can't afford?"

"Fuck," Perry said. He couldn't think of any other word that better expressed his utter misery.

Somewhat to his surprise, Greg didn't continue pressing him. Instead, he also stood. *Great.* Now there were two of them, standing stark bollock naked in the middle of the bedroom.

"Perry. Tell me what's up."

"Oh, for God's sake—"

"Tell me," Greg repeated. "You made me tell you things once. Now it's my turn." He gestured to the bed. Then when Perry stood unmoving, he took his shoulders and guided him back to sit on it. Greg sat beside him, close but not intimidatingly so.

Again, when Perry sat there like a statue, Greg tugged him so that Perry's head lay on his shoulder. *Oh God, yes.* Greg was like a rock: a warm, living, comfortable rock, but steady like the real thing would be. Perry relaxed into the position. He wanted to lie against him forever.

"So?" Greg said softly. "What was it on your phone?"

"It was a message from Antony, my friend at the agency."

"Another follow-up call about the TV program?"

"Worse. I've had a warning delivered to my flat about… about bailiff proceedings."

"What are you talking about?"

Perry swallowed tightly. "I'm broke, Greg. Not just broke, but horribly in debt." How terrible that sounded, said aloud. How humiliating. "It's not my fault!"

"I wouldn't imagine it was."

Perry felt no change in Greg's breathing pattern, so maybe that was sincere. But Perry had too much to blame on his own behalf not to expect it from others. "There was a guy… we went out together for nearly a year. Henry had been in the fashion industry for years but wanted to start up his own agency. Yes, I know what a flaky industry it is. And how bloody difficult it is to succeed, especially on your own."

"I don't doubt it."

"I wanted it to succeed, Greg!" Perry rushed on, He didn't dare stop now. "And for really selfish reasons, I suppose, because I could have launched my own designs with him. He promised me I'd have his full support. Of course, that was in exchange for my financial investment."

Greg was silent for a moment, but his hand tightened on Perry's arm.

"I was happy to do it, you know? I didn't have much in the way of savings, but I was happy to invest it in his future. Plus I supported him when he left his existing job. What's more, I even persuaded Mother to invest. And then…." His stomach clenched. It wasn't just the betrayal that hurt, but his own stupidity. "Well, of course, he struggled to make a go of it. He couldn't make enough contacts, he couldn't attract enough clients. Maybe it was his approach—he was an arrogant bastard, I can see that more clearly now—but like I say, it's not always a friendly business. The money leached away, and he started to run up debt. In the end, he lost his flat to the bank and had to move back in with his sister. We couldn't keep up the relationship by that stage, and to be honest, I was relieved when we split up."

"But what about your investment?"

"Henry said he'd pay it back. I had my doubts about that, but I thought it was important to help his self-esteem, so I agreed to keep in touch. And God knows, I needed the money myself. There was a time when I thought I'd lose my flat as well, but luckily my friends at the agency helped me out. They never really liked Henry." He swallowed hard. "Proves their instincts were better than mine. He ran up extra debt up in my name too. I had no idea until months after he'd left me, when I started getting legal letters threatening me. And Mother too."

"My God, Perry."

"It was a tough time. I've paid Mother back, though she doesn't know it came from me, not Henry. And I'm still challenging most of the claims. But some of the others… dammit." He sank his head into his hands. "I've had to pay up just to get the agencies off my back."

"You shouldn't have done that," Greg said in a low voice.

"Fuck it, don't give me that—!"

"No! I mean you shouldn't have had to do that. You were the victim, Perry, not the one at fault."

For a moment, Perry gulped in a breath, trying to hold back tears. Greg's grip on him had never faltered. "Anyway, that's why my job is so bloody important to me. Without it, I couldn't have afforded to stay in London. Or pay Mother back her savings. And even now, I can't afford to waste anything."

"Like on clothes? And… oh, dammit, me and my big mouth. On gym memberships?"

Perry flushed. He reckoned even his nose was red with shame. "It's true. I can't afford anything except basic living. I don't even know if Eddy is going to reimburse all my expenses for staying here. I have the clothes I arrived with and hardly anything else left behind."

Greg tensed beside him. "None of that stuff matters to me anyway."

"You think I don't know that?" Perry could feel his anguish as a thick lump in his throat. "That's one of the reasons I love you, Greg Ventura! But it's everything to me, in that world—"

His brain caught up with his mouth just those few second too late. *What have I said? What have I done?* Horrified, he twisted away from Greg and leaped back up. His skin was cold without Greg's grip. His heart plummeted at the look of shock on Greg's face.

"Perry—?"

"Don't! I'm sorry!"

They spoke at the same time. The silence fell like the heaviest snowfall. There could be no going back from that kind of declaration. And Perry couldn't deny it, could he? Because it was sadly, shockingly true.

Greg cleared his throat as if it hurt him. “I’m not… I’m no good for anyone else, Perry. I’ve tried to be better, to be different. But I’m never going to be right for you.”

Perry knew his humiliation was complete. He could feel the tears finally seeping out. “Don’t let *anyone* tell you that! You’re just perfect as you are.” He turned quickly so Greg wouldn’t see any more of his shame. “But I apologize for embarrassing us both. Excuse me now. I’ll pack my bag and book my travel back to London. There’s a suitable flight tomorrow afternoon.”

He left the room with as much dignity as he could. Bloody difficult, when he was totally nude and about to bawl his eyes out.

Chapter Twenty-Seven

A COUPLE of hours later, Perry stood in the hallway of the cottage, fully dressed but still rubbing suspiciously wet traces from his eyes. He hadn't dared face Greg after that scene in the bedroom, so he'd spent an unnecessarily long time packing. Not that his clothes were likely to survive many more journeys. In fact, they'd been virtually ruined from his first day here, but… well, they were all he had. He looked at the smart jacket and the ripped but immaculately pressed jeans that still had mud stains on the hems, and they all looked totally alien to him. They'd been some of his favorite pieces when he first arrived.

And he still needed them for that life, didn't he? He couldn't turn up on the streets of Soho in blue Wellington boots and a huge waterproof coat. To say nothing of the layers of comfy clothing he was now used to wearing, especially the oversized blue fleece Greg had loaned him when he first appeared in the cottage like a drowned rat. Perry had always been reluctant to give it back.

For that matter, where the hell *was* Greg? Perry had heard Greg's phone ring in the kitchen an hour or so ago. Greg had shouted up the stairs about having to go to Alasdair's to find a sheep that'd gone missing and there was a storm on its way, then the front door had slammed behind him.

Perry peeked out of the small window by the front door to see if Greg was on his way back yet. How long did it take to find a missing sheep? The fields of peat that stretched from the end of the croft seemed to go on for ever, with no landmarks to break it up. And now the rain had started falling, slowly but steadily. *Typical.* It matched Perry's mood. Miserable, cold, and inevitably wet. Water had dogged him every step of the way on this trip. He'd arrived soaked to the skin, fallen in the loch, needed extra swimming lessons when he should have done it years ago as a kid….

But every time, he recalled, Greg had been there to help him. Greg had dried him off when he fell in, made sure he was warm. Had kissed him. Greg had held him in the water until his swimming confidence grew. Greg had laughed with and kissed him—again, and again—and taken him to bed. Perry sighed.

Oh my God, I am so in trouble.

He'd just received his e-ticket for his flight home tomorrow. It was all booked. But this departure was impossibly painful, and not just because he'd fucked up his mission. It was because he didn't want to leave Greg.

"What am I going to do?" he mused aloud. "What *can* I do?"

Rory gazed up at him, his tail wagging.

"Things are so much easier for a dog, right?" Perry reached down and absentmindedly scratched behind Rory's ears. "You can just love someone without needing to explain yourself. Without worrying whether they feel the same, or how much, or in what way. In fact, not needing to talk about it at all."

Rory tilted his head to one side. Perry had never had such a fascinated, nonjudgmental audience. And my God, he needed to let loose to someone or he'd burst. His emotions started to seep out of him like sand through his fingers, and as soon as he started, he found he couldn't stop.

"I want to sleep in his room like you do, boy. Every night. Be with him every day like you are, walking the croft, eating the food he grows, building the fire, watching his art take shape, drinking that ghastly wine he makes. Good grief." Perry shook his head mournfully. "He's turned me into Bear Grylls."

Rory snuffled. It was almost a laugh. He tilted his head the other way, his bright eyes fixed hopefully on Perry's face.

"Okay. Yes. It's time to be honest, at least with myself, isn't it? And with you. What I said to him was the complete truth. Love is the word. Love is the *bloody* word. I've fallen for him. The big, gorgeous, tongue-tied, brother-bullied, issue-riven berk that he is. I'd never have imagined it. He doesn't like musicals, he doesn't possess any cocktail glasses, he doesn't believe in fabric conditioner, and that haircut…? Oh God, I can't wait until Lisa gets her salon up and running and can knock that into a decent shape on a regular basis."

There was a moment's silence. Rory didn't make any doggy sounds.

"Shit. I won't be here to see it anyway, will I?"

Perry reached down again, letting Rory lick at his hand. His eyes felt suspiciously sore but he refused to cry again. At least not today, and not where Greg might catch him. "I love him. I love Greg Ventura. Trust me to fall for the wrong guy again, eh?"

Rory whined quietly.

"I have to go back to London. I *have* to! I made a commitment, I have a problem to make good, and I have to face up to it. And besides, there's nothing definite for me here. He hasn't really asked me to stay, has he? At least, not because he feels the same way. It's been such a short time to get to know each other."

Rory's ears suddenly pricked up. Perry's heart gave a lurch. Was Greg back at the cottage? Surely he wasn't finished with Alasdair already? Perry had assumed with his newfound island crofting knowledge that they might have to take the sheep to the vet's, and that was out by Dougie's place. But when Rory shook himself and then trotted over to the window, Perry followed.

"Can you hear something, boy? No idea how you can with that bloody rain hammering on the roof. And you certainly aren't tall enough to see outside." With a smile—at a dog, for God's sake, what had got into him?—Perry glanced out toward the end of the croft.

There was someone outside, darting toward the peat bog. Short, dressed in a white top and jeans, unsteady on its feet. Perry couldn't see from here whether it was male or female, but it looked small enough to be a child. He couldn't see anyone else around. No one would let their child out alone in the rain like that, would they? I mean, he knew they were hardy folks around here, but that one didn't look like it had a coat or hat or anything to protect it.

Rory barked loudly. He was standing to attention, right in front of the door, as if expecting to be taken out. And right *now*.

"What is it, boy?"

Rory barked again, as if to say, *How many times do I have to repeat myself, you idiot?* His tail thumped hard against the doorframe.

"You're the idiot, methinks," Perry said. "Wanting to go out in that weather." He peered out of the window again. The wind lifted around the cottage, wailing through the gap in the kitchen window that Greg hadn't fixed yet. There was no sign of Greg or anyone else for that matter. Just the back of the small, white-dressed creature as it staggered across the horizon and finally out of sight.

"The rain will turn that bog into a mud bath," Perry mused aloud. "Poor kid needs to get back indoors as soon as possible." Who was it? Why wasn't it running for cover like any sensible-minded person would? For that matter, where could it be going? The only houses around here were Greg's, Alasdair's, and the Mackies'. And none of them could be called close neighbors in Perry's citified opinion. The figure had been traveling away from Greg's croft—was that north? Perry couldn't remember, and he wasn't going to waste brain cells trying to remember right now, but he suspected there was nothing to find in that direction for miles.

Rory growled from deep in his throat.

"All right. I get you." Perry sighed. "I'll go out and call them in here to shelter until the rain stops. But if I have to travel tomorrow in soaking wet shoes again, you'll be the one to blame." Then he spotted his blue boots against the wall by the front door. Excellent idea, even if he was only going to be outside for ten minutes. He really was turning into an outdoorsy person. He wriggled into them and opened the front door.

Chapter Twenty-Eight

THE wind hit him first, full in the face, sweeping around the corners of the cottage like a mini tornado. He hadn't realized how fierce it was getting. He grabbed the borrowed fleece and zipped himself into it. There was no time to put on any other layers. He couldn't see the figure out on the bog any longer and he was worried about losing it completely. Who knew what muddy mess was out there, places to fall over, places to get stuck, probably pits and mounds like the worst kind of jungle? Subconsciously he knew a Scottish bog wasn't remotely like the Amazon rainforest, but danger was danger, right?

Perry tugged his sweater around him and started jogging down the path toward the bog, waving his hands. "Hey! Where are you? Can you hear me?" No one answered, though he didn't expect it in this wind. He ran out of the croft gate and onto the scrub. The going was harder here, and the rain was gathering into shallow puddles. By the time he reached the peat, he was already slipping on the slick surface, and despite the long fleece, his jeans felt suspiciously damp around the knees.

The rain was increasing in strength. By the time he'd gone a few hundred yards farther, the jungle analogy was getting more and more credible. If he twisted around, he could still see the croft—a small, dark building on the edge of his vision. But the rain was coming down in rods all around him, and he had to blink hard to keep his eyelashes clear. Chill wetness beat down on his head, even through the hood of the fleece, and was soaking through the shoulders.

Keep going. Just over that next lump. The land had always seemed pretty flat, but maybe the water was affecting the peat at different degrees. Whatever the topographical reason, Perry found himself alternately sliding down an incline, then struggling up out of mud that clung to his ankles.

He couldn't see the croft anymore. There should have been a route to the main road somewhere behind it, but he couldn't see any sign of that either. Just gray, thick cloud above his head, sloppy mud below his boots, and the bloody wind and rain everywhere else. When he tried to shield his eyes to find a guiding landmark, the rain smacked him in the face, and the wind was so strong he had to struggle to lift his arms at all.

Maybe he should have done more of that swimming. Or joined Greg more often in his daily workout. The thought of Greg in just a thin workout vest warmed him right through for a moment. Then the wind snatched back his attention. He tottered and nearly fell on his arse.

The smallest tremor of fear ran through him.

Pull yourself together! He was no TV weather boy, but he was sure this would pass quickly. He just had to find the child and get back to the croft, and then he could take a warm shower and change his clothes. He worried briefly about ruining more outfits and having to repack yet again, but that was hardly a priority at the moment. He leaned forward, put down his head like a little bull terrier, and pushed onward.

He'd lost track of time and distance by the time he saw the flash of white clothing again. The child had stopped running and was standing stock-still, bent at the waist as if exhausted. The rain beat down on the bowed head, and the white clothing was turning gray with damp. Whoever it was, they were in trouble.

"Come over here!" Perry yelled. "Come and get out of this hideous weather!" His words were whipped away by the wind, but he was sure the figure heard him. It raised its head and looked his way. Perry clumped a few steps nearer, though the mud was more and more tenacious now.

Oh good God.

It was Fiona Mackie. The little girl was white-faced and soaked through, staring at him with eyes so large they were like beacons. Perry tried to rush to her—he really did—but every step felt like wading in treacle. A foot away, he slipped again and his ankle twisted sharply underneath him. He bit back the curse he would have let loose if there wasn't a minor in hearing distance. Instead, he reached for her and pulled her close. She was as cold as stone.

"Fiona! What are you doing out here?"

Fiona shook her head. Her teeth were chattering and her body shuddered with cold. Fear shot through Perry again. He struggled out of his wet fleece and wrapped it around her as quickly as he could, trying to capture any remaining warmth for her benefit.

"Let's get back," he said. His own teeth felt frozen now, since he'd stopped walking. "Um. Do you know which way you came?" They should retrace their steps: get back to the croft as soon as possible. But where the hell *was* the croft?

"Have to f-find Emily."

Emily? Perry felt sick at the thought of another child left out here, then remembered that Emily was Fiona's doll. "Where is she?"

"Wind. W-wind blew her away. I ran after her. Got to catch her." Fiona's face crumpled in distress, but she was obviously too tired by now to look farther. Perry glanced around but all he could see was black, churning mud. Wherever Emily was, she'd be the same color and consistency by now. They'd never see her against everything else.

"We'll find her, but not now, okay? Please, let's get back out of the rain. We'll come straight back out and find her."

"It's a storm," Fiona said, simply but rather obviously. The words stuttered out of her in her high-pitched child's voice. "Grannie said it'd last for hours. I wanted to go and see Morag's puppies, but Grannie said not until after the storm. And I couldn't have one for myself because who'll look after it when I go home with Mummy to the mainland? It'd be all on its own and would miss me, and they like company, especially farming dogs, don't they? And they need really good training, and I wouldn't be here to do it, but Grannie was being really mean—"

Perry squeezed her arm in the hope of halting the tirade. God, she was wet, the fabric of her shirt was like wringing a sodden dishcloth. "Well, I think that actually sounds very sensible of Grannie, love, but come into the cottage and we'll talk about it. Where *is* Grannie?" Was Aileen out here in this storm as well?

"I ran away," Fiona said. Her face set in a very mulish expression, despite the raindrops rolling off the end of her pert nose. "Me and Emily. I'm coming to live with Rory and Greg. And you, Perry."

Perry resisted rolling his eyes. "Um, well, yes. Let's get Greg to sort all this out, shall we?" The bog underneath his feet was… well, bogging him down. He glanced back the way he thought he'd come, but couldn't see anything to guide him. His ankle was starting to throb. How far had they come, for God's sake?

Fiona was crying and clung to him. "I'm so cold. Emily's lost. Grannie will be so cross, I'll never have a puppy now."

"Fiona Mackie," Perry said almost sharply. "You can have as many puppies as you please, but only if we get back right now!"

She shut up immediately, but she was still shivering violently. Would he have to carry her? She couldn't weigh much, but he was starting to worry about his ankle. Any movement sent a sharp pain through his heel, and his calf had started to go numb. "Come on, love," he said. "We'll try this way. We're bound to find one of the cottages soon." He took her arm as gently but firmly as he could and guided her ahead of him.

IT had been hours. Maybe days. No, that was stupid, wasn't it? But Perry was having trouble concentrating on anything for more than a couple of seconds. He thought he could hear barking in the distance, but it was probably the rain on a fence somewhere. Or his hallucination, imagining St. Bernard rescue dogs on their way. But that was in the snow, wasn't it? Not the jungle. Was he still in the jungle? It may have been called the rainforest, but did it actually rain this much, all the time?

He'd just take a moment to gather his strength, then they'd set off again.

Just a moment. He dug his heels into the mud and paused, breathing heavily.

Fiona had collapsed a while back, her little legs too tired to hold her up any longer. When Perry bent to lift her up out of the mud, she clung around his neck and wouldn't loosen her grip for anything. So he hoisted her up into his arms and struggled forward, carrying her. They'd staggered on like that for yards… miles… centuries. Shit, he was losing touch with his brain again. It was impossible *not* to find one of the three crofts any minute, wasn't it? Unless, of course, he'd gone completely the wrong way and struck out into the uninhabited peat bog beyond the crofts. If so, it was miles before he'd reach any other houses. He could be moving in circles for all he knew.

He peered ahead through the relentless rain. Still nothing to see. A trickle ran off his nose into his mouth and he licked it in, careless now of the muddy taste. The bloody sky must be empty of water eventually. And he was sure this was the right direction. Wasn't it? Fiona was a dead weight in his arms, but he couldn't put her down in all this filth. Poor little love. She hadn't made any noise for what felt like a long time. The rain slithered down his back like he was in a shower at home. No, not home, was it? It was Greg's house, not Perry's. He was just a visitor. An unwelcome one, from the first.

He wondered where Emily was. He wondered where Greg was. Would he be angry that Perry had ruined the fleece? That he'd probably have to delay his flight while his clothes all dried out again? That he'd be an unwelcome, embarrassingly besotted, needy guest for even longer?

Anyway. Rest was over. He had to keep going, get Fiona home safely. He wrenched the boot on his good foot up out of the mud and reached gingerly forward for a more secure foothold. Pulling up his injured foot took longer. Much longer. He nearly dropped Fiona.

Mustn't do that.

Pain in his foot. Wind biting, beating his nose and mouth with sharp, cruel slaps. He'd stopped noticing the rain at the point he realized he *was* the rain, wasn't he? One little, tottering, sodden blob of rain, determined to get across this bloody bog and get back to Greg. To safety, that was.

He lifted the boot again. Made the next step.

And the next.

Chapter Twenty-Nine

GREG didn't feel settled at Dougie's house, even though he'd claimed the comfy armchair, had drunk two cups of tea, and eaten most of Bridie's cherry cake. His friends had been skirting around him, both physically and conversationally, ever since he came stomping over after taking one of Alasdair's sheep to the vet's nearby. He'd just wanted a bit of company, but all he got from them were pitying looks.

"Perry's leaving tomorrow?" Bridie sounded shocked. "Why didn't you tell us? We'll have to come and see him off. When's he coming back again?"

Greg decided to ignore that question, mainly because he'd been asking himself the same thing ever since he arrived. But would Perry ever want to see him again? Greg had just gawped when Perry said that… that *thing* about how he felt. He should have been quicker to reassure Perry, to say something soothing and mature. Instead, he'd blathered on again about himself as usual, and what a crap bet he was, and how Perry deserved so much more….

At least, he thought that was what he said. He'd been so startled, he couldn't remember any of the following minutes until Alasdair's phone call. In fact, he'd sat on the bed like a silent, useless, shocked lump, listening to Perry moving around in the spare room, presumably packing up his stuff. To leave. *To go.* Why did that feel so painful? After all, they could still be friends. They could be even more trendy e-mail pals when Perry got back to London.

E-mail pals? You bloody hypocrite! Greg couldn't ignore the way his traitorous conscience was harassing him. He didn't want a bloody correspondent; another friend he touched base with once in a blue moon. He wanted Perry beside him, in the flesh. How had things got to this stage?

"There's a really big drenchin' on its way," Lisa muttered beside Bridie. They were sitting together on the sofa, holding hands. Greg felt such a fool he'd never noticed their closeness before Perry pointed it out. "You havenae left Perry out there in this, have ye?"

"Of course I haven't," he snapped. "He's safe in the cottage. Packing his stuff. Rory's with him, if you're so worried about the lad!"

Lisa scowled; Dougie still looked bemused.

"Why's he going, anyway?" Bridie persisted. "You should have asked him to stay for good."

Aye, you should, you bloody idiot.

He turned on Bridie too swiftly. "You want me to do his stupid fucking TV show?"

"Ach, steady on!" Dougie raised his eyebrows at Greg's angry tone. Lisa bristled, protective of Bridie.

But Bridie didn't need protecting. "Of course I bloody don't! And don't use that tone with me. I wanted Perry to stay longer because he makes you happy, right?"

"But…." Greg was weary of all his arguments, which, honestly, were looking less justifiable as time went on. "I'm not going into all this again. It was Perry's choice. He has… things to do back in London. He's packing now and has booked a flight for tomorrow."

"You'll be taking him to the ferry?" Bridie asked fiercely.

"Well… can't Dougie take him?" Greg hadn't thought about it before now, to be honest. Seeing Perry off on the ferry? Watching him leave the island? Sounded like a recipe for surefire pain. Greg shifted on his chair. He felt inexplicably chilled, despite Dougie having lit the fire. His despair at having messed everything up was growing, and his stomach hurt. It was unlikely to be because he'd tried to drown his sorrows in tea and cake.

"What am I now?" Dougie groused. "A bloody taxi rank?"

"You want the truth?" Greg startled himself with the misery in his voice, and all three of the others turned to stare at him. "I don't want to see him all togged up in his London gear again, back off to his glamorous job. And he certainly won't want me moping all over him."

Bridie frowned, but with concern in her eyes now. "What's happened, Greg?"

"What's tha' noise?" Lisa called over.

She'd gone to the window by the front door. Greg thought it was probably to check the weather, since she was so bloody worried he'd let Perry out in the wind and rain, like he'd bloody melt or something—

Bridie was up off the sofa, as well, and had moved next to Lisa. "It's a dog barking at the gate. It's Rory!"

She opened the door and the dog came racing in, soaking wet, panting heavily. He ran straight to Greg and leaped onto his lap.

"Looks like he's run all the way from y'r place," Lisa said, with something like awe.

"Perry," Greg said hoarsely, ignoring the damp patch immediately appearing on his lap. He didn't know how he knew, except from Rory's rolling eyes, but… "Something's happened to Perry!"

THEY scooped Rory up into Dougie's car with them and powered their way as fast as they dared to Greg's cottage. The distance was walkable on a fine day, but the wind was fierce now, and Rory's distress dictated speed. Greg sat in the front with Dougie, while Bridie and Lisa insisted on traveling with them in the back.

"Good boy," Greg murmured to his dog, holding him tightly on his lap as Dougie guided the car through growing pools of standing water. The wipers ran at double speed, spraying the rain either side of the car. Rory was still panting and wriggling restlessly against Greg's grip. "Wish you could tell me what's wrong. Has the storm scared you?"

"That dog's got baws of steel," Dougie scoffed. "And he's seen more than his fair share o' storms. Something else has disturbed him."

Greg knew that for himself. *Just trying to calm myself. And failing.*

When Dougie drew up outside Greg's croft, Greg was the first human from the vehicle: Rory had already leaped out ahead of him. The dog wheeled back and forth by the front door, barking, tail swishing raindrops in an arc over his back legs.

Bridie ran ahead of everyone, into the cottage. "Perry's not here!" she called back to the others.

Greg's chest hurt now, not just his stomach. They all clustered inside the front door, dripping water everywhere, the wind slapping around their legs and raising the fringes of the hallway rug.

"Would he ha' booked an earlier flight for t'day? Made his own way t' the ferry?" Lisa asked.

"Of course not." The cold shiver down Greg's back tightened into a grip. "He couldn't walk that far. He doesn't know the bloody way. He wasn't that upset."

"Upset? Why was he upset?" Bridie said sharply.

"Not now," Greg said quickly. "We have to find him." But where did they start? What was Perry playing at? Would he really have set off without any transport or help, so desperate to get home? Greg glanced at the hooks on the wall beside the front door. Perry's boots had gone, but his heavy waterproof coat was still hanging there. *He'll be soaked*, Greg found himself thinking. *He'll freeze out there.* He felt suddenly nauseated.

Had he been the one to send Perry out there on his own after all? Was it Greg's stupid, selfish refusal to climb out of his self-imposed exile and face the world that had driven Perry to the end of his tether? Had he, Greg, really thought he could have a few nights of fun with a handsome young man and not be guilty of using him? Of misleading him?

What's more, he realized suddenly that wasn't the real issue any longer. Maybe he had used Perry at first, stealing a kiss or two, letting things run to much more than that. They'd both been guilty of that, though, hadn't they? But now that felt like a long-ago persona. Perry had changed him. Not in the way he'd probably expected when he turned up at Greg's door in his sopping London clothes and his daft haircut and plans to make Greg his makeover project. It had happened in a much deeper, sweeter, more poignant way than that—it had happened from the inside out.

His thoughts of Perry now were full of panic and fear. What would he do, if Perry had come to some harm? He could have fallen into another loch, tumbled into one of the pits out on the bog. He could have hit his head, knocked himself unconscious, been unable to pull himself out.

Oh God. Oh God! Greg's throat was almost too tight to breathe. If Perry had… how would Greg ever get over it?

The fierce knocking on the doorframe startled them all.

"Perry?" Greg cried with unutterable relief and spun back around. But it wasn't Perry behind them at his door. It was Cameron and Aileen Mackie, their waterproofs drawn tight and glistening black with rain, their heads almost hidden inside heavy, sodden hoods.

"Is she here?" Aileen said abruptly. "The bairn?"

"She definitely ran this way," Cameron said, as if he'd been arguing with Aileen about it. His face was too pale to blame on just the cold wind.

"For God's sake, come in," Greg said.

"No!" Aileen's anguish rang from the word. "Where's Fiona? We had words, and she ran off with her dolly. Ye have the nearest croft, but if she's nae here, where is she?"

And Rory barked hard again.

Chapter Thirty

IT took them only a couple of minutes to organize the search party but, for Greg, that was agonizingly slow. He was scared for Fiona, but more terrified for Perry. Had the two of them set out somewhere together? Had Perry followed Fiona, or had she followed him? Cameron had brought with him a handful of their croft workers, suited for the weather and carrying strong torches, and with the others adding to the team, Greg sent everyone out in a fan arrangement. It seemed right for him to take charge. Cameron didn't make any protest, anyway.

"She's a wee girl," Aileen said. She'd said the same thing again and again in the last few minutes: she was obviously beside herself with worry. She'd wanted to search with Cameron and the others but had been persuaded to stay at Greg's with Bridie, in case Fiona turned up there in the meantime. "How can she have got so far?"

Greg patted her arm awkwardly. "We'll find them, Aileen."

"Them?" She looked as bemused by his touch as she did his words.

"Perry's out there too. For all we know, he's with Fiona and they're both fine." Greg didn't say anything else, but he knew from experience how fast and how far a determined young child could travel. He could remember yet another time George and Gareth went missing, when they decided to row to France from Brighton seafront in an inflatable dinghy. They were only eight, and it took Geoff and their nanny ages to swim out and drag the dinghy back to shore. And one day in the center of London, on a theater trip, Gerry had taken a right turn when the rest of the family took a left… it wasn't until after an hour and a distraught call to the police that they found him. He'd got all the way from Leicester Square to Charing Cross as a weary ten-year-old, with no idea at all of where he was. It had been one of the rare times Greg had seen his brother Gerry frightened.

Pawing madly at Greg's leg, Rory barked. Greg crouched beside him.

"Are you coming?" Dougie called from the doorway.

"I'll follow Rory," Greg said. "He knows something about Perry."

Dougie didn't waste any more words, just nodded, turned, and strode out into the storm.

THE only benefit of the low-lying, treeless landscape was that anything unusual stood out. Greg saw the bundle on top of the peat at almost the same time as Rory started running toward it, barking.

Perry lay on his back in the mud. His whole body was drenched, covered in the brown muck, and he'd sunk down several inches so that it looked like it was slowly consuming him. His eyes were closed. On top of him lay another person, much smaller, just as wet, dirty, and limp. *Fiona!* Perry's arms were clutched tightly around her, holding her above the worst of the mud, cushioned on his own body. And wrapped around her, Greg just about recognized his own fleece jacket, now ruined beyond hope, but offering some small protection for the little girl.

"Fiona? Perry!"

Neither of them stirred. Rory scampered around the bundle of bodies, barking, nosing at Fiona.

"I've got it, boy. I've got them." Greg's voice was distorted by the wind and rain, but even without that, it was barely recognizable. His throat was so tight, the words hurt to speak. He dropped to his knees, squelching mud everywhere, and shoved his gloved hands under Perry. It took several tugs just to get him released. Then Greg gripped under Perry's shoulders and knees as hard as he could, leaned back on his heels, and lifted him up.

Who knew the skinny little bugger could weigh so much? Of course, he was lifting Fiona as well. He staggered as he stood upright and was terrified he'd drop either or both of them, but Perry still clung tightly to the girl.

As Greg stood for a moment, gathering his breath, he glanced down at Perry's legs and feet, hanging limply down. Everything was black from the mud, apart from one toe of his bright blue boots. The rain on Greg's face felt warmer than before, until he realized it was tears. He was crying. He hadn't cried for years.

"And you know what?" he yelled fiercely at Rory, though God knew, it wasn't the poor dog's fault. "I don't fucking care if anyone sees! If anything happens to Perry, I'll never get over it!"

"Greg? *Greg*!"

The others in the search party were struggling their way over to him, alerted by Rory's barking more than anything else. He was shortly surrounded by people, all swathed in their waterproofs so he hardly knew who was who. They tried to help him carry Perry and Fiona, but he wouldn't let anyone near. He couldn't seem to loosen his grip on them. So everyone clustered around to help him stay upright and supported, and Dougie lit the way back to the croft by arranging a small army of people with torches.

BRIDIE had started up the fire in the living room, and as soon as they all stumbled through the front door, Dougie and Lisa all but pushed Greg up the stairs.

"You need a quick, warm shower, man."

"Not now—"

"Yes, now!"

Greg couldn't remember when Dougie had ever sounded so serious. He wriggled out of his coat and boots, but no one tried to undress him further. And no one dared pull Perry out of his arms. Instead, they all followed him to the bathroom. *Bizarre.* However, when Cameron followed them into the room and threatened to get into the shower with him, Greg allowed the old man to peel Fiona out of Perry's grasp.

Fiona stirred and yawned. "Grampy?"

There was a chorus of sighs and relieved laughter.

"Och, my dear wee bairn. My dear wee bairn." Cameron looked close to tears himself.

"Did Rory fetch you, Grampy? Perry sent him to find Greg." Fiona yawned again, more widely. Her face was mud-streaked, but the cheeks beneath it were gaining more color in the warmth of the room.

"Rory's a bloody hero," Lisa said gruffly. "So's Perry."

Bloody hell, was she crying too? Greg thought about commenting, then decided he was way too tired.

"Aye. We'll talk about it all later. Greg? Go on with ye." Dougie hustled him toward the shower again and reached in to start the water. The Mackies shuffled out of the room, chatting over Fiona's head, crying and laughing. The door shut behind them, leaving Greg with Dougie and, surprisingly, Lisa. Greg wondered if they'd stay there even if he stripped off. Maybe they were afraid he'd fall and crack his head open. Or Perry's. *How kind.* He smiled aimlessly at Dougie, startling the other man. *He's a good friend.*

"You're not all there, man," Dougie muttered. "You want help?"

Greg nodded and stepped carefully into the shower. Why didn't Perry wake up, like Fiona had? His eyes were still tightly shut, his body a dead weight. Dougie lifted down the shower head and started washing the mud off Greg's back.

"Don't drown the poor wee bastard," Lisa said sharply, as Dougie moved around to the front. Everyone was drenched by now anyway, either from the rain or Dougie's clumsiness with the shower.

"I've got this in hand, thank ye," Dougie snapped back.

Lisa reached over to undo Perry's shirt. It clung to his torso, the nipple piercing glinting dully through the thin fabric.

"Cute," Lisa murmured.

"Don't touch him!" Greg snapped.

Dougie snorted.

And Perry stirred at last. His eyes sprang open, unfocused and scared, his body jerked in Greg's arms, so they both stumbled against the tiled wall, and he gave a god-awful sneeze.

"Ach, he'll be fine now," Dougie said with all the confidence of an episode of *Dr. Finlay's Casebook*. He dropped the shower head with visible relief. "We'll leave ye to it!"

"I CAN have as many puppies as I like. Perry says so!" Fiona's voice was high and excited. Apart from a high flush on her cheeks and ruined clothes, she seemed to be returning to normal after her ordeal. They were all clustered in the living room by now, Perry on the sofa wrapped in another pair of Greg's pajamas and the spare room duvet. Aileen was crying and alternately hugging Dougie and Bridie. Cameron just stood with Fiona in his arms, rocking her. She looked annoyed at the restriction, but equally thrilled with the attention.

After all the drama, Lisa and Bridie had served everyone with hot drinks and sandwiches, and watched over the invalids until the afternoon had almost slipped away. The rain had eased a little, and the Mackies were preparing to leave.

"Remember to call Dr. Mackenzie," Greg ordered. "He can decide if Fiona needs to be checked out at the hospital in Benbecula." Tomorrow, he'd wonder at the wisdom of ordering Cameron Mackie to do anything, but for now, this was his croft, and he was in charge. He gestured at Fiona with a frown. "And she needs to listen to her elders and betters and stay indoors on days like this."

Fiona stared at him, opened her mouth—then shut it again abruptly, having seen the look on his face, settling for a pout.

"What about Perry?" Bridie asked.

"No, no hospital." Perry coughed and sat up. "I'm fine. Just… cold. Tired." He looked like he'd drop any second, but he looked pleadingly at Greg.

"I'll look after him," Greg said quickly. "If I think we need the doctor, I'll call him as well."

Aileen had crossed the room before he realized it, and she took Perry's hand. He looked up at her with a bleary, puzzled expression.

"Thank ye, lad," she said. "For finding my bairn. For guarding her." She turned briefly to Greg. "And t' you all for bringing her home."

Greg saw the Mackies out of the house, with more thanks and more insistent calls to come around soon. Bridie and Lisa started clearing away the plates and Greg's mismatched mugs.

Dougie came to stand beside Greg on the doorstep. "So will you be needing Dougie's taxis t'morrow after all?"

"Get away with you." Greg scowled at him. "Perry needs to rest. But hopefully he'll be okay enough tomorrow to travel as planned. It's up to him what he does."

"If it were up t' Perry," Dougie said with spirit, "he wouldn't be going anywhere."

Greg stared at him. "Don't be stupid. He's from another world, and he'll go back sooner or later."

Dougie shrugged and grinned. He pulled his waterproofs back on, ready to leave the cottage.

Bridie came out of the kitchen, also wearing her coat. "Greg? What about you? Are *you* okay?"

Surprising them both, he hugged her. Her wet raincoat made a squelching sound between them. Glancing over her shoulder toward the fireplace, he could see Perry, already asleep on the sofa, swaddled in the duvet like it was a cocoon with his tousled hair poking out of the top. The flames flickered on his flushed cheeks.

What would I have done if he'd been lost?

There were puddles of water on Greg's rug and mud trampled all over the hallway. Rory lay panting in his basket as if he'd run a marathon, and he'd need a damn good bath. Greg's sanctuary had been invaded by crofters he barely knew, he'd bossed Cameron Mackie about, and more or less criticized Aileen Mackie's grandparenting skills. But none of it mattered. Perry was okay; Perry was back home. All that mattered was Perry. How had he been so blind to those priorities before now?

And what will I do when he's gone?

"Greg?"

"You were right," he murmured into Bridie's ear.

She chuckled. "Wonders will never cease. What about, specifically?"

"He does make me happy."

"I see." She searched his face for a moment, serious now. "This has moved very fast, my dear man."

"Aye," he said with gentle mimicry of her accent. "Verra fast, and verra definite."

She smiled. "You're a stupid wee arse," she muttered fondly. "Now you just need to let *him* know!"

Chapter Thirty-One

FROM the moment Perry woke the next morning, the community didn't leave him alone.

There seemed to be people wanting to see him, either by ambushing him from the Mackie house—they were just passing, what a coincidence!—or traveling back and forth in Dougie's car on the pretext of delivering supplies, or calling Greg on some spurious business query and asking could they drop in later to discuss it face-to-face? Really, they just wanted a look at the weird London lad who'd saved Fiona Mackie from the peat bog.

Perry knew his Big Adventure on the peat bog—as he was now calling it in his mind—had been one of the worst times of his life. At one stage, when his ankle hurt almost unbearably, when he couldn't lift Fiona any longer without a rest, when he couldn't seem to rouse himself again after he'd sunk down on the sodden ground… well, that ranked as one of the most frightening things he'd ever suffered. Intellectually, he knew he was unlikely to have died out there—though could one drown in mud, like the sea?—and he hadn't been that far from habitation, if only he'd known where the hell he was. But he was far from fighting fit, and there'd been definite risks of hypothermia, shock, and further injury. Or so Dr. Mackenzie had said in a too-loud whisper to Greg, when he made a quick house call that morning. Perry's ankle still hurt like hell, though the doctor said it wasn't broken, but he'd walk with a limp for a while.

Perry was just glad to be alive and in one piece. For the first few hours, he didn't mind all the visitors—he'd taken all of the villagers to his heart—but he was horribly conflicted about being confined to the cottage. On the one hand, he desperately wanted more time with Greg. He missed the silly but sweet routines they'd had so little time to establish together: the snuggling on the sofa; the menu experiments; playing with Rory; sharing the shower in the morning. The way he'd started drifting into the studio when Greg was painting, then just sitting cross-legged on the floor behind him with a book, watching him work. Learning to swim; arguing over the fact Greg never had the TV on because it was full of crap, then watching a stupid program that never got any real attention because they rarely made the end of it before they started making out—

But on the other hand, it hurt to be around Greg. Perry should have remembered it had just been a fun interlude, a romantic, sexy, holiday romp. He was an adult; he knew how these things went. He'd entered into it with his eyes open. But he'd allowed himself to care too much, and there was no reason to prolong that agony.

And really, he couldn't put off the reckoning with both his bank and Eddy Latham for much longer.

Even Rory seemed to know something rotten was happening. He lay in his basket for most of the morning, still exhausted after his mercy dash in the storm, but whining every time he caught sight of Perry. When Greg brought Perry's case down into the hallway, Rory actually howled.

It was a relief when everyone else left the cottage to Greg and Perry, just after lunchtime. Now Perry could concentrate on leaving. Limping into the hallway, he found his blue boots standing neatly by his case. Greg must have cleaned them this morning. Perry gave Rory a good hug, and he didn't protest when Greg shut the dog in the kitchen.

Greg cleared his throat. He looked strangely anguished. "I won't come with you to the ferry."

"I… sorry?"

"Well, there's not a lot of room in Dougie's car, as I hear Bridie and Lisa are coming too. And really, there's not much point, is there?"

Perry stared at him. Greg looked a bit sickly too. Perhaps he'd slept as badly as Perry had, though Perry couldn't confirm that. He'd been hustled into the spare bedroom last night, on the premise he needed undisturbed rest.

"Fuck." Greg grimaced. "I didn't mean that to sound like… well, like it did. I meant, we can say good-bye here in the warm and the quiet. No point stamping our feet against the cold at the ferry, with the girls milling about and weeping over you."

"No, I suppose not. Shall I call you when I get back safely to London?" Perry didn't want to beg, but he was startled by the pleading tone in his voice.

"Yes. You better."

Greg smiled but he still looked pale. Perry didn't want to string this really awkward situation out, but there was no sign of Dougie's car yet. "Don't forget to tell me how Fiona gets on. If she makes it back to school okay for the new term. If Dr. McKenzie's housekeeper finds her son's iPod. If Bridie orders those LGBT books I suggested for the shop. If Marty sells more scallops to that French restaurant on Harris—"

Greg put his hand on Perry's arm. It was a real shock; Greg hadn't touched him all day. "I think you'd better come back yourself to catch up on all that. It sounds like a soap opera in itself."

"Yes." Perry smiled at last. "I'll hold you to that."

They stood in the hallway, more awkwardness descending. Greg's phone buzzed and he pulled it out of his pocket. That was another thing Perry had set him straight on—keeping it charged up at all times.

"Shit. Dougie will be half an hour late. But there's no risk you'll miss the ferry. We allowed for plenty of time."

They looked at each other. Perry felt a flicker of something in his belly that seemed most inappropriate, but totally unmistakable. "Could we… go to bed while we wait? Is that the most selfish thing I've ever asked?"

Greg chuckled. His face colored and his eyes lit up. It was almost the return of the old Greg. "God, yes. I mean, yes, we can go, not yes it's selfish. Or else I'm selfish too."

For a while, quickly naked in Greg's bed, they didn't do anything sexual. They just hugged. It was obvious when Greg remembered Perry was only here for a little more time. One minute he was stroking Perry's thigh, teasing him, nudging his leg, and making some joke about such a skinny bloke taking up so much mattress. The next minute he stilled his hand, and his breath caught. And he shifted almost imperceptibly away, as if drawing back even his muscles. "Um. You've got the journey sorted once you're back on the mainland? You'll need help to get around the airport. Your ankle…."

"Candace is organizing something for me. Transport to get me from the airport to home, and then into the office tomorrow."

Another brief silence. "Do you have to confirm your flight? Check in?"

"It's all done."

"Mr. Efficient." Greg ran his hand down Perry's chest to his navel.

Perry chuckled. "That tickles."

"Was meant to." Greg's voice sounded strained.

I have to ask, don't I? "Look… when I go back… you know what I mean?"

Greg tilted his head as if to hear better. "Not really. I haven't completely clued in to your subtle London-speak."

Perry thumped him on the upper arm, though he reckoned it hurt him more than it hurt Greg's solid muscle. "We'll keep in touch, right?"

"Right," Greg said.

Perry tried to ignore the tiny hesitation there'd been before the response, but failed miserably. "Greg?"

Greg sighed. "I'm sorry. Of course we'll keep in touch."

"You don't sound very enthusiastic." Had he misjudged *everything*?

"Christ, Perry. We can't all leap up in the air cheering with rainbow-colored balloons and streamers every time we speak."

Perry bit his lip.

Greg groaned. "God, that was shit stupid, wasn't it? And not what I meant either."

"So now it's your quaint island speak I can't parse." When Greg blinked at him, Perry laughed at the owlish look. "You're so gorgeous, you know." He shuffled up onto his knees, shrugging the duvet off his shoulders, and leaned into Greg for a kiss. Greg's lips were dry to start with, then eased against Perry's, the brush of their combined saliva softening the taste for them both. Greg slid his hand around the back of Perry's neck, holding him in place. Perry's skin prickled with growing delight, but he wasn't immediately hard. This was a caress, not an invitation to sex, at least not yet. He dropped his hand to Greg's groin, tugging at the little hairs, sliding his little finger against Greg's dick where it rested on his upper thigh. Just to touch, to connect.

"Perry." Greg's voice sounded strangely ragged. "I never said this to anyone before. It's you that's gorgeous."

"For heaven's sake, are we going to bicker about that all over ag—"

"I don't want you to go."

Oh. Perry was silent for a long moment. He could feel Greg's heart beat against the palm of his hand where it rested on Greg's chest.

"Greg. I don't ask much"—apart from the big-arse grief of Greg going back to London, and how well had *that* gone?—"but please be honest with me." *Especially about this.* "I need to know how you're really feeling."

"This," Greg said. He was obviously still struggling with expressing himself.

Perry knew he could probably express enough for them both, but… why should he have to? "You have to give me more to go on. This… what?"

Greg smiled ruefully, his expression pained. "Us. This." He gestured this time at the bed.

Perry nodded slowly. "It's bloody marvelous?"

Greg barked a laugh. "Too bloody right! But it's more than that. Isn't it?"

Perry felt happiness seep through him like sinking into a warm bath. "Well, it is for me."

Greg nodded slowly. Perry watched his progression of thoughts: they appeared in Greg's expressions like a personal movie. "I see that's what you meant. But you're going back to London." It wasn't a question.

"I have to—"

"I know, I know. Your job. The money. I understand."

"And you don't want to come with me."

Greg scowled briefly. "Not fair."

"I know. Sorry."

Greg grimaced, pain still in his eyes. "I love it here. This is my world."

"I know," Perry repeated.

"And that's *your* world, isn't it? What you deserve. All those bright young media types. Glamorous stars. People with power and money to seduce you."

"I hope you're not implying I've slept my way to the top, Greg Ventura. And especially not with Eddy Latham." They looked at each other, shuddered, and laughed. Then Perry let the laughter go, gentling his voice. "I don't want those bright young types, Greg. But I understand how things are, with us in such different places." *And saying I loved you...?* "Look, I can't apologize enough for the stupid thing I said before, I know I overreached—"

"Wait, I don't mean—"

"Come here." Perry didn't want this last time to be full of argument and angst. He licked his palm and slid his hand around Greg's cock. Slowly and lovingly, he began to stroke. Greg made a small strangled sound and arched up beneath him.

Quiet descended over the room, no sound except for their harsh breathing and the occasional groan from Greg. Perry slid his other hand under Greg's balls, relishing the crinkled skin on his palm, gently squeezing to enhance Greg's reaction.

"Oh, Jesus." Greg grunted and gripped hard at Perry's shoulders. "So bloody good."

Perry encouraged Greg up into a kneeling position as well, facing each other. He gripped a little harder, his hand slick now with precome as well as saliva. Greg was panting, leaning into him, his head resting on Perry's neck. From that angle, he could watch Perry's hand moving on him, up and down.

There was a knock at the front door.

"For fuck's sake!" Greg moaned, his hands fisted in the sheets beneath his knees. "Can't they leave us alone?"

"Hush. It's okay. It's probably Dougie. He must have made better time than he expected. He can wait. My case is in the hall so he'll know I'll come down when I'm ready." He knew he was just prattling on, and when he caught Greg's eye again, Greg's stark look was sobering.

"He'll just walk in!"

"It's locked," Perry said softly. "You locked it after that last batch of crofters called around." He tightened his hand.

"Perry?" Greg looked startled, disapproving, desperate. He pressed his hands flat against Perry's chest. "We can't."

"Can," Perry whispered. "You're close, aren't you?" He recognized the tension in Greg's limbs, the tightening of his throat. *I won't give this up, not yet!* He stroked faster.

Greg gave a low, swift growl in the back of his throat. His whole body shivered.

The knock came again downstairs. And again.

"He can wait," Perry repeated in a determined whisper. They could all wait.

"Oh fuck," Greg groaned. The bed rocked beneath him. "Oh *fuck*! Can't stop it."

"Please." Perry made the word almost a sigh. "Please *don't*."

Greg gave a strangled laugh as if both amazed and anguished, and shifted his grip to Perry's arms, anchoring himself. He came with a yell and a shudder through his legs and torso that nearly threw Perry off the mattress.

They remained kneeling up on the bed, facing each other, foreheads touching. All Perry could hear was their gasping. His cock was half-hard, but he didn't need to touch it; he'd been excited enough giving Greg pleasure. He wiped his fingertips gently over Greg's belly. The come was already cooling, and he liked the way it clung to Greg's hairs. Greg shifted his head and kissed the tip of Perry's nose.

"God. You are such…."

"What am I?" He didn't lift his head, though he could see the smile on Greg's face.

"You're a magnificent, dirty, little bugger."

Perry smiled too, though more sadly. That would have to be good enough for him. He leaned away and shifted to the edge of the bed. "I'll answer the door, shall I?" he asked, reaching for his jeans. He kept his back to Greg, because the false brightness in his voice made him wince. "You know, this is going to sound stupid, but I actually *don't* want you to come to London."

Greg sank down on the bed behind him; the mattress dipped heavily. "What the hell?"

"I mean—not for the TV show. I know it'd make you miserable. I know it's not really *you*. And I can't think of anything worse now than making you act against your will. Of you being any less than you. I lov—I really respect that."

"Me?"

"Yes. You. I'm glad I didn't persuade you."

He slipped off the bed, picked up his clothes, socks and shoes, and made for the bedroom door.

Greg seemed frozen in place but he said hoarsely, "You'll call?"

"I'll let you know I arrived safely. Can't have any more watery disasters, right? We'll talk soon."

Perry tried not to limp too much as he left the bedroom.

Chapter Thirty-Two

THAT evening, Bridie was the last person Greg wanted to see. He knew that, she knew that, to hell with it. But there she was at his door with, of all people, Aileen Cameron behind her. And a very different Aileen than usual. Instead of being wrapped up in her habitual thick, albeit beautiful, sweater and jeans, she was wearing a silk blouse and a smart trouser suit.

"Is Perry okay?" he said abruptly, and to hell with sounding rude.

Bridie raised an eyebrow—could she smell the whiskey on his breath from here?—but she didn't scold him. "Yes, there's nothing wrong. Well, not with Perry. He made the ferry okay and I believe his connection to his flight. He'll be back in London by tonight."

"So why are you here?"

"Good God, lad." Aileen snorted and pushed past him into the house. "Your manners are appalling. We came t' get Perry's London contact details." She peered at him as he stood there in some shock. "Thought ye'd know. Mebbe not."

Greg opened and shut his mouth like a fish. Then tried again. "Somewhere. I have them somewhere, in one of my brother's communications."

"What's his agency called?"

Greg dredged up the name from his memory. "Latham. Eric—no, Eddy Latham. What's this about?"

Bridie looked between him and Aileen, then went to put the kettle on. Aileen led Greg into the living room and sat them both down. "Fiona came home with a square of knitting she said was Perry's."

"Aye. He's been designing stuff." There'd been several squares left around the living room, which Greg had bundled into a drawer under the TV so he didn't have to look at them and remember Perry on the sofa, concentrating on his knitting with his tongue flicking out now and then….

"I sell my woolens t' a designer in Glasgow," Aileen said, breaking into his miserable memories. "Just came back from my monthly management meeting. Aye, ye never imagined that, did ye? Thought I was only good for socks and frumpy winter scarves."

"No," Greg protested, way too late.

"The store was very interested in Perry's designs. I think we could develop a range of woolen cloth, created here in North Uist but sold t' the mainland."

It was what Perry had been thinking of too. "Like a cottage industry?"

Aileen resisted—barely—rolling her eyes at him. "Ye know nothing, lad. This is big business, nae amateur hour. I need t' know if Perry is willing t' go into partnership with me, with his designs."

Greg's mouth did the fish impression again. "I don't know," he finally said. "He's gone now."

Aileen sighed and shook her head. Somehow, Greg inferred she was sighing at *him*, not Perry's absence. Bridie came in with the tea and forced a large mug of strong brew into Greg's hands while he thought over what Aileen had said. For a brief, wild moment he imagined what it'd be like if Perry worked here on North Uist, lived with him. Well, not even *with him*, but if he were on the same land mass, rather than a bloody ocean of sea and sky away. *If only....*

"So, Greg," Bridie said, settling beside Aileen on the sofa. "You look like shite."

"Ah. Thanks."

"Did you not ask him to stay? Did you not tell him how you feel?"

Oh Jesus. When was he meant to have done that, when he'd barely realized it himself? "I don't know how I feel, really, Bridie. Except… scared."

"Scared?"

"Aye. Scared, pissed off, whatever. I can't really work it out in my mind." Greg swallowed hard. "Definitely miserable."

"Was it something Perry did? Said?"

"Yes. No." Greg gave a harsh laugh. "It is all his fault. But not. You know?"

Bridie wrinkled her nose. "Astonishingly enough, I do. Must be years of living with my incomprehensible brother."

"I'm scared of losing him."

Bridie kindly didn't point out the fact that it looked like Greg already had. "You mean to the London life? To another man? To someone like your own fucking brothers?"

Greg just stared at her. Aileen sucked in a breath but surprisingly didn't scold Bridie for her language.

"I thought you knew him better," Bridie continued. "Even after such a short time. But you can't have it both ways, Greg Ventura. You can't have him at your beck and call but also push him away when it gets too heavy."

"What did he tell you?" Greg growled.

"Nothing. He's a loyal wee lad."

"Yes," Greg said. "He was. Is."

Rory was sitting in his basket by the fireplace. He'd been moping ever since Perry left that morning. Now he lifted his head and barked sharply at Greg, just once, but with a wealth of doggy meaning.

"I love him." Greg had never told anyone in his life that he'd loved them—not since his mother, anyway, and he'd only been a kid—and he was suddenly swamped with the need to confess it aloud.

But what bloody use was it, saying it to himself?

"Do you know how good you look?" Bridie said with smug satisfaction.

"Bridie, I don't mean—"

"And I don't mean in the mirror. You just are better, you enjoy yourself, you communicate better—"

"Ye smile more," Aileen added, with a brief grimace of her own.

"Face it, Greg, he's made you a new man." Bridie was in full smirk mode now. "Would you have ever said that love stuff before now? You're an antisocial, self-pitying lug at times—and for no good reason, as we've always tried to tell you—but you've never been happier than with Perry around."

Was that why now he'd never felt more bloody *un*happy? "Aileen. Are you here to read me the riot act too?"

"Get over y'self, sassenach," she said crisply.

"Greg." Bridie perched on the edge of the armchair, looming over him. She slid an arm around his shoulders. "We're here to help. And here's what we're gonna do for you!"

Chapter Thirty-Three

"**WHAT** do you mean, I'm fired?"

Perry stared at Eddy Latham from the other side of his boss's outrageously large desk, and felt his stomach roil. Eddy had made him wait two days for a debrief, and now he'd been met with *this* bombshell.

Eddy leaned back in his chair, steepled his fingers, and peered at Perry through his gold-rimmed glasses. "Peregrine, one thing you've always been excellent at is English comprehension. You know what it means. I'm sorry, of course, that it should come to this, but that's the nature of the job. It was made clear to you at the start that this was a rolling twelve-month contract. We've all enjoyed having you around, and I'll draw up a fine reference for you. But this debacle confirms for me that this isn't the job for you."

“Why not?” was all he could think of to say.

“It’s the hunger, Perry. You don’t have it. You don’t have that edge, that desire to win at all costs. To make things happen. You had a mission and a time frame and, unfortunately, you met neither. Now excuse me, I have clients to see before lunch at The Ivy.”

“HE’S livid,” Candace whispered. She and Antony were fussing over a stunned Perry in the staff area, with stewed machine coffee and stale biscuits. “They awarded the TV show to the Howlers a week ago.”

“The Howells,” Perry corrected absentmindedly.

Antony giggled nervously. “Perry, we all call them the Howlers nowadays, like you once did.” He patted Perry’s arm sympathetically. “You’ll need more moisturizer, love. That wilderness has taken its toll on your skin.”

Something Candace had said clicked in Perry’s mind. “A week ago? We’d already lost the contract while I was still on Uist?” No wonder Eddy had abandoned Perry on his own, had suggested Perry stay on for extra time! Eddy hadn’t wanted him back in London to see the disaster—or to admit it hadn’t been Perry’s fault at all. *Bloody nerve!*

“Apparently the Howlers had friends in management at the production company and pulled strings to win the program. Their agent has been crowing over Eddy ever since. They’ve been archenemies for years.” Candace’s face was twisted in upset. “We’re going to miss you working with us. You really livened up this place.”

It was the unfairness of all this that hurt Perry the most. “I’m just the scapegoat here!”

“Darling. It sucks, I know.” Antony shrugged. “That’s the role of us minions, right?”

A ripple of excited chatter ran through the open plan office. Antony gave a pained squeal, because he was meant to be watching Reception, and darted off toward his desk.

Perry took a gulp of the disgusting coffee—he definitely wouldn't miss this—and peered over Candace's shoulder. "Is that…? It's the Venturas. Why are they in the office?"

"Oh. That. Eddy's pitching one last time for a Christmas special. The family at home, but *without* Greg." Candace shrugged. "He's clutching at straws, Perry. Let him make a fool of himself. It serves him right."

The four brothers made their usual fabulous sight: designer suits, perfect hair, the whole arrogant/entitlement thing they had going on. Antony on Reception was cooing and blushing like royalty had arrived, which, in fact, it probably *was* in the media world. The Venturas murmured hellos to everyone, accepted cups of freshly brewed, decent coffee. Geoff led the way as always, with Gerry blustering in his wake. The twins were mugging mischievously for people's camera phones all the way, posing for selfies with the admin staff.

This was their world, and they were princes of it.

But Perry realized his attitude had changed. Instead of being impressed, he could look at them dispassionately now. They were like models, manufactured from a mold—the same look, the same grooming. The same character, the same selfish self-indulgence. *Media plastic.* He wondered who the hell would *want* to see a TV program featuring these self-centered, too-handsome men.

And we let them be that way. We encourage it!

That said, he was without a job because of them. He had quarterly rent to pay next week, and food to buy, to stock up after his trip. His mother needed her scheduled monthly allowance. She still had no idea Perry was making the repayments on her loan, and not his feckless ex, Henry. Eddy would probably sign off on his expenses—if only to make sure he left the building without any fuss—but that was little enough to live on.

He glanced over at the Venturas, now being greeted effusively by Eddy.

He could approach Geoff Ventura direct, couldn't he? Apologize for failing to bring Greg back to London. He could beg Eddy for a chance to work on the Christmas special instead. He could beg Eddy for a job cleaning the toilets, for that matter.

Forget that!

Anger stabbed inside his chest. Yes, he knew his junior job was the lowest of the low, and he'd fucked up the one chance they'd given him. But he knew he was good at what he did, and he had tried as best he could. And this wasn't fair!

He was damned if he'd approach Geoff, Gerry, George, or Gareth Ventura for any bloody favors. And definitely not Eddy Celebrity-Boot-Licking Latham. Perry's last words to Greg had been truthful—he *didn't* want Greg to be caught up in this pile of media shit! He didn't want Greg dragged back to this superficial, two-faced, hypocritical, back-stabbing business at all, in fact—

"Perry?" Candace jabbed him in the ribs. "Who's that just come in behind them?"

A tall man strode up to Reception. "I'd like to see Eddy Latham," he said, loudly enough for Perry and Candace to hear him from the other side of the office.

Geoff Ventura obviously heard him too, because he stopped abruptly on his way over to Eddy's room. The other brothers also turned to look.

"Fucking hell," Gerry said succinctly. "Look what the cat dragged in!"

Greg Ventura stepped away from Reception and glanced over the rest of the office. Everyone was staring at him. Perry recognized a hint of nervousness in the way his hands were half-curled into fists, but it was unlikely anyone else would.

"My fucking gorgeous God's gift," Candace breathed.

Greg wore a splendid designer three-piece suit—and Perry knew a splendid designer when he saw it—with a startlingly white shirt and sumptuous purple silk tie. Perry wondered where he'd bought the suit. It looked personally tailored to fit Greg's every measurement, and it wasn't one of the commonly available styles Perry had seen in this season's catalogs. Greg's shoes matched perfectly and were highly polished. Perry realized he'd never seen Greg in shoes, only ever in hiking boots or slip-on clogs. Greg's whole aura was one of self-confidence and assurance.

Perry's appraisal slid up to Greg's face. Their eyes met. Perry's breath caught in his throat.

Perry knew he was biased but, honestly, Greg had never looked more handsome. There was something about his healthy, craggy features that added style to his sophisticated clothing, rather than conflicting with it. Where so many models nowadays looked pretty, but pale and aloof—or as Perry's mum often said, "white and spiteful"—Greg looked stunning. His wide mouth accentuated his smile, and his striking features caught everyone's attention. No one would ever mistake Greg Ventura for anyone else. He looked fully *alive*. Suddenly his smart, well-groomed brothers were the pale ones in the equation.

"Tongue back in, darling," Candace murmured to Perry. "Do you know him?"

There was total silence in the office apart from a phone ringing persistently, which was blatantly ignored. Perry noticed with some smugness that every woman was fascinated and admiring—and several of the men too.

Then a second phone rang and the temporary spell was broken. People shuffled back to their desks and started tapping again on keyboards. It was only an act of course—it was obvious that everyone was watching to find out who Greg was and why he was here.

"Are you from the TV company?" Antony asked, wide-eyed. He and one of the makeup girls, Amy, were gazing at Greg like he was fillet steak inexplicably served up at a fish and chip restaurant.

"In movies?" Amy asked. "You must be. Don't tell me—I'll remember in a minute. I'm sure I saw you at that premiere last month in Leicester Square." Amy was a shameless celebrity hunter. "Or one of those wonderful dancers on *Strictly Come Dancing*. You move like one. Or that fabulous French revolution series, full of gorgeous hair and ruffled shirts. Wait a minute, maybe you're one of the recent Eiger exploration team, is that it?" She tilted her head to one side, puzzling out what context she'd seen him in.

Greg looked a bit dazed at the attention. He darted a glance at Perry that seemed to say "help me out, here" and Perry weaved his way through the desks to Reception. Amy and Antony never even turned to acknowledge him, maintaining their mouse in the eye of a big cat pose in front of Greg.

When Greg smiled at him, the brilliance made Perry blink, and his stomach flipped with joy.

"Why are you here?" Perry asked. "You said you wouldn't come."

"That was for the program. I came to see you," Greg said.

"Me?" Perry winced at his simpering tone, but it had slipped out with his happiness.

"Well, it's lucky you caught him here!" Candace crowed, appearing at Perry's side. "Because Perry's leaving the company tomorrow."

"What?" Greg frowned. "Leaving?"

Perry shrugged. "We lost the TV option. And officially it's my fault. At least, I'm the one who has to fall on my virtual career sword."

"That's not fair!"

Perry shrugged again, though he was ridiculously touched by the sympathy. "Well, it has its advantages. You're no longer needed back in London and won't get swept up in all this crap. But.... Um." He tried hard not to blush, but reckoned he'd failed when even the tips of his ears felt hot. "I could have let you know by phone. Why did you make the journey all the way from the Western Isles?"

"I thought *I* was the fisherman," Greg said softly, with an increasingly wide grin.

"What?" Then Perry realized what Greg meant and blushed even more. "Oh God, no, I wasn't fishing for compliments!" *Well, not really.* "I just wondered...." He'd been saving himself to e-mail Greg that very night, or maybe call him. He'd just needed an excuse. Dammit, he wasn't even bothered about that. He'd just worried how soon it'd be before Greg told him to piss off from stalking him, if he created spurious reasons to call every night, until he could bum the money off someone to go back out and visit the Isles—

"I couldn't wait to see you. I miss you." Greg looked almost sheepish, which was a very fine look on someone so unutterably gorgeous. "From the minute you left until the minute I could get to the ferry and fly over here after you."

"Wow," Candace breathed, transfixed.

"I miss you too." Perry wanted to grab Greg, to kiss him, to hold him. He pulled up just in time, realizing Candace and Amy and several other just-happened-to-be-passing staff members were enthralled at the little drama unfolding in front of them. "How long are you here for?"

"I can't stay long, just overnight—Alasdair needs help with the sheep, with lambing coming up. And Rory won't take medicine from anyone but me—"

"Oh my God, Rory's sick?"

"Who's Rory? Another hunky friend?" Candace hissed to Antony.

Antony shrugged, his adoring gaze still on Greg. "Who knows? You think he'll have a brother too?"

"Just a chill," Greg reassured Perry. "He's hardy, but he's not a youngster anymore, and I think he outpaced himself that night you saved Fiona Mackie. He went out the next day as well, you know, and found that damn doll of hers. But he's on the mend now."

"Perry? You saved someone's life?" Candace was still hanging around at his elbow, eyes wide. "Were you with this gorgeous man at the time?"

"A hero," Amy sighed. "I knew he had to be that."

"Perry's the hero, not me." Greg dismissed the fans like they were nothing but a small flock of annoying sea birds. He turned back to Perry. "Come back with me. I know I shouldn't ask, but I want you to."

"To North Uist? To the croft?"

"What's a croft?" Candace asked.

Greg rushed on as if Perry had already begun to refuse. "I can try to make it more comfortable for you. I could put in central heating. Double glazing. No, triple glazing, if you want."

"No central heating?" Antony's face screwed up in shocked disgust.

"I'll make sure Rory stays in the spare room. Well." Greg flushed deeply. "That's if you don't want to sleep there yourself."

"A threesome?" Antony murmured. "How very bohemian."

"Perry? Christ, am I messing this up? I knew I would." Greg frowned. "Are you still angry with me?"

Perry took a deep breath. "Angry? Why would I be?"

Greg frowned. "Is that sarcasm?"

Perry laughed much too loudly, but his heart was beating so quickly he felt light-headed. "No, it's genuine. I'm not angry with you, you idiot. I understand precisely what you see in that place, why you don't want to leave it. You're not just hiding away there—you've made your life and love there. I understand your decision, believe me. I wish I could—"

"What?" Greg jumped on his pause. "Sounds like you want to come back there yourself."

"You mean, come back to that erratic weather? Being woken by the noise of sheep every morning? Of not a tree in sight? No manicurist? No decent hairstylist? For that matter, no *shops*?"

"There's good Internet." Greg looked a little sly. "You can do all your shopping online. And Lisa's moving in with Bridie and setting up her own business. So you can get a decent haircut at last. Assuming you like what she did with mine?"

"I like it very much," Perry said softly, though his eyes weren't on Greg's smart haircut. He couldn't get over the utter joy of having Greg in front of him, in person, in *fabulous* person, and speaking such astonishing stuff.

"Oh, and while I remember," Greg said. "Aileen called around with a business proposal for you. She—no, *I* would like you to consider it."

"Business proposal? What—?"

"Greg Ventura!" came a sudden cry. Eddy Latham stood at the door of his office, arms wide in an expansive welcome. "Well, the wanderer has returned. And looking astonishingly good!"

"Greg Ventura?" Candace gasped, gazing up at Greg's full six foot three. "Are you really? You're so better-looking than the other Venturas. Where have they been hiding you?"

"Let's talk about this TV option, shall we?" Eddy said, grasping Greg's elbow and gesturing toward his private office.

"Greg. No!" Perry grabbed his other elbow. He glared at Eddy, who glared right back, but with the smug assurance of a man who knows he has the financial upper hand.

Greg looked confused. He glanced down at Perry. "Your job rests on it, right?"

"I've got new ideas," Eddy crowed. "A rival program to the Howells. The Big Ventura: the ugly duckling of the family becomes the fashionable swan!"

"I don't give a fuck about my job," Perry said through gritted teeth. "You won't do this." He shut his eyes briefly to tune out the awfulness of it all.

"Well, well" came another new voice, the other side of Greg. "I can't believe it's you."

Perry opened his eyes to see Gerry Ventura face-to-face with his newly returned brother. "Brush up surprisingly well, don't you?"

"Better than anyone," Perry said quietly. He didn't care whether he was heard or not, but Gerry Ventura obviously thought he was being insulting, because he swung around immediately to stare at Perry, his handsome face twisted with scorn.

"What's it to you?"

"I'm sorry?" Perry drew himself up to his full height, albeit he was still four or five inches less than the shortest of the Venturas.

"Are you the one who tarted him up like this? Is this why he's so full of himself?" Gerry turned the scorn on Greg as well, then smirked. "You're fucking each other?"

"What the hell does that have to do with you?" Perry snapped.

"Gerry, back off," Greg said coldly. His face looked like thunder.

But Gerry didn't. "It must have taken a hell of a lot of greasepaint to touch up my brother's significant failings," he sneered. "You had bugger all to work on. He's always been an ugly bastard."

Perry opened his mouth in angry shock, but nothing came out. He stepped forward with a firm intention to thump Gerry somewhere it'd really hurt, but then Greg pushed him gently but firmly to one side, leaned forward, and punched Gerry squarely on the nose.

Chapter Thirty-Four

THE office had finally calmed down, the blood from Gerry's nose had been mopped up, and Eddy had pestered everyone back to work. It was unlikely to stop the rumors brewing around Reception or the pictures currently being gleefully uploaded to YouTube, but that was the modern media world in action.

To Perry's startled surprise, Geoff Ventura supervised having his brother thrown out of Latham's. The twins helped him. They directed Gerry and his throbbing face toward a nearby coffee shop to sit and cool down, and then keep out of the way for a while.

"He's an arrogant, mean-mouthed tosser," George said cheerily, as they all ambled back into Eddy's office. "About time someone other than us smacked him down." He smiled at Perry. "You're braver than most, despite your size."

"Fine right hook, Greg," said Gareth beside his twin, eyes twinkling. "You always were a good scrapper."

It was obvious the twins loved every minute of the drama, but Perry could see Eddy almost apoplectic with shock, so he nudged the four remaining brothers into his boss's room. To his utter relief, there was a jug of fresh iced water and good coffee brewing on the table. When Eddy came blustering into the room on their heels, Perry frowned and nodded toward the refreshments. To his eternal astonishment, Eddy scuttled over to pour drinks for everyone.

Geoff turned to Greg. "What can I say?"

"The guy's an arse?"

Geoff barked a laugh. "Always was, right? I suppose I gave him too much leeway, as he was always the loudest of us all. But his humor was always too sharp, his aggression too heavy. Mother struggled with him at the best of times, and Dad just gave up in our teenage years."

"What about the bullying?" Perry said crossly. "You gave plenty of leeway for that too."

Geoff turned to look at him as if he'd forgotten anyone else was there. But he impressed Perry by recalling his name. "Perry Goodwood, isn't it? I remember us trying to persuade you in the first place to turn Greg here into a Ventura figurehead."

"A performing monkey, more like," Perry answered with spirit.

To Perry's continuing surprise, Geoff laughed. "That sums us up pretty well. We were directed when we were sportsmen, stage-managed when we won success, and now we're being manipulated into being TV personalities."

"You regret all that?" Greg looked confused.

Geoff shrugged his broad, elegant shoulders. "You know I always lived for the sport. And now I'm too old to play, a living's got to be made."

"You need this TV gig?"

"Not that badly."

"But I'm here now," Greg said.

"Excellent news, isn't it?" Eddy was hovering around Geoff's elbow, glancing between the two brothers.

Perry was disgusted. The man's tongue was almost hanging out.

"Peregrine, call the TV company, see if we can pick up some of the options. After all, who knows how long it'll be before the Howells self-combust? They're hardly the most stable of families."

Perry snorted loudly and everyone turned to look at him. "Eddy, you're a bloody fool if you don't realize that's exactly what the TV schedulers want to happen. And preferably on screen. Besides, you seem to have forgotten I'm not working for you any longer. You fired me."

"What a pity, Mr. Latham," Greg said. His voice was almost a growl, and his gaze was fully on Perry. "When the only person I will ever work with is Perry."

Eddy went pale.

Geoff cleared his throat. "Let's stop this nonsense, shall we?" He caught Greg's eye. "You're not here for any career reasons, are you? You've never had any intention of appearing on TV as part of the family, whether it's a series, a Christmas special, or an advert for men's knickers."

Greg grinned back. "Not in a million millennia. At least, not if I can humanly avoid it."

"What?" Eddy spluttered. "But you just said—! You can't just come in here—!"

"Eddy, shut up, will you?" Geoff Ventura's tone was smooth and calm, but Eddy shut up immediately.

Geoff turned back to Greg, and a grudging smile crept over his face. "I know that look of yours, you see. You used to look just like that when you wanted to do something we didn't—and vice versa. You always were a determined little arse."

"Now look here—" Perry leaped to Greg's defense again.

"Perry, it's okay." Greg slid an arm so firmly around his waist that Perry had to draw an extra gasp of happiness to keep breathing. Greg turned back to his elder brother. "So what will you do instead?"

"Oh, I've been offered a football commentating job for a satellite channel. I'll enjoy that, and it'll pay my designer's bills. And the twins are planning to open up a nightclub in Knightsbridge. Gareth has a Russian oligarch's daughter devoted to him, to the extent of investing a couple of million in his pet project. And funnily enough, her cute brother keeps calling George at all hours of the day and night and sending enough flowers to bring on hay fever. I think the pair of them are set to be adopted into the new London upper classes. Oh, they'll do all right by their partners, no question—they're decent blokes, especially when they're out of the limelight—but a TV show would probably have been the worst thing in the world for them and their egos. And of all of us, they always land on their feet."

Eddy was still spluttering as the Venturas turned to leave, Perry along with them. Geoff smoothly shook Eddy's hand, took his card, and promised to keep in touch. Then turned to Greg and Perry and gave a big wink. When he walked away from Eddy's office, it was obvious he didn't expect Eddy to follow.

"Peregrine?" Eddy called after them. "We can reconsider your contract!"

"Reconsider my arse," Perry said in his politest tone. "I've had a much better offer." Over by Reception, he could see Candace and Antony laughing. Candace gave him a thumbs-up.

At the exit, Geoff stopped Greg with a hand on his arm. "Whatever Gerry said all those years ago—okay, what we all said—we always loved you, you big fool."

Greg tensed. He didn't smile back. "Not really any excuse, though, is it?"

Geoff looked abashed. "No, you're right. But it looks like you've turned out the best-looking of us all." He pulled Greg into a big, awkward hug, then pushed him away. He was blushing. "Of course I'm noticing this in a brotherly way, not some big gay way."

Perry smirked, and tightened his own arm in Greg's. "Damn right you're not," he said. "*I'm* the one to do the big gay way."

Greg smiled, but he still didn't look convinced by Geoff's protestations of brotherly love.

"Greg," Geoff sighed. "You have every right to hate us forever. I hope I've matured over the last few years, and I can see more clearly now what horror we must have caused you. I hope you'll let us try and mend the breach in some way."

Greg was silent. Perry peered up at him, trying to read his expression.

"And I mean, have you looked at yourself recently?" Geoff said. "I mean, properly? You stupid bugger… look, come here." Geoff pointed to a huge TV screen on the office wall. It was meant for the staff to review screenings of advertising campaigns, but everyone knew Eddy wanted it tuned to American crime series in the afternoons. There was nothing on the TV now, but the screen was polished cleanly enough to act as a mirror.

Geoff pulled Greg beside him and pointed fiercely at their reflection. “You were always going to be a late bloomer, you old bugger. And look at you now! Bloody perfect. No, even better than that.”

“What the hell?” Greg seemed shell-shocked.

“You don’t have that plastic glow *we* all have,” Geoff said quietly. “You reek of natural health and a boatload of charisma—maybe a little like me, while I was still playing. But so much more. You know, you look *content*. Like you’re happy where you are in your life. I’m proud of you, guy.”

Perry held his breath as Greg paused and followed Geoff’s look.

“Perry?” Greg whispered.

“Take a good look,” Perry added softly. “A proper look. An honest look.” Greg had to start seeing himself not colored by his history or by anyone else’s opinion. *A fresh start.*

Greg shook his head slowly, thoughtfully. Then he reached down and grasped Perry’s free hand. To Geoff, he said, “You’re a stupid bugger too.” But his tone had softened.

“For Christ’s sake. It’s not a contest.” Geoff rolled his eyes. “I thought I was the one who’s meant to be so bloody competitive.”

Then they looked at each other and laughed.

“But we should have done better,” Geoff said, his face suddenly twisted in distress.

“You will,” Greg said, and he clapped Geoff heavily on the shoulder. “You will!”

Chapter Thirty-Five

GREG'S brothers had left the building, Eddy had retired to his office to lick his wounds, and Greg and Perry waited a moment more by Reception. If Perry were being truly honest, he'd admit it was because he wanted to lust a little longer after Executive Greg.

"You look so good." Perry smiled. "I'm so proud of the man I love."

"Look, Perry—"

"Oh, shit, I've overreached again, haven't I?"

Greg deliberately put a hand over Perry's mouth. "Will you shut the hell up for a minute?"

Perry mumbled in shock. It was probably a good thing Greg couldn't make out the actual words.

"God, Perry, this is difficult enough as it is without you... you... *being* there!" Greg took a deep breath. He looked almost guilty. "Bridie says I have to tell you. Bridie won't let me—"

Perry broke free of Greg's hand. "—get away with anything?"

Greg roared with laughter. "That's it! You see, when you were out on the bog… I didn't know where you were. I didn't know if you'd left voluntarily, or were lost, or hurt. That's when I realized. Just didn't know what to do about it. *How* to do it."

Perry went very still.

"Perry, I'm trying to say something and scrambling it as always." Greg gave a huge, heavy sigh and ran his hand through his hair, half ruining the careful style. "Perry, I love you too."

There was a long moment of pregnant silence. Then Amy and Candace—whom Perry had even forgotten were there behind them, shamelessly listening in—gave a combined sigh of happiness that echoed through the whole room. There was even a smattering of applause from some staff over by the photocopier.

Perry held his breath for a few seconds more. "Is there a but?"

"No, there is no fucking but!" Then Greg realized what he'd said and roared with laughter again.

"Then I'd love to."

"What?"

Perry rolled his eyes. "Come back to the island. Look into this business opportunity you have. Help you nurse Rory back to health. Buy you a new set of matching crockery for when people come to call. Keep Bridie and Dougie in hand."

"You will?"

Perry reached up and kissed Greg rather chastely on the well-shaven cheek. "I want to come back to the croft with you. For as long as you want me there."

"That's a long bloody time," Greg said. His voice was ragged, but his smile broad. "As I left, the sun was up over the loch. Perry, you'll love how it looks."

"You'll paint it?"

"Aye, I will." Greg gave a rueful grin. "And talking of my painting, you'll have to live on my money until your business gets going—but I promise you, it'll be nothing like your ex's fuckup, not with Aileen Mackie in charge. And I have enough to get you completely out of debt for the moment."

"I don't need much to live on," Perry whispered. "Not there. Not with you."

Greg flushed happily. "Oh, and Aileen has all kinds of plans for new fabrics, including—you'll like this—tartans for kilts."

"Rainbow ones?"

"Jesus, Perry. You dunderheed, as Dougie would pronounce it." But Greg laughed again. "If that's what you want. And I'm taking you out to dinner tomorrow night. Smoked scallops in white wine with green mustard sauce. The Sea Bird sisters are putting on a special event, just for your return."

"You were so sure I'd return?"

"I realize now it was never in doubt." Greg was beaming by now. "Despite all Bridie's plotting, she and Lisa making me over for this trip, Dougie planning my travel, Aileen getting me kitted out in some exclusive Glasgow store—I remember now I've always had the trump card. Your selkie skin!"

"My—what?"

Greg smirked. “That old fleece hoodie of mine you wore all the time you were in the peat bog? I reckon that’s like your magical seal skin. So now I have it, and have hidden it, and so you’re trapped with me forever.”

Perry shook his head, laughing. He and Greg were going to do a lot of that, all the way back to North Uist. “You reckon?”

For a brief moment, Greg’s confidence faltered. “Perry, listen to me, you can’t argue with centuries-old folklore—”

And then Perry leaned in and kissed all the teasing away. At least for the time being.

FOR
MORE
OF THE
BEST
GAY
ROMANCE
DREAMSPINNER
PRESS
dreamspinnerpress.com

Lightning Source UK Ltd.
Milton Keynes UK
UKOW03f0851070517
300626UK00001B/1/P

9 781635 333862

THE ILLU D

Vampire

MOVIE GUIDE

Grateful acknowledgement is made to the following studios, distributors and collections whose stills and posters illustrate this book in the spirit of publicity:

The Forrest J Ackerman Imagi-Movie Archives (2495 Glendower Avenue, Hollywood, California 90027-1110; photos indicated by [FJA] throughout this guide), Allied Artists, Alpha, American Cinema, American International Pictures, Amicus Productions, Anglo Amalgamated Film Distributors, Associated British-Pathe, Azteca Films, Keith Barrish, BBC-TV, British Film Institute, British Lion, Bryanston, Canadian Broadcasting Co, Cannon, Cinematografica Flama, Columbia, Commonwealth United Entertainment, Compass International, Crown International, Dan Curtis Productions, De Laurentiis Entertainment, Dirk Productions, Embassy Pictures, EMI, Eros Films, Europix, Fangoria Films, F/M Entertainment, Golden Era, Grand National, GVi, Hammer Films, Hemdale, Hemisphere Pictures, Iduna Film, Independent-International, International Amusement, Invincible Pictures, ITC, Klangfilm, Larco Productions, Laurel Entertainment, Les Films ABC, London Independent Producers (Distribution), Majestic Pictures, Merrick International, Metro-Goldwyn-Mayer, Mirisch, Morgana Films, Morgan Creek, New Realm, New World Pictures, NBV Productions (*Simon Tams*), Paramount, Pennea, Prana Film, PRC, Rank Films, Recorded Releasing, Regal Films International, Renown Pictures, RKO Radio Pictures, The Samuel Goldwyn Company, SC Entertainment International, Ser-Cine, SF Film Distributors, Shere Productions, Showking, Skouras International, State Screen Productions (*Sam Myers*), Surf Film, Taft Entertainment, Target International, Tigon British, Titanus, Toho, Topaz Film Corporation, Towers of London, Tri-Star, Troma, Twentieth Century Fox, United Artists, Universal, Vestron Pictures, Warner Bros, Warner Home Video, and Zenith.

Top right: *The Brides of Dracula.*
Centre right: *Dracula vs. Frankenstein. (FJA).*
Bottom right: *The House That Dripped Blood.*

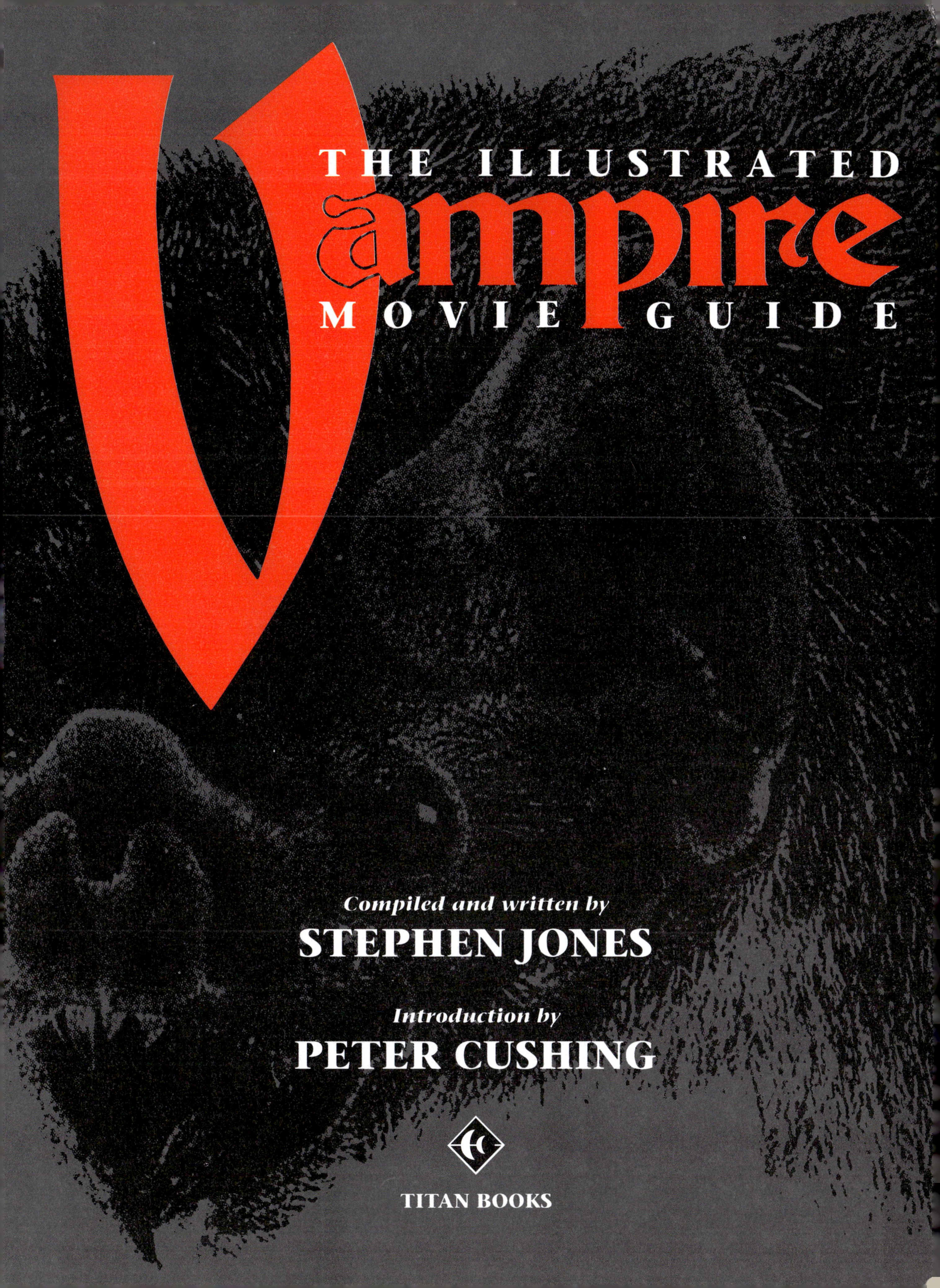

THE ILLUSTRATED Vampire MOVIE GUIDE

Compiled and written by

STEPHEN JONES

Introduction by

PETER CUSHING

TITAN BOOKS

THE ILLUSTRATED VAMPIRE MOVIE GUIDE
ISBN 1 85286 449 4

Published by
Titan Books
19 Valentine Place
London SE1 8QH

First edition January 1993
10 9 8 7 6 5 4 3 2 1

British Library Cataloguing-in-Publication Data. A catalogue record for this book is available from the British Library.

Designed by Chris Teather
Production by Bob Kelly

Any book as detailed as this needs friends, and I would like to thank Kim Newman, Jo Fletcher, Marcel Burel, Forrest J Ackerman, David Barraclough, Stefan Jaworzyn, Alan Jones, Mike Wathen, Neil Alsop, Robert Eighteen-Bisang, Robert T. Garcia, Dennis Etchison, Andrew Porter, Randy Broecker, Dave Carson, Richard Dalby, David J. Howe, Dave Reeder, Paul J. McAuley, Giovanni Scognamillo, the long-suffering Katy Wild, and Chris Teather and, of course, Peter Cushing OBE for all their help and support in compiling what I hope you will discover is a useful and entertaining reference work. Special thanks to Ron Borst, Donald F. Glut and Jean-Claude Michel, who have all been there before me.

Printed and bound in Great Britain by Stephens and George Ltd, Merthyr Industrial Estate, Dowlais, Merthyr Tydfil.

Right: *Dracula (1958).*
Opposite top: *The Brides of Dracula.*
Opposite centre: *Slaughter of the Vampires.*
Opposite bottom: *Fright Night Part 2.*

For Sara and Randy, who will probably get more use out of this book than anyone else I know.

Contents

Author's Notes

The *Illustrated Movie Guide* series is designed to be of use to both the casual viewer and the hardened movie buff. Films are arranged alphabetically by the whole title and reviewed under their most common usage title, with spelling and punctuation taken directly from the screen where possible. Theses are cross-referenced in the index with the original or British and American alternative titles. The year given is usually the copyright date taken from the print, with the actual release date of the version reviewed (if significantly different) listed in parentheses. Wherever such information is available, I have included the names of director and major stars (with alternative spellings or real names in parentheses), production company and/or distributor, and whether the film was made in colour or black and white. Any disparity in the spelling of character names is also reflected in the text.

Below: *Behind-the-scenes, Dracula (1930).*

Within these pages you will discover myriad variations on vampires: those who need blood to further their mad experiments; serial killers who take on the aspects of blood-drinkers; the undead used as political allegory; people who simply dress in vampire garb; plus dream sequences, shorts, cartoons and experimental films. However, you'll also find plenty of traditional vampires as well, complete with fangs and evening dress, allergic to garlic or sunlight, and dispatched by a wooden stake through the heart.

I should also point out that a number of the films reviewed in this volume obviously contain adult material and may therefore not be suitable for viewers of all ages. It should also be noted that readers may encounter some difficulty tracking down every movie listed herein.

Obviously, no book about vampire movies can be definitive, although this volume should be more complete than most, and I would be grateful to receive any updates or corrections c/o the publisher. Credit will be given in all future editions.

RATINGS

A brief explanation of the ratings system is probably needed. As with any at-a-glance recommendation, this unapologetically reflects my own biased opinions of whether a film is worth viewing or not. As a criteria, if I were to base all the films listed in this book on, for example, Orson Welles' *Citizen Kane (1941)*, then most of them would hardly rate more than one bat. Therefore, as a general guide, I've tried to take into account whether these films would appeal to the general horror fan and the vampire *aficionado* in particular. After all, as is so often the case with genre movies, a really *bad* example can still be worth watching...

🦇🦇🦇🦇🦇	A classic!
🦇🦇🦇🦇	Recommended
🦇🦇🦇	Worth catching
🦇🦇	Average
🦇	For completists only

Please note that the above ratings should be used as a guide only. Obviously, it has not been possible to see every film listed in this book, therefore some of the ratings are based on provisional material. Any reassessment will be noted in subsequent editions.

Stephen Jones
London, 1992

Introduction

Peter Cushing

Vampires. *H'mm.* Not exactly cuddly creatures, are they? Although, mind you, they must have something going for 'em — a fatal fascination — as many a film heroine has discovered to her cost.

In Bram Stoker's definitive work about such things, Count Dracula is described by Jonathan Harker as having a strong face, 'very strong — aquiline, with high bridge of the thin nose and peculiarly arched nostrils; with lofty domed forehead, and hair growing scantily round the temples, but profusely elsewhere. His eyebrows were very massive, almost meeting over the nose, and with bushy hair that seemed to curl in its own profusion. The mouth, as far as I could see it under the heavy moustache, was fixed and rather cruel-looking, with peculiarly sharp white teeth; these protruded over the lips, whose remarkable ruddiness showed astonishing vitality in a man of his years. For the rest, his ears were pale and at the tops extremely pointed...' (Shades of Mr Spock of *Star Trek* fame!)

Dracula's arch-enemy, Professor Van Helsing from Amsterdam, also possessed bushy eyebrows, according to the author, had reddish hair, was elderly and spoke his own brand of rather strange pidgin English. Double-Dutch, one might say. He was given to stamping his foot and exclaiming "Pouf!" when vexed, and "Ho! Ho!" when pleased.

In 1958, when we made Hammer's first *Dracula* movie, Christopher Lee and I were on the verge of becoming familiar to cinemagoers, so it was decided that we should play the parts without any of the foregoing additions. Of course, Christopher, who was magnificent as the Count, did pop in the false fangs when necessary, but otherwise he was just 'Tall, Dark and Gruesome' — which was the title his publishers insisted upon for his

Above: *The Vampire Lovers.*
Left: *The Legend of the 7 Golden Vampires.*

autobiography — and his appearance was the answer to maidens' prayers.

Stoker's novel was published in 1897, when late Victorian Gothic romance invariably featured a beautiful young woman, very marriageable, being pursued by a dark and wicked stranger, usually Italian, intent upon dishonouring her. Christopher fitted the bill to perfection — as this character, I hasten to add!

Mr Stephen Jones, who has compiled this guide to vampire films, credits me with being the only actor to have played Van Helsing *and* Dracula, but his assertion needs a little modification. In 1974 I thoroughly enjoyed making a film in Paris entitled *Tender Dracula, or the Confessions of a Bloodsucker*, directed by Pierre Grunstein.

My part was that of a famous and superb actor (I quote from the script!) named MacGregor, and I did indeed appear as old Draco in a montage dream sequence in which my character attempted to scare the living daylights out of a group of people who were annoying him. To my knowledge, the film has never seen the light of day, so I fear I must disown Mr Jones' claim on my behalf!

For those who don't know, it may be of interest to learn that Bram Stoker, a bearded, industrious and genial Irishman, studied pure mathematics at Trinity College, Dublin, qualified as a barrister, and worked in the Registrar of Petty Sessions Clerk's Department in the Irish Civil Service before the lure of the theatre proved too strong to resist. He became business manager to his old friend and great actor, Sir Henry Irving, the Olivier

Above right: *Twins of Evil.*
Below right: *Dracula.*
Below: *The Legend of the 7 Golden Vampires.*

of his day.

My paternal grandfather, Mr Henry Cushing, was a member of Irving's company for twenty years; Stoker banked with Coutts and Co, London; so did Dracula; and so do I. Ergo, in this particular, I *can* claim some distinction!

Stoker wrote nineteen other books besides *Dracula*, but they have sunk into oblivion. I suspect that his gift for dramatic tension, which is so evident in the survivor, owed much to his theatrical associations, but I doubt whether he could have foreseen that the first film of his masterpiece would be made in 1930 and that during the next sixty-two years it would spawn countless other movies in this genre — the latest, directed by Francis Coppola with the super Anthony Hopkins as Professor Van Helsing, appeared this year, and no doubt it will be followed by many more in the future.

The Count is Undead; long live the Prof!

Peter Cushing OBE, Whitstable, 1992

the

There have always been legends and folktales of reanimated corpses and blood-drinking ghosts, but the vampire as we know it is a surprisingly recent creation. On a memorable evening beside Lake Geneva in June 1816, Lord Byron read Coleridge's unfinished vampire poem 'Christabel' to Percy Shelley, his wife Mary Shelley and Byron's physician, John Polidori (1795-1821). This not only inspired the eighteen year-old Mary to write her novel **Frankenstein, or a Modern Prometheus**, but also led to Polidori's less successful **The Vampyre; a Tale**, which has the distinction of being the first vampire story in English literature.

It was followed in 1845 by **Varney the Vampire; or, the Feast of Blood**, a Victorian hackwork credited to J.M. Rymer which stretched to 220 chapters. In 1870 J. Sheridan Le Fanu (1814-1873) created 'Carmilla', the first great literary vampire tale, which revived the suggestions of a vampiric lesbian relationship hinted at in Coleridge's poem. As a direct result of reading Le Fanu's classic novella, fellow Irishman Bram Stoker (1847-1912) started researching his own vampire story.

Dracula, published in 1897, was the first best-selling vampire novel and influenced everything that followed. Stoker based his character on the fifteenth century Transylvanian ruler, Vlad IV, known as Vlad the Impaler because of his predilection for impaling live victims on wooden stakes while he dined. For Dracula's physical form, the author took as his inspiration the greatest actor of his age, Henry Irving, who just happened to be managed by Stoker.

Nosferatu.

By the early 1900s, the fledgling film industry had adapted the term 'vamp' or 'vampire' to describe such femme fatales of the silent

Silents

screen as Theda Bara. This resulted in a number of titles which, while sounding like vampire movies, had nothing to do with the supernatural or the blood-drinking undead.

The first movie version of Stoker's book might possibly have been the Hungarian feature **Drakula***, which was made in 1921, but it is a lost film today. It is therefore generally accepted that Max Schreck is the screen's first, and perhaps ugliest, vampire, as he stalked through F.W. Murnau's* **Nosferatu***, an unauthorised 1922 German adaptation of Stoker's novel. Hollywood wasn't far behind, and in 1927 Lon Chaney Sr (1883-1930), one of the screen's most versatile performers, portrayed a bug-eyed, top-hatted vampire in MGM's atmospheric murder mystery* **London After Midnight**.

For an insatiable American movie-going public, the vampire had arrived. But it would be another three years before an actor would create the screen's first legitimate Dracula, and set a trend in vampire movies that continues to resonate up to the present day...

London After Midnight.

DRAKULA

Hungary, 1921. Dir: Karoly Lajthay. B&W.

Possibly the first known movie adaptation of Bram Stoker's novel (preceding Murnau's *Nosferatu* by a year). Now a lost film.

THE EXPLOITS OF ELAINE

USA, 1914-15. Dir: Louis J. Gasnier and George B. Seitz. With: Pearl White, Arnold Daly, Creighton Hale, Sheldon Lewis, William Riley Hatch, Mrs Besse E. Wharton. Star/Pathe. B&W.

Fourteen episode silent serial, with such chapter titles as 'The Twilight Sleep', 'The Poisoned Room', 'The Death Ray', 'The Blood Crystals' and 'The Devil Worshippers'. Chapter six is titled 'The Vampire', in which master villain Perry Bennett, aka the Clutching Hand (Lewis), tries to drain the blood from heroine Elaine Dodge (White) through a hypodermic needle.

THE GREAT LONDON MYSTERY

UK, 1920. Dir: Charles Raymond. With: David Devant, Lady Doris Stapleton, Lester Gard, Lola de Liane. T&P. B&W.

De Liane plays Froggie the Vampire in this twelve part serial with great chapter titles like 'The Sacred Snake Worshippers', 'The Fraudulent Spiritualistic Seance' and 'The Living Dead'. Also includes such characters as the Master Magician (Devant) and the Man Monkey (Gard).

THE HAUNTED CASTLE

(Orig: LE MANOIR DU DIABLE. UK/USA: aka THE MANOR OF THE DEVIL/THE DEVIL'S MANOR/THE DEVIL'S CASTLE)

France, 1896. Dir: Georges Méliès. With: Georges Méliès. Robert-Houdin/Pathe/Star. B&W.

One of film pioneer Georges Méliès' short (two minutes) trick films. A bat flies around a medieval castle and turns into the Devil (Méliès). He then conjures up a parade of ghosts, skeletons and witches from a magic cauldron until one holds up a crucifix and Mephistopheles disappears in a puff of smoke.

IN THE GRIP OF THE VAMPIRE

France, 1912. Gaumont. B&W.

A super-villain called The Vampire uses a drug to turn the heroine into a mindless idiot. Her sense is restored by hypnotism at the end. Based on a story by Leonce Perret.

MAGIA

Hungary, 1917. Dir: Alexander Korda. With: Mihaly Varkonyi. Corvin. B&W.

While gazing into Baron Merlin's magic mirror, the hero learns that his host is an ancient magician who must drink the

Left and above: *London After Midnight.*

LONDON AFTER MIDNIGHT

(UK: THE HYPNOTIST)
USA, 1927. Dir: Tod Browning. With: Lon Chaney, Marceline Day, Conrad Nagel, Henry B. Walthall, Percy Williams, Polly Moran. Metro-Goldwyn-Mayer. B&W.

Based on Browning's own story, 'The Hypnotist', Lon Chaney Sr portrays a grotesque vampire prowling the moors with his wraith-like daughter (Edna Tichenor). In the end, it turns out to be a trick by Scotland Yard Inspector Burke (also played by Chaney) to trap a murderer (Walthall). Chaney's vampire is a masterful creation — he used wire hoops to make his eyes bulge and a bridge of needle-sharp animal teeth which he could only wear for short periods. Browning remade the film, with Chaney's roles split between three actors. Thought lost for many years, most of the reels have apparently now been rediscovered.

Remake: MARK OF THE VAMPIRE (qv; 1935)

Left and below: Nosferatu. (FJA).

blood of a young man every thousandth full moon to survive.

NOSFERATU

(Orig: NOSFERATU, EINE SYMPHONIE DES GRAUENS/aka DIE ZWOELFTE STUNDE, EINE NACHT DES GRAUENS)
Germany, 1922. Dir: F. (Friedrich) W. (Wilhelm) Murnau. With: Max Schreck, Alexander Granach, Gustav Von Waggenheim, Greta Schroder, G.H. Schnell, Ruth Landshoff. Prana Film. B&W.

This early version of Bram Stoker's novel *Dracula* was fated for a short commercial life. Although screenwriter Henrik Galeen freely adapted the book, he failed to obtain permission from the copyright holder. The author's widow, Florence Stoker, successfully sued Prana and the company went bankrupt. In July 1925, a court ruled that the negative and all prints of the film should be destroyed. Luckily, some copies survived. Actor Max Schreck (whose name means 'horror' in German) creates a truly disturbing vampire with the skeletal, taloned Graf Orlok/Nosferatu who is seduced by the heroine until the rising sun destroys him. Director Murnau (*Faust* [1926]) uses shadows, speeded-up photography and negative images to give the film a dream-like quality. Overlong and dull in places, this still has the power to fascinate. Released in America in 1929.

Remakes: DRACULA (qv; 1930) and NOSFERATU THE VAMPYRE (qv; 1979)

THE VAMPIRE

USA, 1913. Dir: Robert Vignola. With: Harry Millarde, Alice Hollister, Marguerite Courtot, Bert French, Alice Eis. Kalem. B&W.

An artist is lured to his death by a seductive wood nymph.

THE VAMPIRE

UK, 1913. Searchlight. B&W.

A lost film, featuring a native woman in India who kills a hunter. When his friend shoots her, she transforms into a were-snake and kills him as well.

THE VAMPIRE

France, 1914. Eclair. B&W.

A member of a mysterious organisation is bound by an oath to kill his second wife with drugs and a huge vampire bat.

THE VAMPIRE OF THE DESERT

USA, 1913. With: Helen Gardner, Flora Finch, Tefft Johnson. Vitagraph. B&W.

Based on the poem 'The Vampire' by Rudyard Kipling, about a vamp who uses her hypnotic power.

LES VAMPIRES

(aka VAMPIRES, THE ARCH CRIMINALS OF PARIS)
France, 1915-16. Dir: Louis Feuillade. With: Juliet Musidora, Edouard Mathe, Florense Simoni, Marcel Levesque, Eugene Ayme, Jacques Hermann. Gaumont. B&W

Creaky ten part serial about a secret society of super-criminals. Chapter titles include 'The Ghost', 'The Dead Man's Escape' and 'The Poison Man', and involve hypnotism, a fake psychic, poisoned paper, revived corpses and an electric cannon attack on Paris. Ayme plays Le Grand Vampire, Louis Leubas is Satanas and Musidora's heroine is named Irma Vep (an anagram of vampire).

VASCO, THE VAMPIRE

USA, 1914. Independent Motion Picture Company. B&W.

A detective is hypnotised and taken to the villain's lair.

the

When Universal decided to film Bram Stoker's **Dracula**, *their first choice of an actor to portray the Count was Lon Chaney Sr, who would be reunited with his* **London After Midnight (1927)** *director, Tod Browning. Unfortunately, before the project could be realised, Chaney died from throat cancer in 1930 after making only one sound film,* **The Unholy Three (1930).**

Over the following months, a number of other actors were considered (and announced) for the role, including John Wray, Conrad Veidt, Ian Keith, William Courtenay, Joseph Schildkraut, Paul Muni and Chester Morris. They finally chose Hungarian actor Bela Lugosi (Bela Ferenc Dezso Blasko, 1882-1956), who had played the part on stage since 1927, and signed him for a mere $3,500. It would be the high point of Lugosi's career and the precursor of a long decline.

Billed as 'The strangest passion the world has ever known!', Universal released **Dracula** *on February 12th, 1931, during the height of the Depression. It quickly became their first hit for two years, stabilizing the studio's ailing fortunes. Despite its obvious stage origins,* **Dracula** *firmly established the vampire in the public's consciousness, spawned the first great cycle of American horror movies and typecast its star for life.*

A far more interesting version was filmed simultaneously by Universal for Spanish-speaking audiences. Thirty-eight year-old Carlos Villarias played the title role for director George Melford, better known for his westerns, who shot at night on Browning's sets.

Despite the success of **Dracula**, *filmmakers were*

1930s

slow to exploit the popularity of the vampire, and over the next few years the undead were utilized only in low budget independent productions such as **The Vampire Bat (1933)** *and* **Condemned to Live (1935).**

By 1935, Lugosi was already trading on his Dracula image for another

Dracula.

Dracula.

studio. When Browning decided to remake **London After Midnight** *as* **Mark of the Vampire** *over at MGM, the actor was third-billed as Count Mora in what amounted to little more than a supporting role.*

Meanwhile, Universal inexplicably waited six years before making **Dracula's Daughter (1936)**, *a sequel to their box office hit. Only Edward Van Sloan (who portrayed Professor Van Helsing) returned from the original film, and Universal evidenced its waning interest in the property by churning out nothing more than a routine programmer.*

As the 1930s horror cycle came to an end, only an injection of new blood could guarantee that the vampire would still be around to thrill audiences in need of escaping the real-life horrors of a Second World War...

CONDEMNED TO LIVE

USA, 1935. Dir: Frank Strayer. With: Ralph Morgan, Maxine Doyle, Russell Gleason, Pedro De Cordoba, Mischa Auer, Lucy Beaumont. Invincible Pictures. B&W.

From the director of *The Vampire Bat* (1933) comes another low budget independent movie filmed on the Universal backlot. Unknown even to himself, kindly Professor Kristan (Morgan) is transformed by the full moon into the vampire terrorising a European village. His faithful hunchbacked servant, Zan (Auer), disposes of the victims in a hidden pit. Ralph Morgan was the brother of the more famous Frank (*The Wizard of Oz* [1939]) Morgan.

DARKEST AFRICA

(aka KING OF THE JUNGLELAND/ BATMEN OF AFRICA)
USA, 1936. Dir: B. Reeves Eason and Joseph Kane. With: Clyde Beatty, Manuel King, Elaine Shepard, Lucien Prival, Naba, Ray Benard. Republic Pictures. B&W.

Famed animal trainer Clyde Beatty plays himself in Republic's first serial. He travels to the hidden city of Joba, built by Solomon in ancient times, to rescue a girl who the high priest, Dagna (Prival), has established as the Goddess of the Golden Bat. Beatty, jungle boy Baru (King) and the boy's gorilla, Bonga, battle Dagna's army of flying Bat Men through fifteen chapters with titles like 'Jars of Death', 'Revolt of Slaves' and 'The Divine Sacrifice'. Samabe, the leader of the Bat Men, and Bonga the gorilla hero were both portrayed by Ray Bernard who, after changing his name to Ray 'Crash' Corrigan, went on to star in Republic's second serial, *Undersea Kingdom* (1936). This also includes back-projected lizards as dinosaurs. It was released as a feature in 1966.

DRACULA

USA, 1930. Dir: Tod Browning. With: Bela Lugosi, David Manners, Helen Chandler, Dwight Frye, Edward Van Sloan, Frances Dade. Universal. B&W.

Originally billed as 'The strangest love story of all', this slow moving, stagey version of Bram Stoker's novel (previously filmed as *Nosferatu* [1922]) was

***Above:** Condemned to Live. (FJA).*
***Left:** Dracula.*

released on St Valentine's Day, 1931. After playing the Count in the hit stage production since 1927 (alongside Van Sloan), this was forty-nine year-old Hungarian actor Bela Lugosi's (Bela Blasko) first starring role in Hollywood (replacing the late Lon Chaney Sr). Based on the play by Hamilton Deane and John L. Balderston, Garrett Fort's script still has its moments, but looks terribly dated today. Despite Frye's manic Renfield and Van Sloan's dignified Van Helsing, the film is dragged down by the weak love interest (Manners and Chandler) and Browning's unimaginative direction. However, along with Universal's *Frankenstein* the following year, this started the horror boom of the 1930s. Original prints reportedly included an epilogue by Van Sloan telling the audience that vampires really existed.

Sequel: DRACULA'S DAUGHTER (qv; 1936)
Remake: DRAKULA ISTANBULA (qv; 1953)

DRACULA'S DAUGHTER

USA, 1936. Dir: Lambert Hillyer. With: Otto Kruger, Gloria Holden, Marguerite Churchill, Edward Van Sloan, Gilbert Emery, Irving Pichel. Universal. B&W.

It took six years for Universal to get around to making this direct sequel to *Dracula* (1930), credited to Bram Stoker's story 'Dracula's Guest' but in fact based on an original screenplay by Garrett Fort. It begins only moments after the original

[redacted] Countess Maria Zaleska (Holden), who wants to escape her vampiric heritage but is forced to drink the blood of young female models. Pichel is the Countess' macabre servant, Sandor, and there's a great supporting cast (including Billy Bevan, E.E. Clive and Hedda Hopper). However, director Hillyer (better known for his westerns) fails to bring any sparkle to the proceedings, and this remains only an interesting curio.

Sequel: SON OF DRACULA (qv; 1943)

Right and below: *Dracula.*

FLASH GORDON

USA, 1936. Dir: Frederick Stephani. With: Larry 'Buster' Crabbe, Jean Rogers, Charles Middleton, Priscilla Lawson, Frank Shannon, John Lipson. Universal. B&W.

The first of three serials based on Alex Raymond's super-science fiction newspaper strip. Over thirteen chapters, Flash (Crabbe), Dale (Rogers) and Dr Zarkov (Shannon) journey to the planet Mongo to stop Ming the Merciless (Middleton) from destroying the Earth. In one chapter, Flash battles Ming's fanged warriors in the arena.

G-MAN JITTERS

USA, 1939. Terrytoons/Twentieth Century-Fox. B&W.

Seven minute animated Gandy Goose short, featuring Dracula and the Frankenstein monster.

HOLLYWOOD ON PARADE NO.8

USA, 1933. Dir: Lewis Lewyn. With: Eddie Borden, Mae Questel, Bela Lugosi, Rex Bell, Dorothy Burgess, George Sidney. Lewyn/Paramount. B&W.

Ten minute novelty short, filmed in Charles Pressley's Motion Picture Museum and Hall of Fame in Hollywood. Borden visits a wax museum where the exhibits come to life. In a brief sequence, visitor Mae Questel, dressed as Betty Boop, sings 'My Silent Love'. The wax figure of Lugosi, in his Dracula costume, comes to life and bends towards her throat, warning: "Boop! You have booped your last boop!" Also includes Gayne Whitman as Chandu the Magician and silent Lubitsch star Marie Prevost as a harem girl. The eighth in a series of twenty-four shorts produced by Paramount between 1932-33.

JAWS OF THE JUNGLE

(aka JUNGLE VIRGIN)

Ceylon/USA, 1936. Dir: J.D. Kendis. With: Teeto, Minta, Gukar, Walla the Ape, Agena the Bear. Jay Dee Kay. B&W.

Independent feature in which a horde of giant vampire bats attack a village in Ceylon. Narrated by C. Howell.

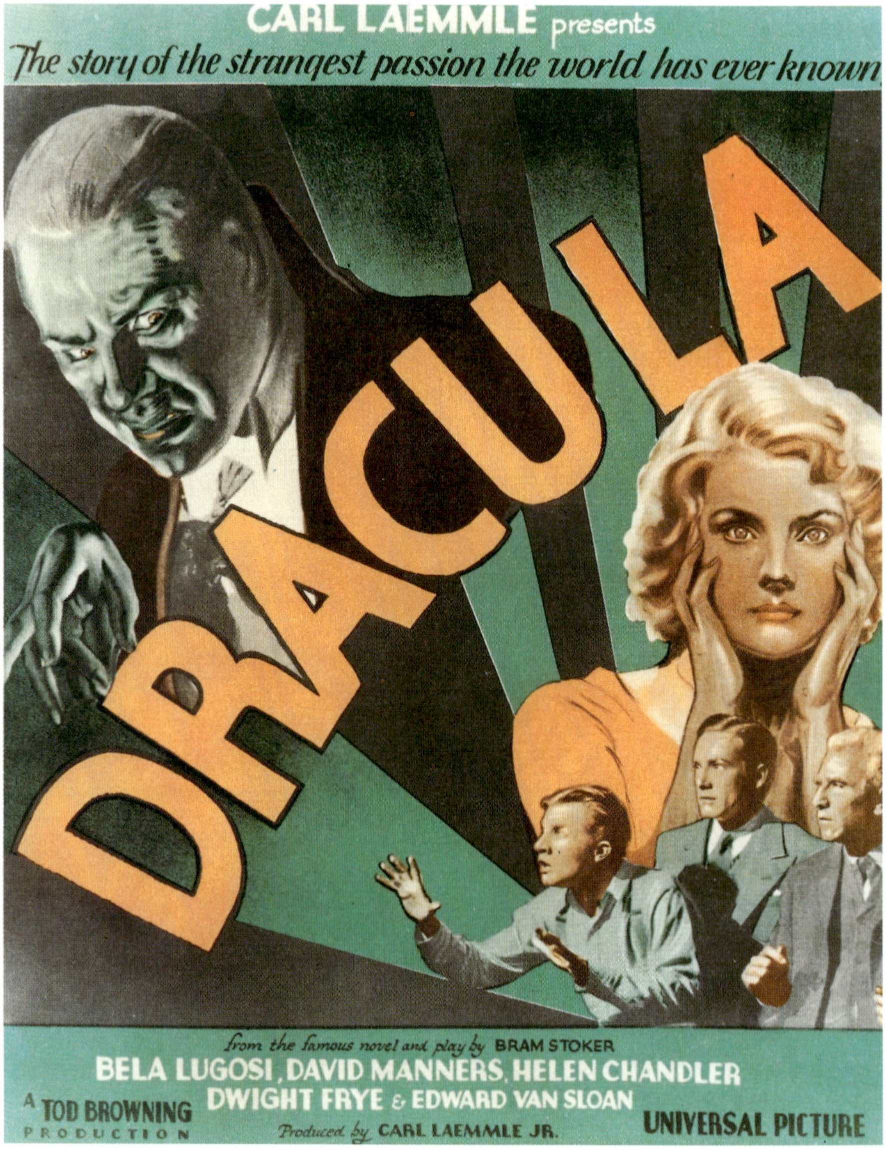

M

Germany, 1931. Dir: Fritz Lang. With: Peter Lorre, Otto Wernicke, Ellen Widmann, Inge Landgot, Gustav Grundgens, Fritz Gnass. Nero Films. B&W.

Lang's first sound film is a visually superb thriller which made a star of Lorre, a then-unknown Hungarian stage actor. Loosely based on the true-life case of homosexual child murderer Peter Kürten, the Vampire of Dusseldorf. Some of the most powerful sequences include the mother waiting for a child who never returns home; the police raids on the criminal underworld; the hunt for the killer by the city's beggars; and, best of all, Lorre's climactic confession, where he describes the *doppelgänger* that follows him and urges him to kill. Lang considered this his most satisfying film.

Remake: M (1951)

Above: Dracula (Spanish).

THE MACABRE TRUNK

(Orig: EL BAUL MACABRO)
Mexico, 1936. Dir: Miguel Zacarias. With: Esther Fernandez, Ramón Pereda, René Cardona, Carlos Lopez (Chaflan), Manuel Noriega, Enrique Gonce. Produccion Pezet. B&W.

Pereda plays the mad Dr del Vialle who kills young women and uses their blood to keep his wife (Fernandez) alive. Co-star Cardona went on to become a prolific director.

MARK OF THE VAMPIRE

USA, 1935. Dir: Tod Browning. With: Lionel Barrymore, Elizabeth Allan, Bela Lugosi, Lionel Atwill, Jean Hersholt, Donald Meek. Metro-Goldwyn-Mayer. B&W.

Browning's remake of his own *London After Midnight* (1927), with the multiple roles taken by Lon Chaney Sr in the original here split between Barrymore, Atwill and Lugosi. When a body is discovered drained of blood, it is apparently the work of a pair of vampires (Lugosi and Carol Borland). However, disappointingly, it all turns out to be a plot by Barrymore's professor and Atwill's police inspector to trap the real killer. Browning gets the chance to reuse a number of ideas from *Dracula* (1930), and such archetypal images as fog-shrouded graveyards, cobwebbed castles, bats and wolves are atmospherically photographed by the great James Wong Howe. Lugosi is effective as Count Mora (a mostly non-speaking role) and the best scene has twenty-one year-old Borland (as his daughter Luna) descending through the air on giant bat wings.

MICKEY'S GALA PREMIERE

USA, 1933. Walt Disney/United Artists. B&W.

Seven minute animated short, produced by Disney, in which Mickey Mouse dreams that he is attending the première of his new movie. It features caricatures of numerous Hollywood stars, including Count Dracula and the Frankenstein monster.

PREVIEW MURDER MYSTERY

USA, 1936. Dir: Robert Florey. With:

return to horror after three years' absence and was originally set to star Boris Karloff (in the Bogart role) and Claude Rains. The interesting supporting cast includes Lya Lys as another reanimated corpse.

TARZAN ESCAPES

USA, 1936. Dir: Richard Thorpe (and James McKay and John Farrow). With: Johnny Weissmuller, Maureen O'Sullivan, John Buckler, Benita Hume, William Henry, E.E. Clive. Metro-Goldwyn-Mayer. B&W.

The third in MGM's series starring Weissmuller, this is one of the more routine Tarzan adventures, in which the Ape Man is kidnapped by an animal safari. Sequences involving giant vampire bats (often shown in stills) and dinosaur-like lizards were cut by the studio prior to release because they were considered too horrific.

Sequel: TARZAN FINDS A SON! (1939)

THE VAMPIRE BAT

USA, 1933. Dir: Frank Strayer. With: Lionel Atwill, Fay Wray, Melvyn Douglas, Maude Eburne, George E. Stone, Dwight Frye. Majestic Pictures. B&W.

Stars Atwill and Wray are teamed for the third time (after *Doctor X* [1932] and

Left: *Mark of the Vampire.*
Below: *The Vampire Bat.*

Mystery of the Wax Museum [1932]) in this low budget independent chiller, filmed on the Universal backlot. Atwill plays the mad Dr Otto van Niemann who uses hypnotism to create fake vampire deaths and obtain blood to feed the synthetic creature he has created. Douglas is miscast as the stiff police inspector, but there's always Lionel Belmore recreating his Burgomaster role from *Frankenstein* (1931) and a sleazy Dwight Frye as an idiot Renfield-like bat-lover.

VAMPYR

(Orig: VAMPYR OU L'ETRANGE ADVENTURE DE DAVID GRAY/DER TRAUM DES ALLAN GRAY. UK: aka THE STRANGE ADVENTURES OF DAVID GRAY. USA: aka CASTLE OF DOOM/THE VAMPIRE) France/Germany, 1931-32. Dir: Carl Theodore Dreyer. With: Julian West, Henriette Gérard, Jan Hieronimko, Rena Mandel, Sybille Schmitz, Maurice Schultz. Tobis/Klangfilm. B&W.

Danish-born Dreyer co-wrote, produced and directed this ponderous vampire mystery, loosely based on J. Sheridan Le Fanu's story 'Carmilla'. It was filmed silently in Paris in 1931 and a German soundtrack was added in Berlin the following year. Baron Nicolas de Gunzberg financed the project and, under the name of Julian West, played David Gray (Allan Gray in the German version), who arrives at a strange inn in the Carpathians. There he discovers a book about vampires, an old woman who is one of the undead and the evil doctor who aids her. In a dream, he watches his own funeral. Dreyer uses such camera effects as double exposure and reverse photography to create a sense of unreality, but the film is often incomprehensible due to the dream-like narrative and hilariously misspelled title cards. Scenes were later included in the 1943 compilation *Dr. Terror's House of Horrors*.

Above: *The Return of Doctor X. (FJA).*
Below: *Vampyr. (FJA).*

the

A*lthough never the actor his father had been, Lon Chaney Jr (Creighton Chaney, 1906-1973) managed to carve something of a niche for himself at Universal, following in the footsteps of Boris Karloff by portraying the Frankenstein monster* **(The Ghost of Frankenstein [1942])** *and the Mummy* **(The Mummy's Tomb [1942])**, *and creating at least one genuine character of his own, the lycanthrope Lawrence Talbot of* **The Wolf Man (1941)**, *which launched the second great cycle of American horror films.*

Having played most of the studio's major movie monsters, it was almost inevitable that he would be cast as the Count in Universal's second, much improved vampire sequel, **Son of Dracula (1943).**

However, audiences caught up in the horrors of world devastation were quickly becoming inured to the Gothic chills served up by Hollywood. Universal's answer to this waning interest was **Frankenstein Meets the Wolf Man** *in 1943, and increased box office returns led to the natural assumption that if two monsters meant more revenue, then combining three or four in a single movie would result in even greater success. Proving the rule of diminishing returns, the result was* **House of Frankenstein (1944)** *and* **House of Dracula (1945)**, *both of which featured Shakespearean actor and poverty row mad scientist John Carradine as a suave Count.*

Bela Lugosi was apparently not even considered by the studio, even though he'd played another Dracula-like vampire, Armand Tesla, in Columbia's entertaining **The Return of the Vampire (1943)**. *Unfortunately, cheap quickies like* **The Devil Bat (1940)** *and* **Zombies on Broadway (1945)** *were more indicative of his*

1940s

declining career during this period.

His sometime co-star, Boris Karloff (William Henry Pratt, 1887-1969), was faring somewhat better, and his presence considerably enhanced Val Lewton's underrated study of vampire mythology, **Isle of the Dead (1945)**. *However, Hollywood more usually restricted its bloodsuckers to such B-movie mediocrity as* **Dead Men Walk (1943)**, **The Vampire's Ghost (1945)** *and* **Valley of the Zombies (1946)**.

It was left to Universal to bring the second great horror cycle to a close in style when they united their stable of movie monsters one last time and added the slapstick antics of comedians Abbott and Costello in **Meet Frankenstein (1948)**. *It was only proper that Lugosi should return to recreate his most famous role one more time on the screen, thus effectively beginning the Hollywood horror boom in the 1930s and being present at its (surprisingly dignified) end almost two decades later.*

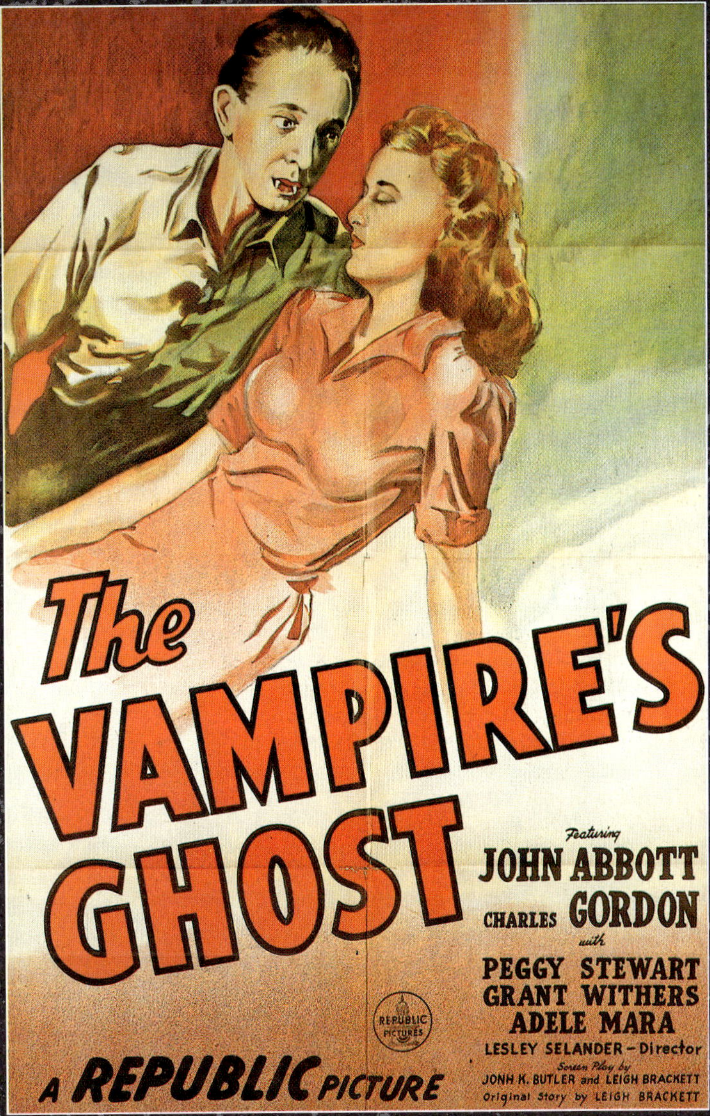

In the meantime, man had learned to split the atom, the radioactive horrors of Hiroshima were still fresh in everyone's mind and the world would never be the same again...

THE CRIME DOCTOR'S COURAGE

USA, 1945. Dir: George Sherman. With: Warner Baxter, Hillary Brooke, Jerome Cowan, Robert Scott, Lloyd Corrigan, Emory Parnell. Columbia. B&W.

In 1943, Columbia initiated a series of ten films based on Max Marcin's successful radio show, *Crime Doctor.* Baxter starred in them all as amnesia victim Dr Ordway, who becomes a leading criminal psychologist before discovering he was once a gang leader himself. In this mystery/thriller his investigations into a possible homicidal maniac lead to a Spanish dance team (Anthony Caruso and Lupita Tovar) who are suspected of being 300 year-old vampires. It's all explained scientifically in the end.

Sequel: THE CRIME DOCTOR'S WARNING (1945)

DEAD MEN WALK

USA, 1943. Dir: Sam Newfield. With: George Zucco, Mary Carlisle, Nedrick Young, Dwight Frye, Fern Emmett, Robert Strange. Producers Releasing Corporation. B&W.

The wonderful George Zucco, in a dual role, plays a vampiric black magician determined to kill his kindly twin brother, who is a doctor. They are eventually both destroyed by fire. The evil Zucco is aided by Zolor the hunchback (a sick-looking Frye, in his final horror movie — he died of a heart attack the same year). An incomprehensible mess!

THE DEVIL BAT

(USA: aka KILLER BATS/DEVIL BATS)

USA, 1940. Dir: Jean Yarbrough. With: Bela Lugosi, Suzanne Kaaren, Dave O'Brien, Hal Price, Donald Kerr, Guy Usher. PRC. B&W.

Lugosi portrays the mad Dr Carruthers, who creates a pair of gigantic vampire bats to destroy those he believes have cheated him. The bats are attracted to their victims by a pungent aftershave lotion! Lugosi goes over the top and everything else is rock bottom.

Sequel: THE DEVIL BAT'S DAUGHTER (qv; 1946)

Remake: THE FLYING SERPENT (1945)

THE DEVIL BAT'S DAUGHTER

USA, 1946. Dir: Frank Wisbar (Wysbar). With: Rosemary La Planche, Eddie Kane, John James, Michael Hale, Molly Lamont, Edward Cassidy. PRC. B&W.

Ludicrous sequel to *The Devil Bat* (1940). La Planche (who was Miss America of 1941) plays the daughter of the late Dr Carruthers (Lugosi in the earlier film) being driven mad by her psychiatrist (Kane). In a cheat twist, the doctor's name is cleared when the real villain is revealed.

DR. TERROR'S HOUSE OF HORRORS

USA, 1943. National Roadshow. B&W.

The producers of this compilation movie edited together sequences from five independent movies, including Dreyer's *Vampyr* (1932), *The Living Dead* (Germany, 1933; aka *Histoires Extraordinaires*), *The Golem* (1936), and two Bela Lugosi features, *White Zombie* (1932) and *The Return of Chandu* (1934).

Above left: *Dead Men Walk. (FJA).*
Below: *The Devil Bat. (FJA).*

DROOMS OF FU MANCHU

USA, 1940. Dir: William Witney and John English. With: Henry Brandon, William Royle, Robert Kellard, Gloria Franklin, Dwight Frye, Olaf Hytten. Republic. B&W.
Brandon gives a great performance as Sax Rohmer's supercriminal in this fifteen chapter serial from Republic, subsequently released as a feature in 1945. This time Fu Manchu and his fanged followers are seeking an ancient tomb that will reveal the secret of world domination. Includes Dwight Frye in a supporting role.

THE FACE OF MARBLE

USA, 1946. Dir: William Beaudine. With: John Carradine, Robert Shayne, Claudia Drake, Maris Wrixon, Rosa Rey, Willie Best. Monogram. B&W.
Mad Professor Randolf (Carradine) experiments with reviving the dead, but his victims quickly expire again with rigid faces. When he resuscitates a Great Dane, the dog becomes semi-transparent, walks through walls and drinks blood. Low budget Monogram madness that includes voodoo love potions and the usual comedy relief from Best.

GANDY GOOSE IN THE GHOST TOWN

USA, 1944. Dir: Mannie Davis. Terrytoons/Twentieth Century Fox. Colour.

Above left: *The Devil Bat's Daughter.*
Above right: *House of Dracula.*
Right: *House of Frankenstein.*

Animated short in which Gandy has a nightmare and meets ghosts, the Frankenstein monster and Count Dracula.

HOUSE OF DRACULA

USA, 1945. Dir: Erle C. Kenton. With: Lon Chaney, Martha O'Driscoll, John Carradine, Lionel Atwill, Onslow Stevens, Glenn Strange. Universal. B&W.

Uninspired sequel to *House of Frankenstein* (1944). Dr Edelmann (Stevens) attempts to cure the monsters with the aid of his scientifically created mould! But Carradine's suave Count Dracula decides he enjoys being a vampire and turns Edelman into one as well. The mad doctor tries to revive the Frankenstein monster (Strange) in the blazing climax (lifted from *The Ghost of Frankenstein* [1942]), while Larry Talbot (Chaney Jr) is finally cured after changing into the Wolf Man only once. Martha O'Driscoll portrays a beautiful hunchbacked nurse and Atwill turns up as another police inspector. Worth catching for John P. Fulton's wonderful man-into-bat transformations.

Sequel: MEET FRANKENSTEIN (qv; 1948)

HOUSE OF FRANKENSTEIN

USA, 1944. Dir: Erle C. Kenton. With: Boris Karloff, Lon Chaney, John Carradine, J. Carrol Naish, Anne Gwynne, Lionel Atwill. Universal. B&W.

Entertaining sequel to *Frankenstein Meets the Wolf Man* (1943). Karloff's mad Dr Niemann and Daniel the homicidal hunchback (Naish) escape from a prison for the criminally insane and take over a travelling carnival. Pursued by Atwill's police inspector, they revive 'Baron Latos' (Carradine as Count Dracula, complete with top hat) before arriving at Castle Frankenstein where they discover the Wolf Man (Chaney Jr as Larry Talbot, still trying to find a cure) and the Frankenstein monster (Glenn Strange). In the end, the villagers put a stop to it all and the monster drags Karloff into the quicksands. The best scene has Dracula tempting Gwynne with the twilight world she sees in his ring. Originally announced as *The Devil's Brood*, it also includes brief appearances by George Zucco and Frank Reicher.

Sequel: HOUSE OF DRACULA (qv; 1945)

ISLE OF THE DEAD

USA, 1945. Dir: Mark Robson. With: Boris Karloff, Ellen Drew, Marc Cramer, Katherine Emery, Helene Thimig, Alan Napier. RKO Radio Pictures. B&W.

Unfairly neglected film from Val Lewton's B-unit at RKO, this was Karloff's second teaming with the talented producer. The actor gives a strong performance as an obsessed Greek general during the 1912 Balkan War who believes the pagan myths that a vampire-like vrykolaka is killing off the inhabitants of a plague-ridden island. Despite a sometimes confusing script, Robson's atmospheric direction, coupled with the haunting sets and an impressive cast (including Jason Robards Sr and Skelton Knaggs), make this a minor classic. It was banned by the British censor for ten years.

THE JAILBREAK

USA, 1946. Dir: Eddie Donnelly. Terrytoons/Twentieth Century-Fox. Colour.

Animated Mighty Mouse short in which Count Dracula and the Frankenstein monster are prisoners on Alcatraz.

MIGHTY MOUSE MEETS BAD BILL BUNION

USA, 1945. Terrytoons/Twentieth Century-Fox. Colour.

A Mighty Mouse cartoon short featuring Count Dracula.

THE RETURN OF THE VAMPIRE

USA, 1943. Dir: Lew Landers. With: Bela Lugosi, Frieda Inescort, Nina Foch, Miles Mander, Matt Willis, Roland Varno. Columbia. B&W.

Because Universal owned the rights to the Dracula name, Lugosi plays a vampire named Armand Tesla, freed from his stake and tomb during the Nazi blitz of England. Aided by his tatty werewolf assistant, Andreas Obry (Willis), he arrives at the home of Lady Jane Ainsley (Inescort). Lugosi brings some dignity to his role, and director Landers piles on the atmosphere with a fog-wreathed graveyard. The werewolf talks and wears a suit, but there's more intentional comedy relief from Billy Bevan. The sequence of

Right: *The Face of Marble.*

MEET FRANKENSTEIN

(UK: ABBOTT AND COSTELLO MEET THE GHOSTS)

USA, 1948. Dir: Charles Barton. With: Bud Abbott, Lou Costello, Lon Chaney, Bela Lugosi, Glenn Strange, Lenore Aubert. Universal-International. B&W

Originally intended to be a serious entry in the series entitled *The Brain of Frankenstein*, this marked Universal's last outing for all its classic monsters. Bud and Lou (in probably their best film) team up with Chaney Jr's hero/Wolf Man to stop Dracula and a mad female scientist (Aubert) from transplanting Lou's brain into the Frankenstein monster (Strange). Amazingly, this was only the second (and last) time that Lugosi officially portrayed the Count on screen. Director Barton plays the horror elements straight, thus emphasizing the classic comedy routines, and an uncredited Vincent Price is heard as the Invisible Man.

Remake: CASTLE OF THE MONSTERS (qv; 1957)

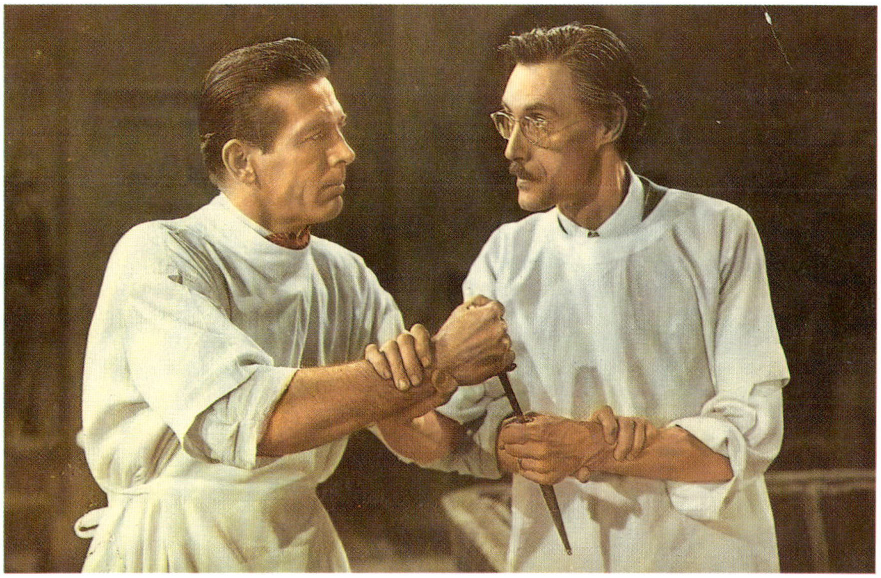

Lugosi's face melting when exposed to the sunlight was originally cut by the British censor.

SON OF DRACULA

USA, 1943. Dir: Robert Siodmak. With: Lon Chaney, Louise Allbritton, Robert Paige, Evelyn Ankers, Frank Craven, J. Edward Bromberg. Universal. B&W.

A stylish blend of vampires and witchcraft, set in the American bayous. Based on an idea by Curt (*Donovan's Brain*) Siodmak and directed by his brother, Universal's follow-up to *Dracula's Daughter* (1936) features beautifully detailed sets, a good cast of contract players and John P. Fulton's impressive man-into-bat-and-mist transformations. The title is a misnomer — Chaney Jr's moustachioed Count Alucard (spell it backwards) is really Dracula himself, who travels to Louisiana to turn willing Louise Allbritton into his vampire bride. One of the most atmospheric sequences has the Count's coffin rise from the swamp water and magically glide towards the shore where a victim eagerly awaits his embrace. A dark, Gothic fairy tale, which is much better than most forties horror movies.

Sequel: HOUSE OF FRANKENSTEIN (qv; 1944)

THE SPIDER WOMAN STRIKES BACK

USA, 1945. Dir: Arthur Lubin. With: Brenda Joyce, Gale Sondergaard, Kirby Grant, Rondo Hatton, Milburn Stone, Hobart Cavanaugh. Universal. B&W.

The year before, Sondergaard played a woman who used poison to drive her victims to suicide in Universal's Sherlock Holmes adventure *The Spider Woman*. She returns in this shoddy sequel-in-name-only as a totally different character, the evil Zenofia, who uses the blood of her female companions to feed the carnivorous plants in her basement. Real-life acromegalic Rondo Hatton portrays her

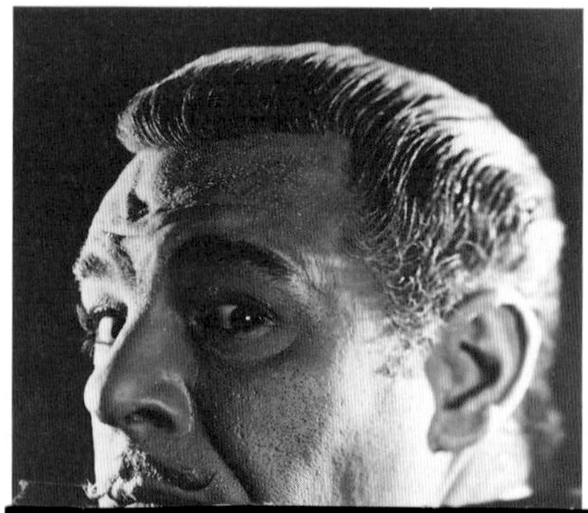

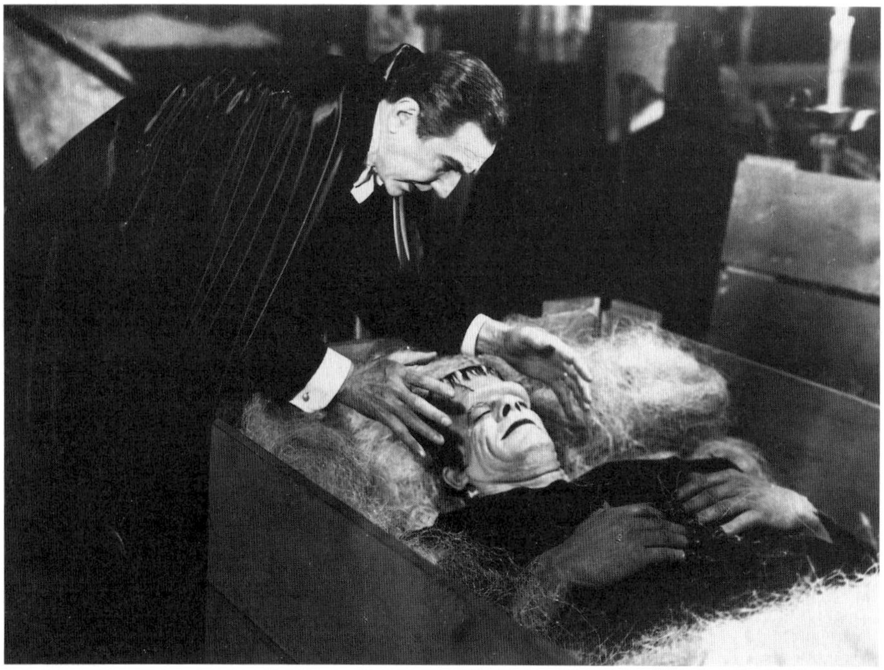

[redacted]

English character actor Abbott plays Web Fallon, an unlikely looking 400 year-old vampire posing as a nightclub owner on the west coast of Africa. When Peggy Stewart discovers his real identity, he tries to burn her to death at the stake. Even with a running time of just under an hour, director Selander (better known for his B-westerns) has trouble making it interesting.

Trowbridge, Earle Hodgins. Republic. B&W.
Despite the title, this low budget vampire movie doesn't actually include any zombies! Ian Keith stars as mad undertaker Ormand Murks, who returns from the dead and needs to drink a formula containing fresh blood to stay alive. He is finally shot to death at the end.

LE VAMPIRE

France, 1945. Dir: Jean Painleve. La Cinegraphic Documentaire. B&W.
Documentary short which includes footage from *Nosferatu* (1922). Music by Duke Ellington.

LES VAMPIRES

France, 1947. Dir: Henri Gruault. With: Boris Vian.
Short film with vampires.

THE VAMPIRE'S GHOST

USA, 1945. Dir: Lesley Selander. With: John Abbott, Charles Gordon, Peggy Stewart, Grant Withers, Adele Mara, Emmett Vogam. Republic. B&W.
Surprisingly faithful reinterpretation of John Polidori's tale 'The Vampyre', co-scripted by science fiction writer Leigh Brackett and based on her original story.

Above left: *The Return of the Vampire. (FJA).*
Right and above right: *Isle of the Dead. (FJA).*

the

With the science fiction boom of the 1950s, American bloodsuckers took on distinctly alien forms in such films as **The Thing from Another World (1951), Not of This Earth (1957), It! The Terror from Beyond Space (1958)** *and* **First Man Into Space (1958).** *More traditional vampires were also given a scientific slant in* **The Vampire (1957)** *and* **Blood of Dracula (1957)**, *or else removed to the entirely incongruous wild west setting of* **Curse of the Undead (1959).** *Even the poor old Count himself was kicked out of Transylvania and transported to suburban southern California in* **The Return of Dracula (1957).**

More than twenty years after **Dracula (1930)**, *Bela Lugosi was still trading on his most famous role in the British comedy* **Mother Riley Meets the Vampire (1952).** *Steadfastly typecast and reduced to appearing in low budget dregs like* **Bela Lugosi Meets a Brooklyn Gorilla (1952)** *and* **Bride of the Monster (1955)**, *the seventy-two year-old actor committed himself to a state hospital in 1955 for drug dependency and died of a heart attack on August 16th the following year while reading a script in bed. In 1957,* **Dracula** *was released to American television as part of Universal's Shock Theater package and prompted a huge revival of interest in the character. The role that had made and destroyed Lugosi's career even haunted him to the grave, and he was buried in his Dracula cape and tuxedo.*

Dracula.

While the American cinema ushered in the atomic age with radioactive mutations and man's conquest of space, south of the border in Mexico they were reinventing Hollywood history with a distinctly Latin American slant. In 1957, Germán Robles starred as vampire Count Lavud in both **The Vampire** *and*

1950s

The Vampire's Coffin, *and he even parodied the role in* **Castle of the Monsters**, *made the same year.*

In Europe they were also rediscovering their Gothic roots, and Riccardo Freda's **The Devil's Commandment (1956)** *set the stage for a burgeoning Italian horror film industry.*

Across the Channel, a small British company had already enjoyed some success adapting the BBC-TV **Quatermass** *serials into two low budget science fiction movies. In 1957, Hammer Films decided the time was right to produce a remake of Mary Shelley's classic novel in colour for the first time.* **The Curse of Frankenstein (1957)** *starred Peter Cushing (b 1913), well-known for his television roles, as the Baron, and a relatively unknown actor named Christopher Lee (b 1922), hidden beneath the gruesome make-up of the creature. It turned out to be the biggest dollar-earner produced by a British studio that year and Hammer quickly looked around for a follow-up. The next obvious subject for remake treatment was the Count.*

Reteaming their star duo of Cushing and Lee, as a dynamic Van Helsing and a demonic Count Dracula respectively, **Dracula (1958)** *proved to be an even bigger box office hit for the studio.*

Vampires were suddenly popular again and the Hammer Age of Horror had begun. It was not long before the floodgates opened...

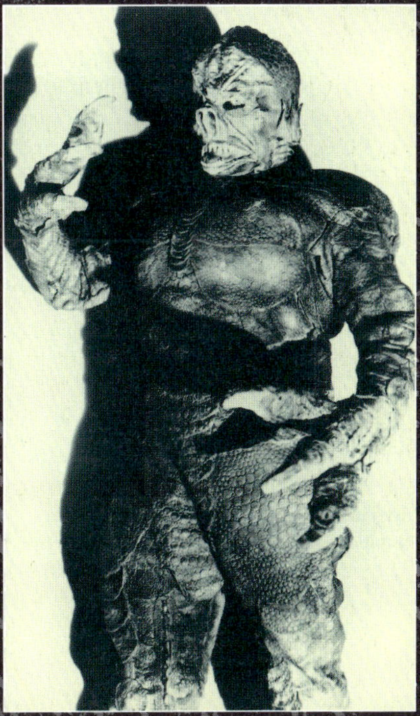

It! The Terror from Beyond Space

ABBOTT AND COSTELLO MEET DR. JEKYLL AND MR. HYDE

USA, 1953. Dir: Charles Lamont. With: Bud Abbott, Lou Costello, Boris Karloff, Craig Stevens, Helen Westcott, Reginald Denny. Universal-International. B&W.

Slapstick version of Robert Louis Stevenson's classic story. Bud and Lou (in the fifth *Abbott and Costello Meet...* movie) play two turn-of-the-century American policemen in London who are called in to help capture a monster which is terrorising the city. Although it doesn't have the polish of earlier Abbott and Costello vehicles, Karloff adds some much-needed class as Dr Jekyll, but stuntman Eddie Parker mostly played Mr Hyde beneath an unconvincing mask. Includes an exciting roof-top chase and a sequence in a wax museum, where two uncredited actors portray Count Dracula and the Frankenstein monster brought to life. Kids will enjoy it, despite originally being given an 'X' certificate by the British Board of Film Censors!

ANAK PONTIANAK

Malaya, 1958. Dir: Ramon Estella. With: Hasimah, Haj Sattar, Dayang Sofia, Jins Sashudin, Kemat bin Hassan. Shaw. B&W.

Sequel to *Sumpah Pontianak* (1958). The son of the vampire turns up in this fourth entry in the popular Pontianak series. Also includes a bodiless creature (a Polong) and a snake devil (a Hnatu).

Sequel: PONTIANAK KEMBALI (qv; 1963)

ATTACK OF THE GIANT LEECHES

(aka THE GIANT LEECHES. UK: DEMONS OF THE SWAMP)
USA, 1959. Dir: Bernard Kowalski. With: Ken Clark, Yvette Vickers, Gene Roth, Jan Shepard, Tyler McVey, Bruno Ve Sota. Balboa/American International Pictures. B&W.

A bunch of swamp dwellers are menaced by intelligent, bloodthirsty giant leeches (obviously divers in unconvincing suits) in this cheapie from executive producer Roger Corman. His brother Gene produced.

BLACK INFERNO

USA, 1956. Dir: Tony (Anthony) Brzezinski. Adventure Film Productions. B&W.

This is a rarity: an amateur Dracula film shot on 8mm by teenager Brzezinski and his fellow students in Riverside, California. It was a sequel to *Curse of Dracula*, made the same year, and Brzezinski followed it with a feature length version of *Dracula*. It's only listed here so that we can run the still from Forry Ackerman's collection. The director ended up making explicit hardcore movies such as *Dr. Sexual and Mr. Hyde* (1971).

BLOOD OF DRACULA

(UK: BLOOD IS MY HERITAGE)
USA, 1957. Dir: Herbert L. Strock. With: Sandra Harrison, Louise Lewis, Gail Ganley, Jerry Blaine, Malcolm Atterbury, Richard Devon.

Left: *Black Inferno. (FJA).*
Below: *Blood of Dracula.*

Carmel/American International Pictures. B&W.
A companion piece to producer Herman Cohen's teenage Frankenstein and werewolf entries (made the same year), this should really have been called *I Was a Teenage Vampire*. Sandra Harrison becomes a vampire when she is hypnotised by an evil teacher at her girls school. She turns into an ugly monster wearing a prerequisite fifties tight sweater. Ignore the title, this has nothing to do with Dracula.

BLOOD OF THE VAMPIRE

UK, 1958. Dir: Henry Cass. With: Donald Wolfit, Barbara Shelley, Vincent Ball, Victor Maddern, William Devlin, Andrew Faulds. Eros Films. Colour.
Gruesome horror movie scripted by Hammer veteran Jimmy Sangster, and probably the best production from the team of Robert S. Baker and Monty Berman (the latter also responsible for the excellent colour photography). Sir Donald Wolfit must have needed the cash to have agreed to play the villainous Dr Callistratus, revived from the dead and experimenting with the blood of the inmates of an insane asylum in order to stay alive. Director Cass, who usually handled Shakespearean plays at the Old Vic, includes plenty of sleazy torture and murder, and Maddern is great as Carl, the doctor's mute hunchbacked assistant.

THE BLOOD SWORD OF THE 99TH VIRGIN

(Orig: KYUJU-KYUHONME NO KIMUSUME)
Japan, 1959. Dir: Morihei Magatani. With: Bunta Namiji Matsuura. Shintoho. B&W.
The inhabitants of a superstitious rural community sacrifice the blood of virgins to appease a local diety. The investigating policeman's daughter is hung upside-down from a tree as the ninety-ninth, and final, victim.

THE BOWERY BOYS MEET THE MONSTERS

USA, 1954. Dir: Edward Bernds. With: Leo Gorcey, Huntz Hall, Bernard Gorcey, Lloyd Corrigan, Ellen Corby, John Dehner, Paul Wexler. Allied Artists. B&W.
The Bowery Boys (who started as the Dead End Kids in the classic 1937 gangster thriller *Dead End* and went on to appear [later as the East Side Kids] in series for Warner Bros, Universal and Monogram) had a number of run-ins with the horror genre, including two meetings with Bela Lugosi. In this B-movie comedy, the boys approach the creepy Gravesend family about using their old dark house as a playground for local kids. Pretty soon Huntz Hall is turned into a werewolf, and they get involved with a gorilla, a robot, a carnivorous plant and even a vampire (Wexler). Like the rest of the series, you have to be a fan.

CASTLE OF THE MONSTERS

(Orig: EL CASTILLO DE LOS MONSTRUOS)
Mexico, 1957. Dir: Julian Soler. With: Clavillazo (Antonio Espino), Evangelina Elizondo, Germán Robles, Carlos Orellana, Guillermo Orea. Producciones Sotomayor. B&W.
Just what we needed, a Mexican version of (Abbott and Costello) *Meet Frankenstein* (1948). Comedians Clavillazo and Elizondo play newly-weds trapped in a castle with a gorilla, a mummy, a werewolf, the Creature from the Black Lagoon, Frentenstein's (*sic*) monster and a vampire. As the latter, Robles parodies his role as Count Lavud from *The Vampire* and *The Vampire's Coffin* (both made the same year).
Remake: FRANKENSTEIN, EL VAMPIRO Y CIA (qv; 1961)

***Above:** Curse of the Undead.*

CURSE OF THE UNDEAD

USA, 1959. Dir: Edward Dein. With: Eric Fleming, Kathleen Crowley, Michael Pate, John Hoyt, Bruce Gordon, Edward Binns. Universal-International. B&W.
A hired gunslinger, Drake Robey (Pate), turns out to be Don Drago Robles, one of the undead in this, the first vampire western. Fleming's Preacher Dan finally kills the black-clad bloodsucker with a bullet containing a fragment of a crucifix. A real curio.

DENDAM PONTIANAK

Malaya, 1957. Dir: B.N. Rao. With: Maria Menado, Puteh Lawak, S.M. Wahid, Mustapha Maarof, Salmah Ahmad, Rahimah Alias. Keris. B&W.
Sequel to the popular *Pontianak* (1957). Menado returns as the vampire, out for revenge.
Sequel: SUMPAH PONTIANAK (qv; 1958)

THE DEVIL'S COMMANDMENT

(Orig: I VAMPIRI. UK: LUST OF THE VAMPIRE)
Italy, 1956. Dir: Riccardo Freda. With: Gianna Maria Canale, Antoine Balpêtré, Paul Muller, Carlo D'Angelo, Wandisa Guida, Dario Michaelis. Titanus/Athena Cinematografica. B&W.

This marked the beginning of the Italian horror film renaissance. Loosely based on the Elizabeth (Erzsebeth) Bathory legend, a mad doctor (Balpêtré) uses the blood of female victims to restore youth to his beloved Countess (Miss Italy finalist Canale). Because of added bath murders and rape scenes, this was originally released as an adults-only feature in America. It was photographed in CinemaScope by Mario Bava, who completed the twelve days filming when the director walked off the production.

DRACULA

(USA: HORROR OF DRACULA)
UK, 1958. Dir: Terence Fisher. With: Peter Cushing, Christopher Lee, Michael Gough, Melissa Stribling, Carol Marsh, Olga Dickie. Hammer Films. Colour.

Following their success with *The Curse of Frankenstein* (1957), Hammer revived another classic horror character with this first colour version of Bram Stoker's novel. Jimmy Sangster's action-packed script is a definite improvement over previous adaptations, helped by lavish sets, stylish direction and — pretty daring for a fifties film — strong sexual and graphic overtones. Cushing gives one of his finest performances as a dynamic Van Helsing and Lee became an instant sex symbol as the demonic Count. Although a little slow in places, the climactic duel remains a masterpiece of modern horror cinema. A Gothic fairy tale.

Sequels: THE BRIDES OF DRACULA (qv; 1960) and DRACULA PRINCE OF DARKNESS (qv; 1965)
Remake: BRAM STOKER'S COUNT DRACULA (qv; 1970)

DRAKULA ISTANBULDA

Turkey, 1953. Dir: Mehmet Muhtar. With: Atif Kaptan, Annie Ball. Demirag. B&W.

The first non-Western adaptation of the story stars Kaptan as the historical Vlad Tepes character. Based on Bram Stoker's novel and *The Impaling Voivode* by Riza Seyfi.

Remake: DRACULA (qv; 1958)

EL FANTASMA DE LA OPERETA

Argentina, 1955. Dir: Enrique Carreras. With: Amelita Vargas, Alfredo Barbieri, Tono Andreu, Gogo Andreu, Inez Fernandez. Belgrano. B&W.

A horror comedy that includes a vampire and a Frankenstein-like monster. Not to be confused with the 1959 Mexican movie with the same title.

FIRST MAN INTO SPACE

UK, 1958. Dir: Robert Day. With: Marshall Thompson, Marla Landi, Bill Edwards, Robert Ayres, Bill Nagy, Carl Jaffe. Metro-Goldwyn-Mayer/Producers Associates. B&W.

Low budget science fiction/horror film that owes quite a lot to the *Quatermass* movies. Bill Edwards plays the first man into space, whose ship passes through a cloud of radioactive meteorite dust. He returns to Earth as an ugly monster craving human blood. Imported American star Thompson is the stuffy hero and only Roger Delgado stands out in a brief comedy cameo. The sets look cheap and most of the 'special effects' are stock footage.

IT! THE TERROR FROM BEYOND SPACE

USA, 1958. Dir: Edward L. Cahn. With: Marshall Thompson, Shawn Smith, Kim Spalding, Ann Doran, Dabbs Greer, Paul Langton. Vogue/ United Artists. B&W.

Filmed under the title *It! The Vampire from Beyond Space*, this very effective low budget science fiction/horror movie was probably the high point of director Cahn's career. Jerome Bixby's tight screenplay later 'inspired' everything from *Queen of Blood* (1966) to *Alien* (1979), although it in turn seems to have been 'inspired' by A.E. van Vogt's story 'The Black Destroyer'. Thompson (who also starred in *First Man Into Space* the same year) has his best role as Captain Carruthers, being returned to Earth by the second Mars mission to stand trial for the murders of his entire crew. What they don't know is that the real killer — a blood-drinking scaly monster (played by Ray 'Crash' Corrigan) — has sneaked aboard and soon begins ripping up the supporting cast. Cahn wisely kept Paul Blaisdell's creature suit in the shadows for most of the movie. A minor classic.

KYUKETSUKI GA

Japan, 1956. Dir: Nobuo Nakagawa. With: Ryo Ikebe, Akio Kobori, Asami Kuji, Kinuko Ito. Shintoho. B&W.

A somewhat odd vampire film, in which the only clues to a series of murders are teeth marks found in the victims' necks and a bloodstained moth. In the end, the killer turns out not to be a vampire. This was the first of nine horror movies directed

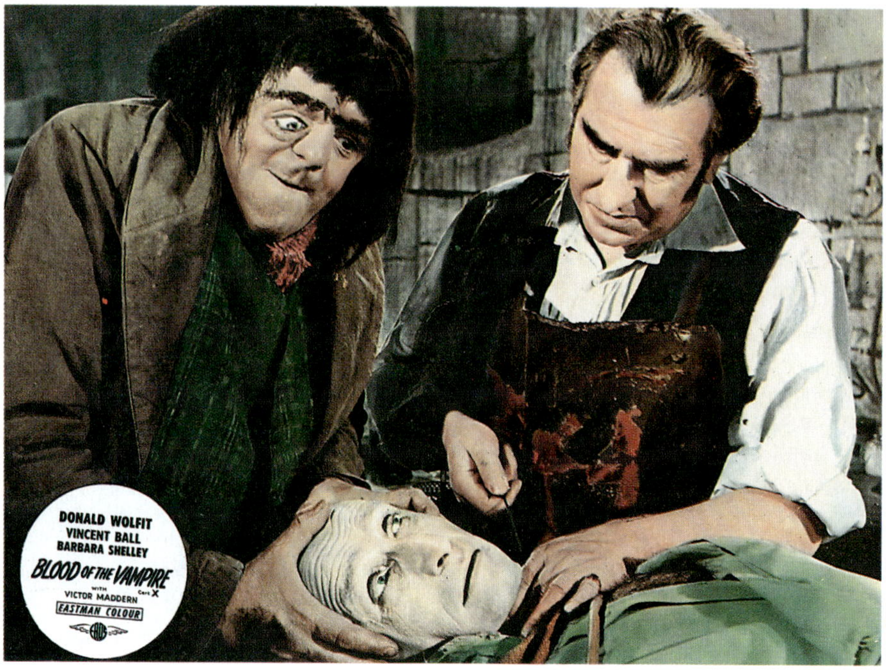

by Nakagawa under the series title *Kaidan Eiga* (ghost story films). Based on the novel by Seishi Yokomizo.

M

USA, 1951. Dir: Joseph Losey. With: David Wayne, Howard Da Silva, Luther Adler, Karen Morley, Steve Brodie, Raymond Burr. Columbia. B&W.

Grim remake of Fritz Lang's 1931 classic from the same producer (Seymour Nebenzal). Wayne portrays a flute-playing child murderer, based on the true-life crimes of the Vampire of Dusseldorf.

Remake: EL VAMPIRO NEGRO (qv; 1953)

MOTHER RILEY MEETS THE VAMPIRE

(USA: MY SON THE VAMPIRE/ VAMPIRE OVER LONDON)

UK, 1952. Dir: John Gilling. With: Arthur Lucan, Bela Lugosi, Dora Bryan, Philip Leaver, Richard Wattis, Graham Moffatt. Renown Pictures. B&W.

The last of Lucan's fourteen Old Mother Riley comedies (this time without partner Kitty McShane) is not quite as awful as expected. Lugosi, looking surprisingly well, was paid only $5,000 to play a mad doctor, Count Von Housen, who thinks he is a vampire (he wears a Dracula cape and sleeps in a coffin). When his prototype robot is delivered by mistake to Irish washerwoman Old Mother Riley, it leads to chaos. Ian Wilson plays Lugosi's maniacal Renfield-like assistant, Hitchcock, and there's a song-and-dance number that includes Hattie Jacques and Dandy Nichols. Moffatt has a brief cameo as a yokel, and Charles Lloyd-Pack and Laurence Naismith also turn up. Released in 1953 in America in a re-edited version, and again in 1963. Yet another version, titled *King Robot*, was never completed.

LA NAVE DE LOS MONSTRUOS

Mexico, 1959. Dir: Rogelio A. Gonzalez. With: Eulalio Gonzalaz Piporro, Ann Bertha Lepe, Lorena Velazquez, Consuelo Frank, Manuel Lopez, Jesus Rodriguez. Producciones Sotomayor/Columbia. B&W.

A science fiction/western/musical/comedy, with cowboy Piporro confronting the

inhabitants of a Venusian spacecraft. These include a vampire woman (Velazquez) who can turn into a giant bat, the sexy Captain (Lepe), and such monstrous specimens as a cyclops, a saucer-man, a hairy dinosaur and Tor the robot. Small kids will probably love it.

NOT OF THIS EARTH

USA, 1957. Dir: Roger Corman. With: Paul Birch, Beverly Garland, Morgan Jones, Jonathan Haze, William Roderick, Richard (Dick) Miller. Allied Artists. B&W.

An alien from the dying planet Davanna arrives on Earth to learn whether human blood can be used to replace that of his own race. Soon, the inhabitants of a small American town are being found murdered, with all the blood drained from their bodies... Roger Corman's low budget science fiction thriller may be short on special effects, but makes up for it with an intelligent script by Charles Griffith and a powerful performance by Paul Birch as the shades-wearing alien, who can destroy minds with his bleached-out eyes. Includes Dick Miller and a flying bat creature created by Paul Blaisdell. A cult classic.

Remake: NOT OF THIS EARTH (qv; 1988)

ONNA KYUKETSUKI

Japan, 1959. Dir: Nobuo Nakagawa. With: Shigeru Amachi, Yoko Mihara, Keinosuke Wada, Junko Ikeuchi. Shintoho. B&W.

Oddball vampire comedy in which the wife of an atomic scientist is kidnapped by one of the undead (Amachi) and imprisoned in his subterranean castle. This vampire can't stand the light of the moon and wields a pair of swords. Also features a dwarf, a witch and a bald wrestler. Nakagawa previously tried his hand at a vampire movie with the equally strange *Kyuketsuki Ga* (1956).

PONTIANAK

Malaya, 1956. Dir: B.N. Rao. With: Maria Menado, M. Amin, Salmah Ahmed, Dollah Serawak, Aminah Yem, N. Kassim. Keris. B&W.

The first of the popular Pontianak series. Menado plays a hunchbacked girl who is made beautiful by magic. But when her husband is bitten by a snake, she sucks his blood to get the poison out and turns into a vampire (Pontianak). She then tries to turn her daughter into one of the undead as well, but is finally destroyed by having a nail driven into her skull.

Sequel: DENDAM PONTIANAK (qv; 1957)

THE RETURN OF DRACULA

(USA: aka CURSE OF DRACULA. UK: THE FANTASTIC DISAPPEARING MAN)

USA, 1957. Dir: Paul Landres. With: Francis Lederer, Norma Eberhardt, Ray Stricklyn, John Wengraf, Jimmie Baird, Norbert Schiller. Gramerly/United Artists. B&W.

Surprisingly effective low budget independent Dracula movie, released just before Hammer's colour remake made the Count a major box office draw again. Lederer is a rather cold vampire, forced out of his Transylvanian resting place, who moves in with an ordinary American family as Count Bellac while preying on the inhabitants of a small Californian town. He is finally impaled on a wooden stake in an old mine shaft (red-tinted in original prints!).

SUMPAH PONTIANAK

Malaya, 1958. With: Maria Menado. Keris. B&W.

The third entry in the popular series, and a follow-up to *Dendam Pontianak* (1957). Menado returns as the cursed vampire, along with various ghosts and monsters.

Sequel: ANAK PONTIANAK (qv; 1958)

UNCLE WAS A VAMPIRE

(Orig: TEMPI DURI PER I VAMPIRI. UK: HARD TIMES FOR VAMPIRES)

Italy, 1959. Dir: Steno (Stefano Vanzina). With: Renato Rascel, Sylvia Koscina, Christopher Lee, Lia Zoppelli, Kay Fisher. Maxima Film/Cei Incom/Montflour Film. Colour.

Following the success of Hammer's *Dracula* (1958), Lee went to Italy to play another vampire in this horror comedy. As Baron Rodrigo, he bites his indebted aristocratic cousin (comedian Rascel imitating Bela Lugosi) who is working as a porter in a castle hotel. In the end, a kiss from the beautiful gardener (Koscina) cures Rascel's vampirism.

Below: *Mother Riley Meets the Vampire. (FJA).*

THE THING FROM ANOTHER WORLD

USA, 1951. Dir: Christian Nyby. With: Margaret Sheridan, Kenneth Tobey, Robert Cornthwaite, Douglas Spencer, James Young, Dewey Martin. RKO Radio Pictures/Winchester. B&W.

Classic science fiction/horror thriller based on John W. Campbell's story 'Who Goes There?' When a crashed flying saucer is discovered beneath the Arctic ice, a research team rescues the frozen alien inhabitant which is unfortunately allowed to thaw out. The original story's shape-changing monster here becomes an eight-foot tall vegetable (played by *Gunsmoke*'s James Arness) which needs human blood to germinate its seeds. The movie develops into a remarkable exercise in prolonged claustrophobic terror, as Tobey and his crewmen track the creature with geiger counters through the corridors of the snowbound camp. Militarism, not science, wins in the end and the final Cold War message is to "Keep watching the skies!" Film editor Nyby received his first director's credit, but the film is heavily influenced by producer Howard Hawks, who prepared the script and 'supervised' the production. Originally titled simply *The Thing*, but changed prior to release because of the novelty song of the same name.

Remake: THE THING (1982)

THE VAMPIRE

(aka THE MARK OF THE VAMPIRE)
USA, 1957. Dir: Paul Landres. With: John Beal, Coleen Gray, Kenneth Tobey, Lydia Reed, Dabbs Greer, Herb Vigran. Gramercy/United Artists. B&W.

From the same team who brought you *The Return of Dracula* (also 1957), this variation on the theme takes a fifties science fiction approach to vampirism. Scientist John Beal swallows some pills derived from vampire bats and turns into a horrible scaly monster. Billed as 'A new kind of horror!' It wasn't.

THE VAMPIRE

(Orig: EL VAMPIRO)
Mexico, 1957. Dir: Fernando Mendez. With: Germán Robles, Ariadna Welter, Abel Salazar, José Luis Jimenez, July Danery (Julio Daneri), Joseph (José) Chavez. Abel Salazar/Cinematografica A.B.S.A./American International. B&W.

About the same time Riccardo Freda was reviving the vampire movie in Italy, Fernando Mendez was doing the same thing south of the border. In this classic Mexican horror movie, Germán Robles stars for the first time as Hungarian Count Karol de Lavud who puts the bite on various supporting players until staked by Dr Enrique (producer Salazar). An inferior American version, with new footage, was prepared by Dick Barker.

Sequel: THE VAMPIRE'S COFFIN (qv; 1957)

Right: *The Thing from Another World.*
Below: *The Return of Dracula.*

THE VAMPIRE'S COFFIN

(Orig: EL ATAUD DEL VAMPIRO)
Mexico, 1957. Dir: Fernando Mendez. With: Abel Salazar, Ariadna Welter, Germán Robles, Yerye Beirute, Alicia Montoya, Guillermo Orea. Cinematografica A.B.S.A./American International. B&W

Director Mendez made this sequel to his own *The Vampire* (1957) just six months after the original, using the same cast and crew. Robles returns as the suave Count Karol de Lavud when the stake piercing his heart is removed by a body snatcher. It's then up to producer/hero/comedy relief Salazar as Dr Enrique to hunt the vampire down in his waxworks lair, finally spearing the Count while he has transformed into a bat. Much of the plot is chaotic, but Robles makes an impressive vampire and the scenes of Lavud's shadow(!) stalking a victim through the nighttime streets are heightened by imaginative lighting effects.

EL VAMPIRO NEGRO

Argentina, 1953. Dir: Roman Vinoly Barreto. With: Olga Zubarry, Roberto Escalada, Nathan Pinzon, Nelly Panizza, George Rivier, Pascual Pelliciotta. Sono Film. B&W.

Thriller inspired by the true case of the Vampire of Dusseldorf, also the basis for, amongst others, Fritz Lang's classic *M* (1931).

Remake: LE VAMPIRE DE DUSSELDORF (qv; 1964)

the

having initiated the third great horror cycle with its colour remakes of the classics during the late 1950s, Hammer Films was quick to exploit its growing reputation as Britain's 'House of Horror'. Peter Cushing was back as Van Helsing to battle the Count's disciples in **The Brides of Dracula (1960)***, and the studio expanded the mythology with* **The Kiss of the Vampire (1962).** *Christopher Lee finally relented in 1965 and returned as the eponymous* **Dracula Prince of Darkness***, donning cape and fangs again for* **Dracula Has Risen from the Grave (1968***, the year Hammer won the Queen's Award to Industry) and* **Taste the Blood of Dracula (1969).**

Lee was also not adverse to playing other vampires in such movies as **Uncle Was a Vampire (1959), Hercules in the Haunted World (1961), Theatre of Death (1966), The Blood Demon (1967)** *and* **The Magic Christian (1969).** *He also turned up in* **Crypt of Horror (1963)***, an adaptation of J. Sheridan Le Fanu's 'Carmilla', which had been previously filmed as* **Blood and Roses** *by Roger Vadim in 1960.*

Hammer was soon joined in its revival of the horror film by Amicus Productions in Britain, with their series of episodic horror anthologies, and American International Pictures in America, whose adaptations of Edgar Allan Poe regularly combined the talents of director Roger Corman and star Vincent Price.

In Italy, such highly stylistic directors as Mario Bava **(Black Sunday [1960], Black Sabbath [1963], Planet of the Vampires**

19 [redacted]

[1965]), *Antonio Margheriti* (**Castle of Blood [1964]**) *and Riccardo Freda* (**The Horrible Dr. Hichcock [1962]**) *were giving their own dark twists to the vampire legend, while in Mexico they were content to churn out the adventures of a vampiric Nostradamus or pit silver-masked wrestler Santo against a variety of undead opponents.*

Shakespearean actor John Carradine (Richmond Reed Carradine, 1906-1988), who had been appearing in movies of dubious quality since the 1940s, returned to playing a top-hatted

Dracula Has Risen from the Grave.

Count in the imaginatively titled **Billy the Kid versus Dracula (1965)**, *as well as turning up as an evil butler in* **Blood of Dracula's Castle (1967)** *and a vampire leader in the Mexican-made* **Las Vampiras (1968)**.

It wasn't long before the genre was spoofing itself with such titles as **The Horror of it All (1963)**, **Munster, Go Home! (1966)** *and* **Carry On Screaming (1966)**, *while Roman Polanski's dark comedy* **Dance of the Vampires (1967)** *topped them all with its inspired homage to both the undead and Hammer Films.*

As the decade of Peace and Love came to an end, the vampire had never been so popular. But the sexual revolution was just beginning...

[redacted]

AHKEA KHOTS

South Korea, 1961. Dir: Yongmin Lee. With: Yechoon Lee, Chimi Kim. Sunglim Film. B&W.

Yechoon Lee is the vampiric 'Bad Flower' of the title in this South Korean imitation of Hammer's *Dracula* (1958).

ANNABEL LEE

USA, 1969. Dir: Ron Morante. Narrator: Vincent Price. Warner Bros. Colour.

Ten minute short based on the Edgar Allan Poe poem, about a dead woman calling her lover back to the grave. Director Morante uses retouched photographs to tell the story, aided by Price's eerily effective narration.

ATOM AGE VAMPIRE

(Orig: SEDDOK, L'EREDE DI SATANA. UK: SEDDOK)

Italy, 1960. Dir: Richard McNamara (Anton Giulio Majano). With: Susanne Loret, Albert (Alberto) Lupo, Sergio Fantoni, Franca Parisi Strahl, Ivo Garrani, Andrea Scotti. Topaz/Lion's Film. B&W.

Despite the title, this is not really a vampire movie but an imitation of Georges Franju's classic *Eyes Without a Face* (1959). When a professor (Lupo) restores the horribly scarred face of car accident victim Loret, he falls in love with her and is forced to kill women for their glands to keep her alive. The doctor also periodically transforms himself into a scaly-faced monster. Most reference books erroneously credit Mario Bava as producer.

EL BARON BRAKOLA

(aka SANTO CONTRA EL BARON BRAKOLA)

Mexico, 1965. Dir: José Diaz Morales. With: Santo (Rodolfo Guzman Huerta), Mercedes Carreno, Antonio de Hud, Susana Robles, Fernando Oses, Ana Martin. Filmica Vergara/Columbia. B&W

Santo the Mexican wrestler, also known as El Enmascarado de Plata (The Man in the Silver Mask), battles the Dracula-like Baron Brakola and his vampire brides.

BATMAN DRACULA

USA, 1964. Dir: Andy Warhol. With: Jack Smith, Baby Jane Holzer. Film-maker's Cooperative. B&W.

Smith portrays the Count in this two hour underground film.

BATMAN FIGHTS DRACULA

Philippines, 1967. Dir: Leody M. Diaz. With: Jing Abalos, Dante Rivero, Vivian Lorrain, Ramon D'Salva. Lea/Fidelis. Colour.

The title says it all: Batman (Abalos) fights Dracula (Rivero).

BILLY THE KID VERSUS DRACULA

USA, 1965. Dir: William Beaudine. With: John Carradine, Chuck Courtney, Melinda Plowman, Virginia Christine, Walter Janowitz, Bing Russell. Embassy Pictures/ Circle. Colour.

Classic grade-Z horror/western has Carradine recreating his Dracula role in

Below: El Baron Brakola. (FJA).

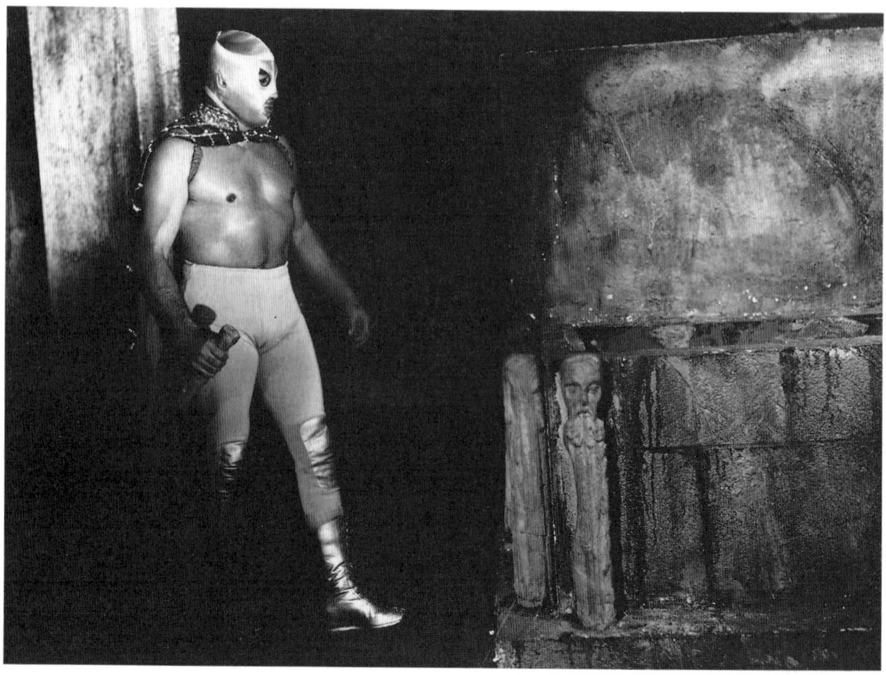

BLACK SUNDAY

(Orig: LA MASCHERA DEL DEMONIO. UK: REVENGE OF THE VAMPIRE/ THE MASK OF SATAN)
Italy, 1960. Dir: Mario Bava. With: Barbara Steel (Steele), John Richardson, Andrea Checchi, Ivo Garrani, Arturo Dominici, Enrico Olivieri. Galatea/Jolly. B&W.

Based on Nikolai Gogol's story 'The Vij'. English actress Barbara Steele became a cult star in the dual roles of heroine Katia and Princess Asa, the latter a seventeenth century witch accidently released from her tomb by a drop of blood. With the aid of her vampire helper (Dominici), she plans to replace Katia, who is her exact double. Atmospherically photographed by co-writer/director Bava, it begins with a great scene in which a spiked mask is hammered onto Steele's face. The American version replaced Roberto Nicolosi's moody score with an inferior one by Les Baxter. It was banned in Britain until 1968, when it was finally released in a cut version.

Remake: LA MASCHERA DEL DEMONIO (qv; 1990)

the movies for the first time since *House of Dracula* (1945). Actually, it's better than expected. Veteran director William ('one-shot') Beaudine (making his penultimate film) does his best with a weak script, using clever lighting effects to add extra menace to sixty year-old Carradine's smooth-talking, top-hatted vampire (who happily walks around in broad daylight!). The Count poses as the uncle of ranch owner Betty (Plowman) until dispatched by her foreman (Courtney), who turns out to be reformed outlaw Billy the Kid. Although the production values are bottom-of-the-barrel (including a particularly fake-looking bat), this is worth watching for the star's remarkable, over-the-top performance and such old time western performers as Virginia Christine, Roy Barcroft and Harry Carey Jr.

BLACK SABBATH

(Orig: I TRE VOLTI DELLA PAURA)
Italy/USA, 1963. Dir: Mario Bava. With: Boris Karloff, Mark Damon, Michele Mercier, Jacqueline Pierreux, Lidia Alfonsi, Susy Andersen. Emmepi Galatea/Lyre/ American International. Colour.

Originally called *The Three Faces of Fear*, AIP changed the title to cash-in on the success of their earlier Bava release, *Black Sunday* (1960). They also cut four minutes, changed the order of the episodes, and added a jokey Les Baxter score and scenes of Karloff linking the three stories in his best *Thriller* manner. 'The Drop of Water' by Anton Chekhov is an effective tale of a murderous ghost, while 'The Telephone' by 'F.G. Snyder' is a confusing story about a man returning from the dead for revenge. However, it is the last episode — based on 'The Wurdalak' by Alexei Tolstoy — which is the real winner. Karloff is marvellously evil as Gorca, a Balkan hunter, who becomes a curly-haired vampire (a Wurdalak) forced to drink the blood of those he loves most. Worth catching for the final story alone.

BLOOD AND ROSES

(Orig: ET MOURIR DE PLAISIR)
France/Italy, 1960. Dir: Roger Vadim. With: Mel Ferrer, Elsa Martinelli, Annette Vadim (Stroyberg), Marc Allegret, Alberto Bonucci, R.J. Chauffard. Paramount/Les Films EGE

Above right: *Blood and Roses. (FJA).*
Below right: *Black Sunday.*

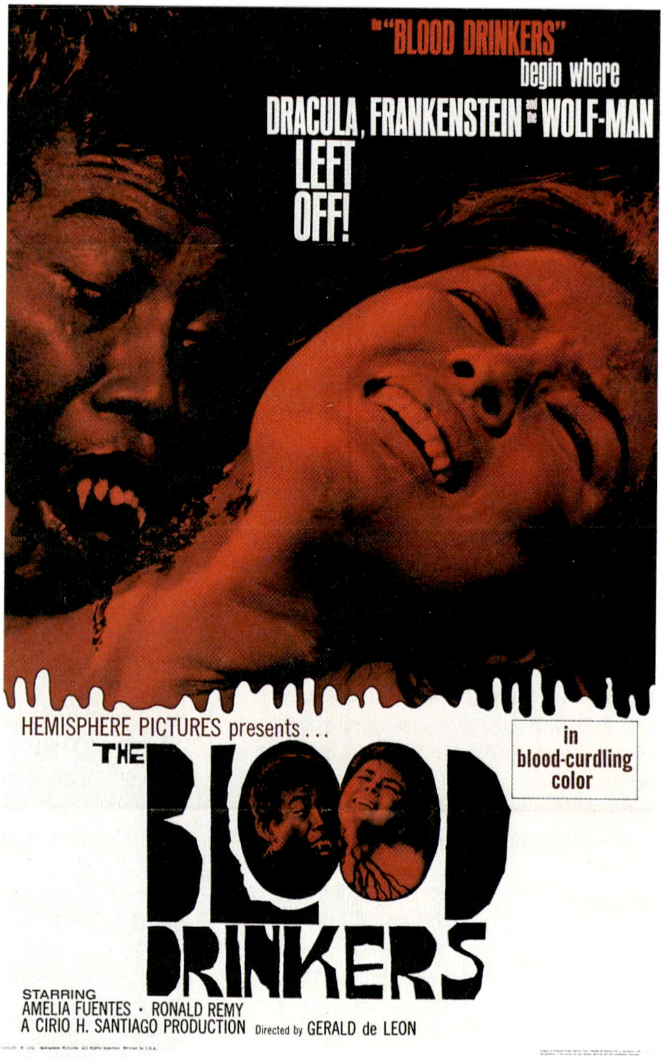

Documento. Colour/B&W.
Fairly bloodless version of 'Carmilla' by J. Sheridan Le Fanu (Le Vanu [*sic*] in the credits!). Stroyberg (then married to co-writer/director Vadim) stars as Carmilla, who is obsessed with her vampire ancestor Mircalla. At a masked ball, she seduces and bites her cousin's fiancée, Georgia (Martinelli). Contains some wonderfully bizarre black and white dream sequences, but the American version removed most of the lesbian subtext from this slow-moving horror movie.
Remake: CRYPT OF HORROR (qv; 1963)

BLOOD BATH

(aka TRACK OF THE VAMPIRE)
USA, 1966. Dir: Jack Hill and Stephanie Rothman. With: William Campbell, Marissa Mathes, Linda (Lori) Saunders, Sandra Knight, Carl Schanzer, Biff Elliot. American International Pictures. B&W.
Filmed in atmospheric Venice, California. Campbell plays macabre artist Antonio Sordi, possessed by a fifteenth century vampire ancestor who paints his victims and then dunks them in a vat of boiling wax. In the end, the wax-coated corpses come back to life and kill him. Roger Corman fired writer/producer Jack Hill and replaced him with Stephanie Rothman, who was given all Hill's footage (including that from a Yugoslavian film, *Operacija Ticijan* [1962]) and told to shoot new material with Sandra Knight. The result is a hallucinatory, impressionistic horror film which is a perfect companion piece to Corman's beatnik classic *A Bucket of Blood* (1959). Includes AIP regulars Jonathan Haze and Sid Haig, and scenes of a wax-covered Patrick Magee (uncredited) from the Yugoslavian footage (finally released as *Portrait in Terror* in 1965). *Star Wars* (1977) producer Gary Kurtz recorded the sound.

THE BLOOD BEAST TERROR

(USA: aka THE VAMPIRE BEAST CRAVES BLOOD)
UK, 1967. Dir: Vernon Sewell. With: Peter Cushing, Robert Flemyng, Wanda Ventham, Roy Hudd, Vanessa Howard, David Griffin. Tigon British. Colour.
Cushing stars in the thankless role of a nineteenth century police inspector investigating a series of bizarre deaths. It turns out that scientist Flemyng has created a giant blood-sucking moth that seduces its prey in the guise of a beautiful woman (Ventham)! Basil Rathbone was originally signed to play the mad doctor, but died before filming began. British comedian Roy Hudd livens things up as a mortuary attendant, but Sewell's direction is, at best, workmanlike. Apparently, Cushing considers it his worst film.

THE BLOOD DEMON

(Orig: DIE SCHLANGENGRUBE UND DAS PENDEL. USA: aka THE TORTURE CHAMBER OF DR. SADISM/CASTLE OF THE WALKING

DEAD)
West Germany, 1967. Dir: Harold Reinl. With: Christopher Lee, Lex Barker, Karin Dor, Carl Lange, Vladimir Medar, Christiane Ruecker. Constantin Film/New Realm. Colour.
Supposedly based on Edgar Allan Poe's 'The Pit and the Pendulum', Lee stars as the evil Count Regular who has been dismembered for killing twelve virgins. Now he's been resurrected and is ready to claim his thirteenth victim and become immortal. Lee walks through his role as the undead Count, but ex-Tarzan Barker makes a solid hero. The period setting is enhanced by striking colour photography and imaginative production design, but the weak script lets the side down.

THE BLOOD DRINKERS

(USA: aka VAMPIRE PEOPLE)
Philippines/USA, 1966. Dir: Gerardo de Leon. With: Amelia Fuentes, Ronald Remy, Eddie Fernandez, Eva Montez, Celia Rodriguez, Paquito Salcedo. Cirio H. Santiago Productions/Hemisphere Pictures. Colour.
When he discovers the girl he loves is dying, bald-headed vampire Marco (Remy) pursues her twin sister so that he can transplant her heart. The undead aristocrat is aided by a sexy assistant (Montez), a hunchbacked dwarf and a trained bat. Fuentes plays the twins and also turned up as a vampire in the same director's *Creatures of Evil* four years later. This is an odd mixture of real colour and tinted black and white footage.

THE BLOODLESS VAMPIRE

Philippines/USA, 1965. Dir: Michael du Pont. With: Charles Macauley, Helen Thompson. Journey.
There is some doubt that this Filipino vampire movie was ever released. Macauley later played Dracula in *Blacula* (1972).

BLOOD OF DRACULA'S CASTLE

USA, 1967 (1969). Dir: Al Adamson (and Jean Hewitt). With: John Carradine, Paula Raymond, Alex D'Arcy, Robert Dix, Gene O'Shane, Barbara Bishop. Paragon Pictures/Crown International. Colour.
Probably one of producer/director Adamson's better low budget efforts (which isn't saying much!). At least the script makes some sense, and the cast actually give performances for a change. This could be because Jean Hewitt helped (uncredited) with the direction and Laszlo Kovacs handled the photography. Shot on the Charles Manson ranch, veterans D'Arcy and Raymond play the Count and Countess Townsend (in fact, Dracula), who keep a stock of half-naked girls chained up in their desert castle for nourishment. George the butler (a slyly humorous performance by Carradine) sacrifices them now and then to the great god Luna. Add Dix as a psychopathic friend of the family, Mango the hulking hunchback (Ray Young) and director John Cardos in there somewhere, and you have a trash classic. Apparently Jayne Mansfield was originally set to star in the Raymond role, while a proposed sequel, *Dracula's Coffin*, was never made.

THE BLOOD OF NOSTRADAMUS

(Orig: LA SANGRE DE NOSTRADAMUS)
Mexico, 1960. Dir: Frederick (Frederico) Curiel. With: Germán Robles, Julio Aleman, Domingo Soler, Aurora Alvarado, Manver (Manuel Vergara), Manuel Casanueva. Estudios America/American International. B&W.
A sequel to *The Genii of Darkness* (1960), and the last of four features cut down from a twelve part Mexican serial and released directly to television in America. Robles stars as the bearded vampire descendant of the sixteenth century prophet Nostradamus. He is pursued by Professor Duran (Soler) and the police, who are armed with silver bullets, and in the end he is staked after causing a total eclipse of the moon! Includes the episodes 'El Aparecido en el Convento', 'El Ave Negra' and 'La Ultima Victima'.

BLOOD SUCKERS

(Orig: LA ISLA DE LA MUERTE/DAS GEBHEIMNIS DER TODENINSEL. USA: ISLAND OF THE DOOMED/MAN EATER OF HYDRA/ISLAND OF DEATH)
Spain/West Germany, 1966. Dir: Mel Welles (Ernst von Theumer). With: Cameron Mitchell, Kay (Kai) Fisher, Elisa Montes, George (Jorges) Martin, Matilde (Muñoz) Sampedro, Ralph (Rolf von) Naukoff. Orbita/Tefi/Allied Artists. Colour.
Mitchell stars as insane botanist Baron Von Weser, who feeds guests on his island retreat to a vampire tree he has created. The blood-soaked finale has the hero (Martin) using an axe to hack away at the tree's pulsating tentacles as the Baron is destroyed by his own creation. The director played Gravis Mushnik in Roger Corman's *The Little Shop of Horrors* (1960).

BLOOD THIRST

Philippines/USA, 1965 (1971). Dir: N. (Newt) Arnold. With: Robert Winston (Adam Roarke), Yvonne

Nielson, Judy Dennis, Vic Diaz, Katherine Henryk, Eddie Infante. Chevron/Paragon/Journey. B&W.
Filmed under the title *The Horror from Beyond*. Wise-cracking hero Winston plays an American detective who uncovers a cult of blood-drinking sun worshippers led by an ageless vampire priestess and her monstrous servant. In the end, the vampire is burned to death and reverts to her centuries-old self.

THE BLOODY VAMPIRE

(Orig: EL VAMPIRO SANGRIENTO/ EL CONDE FRANKENHAUSEN) Mexico, 1962. Dir: Michael Morata (Miguel Morayta). With: Carlos Agosti, Begona Palacios, Erna Martha Bauman, Raul Farell, Bertha Moss, Antonio Raxel. Tele Talia Films/Clasa-Mohme/American International Pictures. B&W.
The sequel to Morayta's *The Invasion of the Vampires* (1961), filmed back-to-back with *Samson vs. the Vampire Women*. Count Cagliostro, a Mexican vampire hunter, uses his daughter to gain entrance to the home of the undead Count Frankenhausen (Agosti, repeating his role from the previous film).

LA BONNE DAME

France, 1966. Dir: Pierre Philippe. With: Valeska Gert, Constantin Nepo. S.O.F.A.C.
Twenty-five minute short featuring vampires. Narrated by Germaine Kerjean.

THE BRIDES OF DRACULA

UK, 1960. Dir: Terence Fisher. With: Peter Cushing, Yvonne Monlaur, Freda Jackson, David Peel, Martita Hunt, Andree Melly. Hammer Films. Colour.
Despite the title, Christopher Lee didn't want to repeat his role as the Count from *Dracula* (1958), so three scriptwriters (including Jimmy Sangster) cobbled together this atmospheric sequel which once again stars Cushing as Van Helsing. The opening narrative explains that, although Dracula is dead, his disciples live on. When a naïve French schoolteacher (Monlaur) releases the Baron Meinster (Peel) from his mother's chains, little does she realise that she has set free a vampire to prey upon a nearby school for girls. Director Fisher gives the film a fairy tale quality, and the best scenes include Van Helsing burning a vampire's bite from his neck; the mad Greta (Jackson) crawling over the grave of a recent victim, willing the new vampire to rise from the dead; and a great climax where a burning mill forms the shadow of a cross.

BRING ME THE VAMPIRE

(Orig: ECHENME AL VAMPIRO) Mexico, 1961. Dir: Alfredo E. Crevenna. With: Maria Eugenia San Martin, Hector Godoy, Mantequilla (Fernando Soto), Borolas (Joaquin Garcia Vargas), (Alfonso) Pompin Iglesias, José Jasso. Prouciones Rosas Priego/Clasa-Mohme. B&W.
Old dark house comedy in three episodes. A group of misfits have to stay in the Black Castle for a month so that they can inherit a possible fortune. Includes a mad killer, disappearing bodies and a fake vampire (Mantequilla). The non-vampire sequel explained everything away with a happy ending.
Sequel: LA CASA DE LOS ESPANTOS (1961)

CARRY ON SCREAMING

UK, 1966. Dir: Gerald Thomas. With: Harry H. Corbett, Kenneth Williams, Jim Dale, Charles Hawtrey, Fenella Fielding, Joan Sims. Anglo Amalgamated. Colour.
The vampish Valeria (Fielding) and her reanimated brother Dr Watt (Williams) are using their monster Odbodd to kidnap

Above right: *The Blood Beast Terror.*
Below right: *Blood of Dracula's Castle.*

nubile young girls so they can petrify them (literally!) into show window manikins. This was the twelfth in the long-running British comedy series, and one of the best.

CASTLE OF BLOOD

(Orig: LA DANZA MACABRA. UK: CASTLE OF TERROR)
Italy/France, 1964. Dir: Anthony M. Dawson (Antonio Margheriti) and Gordon Wilson Jr (Sergio Corbucci). With: Barbara Steele, George Rivière, Margrete Robsahn, Henry Kruger, Montgomery Gleen, Sylvia Sorent. Vulsinia/Jolly/Leo Lax/ Ulysee. B&W.

Writer Rivière is bet by Edgar Allan Poe and Lord Blackwood that he can't spend the night in a haunted castle on All Souls' Eve. He accepts the wager and discovers that everyone who died there re-enacts their murder, including beautiful bloodthirsty ghost Elizabeth Blackwood (Steele). One of the better Italian supernatural movies, with Steele in some minor lesbian scenes. Director Margheriti liked it so much he remade it in colour six years later. Supposedly based on Poe's 'Dance Macabre'!

Remake: WEB OF THE SPIDER (qv; 1970)

CAVE OF THE LIVING DEAD

(Orig: DER FLUCH DER GRUENEN AUGEN)
West Germany/Yugoslavia, 1964. Dir: Akos Von Ratony. With: Adrian Hoven, Karin Field, Carl Moehner, Erika Remberg, Wolfgang Preiss, Emmerich Schrenck. Objektiv/Triglav. B&W.

Executive produced by Richard Gordon. Interpol Inspector Doren (Hoven) and a witch discover that vampire Professor Adelsberg (Preiss) and his secretary (Field) are transforming missing girls into the living dead in a secret cave beneath an old castle. In the end, the vampire turns into a skeleton and explodes.

CHAPPAQUA

USA, 1966. Dir: Conrad Rooks. With: Jean-Louis Barrault, Conrad Rooks, William S. Burroughs, Allen Ginsberg, Ravi Shankar, Ornette Coleman. Conrad Rooks Productions. B&W/Colour.

1960s psychedelica from writer, producer and director Rooks. He also plays a Lugosi-voiced Dracula who bites a woman's neck and hangs around in a coffin. Music by Ravi Shankar.

Above: The Bloody Vampire. (FJA).

CHARRO DE LAS CALAVERAS

Mexico, 1965. Dir: Alfredo Salazar. With: Dagoberto Rodriguez, David Silva, Alicia Caro, Pascual Garcia Pena, Laura Montez, Rosario F. Montez. Columbia. B&W.

In three episodes, a masked rider battles a werewolf ('La Lobo Humano'), a vampire ('El Vampiro Humano') and a headless horseman ('El Jinete Sin Cabeza').

CREATURE OF THE WALKING DEAD

(Orig: LA MARCA DEL MUERTO)
Mexico/USA, 1960/65. Dir: Frederick Corte (Fernando Cortes). With: Rock Madison, Ann Wells, Willard Gross, George Todd, Bruno Ve Sota, Katherine Victor. Alameda Films/ADP. B&W.

Cheapo producer Jerry Warren added new footage (by Richard Wallace) for the American release of this Mexican horror film. A scientist (Fernando Casanova) revives his dead grandfather, Dr Malthus (also Casanova), only to discover that the living corpse kills for the blood it needs to survive. Like Warren's other abominations, this is a mess. The original Mexican cast included Sonia Furio, Pedro de Auguillon, Aurora Alvarado, Rosa Maria Gallardo and Hortensia Santoveña.

CRYPT OF HORROR

(Orig: LA CRIPTA E L'INCUBO/LA MALDICION DE LOS KARNSTEIN. USA: TERROR IN THE CRYPT)
Italy/Spain, 1963. Dir: Thomas Miller (Camillo Mastrocinque). With: Christopher Lee, Audrey Amber (Adriana Ambessi), Ursula Davis (Pier Ana Quaglia), José Campos, Nela Conjiu, Vera Valmont. MEC Cinematografica/Hispamer Films/American International Pictures. B&W.

An uncredited reworking of J. Sheridan Le Fanu's 'Carmilla', with Lee as Count Ludwig Karnstein. Karnstein believes that his daughter Laura (Amber) is the reincarnation of the dead witch Sheena, who is murdering members of his cursed family. In fact, her friend Lyuba (Davis) is revealed as the vampiric killer. Despite all the usual genre trappings, director Mastrocinque lacks the style of Bava and Freda, and any attempt at eroticism is lost in the muddled script.

Remake: THE VAMPIRE LOVERS (qv; 1970)

THE CURSE OF NOSTRADAMUS

(Orig: LA MALDICION DE NOSTRADAMUS)
Mexico, 1960. Dir: Frederick (Frederico) Curiel. With: Germán Robles, Julio Aleman, Domingo Soler, Aurora Alvarado, Manver (Manuel Vergara), Manuel Casanueva. Estudios America/ American International. B&W.

In 1959, Robles starred in a twelve part

serial (each episode running twenty-five minutes) which was re-edited into four features and released by American International directly to television in the US. In this first one, Robles plays the bearded vampire descendant of the sixteenth century prophet Nostradamus. He kills two colleagues of Professor Duran (Soler) and kidnaps the professor's daughter (Alvarado) before escaping through a maze of underground tunnels. There's even a hunchbacked assistant. Like most Mexican features of this period, it comprises of three episodes ('El Dedo del Destino', 'El Libro de los Siglos' and 'Las Victimas de la Noche') because many independent filmmakers were restricted by the unions from producing full-length movies.

Sequel: THE MONSTERS DEMOLISHER (qv; 1960)

THE CURSE OF THE CRYING WOMAN

(Orig: LA MALDICION DE LA LLORONA)

Mexico, 1961 (1963). Dir: Rafael Baledon. With: Rosita Arenas, Abel Salazar, Rita Macedo, Carlos Lopez Moctezuma, Enrique Lucero, Mario Sevilla. Cinematografica ABSA/ Clasa-Mohme/American International. B&W.

The third film based on the Mexican legend about a ghostly wailing mother, la Llorona. Macedo plays a vampiric woman who, along with her horribly scarred homicidal husband (Lucero), attempts to revive the mummified corpse of the crying woman. Arenas and producer Salazar encounter ghosts and hypnosis before they escape. A flashback sequence (in negative) includes clips from Salazar's *The Witch's Mirror* (1960), which also starred Arenas.

DANCE OF THE VAMPIRES

(USA: THE FEARLESS VAMPIRE KILLERS OR: PARDON ME, BUT YOUR TEETH ARE IN MY NECK)

UK, 1967. Dir: Roman Polanski. With: Jack MacGowran, Roman Polanski, Sharon Tate, Alfie Bass, Ferdy (Ferdinand) Mayne, Jessie Robbins. Metro-Goldwyn-Mayer. Colour.

Often very amusing, but strangely downbeat horror comedy, co-scripted, starring and directed by Polanski. Fearless vampire killers Professor Abronsius (MacGowran) and his faithful assistant Alfred (Polanksi) travel to Transylvania to stay in the castle of the sinister Count Von Krolock (Mayne), who they suspect is a vampire terrorising the local villagers. The dance of the title is a marvellously macabre setpiece. In America, the film was cut by at least ten minutes, re-edited, re-dubbed and released with a new animated title sequence. Polanski asked for his name to be removed from the credits. It features a Jewish vampire (Bass), a gay vampire (Iain Quarrier) and Polanski's murdered wife, Sharon Tate.

THE DEVIL'S MISTRESS

USA, 1966. Dir: Orville Wanzer. With: Arthur Resley, Joan Stapleton, Forrest Westmoreland, Douglas Warren, Oren Williams, Robert Gregory. Emerson/Holiday/ WGW. Colour.

Low budget western about an Indian half-caste who sucks the life out of the four outlaws who killed her husband.

DEVILS OF DARKNESS

UK, 1964. Dir: Lance Comfort. With: William Sylvester, Hubert Noel, Carole Gray, Tracy Reed, Diana Decker, Rona Anderson. Planet Films. Colour.

Contemporary vampire thriller set in modern day France. When a young British holidaymaker is killed during a holiday in a Breton village on All Souls' Eve, his two companions and American Paul Baxter (Sylvester) investigate the mysterious death. Noel plays Count Sinistre, the leader of a local vampire cult. A dull plot, abrupt ending and complete lack of chills make this one to miss.

DOES DRACULA REALLY SUCK?

(aka DRACULA SUCKS/DRACULA AND THE BOYS)

USA, 1969. Colour.

Hardcore gay vampires.

DRACULA

USA, 1964. Dir: Andy Warhol. With: Naomi Levine. Film-maker's Cooperative.

Underground film directed by cult favourite Warhol.

DRACULA HAS RISEN FROM THE GRAVE

UK, 1968. Dir: Freddie Francis. With: Christopher Lee, Rupert Davies, Veronica Carlson, Barbara Ewing, Barry Andrews, Ewan Hooper, Michael Ripper. Hammer

Left: *Dance of the Vampires.*

Films. Colour.
The third entry in Hammer's Dracula series and a direct sequel to *Dracula Prince of Darkness* (1965). The overtly religious script by John Elder (Anthony Hinds) has Lee's demonic-looking Count acting as a catalyst when he commands a weak-willed priest and other humans to take revenge on Davies' Monsignor, who has exorcised Dracula's castle. Director Francis wisely keeps the Count in the background and concentrates on the violence and sexuality of the myth. Includes a memorable sequence in which Dracula rips a wooden stake from his bleeding chest when the hero can't finish the required prayer because he's an atheist!
Sequel: TASTE THE BLOOD OF DRACULA (qv; 1969)

DRACULA MEETS THE OUTER SPACE CHICKS

USA, 1968.
Low budget, softcore vampires.

DRACULA PRINCE OF DARKNESS

UK, 1965. Dir: Terence Fisher. With: Christopher Lee, Barbara Shelley, Andrew Keir, Francis Matthews, Suzan Farmer, Charles Tingwell, Thorley Walters. Hammer Films. Colour.
It took seven years before Hammer made a direct sequel to their box office hit *Dracula* (the movie begins with a reprise of the closing minutes of the 1958 film), and this became one of the top fifteen releases of 1966. John Sansom's script is not particularly original (on a visit to the Carpathian mountains a group of travellers are forced to spend the night in an eerie castle) and it is left to director Fisher to build the tension slowly (Dracula isn't resurrected until about a third of the way into the film). Once his body has been reconstituted from the blood of a sacrificial victim, Lee doesn't have any dialogue as the Count, but imbues the character with a powerful sense of evil. Cushing's presence as Van Helsing is sorely missed, but Keir gives strong support as the larger-than-life vampire-hunting monk, Father Sandor, and Barbara Shelley makes a demonic creature of the night. Filmed back-to-back with *Rasputin the Mad Monk*, using many of the same sets and cast members.
Sequel: DRACULA HAS RISEN FROM THE GRAVE (qv; 1968)

Above: The Blood Demon.

DRACULA'S WEDDING DAY

USA, 1967. Dir: Mike Jacobson. B&W.
Underground film, tinted purple, in which Dracula leads a girl into a cave at sunset.

DRACULA (THE DIRTY OLD MAN)

USA, 1969. Dir: William Edwards. With: Vince Kelly, Ann Hills, Bunny Boyd, Adarinne, Bill Whitton, Libby Caculus. Whit Boyd Productions. Colour.
Produced, written and directed by Edwards, this softcore sex comedy has Count Alucard (Kelly), with the aid of his werewolf/jackal man assistant Dr Irving Jekyll (Whitton), kidnapping naked virgins and fulfilling his sexual desires in an abandoned mine. Originally shot as a straight horror movie, this was redubbed into a comedy. It's still pretty terrible.

DRACULA VS. FRANKENSTEIN

(Orig: EL HOMBRE QUE VINO DEL UMMO/DRACULA JAGT FRANKENSTEIN/LOS MONSTRUOS DEL TERROR. USA: aka ASSIGNMENT TERROR) Spain/West Germany/Italy, 1969 (1971). Dir: Hugo Fregonese and Tulio Demichelli. With: Michael Rennie, Karin Dor, Craig Hill, Paul Naschy (Jacinto Molina), Patty Sheppard (Shepard), Angel del Pozo. Jaime Prades/Eichberg/ International Jaguar. Colour.

The sequel to *Nights of the Werewolf* (1968). Michael (*Day the Earth Stood Still* [1951]) Rennie's last film features him as the leader of a group of aliens who have travelled from their dying planet, Ummo, to reanimate the world's legendary monsters — Dracula, Count Waldemar Daninsky the werewolf (Naschy, who wrote the script under his real name, Jacinto Molina), the Mummy and Frankenstein's creature — to conquer the Earth. Argentinian director Fregonese quit towards the end of production and was replaced by Demichelli. Despite being shot in just six days, the whole thing moves at a leaden pace, and Universal learned to stop doing this sort of thing twenty-five years earlier. Despite the title, Dracula and the Frankenstein monster never actually meet!

Sequel: FURY OF THE WOLFMAN (1970)

DRAKULITA

Philippines, 1969. Dir: Consuelo P. Osorio. With: Rossana Ortiz, Lito Legaspi, Gina Laforteza, Joseph Gallego, Rebecca Rocha. RJF Brothers.

Ortiz stars as a vampire in this Filipino haunted house comedy.

DR. TERROR'S GALLERY OF HORRORS

(aka THE BLOOD SUCKERS/ RETURN FROM THE PAST/ALIEN MASSACRE/GALLERY OF HORRORS) USA, 1967. Dir: David L. Hewitt. With: Lon Chaney, John Carradine, Rochelle Hudson, Roger Gentry, Karen Joy, Vic McGee. American General. Colour.

Inept five part horror anthology, shot on cardboard sets and featuring the same small group of performers and clips from AIP's Poe movies. Carradine introduces the segments and plays a warlock in 'The Witch's Clock'. A vampire terrorises Victorian London in 'King Vampire', and a dead man returns from the tomb in 'Monster Raid'. Poor old Chaney Jr (who still had worse roles to come) brings a crazed murderer back to life in 'Spark of Life' (set in the nineteenth century, although all the laboratory equipment is modern!). Finally, Mitch Evans is the eponymous 'Count Alucard' who fights a werewolf in a story that is simply lifted from the first part of Bram Stoker's *Dracula*. Filmed under the title *Gallery of Horrors*.

Right: *Dracula Has Risen from the Grave.*

DR TERROR'S HOUSE OF HORRORS

UK, 1965. Dir: Freddie Francis. With: Peter Cushing, Christopher Lee, Max Adrian, Michael Gough, Neil McCallum, Ann Bell. Amicus. Colour.

The first of the Amicus anthology films and the movie that established the company as a serious rival to Hammer. On a railway journey, the mysterious Dr Schreck (Cushing) introduces himself to his five travelling companions and offers to tell their fortunes with his Tarot cards. Predictably, each of the stories (scripted by co-producer Milton Subotsky) leads to death. These involve a female werewolf, a murderous vine, a voodoo god and a crawling hand. In the last tale, American doctor Bob Carroll (Donald Sutherland) is convinced by another doctor (Max Adrian) that his French bride Nicolle (Jennifer Jayne) is a vampire and it is his duty to destroy her by driving a stake through her heart. The twist is that Adrian is the real vampire.

ESCALA EN HI-FI

Spain, 1963. Dir: Isidoro Martinez Ferry. With: Arturo Fernandez, Germaine Damar, José Rubio, Manuel Zargo, Dorothy Peterson. Documento Izaro. Colour.

This includes a nightmare sequence set in Count Dracula's castle.

THE EYE OF COUNT FLICKENSTEIN

USA, 1966. Dir: Tony Conrad.

Short underground film which includes a Dracula parody.

FANTASMAGORIE

France, 1962. Dir: Patrice Molinard. With: Edith Scob, Venantino Venantini, Jean Henry.

Short film with vampires.

FRANKESTEIN, EL VAMPIRO Y CIA

Mexico, 1961. Dir: Benito Alazraki. With: Manuel 'Loco' Valdes, José Jasso, Joaquin Garcia Vargas (Borolas), Martha Elena Cervantes, Nora Veryan, Roberto G. Rivera. Cinematografica Calderon. B&W.

After *Castle of the Monsters* (1957), here's another Mexican version of (Abbott and Costello) *Meet Frankenstein* (1948). The comedy team of 'Loco' Valdes and José Jasso are employed to deliver wax figures of the Frankestein (*sic*) monster and a vampire (Quintin Bulnes) to a mysterious castle. When the figures come to life, the vampire tries to convince female scientist Dr Sofia (Veryan) to transplant Valdes' brain into the monster. Also includes a werewolf.

FRANKENSTEIN'S BLOODY TERROR

(Orig: LA MARCA DEL HOMBRE LOBO. UK: HELL'S CREATURES)

Spain, 1967 (1971). Dir: Henry Egan (Enrique L. Eguiluz). With: Paul Naschy (Jacinto Molina), Diane Konopka (Dianik Zurakowska), Julian Ugarte, Rossana Yanni, Michael Manz (Manuel Manzanaque), Joseph Morton (José Nieto). Maxper/Independent-International. Colour.

American audiences were promised a free burial to anyone who died of fright during performances of this film — a pretty safe bet. Werewolf Count Waldemar Daninsky (Naschy, who also scripted under his real name) appeals to a pair of weird occultists for help. Unfortunately, they turn out to be vampires. Originally released in Spain in 3-D, this was a box office smash there and led to a series of films with Naschy as Daninsky. The American version was totally re-edited (by F. Neumann) and released in 'Super 70mm Chill-O-Rama'. Frankenstein isn't even in it!

Sequel: NIGHTS OF THE WEREWOLF (1968)

THE GENII OF DARKNESS

(Orig: NOSTRADAMUS, EL GENIO DE LAS TINIEBLAS)

Mexico, 1960. Dir: Frederick (Frederico) Curiel. With: Germán Robles, Julio Aleman, Domingo Soler, Aurora Alvarado, Manver (Manuel Vergara), Manuel Casanueva. Estudios America/ American International. B&W.

A sequel to *The Monsters Demolisher* (1960), and the third of four features cut down from a twelve part Mexican serial and released directly to American television. Robles stars as the bearded vampire descendant of Nostradamus who falls in love, while his nemesis Professor Duran (Soler) steals the ashes of the original Nostradamus from a crypt in the forest. Includes the episodes 'El Genio de las Tinieblas', 'Mas alla de la Vida' and 'El Hijo de la Noche'.

Sequel: THE BLOOD OF NOSTRADAMUS (qv; 1960)

GOKE, BODY SNATCHER FROM HELL

(Orig: KYUKETSUKI GOKEMIDORO)

Japan, 1967. Dir: Hajime Sato. With: Teruo Yoshida, Tomomi Sato, Hideo Ko, Masaya Takahashi, Nobuo Kaneko, Eizo Kitamura. Shochiku. Colour.

The crew and passengers of a crashed airliner are terrorised by a vampiric alien that possesses the bodies of its victims by splitting their heads open and crawling into their brains! Once everyone starts arguing amongst themselves, director Sato runs out of ideas and keeps repeating scenes of Vietnam atrocities to support the film's anti-war message. Two crew members finally escape, only to discover — as in *Invasion of the Body Snatchers* (1956) — that the colonisation of the rest of the Earth is already underway. Includes imaginative scenes of birds committing suicide by smashing themselves to bloody pulp against the windows of the plane.

GOLIATH AND THE DRAGON

(Orig: LA VENDETTA DE ERCOLE)

Italy/France, 1960. Dir: Vittorio Cottafavi. With: Mark Forest, Broderick Crawford, Leonora (Eleonara) Ruffo, Gaby Andre, Phillipe Hersent, Sandro Maretti. American International Pictures. Colour.

Forest stars as Hercules (here called Goliath), who not only has to battle a fake-looking dragon, but also a giant bat, a three-headed dog, the Wind Goddess and American actor Crawford as the evil king.

GOLIATH AND THE VAMPIRES

(Orig: MACISTE CONTRO IL VAMPIRO)

Italy, 1961. Dir: Giacomo Gentilomo and Sergio Corbucci. With: Gordon

Left: *El Imperio de Dracula. (FJA).*

Scott, Gianna Maria Canale, Jacques Sernas, Leonora Ruffo, Annabella Incontrera, Rocco Vitolazzi. Ambrosiana Cinematografica/ American International. Colour.

'See: the virgin-harem of the Vampire God!' promised the ads. This violent *peplum* stars ex-Tarzan Scott as Italian muscleman Maciste (changed to Goliath for American audiences) in one of the best of the series. With the help of the subterranean Blue Men, he battles an army of faceless zombies controlled by shape-changing vampire Kobrak (Guido Celano). During the climax, Goliath also confronts an undead double of himself.

EL HACHA DIABOLICA

Mexico, 1964. Dir: José Diaz Morales. With: Santo (Rodolfo Guzman Huerta), Lorena Velazquez, Betty Gonzalez, Fernando Oses, Mario Sevilla, Colocho. Filmica Vergara. B&W.

Santo, the silver masked wrestler, travels back in time to 1630 to battle the vampiric Black Mask and his enchanted axe.

THE HAND OF NIGHT

(USA: aka BEAST OF MOROCCO)
Morocco/UK, 1966. Dir: Fredric Goode. With: William Sylvester, Diane Clare, Alizia Gur, Edward Underdown, William Dexter, Terence De Marney. Associated British Pathe. Colour.

An unusual blend of ghosts and vampires. After the accidental death of his family, Paul Carver (Sylvester) is drawn to Morocco by a death-wish. There he is tempted by the Servants of the Night, a cult of phantoms led by a beautiful princess (Gur) and her eerie servant (De Marney), who want his soul. These vampires may not have fangs, but they still don't cast reflections and can be destroyed by a stake through the heart. Director Goode gives the film a bizarre, dream-like quality, aided by the unusual desert locations, and William Sylvester finally proves that he really can act.

HERCULES IN THE HAUNTED WORLD

(Orig: ERCOLE AL CENTRO DELLA TERRA. UK: HERCULES IN THE CENTER OF THE EARTH)
Italy, 1961. Dir: Mario Bava. With: Reg Park, Christopher Lee, Leonora (Eleonara) Ruffo, Giorgio Ardisson, Franco Giacobini, Marisa Belli. SPA Cinematografica. Colour.

Probably the best of the Italian musclemen (*peplum*) movies. Hercules (Park) and Theseus (Ardisson) must travel to Hades to save the soul of Daianara (Ruffo), put under a spell by vampire-like villain Licho (Lee, dubbed by someone else, but still impressive). Along the way they have to overcome unconvincing stone giant Procrustes, a flying army of the dead, and a lake of boiling lava. Too much comedy, but co-writer/ photographer/director Bava gives the film a wonderful fairy tale quality.

HIROKU KAIBYODEN

Japan, 1969. Dir: Tokuzo Tanaka. With: Kojiro Hongo, Naomi Kobayashi, Mitsuyo Kamei, Matsuhiro Toura, Koichi Uenoyama, Akane Kawasaki. Daiei. Colour.

Set in the eighteenth century. A ghost-cat haunting the castle of Lord Nabeshima (Uenoyama) can turn into a fanged female demon that drinks the blood of its victims. It is finally impaled by a samurai (Hongo).

THE HORRIBLE DR. HICHCOCK

(Orig: L'ORRIBILE SEGRETO DEL DOTTOR HICHCOCK. UK: THE TERROR OF DR. HICHCOCK/ RAPTUS: THE SECRET OF DR. HICHCOCK)
Italy, 1962. Dir: Robert Hampton (Riccardo Freda). With: Barbara Steele, Robert Flemyng, Montgomery Glenn (Silvano Tranquili), Teresa Fitzgerald (Maria Teresa Vianello), Harriet White, Spencer William. Panda Film. Colour.

A minor classic, shot in only eight days. English actor Flemyng plays a turn-of-the-century doctor who is only sexually aroused by necrophilia. Having accidentally killed his first wife with an overdose of drugs, his new wife (Steele) is menaced by her ghostly predecessor, who has returned from the grave seeking blood. Director Freda uses the colour photography to create some wonderful images, and Steele has never looked better as the put-upon heroine. Scenes of Flemyng fondling dead female bodies were cut from the film's original release in both America and Britain.

Sequel: THE GHOST (1963)

THE HORROR OF IT ALL

UK, 1963. Dir: Terence Fisher. With: Pat Boone, Erica Rogers, Dennis Price, Andree Melly, Valentine Dyall, Jack Bligh. Lippert/ Twentieth Century-Fox. B&W.

Clean-cut crooner Pat Boone (who sings the dreadful title song) stars as an American salesman who falls in love with plump Erica Rogers. He is invited back to her ancestral old dark house to meet the rest of the relatives, who include her vampiric sister (Melly, who played a real vampire in *The Brides of Dracula* [1960]), a crazy actor (Price), a madman locked in the basement (Archie Duncan) and the

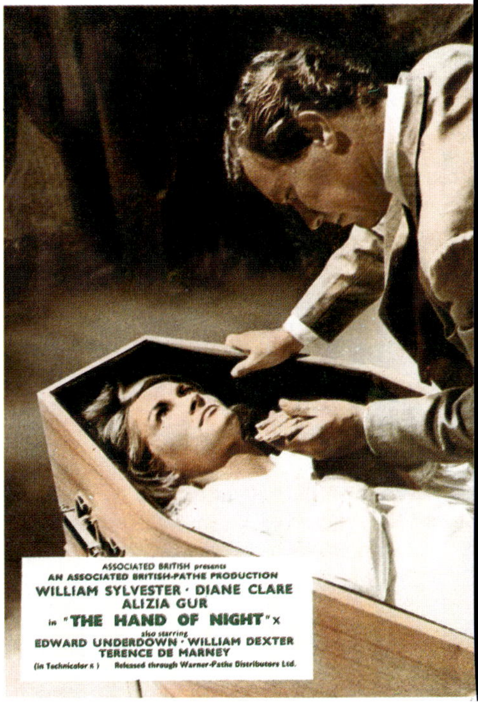

sepulchral head of the family (Dyall). Scripted by horror author Ray Russell, this was similar to William Castle's *The Old Dark House* (1962) and is probably Terence Fisher's worst film. It wasn't released in Britain for three years.

HOUSE ON BARE MOUNTAIN

USA, 1962. Dir: (R.) Lee Frost. With: Bob Cresse, Laura Eden, Angela Webster, Ann Meyers, Hugh Cannon, Jeffrey Smithers. Olympic International. Colour.

Nudie film from the makers of *One Million AC/DC*. Co-producer Cresse plays a bootlegger, who runs Granny Good's School for Good Girls in drag. His assistant is a werewolf, and a fake Frankenstein monster (Warren Ames) and Dracula (Smithers) turn up and do the twist at a costume ball. This cost $72,000 and was one of the most expensive adult movies at the time.

LA HUELLA MACABRA

Mexico, 1962. Dir: Alfredo B. Crevenna. With: Guillermo Murray, Rosa Carmina, Carmen Molina, Jaime Fernandez, Elsa Cardenas, José Luis Jimènez. Rosas Priego/ Clasa-Mohme. B&W.

From the stills, this appears to be about vampire children.

EL IMPERIO DE DRACULA

Mexico, 1966. Dir: Federico Curiel. With: Lucha Villa, Eric del Castillo, Cesar del Campo, Ethel Carrillo, Rebeca Inturbide, Altia Michel. Filmica Vergara/Columbia. Colour.

A young man (del Campo) is sent by his dying mother to Castle Draculstein(!) to avenge his father who was killed by the Count (del Castillo). This owes much to Fisher's *Dracula Prince of Darkness* (1965), and includes a sexy vampire woman and an assistant named Igor. Apparently it was also the first Mexican horror film shot in colour.

INCUBUS

USA, 1965. Dir: Leslie Stevens. With: William Shatner, Allyson Ames, Eloise Hart, Robert Fortier, Ann Atman, Milos Milos (Milosevic). Daystar/Contempo III. B&W.

A rarity starring Shatner (just before he became *Star Trek*'s Captain Kirk), who is tempted by an evil succubus (Ames), while his sister (Atman) is having troubles of her own with an incubus (Milos). This was written and directed by the creator of *The Outer Limits* TV show, and the reason you've probably never seen it is because all the dialogue is in Esperanto — an international language created in 1887. There are also English subtitles. Milos subsequently killed his lover, Barbara Rooney (wife of Mickey), and then committed suicide.

[redacted]

hausen (Agosti) and his daughter Brunilda (Bauman). After the Count is staked against a wall, his undead victims (with stakes still protruding from their chests!) attack the village and can only be stopped by the doctor's distillation of black garlic.

Sequel: THE BLOODY VAMPIRE (qv; 1962)

THE KILLING GAME

(Orig: JEU DE MASSACRE)
France, 1967. Dir: Alain Jessua. With: Jean-Pierre Cassel, Claudine Auger, Michel Duchaussoy, Eleanore

[redacted]

Hirt, Anna Gaylor. A.J./Francinor/ LFM. Colour.
A comic strip writer bases his stories on the real life adventures of a strange young playboy. This includes a clip from a vampire movie.

KISS ME QUICK!

(aka DR. BREEDLOVE OR HOW I LEARNED TO STOP WORRYING AND LOVE)
USA, 1964. Dir: Pete Perry and Max Gardens. With: Frank Coe, Sexton Friendly, Jackie DeWitt, Althea Currier, Claudia Banks. Fantasy Films/G&S Productions. Colour.
Filmed on a single laboratory set, this nudie comedy features an effeminate alien, Sterilox (Coe), from an all-male planet. Looking for a mate he visits the mad Dr Breedlove (a spoof of Peter Sellers' Dr Strangelove from the previous year), who creates naked women, but leaves instead with a vending machine. Includes Dracula, a Frankenstein monster (Coe again) and a mummy. Lester Kovac (Laszlo Kovacs) was the cinematographer, while the direction is often mistakenly attributed to Russ Meyer.

THE KISS OF THE VAMPIRE

(aka KISS OF EVIL)
UK, 1962. Dir: Don Sharp. With: Clifford Evans, Edward De Souza, Noel Willman, Jennifer Daniel, Barry Warren, Brian Oulton. Hammer Films/Universal-International. Colour.
One of Hammer's most stylish films of the sixties. While on a motoring honeymoon in the Carpathian mountains, a young couple find themselves stranded at a local inn. The young wife soon attracts the attention of Dr Ravna (Willman), the leader of a pleasure-seeking cult of vampires. Evans gives a solid performance as the drunken Professor Zimmer, waging a fanatical war against the coven, and there are some impressive setpieces: the opening staking of a vampire with a sexton's shovel, a macabre masked ball, and the climax where Zimmer invokes the forces of darkness in the form of a plague of (animated) bats to destroy the vampires. In America, the TV version dropped some scenes and included new sequences featuring Carl Esmond and clips from Hammer's *The Evil of Frankenstein* (1964).

KURONEKO

(Orig: YABU NO NAKA KURONEKO)
Japan, 1968. Dir: Kaneto Shindo. With: Kichiemon Nakamura, Nobuko Otowa, Kiwako Taichi, Kei Sato, Hideo Kanze, Rokko Toura. Kindai Eiga Kyokai/Nihon Eiga Shinsha/Cinecenta. B&W.
From Shindo, also the writer/director of *Onibaba* (1964), comes a similar horror story, set in the twelfth century. Awaiting her husband's return from the wars, a young woman (Taichi) and her old mother-in-law (Otowa) are raped and murdered by a band of samurai. They return as blood-drinking ghosts who can transform into black cats to destroy any warrior they meet. An imaginative blend of poetic imagery with shock effects that has its moments.

THE LADIES' MAN

USA, 1961. Dir: Jerry Lewis. With: Jerry Lewis, Helen Traubel, Kathleen Freeman, Hope Holiday, Pat Stanley, Jack Kruschen. Paramount. Colour.
Lewis directs and stars as a handyman in a girls' school run by Mrs Wellenmelon (Traubel). In a dream sequence, he imagines a girl as a beautiful vampire. Includes cameo appearances by Buddy Lester, George Raft and Harry James and His Band.

THE LAST MAN ON EARTH

(Orig: L'ULTIMO UOMO DELLA TERRA)
Italy/USA, 1961 (1964). Dir: Sidney Salkow (and Ubaldo Ragona). With: Vincent Price, Franca Bettoia, Emma Danieli, Giacomo Rossi-Stuart, Umberto Rali, Christi Courtland. La Regina/Alta Vista/ American International. B&W.
Richard Matheson originally scripted his classic novel *I am Legend* for Hammer Films in 1957, and they eventually sold it to producer Robert L. Lippert who shot it on the cheap in Italy for Twentieth Century-Fox, who then passed it on to AIP. Re-written by William P. Leicester, Matheson used the pen-name Logan Swanson on the final screenplay credit. Despite the problems, this is still a pretty effective adaptation. After the world has been decimated by a wind-carried plague, scientist Morgan (Price) is the last human left, staking pasty-faced vampires/zombies until he is killed by a group of mutant humans. Price gives a surprisingly restrained performance, and the vampire make-ups were obviously an influence on George Romero's *Night of the Living Dead* (1969). The remake replaced the vampires with blank-eyed mutants.
Remake: THE OMEGA MAN (1971)

THE LEMON GROVE KIDS MEET THE MONSTERS

USA, 1966. Dir: Ray Dennis Steckler. With: Cash Flagg (Ray Dennis Steckler), Carolyn Brandt, Mike Cannon, Larry Byrd, Jim Harmon,

Ron Haydock. Morgan-Steckler. Colour.

From the same team that brought you *The Incredibly Strange Creatures Who Stopped Living and Became Mixed-Up Zombies!!?* (1963) comes this homage to The Bowery Boys. Director Steckler stars under the name Cash Flagg, along with his wife (Brandt) as a vampire, friends and neighbours. The insanity also includes a mummy, a gorilla, a spaceman and a beatnik spy. Originally a homemade 16mm short spliced together with *The Lemon Grove Kids Meet the Green Grasshopper and the Vampire Lady from Outer Space.*

LITTLE RED RIDING HOOD AND TOM THUMB VS. THE MONSTERS

(Orig: CAPERUCITA Y PULGARCITO CONTRA LOS MONSTRUOS)
Mexico, 1960. Dir: Roberto Rodriguez. With: Maria Garcia, Cesarea Quezadas, José Elias Moreno, Manuel 'Loco' Valdez, El Enano Santanon. Peliculas-Rodriguez. Colour.

A sequel to both *Little Red Riding Hood and Her Friends* (1959) and *Tom Thumb* (1958/67). More juvenile weirdness from Mexico. Little Red Riding Hood (Garcia), Tom Thumb and their animal friends battle a Dracula-type vampire and a witch in an evil forest. One of three Little Red Riding Hood movies featuring Garcia. The English language version was directed by Manuel San Fernando.

THE LITTLE SHOP OF HORRORS

USA, 1960. Dir: Roger Corman. With: Jonathan Haze, Jackie Joseph, Mel Welles (Ernst von Theumer), Myrtle Vail, Dick Miller, Jack Nicholson. Filmgroup/American International Pictures. B&W.

Corman's cult follow-up to *A Bucket of Blood* (1959), shot for $27,000 in just over two days from a clever script by Charles B. Griffith. Haze stars as Seymour Krelboined, who works in a skid row florists and grows a talking plant (named Audrey Jr) on a diet of human blood. Great support from Welles as Gravis Mushnik, the flower shop owner, Miller as a customer who eats flowers, and Nicholson as masochistic undertaker Wilbur Force, who enjoys having his teeth pulled! It wasn't released commercially in Britain for thirteen years. "Feed me, feed me!"

Remakes: PLEASE DON'T EAT MY MOTHER! (1972) and LITTLE SHOP OF HORRORS (qv; 1986)

MAD MONSTER PARTY?

USA, 1966 (1969). Dir: Jules Bass. Voices: Boris Karloff, Alan Swift, Gale Garnett, Phyllis Diller, Ethel Ennis. Embassy/Videocraft International. Colour.

Animated children's puppet film, shot in a process dubbed 'Animagic'. Karloff voices a puppet version of himself as Baron Von Frankenstein (and even sings one of the better musical numbers), who holds a convention of all the monsters to reveal the secret of total destruction. Among the guests are Count Dracula, the Wolf Man, the Hunchback, the Mummy, Dr Jekyll and Mr Hyde, the Creature, the Frankenstein monster and his mate, and It (King Kong). Also includes voice impersonations of Bela Lugosi, Peter Lorre, James Stewart, Charles Laughton and Sidney Greenstreet (as the Invisible Man). Overlong, but often amusing. *Mad* magazine's Harvey Kurtzman co-wrote the script.

THE MAGIC CHRISTIAN

UK, 1969. Dir: Joseph McGrath. With: Peter Sellers, Ringo Starr, Richard Attenborough, Leonard Frey, Laurence Harvey, Christopher Lee. Grand Film/Commonwealth United Entertainment. Colour.

All-star comedy, based on the novel by co-writer Terry Southern, that badly misfires. Sellers stars as Sir Guy Grand who, along with his adopted son (Beatles drummer Starr), sets out to prove that money corrupts. Includes Christopher Lee as a ship's vampire, Raquel Welch as a whip-wielding slave driver, an uncredited Yul Brynner in drag and other embarrassing cameos by Richard Attenborough, Laurence Harvey, Wilfred Hyde White, Roman Polanski, Graham Chapman, John Cleese, Spike Milligan, Ferdy Mayne, Dennis Price, John Le Mesurier and Victor Maddern. Music by Badfinger and Thunderclap Newman.

THE MAGIC SWORD

(UK: ST. GEORGE AND THE SEVEN CURSES)
USA, 1961. Dir: Bert I. Gordon. With: Basil Rathbone, Estelle Winwood, Gary Lockwood, Anne Helm, Jack Kosslyn, Maila Nurmi. United Artists. Colour.

Probably producer/director Gordon's best film, which doesn't mean much. This fairy tale fantasy with a grim edge has witch Sybil (the wonderful Winwood) bringing up dreary foster son George (Lockwood) in the forest. She gives him a magic sword, armour and companions, and he sets out to defy the seven curses of the evil sorcerer Lodac (a nicely villainous Rathbone) and rescue a princess. Along the way he has to confront a vampire hag (played by TV host Vampira, aka Nurmi), a giant ogre and a two-headed fire-breathing dragon, plus various evil dwarfs and pinheads (who include Richard Kiel and Angelo Rossitto). The special effects look

Left: *The Magic Christian.*

cheap and unconvincing, but kids will love it and it's worth catching for Rathbone's performance alone.

MALENKA — THE NIECE OF THE VAMPIRE

(Orig: MALENKA — LA NIPOTE DEL VAMPIRO. USA: FANGS OF THE LIVING DEAD)
Spain/Italy, 1968. Dir: Armando de Ossorio. With: Anita Ekberg, Julian Ugarte, John Hamilton (Gianni Medici), Diana Lorys, Audrey Ambert (Adriana Ambesi), Rossana Yanni. Triton/Victory/Cobra/Felix/ Europix. Colour.
Vampire Count Wolduck (Ugarte) tries to convince his niece Silvia (Ekberg) that she is the reincarnation of Malenka, a nun burned for witchcraft. It all turns out to be a plot to gain her inheritance. The first horror film from the director of the Blind Dead series.

THE MALTESE BIPPY

USA, 1969. Dir: Norman Panama. With: Dan Rowan, Dick Martin, Carol Lynley, Julie Newmar, Mildred Natwick, Fritz Weaver. Metro-Goldwyn-Mayer. Colour.
The two stars of the sixties hit TV show, *Rowan and Martin's Laugh-In*, unwisely made their movie début together in this horror comedy set in an old dark house on Long Island. Martin is turned into a werewolf and Weaver plays the Dracula-like Ravenswood. There are several different endings.

MGA MANUGANG NI DRAKULA

Philippines, 1964.
The title translates as *The Secrets of Dracula*.

MEN OF ACTION MEET WOMEN OF DRACULA

Philippines, 1969. Dir: Artemio Marquez. With: Dante Varona, Eddie Torrento, Ruben Obligacion, Norman Henson, Ernesto Beren, Angelito Marquez. Villanueva.
A troupe of tumblers battle Dracula and his vampire women.

MILL OF THE STONE WOMEN

(Orig: IL MULINO DELLE DONNE DI PIETRA/LE MOULIN DES SUPPLICES. UK: DROPS OF BLOOD. USA: aka ICON)
Italy/France, 1960. Dir: Giorgio Ferroni. With: Danny (Dany) Carrel, Scilla Gabel, Pierre Brice, Wolfgang Preiss, Liana Orfei. Galatea Film. Colour.
Filmed in Holland, and based on a story from *Flemish Tales* by Peter Van Weigen. German actor Preiss plays a mad professor who keeps his daughter alive by stealing the blood from young girls and petrifying the corpses into statues for his macabre carousel of death. Ferroni originally dedicated the film to Terence Fisher. Richard McNamara is credited as director of the English version.

MONDO KEYHOLE

(aka THE WORST CRIME OF ALL!)
USA, 1966. Dir: John Lamb. Ajay/Boxoffice International.
'Adults only' sex/horror movie. A pornographer/rapist is punished by lesbians while his wife becomes a victim of Dracula.

THE MONSTERS DEMOLISHER

(Orig: NOSTRADAMUS Y EL DESTRUCTOR DE MONSTRUOS)
Mexico, 1960. Dir: Frederick (Frederico) Curiel. With: Germán Robles, Julio Aleman, Domingo Soler, Aurora Alvarado, Manver (Manuel Vergara), Manuel Casanueva. Estudios America/ American International. B&W.

A sequel to *The Curse of Nostradamus* (1960), and the second of four features cut down from a twelve part Mexican serial and released directly to television in America. Robles stars as a bearded vampire descendant of the prophet Nostradamus who hypnotises a criminal to do his will. Professor Duran (Soler) defeats him with a soundwave machine harmful to bats. Includes the episodes 'El Destructor de Monstruos', 'El Estudiante y la Horca' and 'El Ataud Vacio'.

Sequel: THE GENII OF DARKNESS (qv; 1960)

MUNSTER, GO HOME!

USA, 1966. Dir: Earl Bellamy. With: Fred Gwynne, Yvonne De Carlo, Al Lewis, Butch Patrick, Debbie Watson, Terry-Thomas. Universal. Colour.

Based on *The Munsters* TV series, this was originally made for television but released theatrically at the last minute. The weird family (including Lewis' vampiric Grandpa) travel to Britain to claim Herman's inheritance. The humour is laboured (although there are a couple of nice *Car 54 Where Are You?* and *Batman* jokes), and guest stars like Terry-Thomas and Hermione Gingold just look embarrassed. Only John Carradine, hidden under a red wig and sideburns as Cruikshank, the doddering butler, makes anything out of his small role. The film quickly runs out of steam and ends with a tedious car chase.

Sequel: THE MUNSTERS' REVENGE (qv; 1981)

THE NAKED WITCH

(aka THE NAKED TEMPTRESS)
USA, 1961 (1964). Dir: Andy Milligan. With: Beth Porter, Robert Burgos, Lee Forbes. Alexander. Colour.

Milligan's first horror movie, made for veteran New York exploitation distributor William Mishkin. A nineteenth century vampire-witch (Porter) is revived when a student removes a stake from her heart. Also includes Forbes as a hunchback. Filmed in New Jersey in eight or nine days for $7,500, it was rereleased in 1967 with an extra twenty minutes added. Incredible!

THE NAKED WORLD OF HARRISON MARKS

UK, 1967. Dir: (George) Harrison Marks. With: (George) Harrison Marks, Pamela Green, June Palmer. Manson/Token. Colour.

Dated nudie comedy directed, produced and co-scripted by British photographer Marks, who also plays seven roles, including Count Dracula and James Bond. Narrated by Valentine Dyall.

PLANET OF THE VAMPIRES

(Orig: TERRORE NELLO SPAZIO/TERROR EN EL ESPACIO. USA: aka DEMON PLANET)
Italy/Spain, 1965. Dir: Mario Bava. With: Barry Sullivan, Norma Bengell, Angel Aranda, Evi Marandi, Stelio Candelli, Fernando Villena. Italian International/Castilla/American International. Colour.

After *Black Sunday* (1960), this is probably Bava's best film. Based on the story 'One Night of 21 Hours' by Renato Pestriniero, the English language script by Ib Melchoir and Louis M. Heyward almost makes sense. Space captain Sullivan and his crew crash on a strange planet where the dead come back to life to kill the living. The 'surprise' ending has the alien-possessed vampiric survivors preparing to land on another alien world — Earth! Bava's chilling images — the living dead tearing themselves out of transparent body bags; the giant inhabitants of another crashed spaceship — influenced everything from *Night of the Living Dead* (1969) to *Alien* (1979).

THE NUDE VAMPIRE

(Orig: LA VAMPIRE NUE)
France, 1969. Dir: Jean Rollin. With: Oliver Martin, Maurice Lemaitre, Caroline Cartier, Ly Letrong, Bernard Musson, Jean Aron. Films ABC. Colour.

The second film from co-writer, producer and director Rollin has hero Martin falling in love with a strange young woman (Cartier). He soon discovers that she is a vampire being held prisoner by a secret suicide sect and that another group of vampires want to rescue her. More arty nonsense from the overrated French director.

PARIS WHEN IT SIZZLES

USA/France, 1964. Dir: Richard Quine. With: William Holden, Audrey Hepburn, Gregoire Aslan, Raymond Bussieres, Tony Curtis, Noel Coward. Paramount. Colour.

Weak comedy with writer Holden and secretary Hepburn working on a screenplay and imagining a number of movie clichés, including Holden as a Dracula-like vampire. Also includes a cameo appearance by Marlene Dietrich and Mel Ferrer as Dr Jekyll and Mr Hyde.

THE PLAYGIRLS AND THE VAMPIRE

(Orig: L'ULTIMA PREDA DEL VAMPIRO. USA: aka CURSE OF THE VAMPIRE)
Italy, 1960 (1963). Dir: Piero Regnoli. With: Lyla Rocco, Walter Brandi, Maria Giovannini, Alfredo Rizzo, Marisa Quattrini, Leonardo Botta. Nord Film Italiana/Fanfare. B&W.

Director Regnoli, who scripted Riccardo Freda's *The Devil's Commandment* (1956), here reworks the same theme as Renato Polselli's *The Vampire and the Ballerina* (1960), only with more mild nudity. A group of chorus girls in transparent nighties are chased around a castle by a vampire. Brandi (who was also in Polselli's film) plays both the heroic ancestor of the undead Count Kernassy and the vampire himself. In the end, the Count is impaled and then destroyed by sunlight.

PONTIANAK GUA MUSANG

Malaya, 1964. Dir: B.N. Rao. With: Suraya Haron, Ghazali Sumantri, Malek Siamat, Ummi Kalthoum. Keris. B&W.

A follow-up to *Pontianaka Kembali* (1963), this was the sixth and last entry in the popular series. This time the vampire lives in a cave.

PONTIANKA KEMBALI

Malaya, 1963. Dir: Ramon Estellia. With: Maria Menado, Malik Selamat. Cathay/Keris. B&W

Fifth in the popular series and a follow-up to *Anak Pontianak* (1958). Menado returns as the vampire.

Sequel: PONTIANAK GUA MUSANG (qv; 1964)

QUEEN OF BLOOD

(aka PLANET OF BLOOD)
USA, 1966. Dir: Curtis Harrington. With: John Saxon, Basil Rathbone, Judi Meredith, Dennis Hopper, Florence Marly (Florence Marly von Wurmbrand), Robert Boon. American International Pictures. Colour.

When Roger Corman acquired special effects footage from a Russian science fiction film (*Niebo Zowiet* [1959]), Curtis Harrington wrote a script around it and directed this modest thriller in seven-and-a-half days for $65,000. A mission to Mars to rescue a crashed alien spaceship brings back green-skinned, glowing-eyed Marly, who turns out to be a creepy vampire feeding on the crew. Veteran Rathbone plays a scientist back on Earth and Forrest J Ackerman is eleventh billed as his assistant. Stephanie Rothman was associate producer and *Star Wars* (1977) producer Gary Kurtz the production manager.

IL RISVEGLIO DI DRACULA

Italy. Dir: U. Paolessi. With: Gabby Paul, Gill Chadwich.

The title translates as *The Revival of Dracula.*

SAMSON VS. THE VAMPIRE WOMEN

(Orig: SANTO CONTRA LAS MUJERES VAMPIRO)
Mexico, 1961. Dir: Alfonso Corona Blake. With: Santo (Rodolfo Guzman Huerta), Lorena Velazquez, Maria Duval, Jaime Fernandez, Orfelia Montesco, Laura Marquetti. Tele-Cine-Radio/American International Pictures. B&W.

One of numerous movies featuring Santo, the silver masked wrestling hero (renamed Samson in the dubbed versions), who sets out to save a doctor's daughter from becoming queen to a group of vampire women led by a resurrected priestess.

SANGRE DE VIRGENES

Mexico, 1968. Dir: Emilio Vieyra. With: Ricardo Bauleo, Gloria Prat, Susana Beltran, Rolo Puente, Walter Kliche, Orestes A. Trueco. Azteca Films. Colour.

Sex and horror from south of the border, with vampires and virgins.

SANTO Y BLUE DEMON VS. LOS MONSTRUOS

(aka SANTO Y BLUE DEMON CONTRA LOS MONSTRUOS)
Mexico, 1969. Dir: Gilberto Martinez Solares. With: Santo (Rodolfo Guzman Huerta or Eric del Castillo), Blue Demon (Alejandro Cruz), Heidi Blue, Jorge Rado, Carlos Ancira, David Avizu. Cinematografica Sotomayor. Colour.

During the late sixties and early seventies, as their respective series were coming to an end, Mexico's two greatest wrestling heroes, Santo and the Blue Demon, teamed up for a number of adventures. This is probably the best, in which they not only have to confront the mad Dr Bruno Halder (Ancira), but also battle

Left: *Queen of Blood. (FJA).*

Above: Taste the Blood of Dracula.
Right: Slaughter of the Vampires.

Dracula (Avizu), two vampire women (Elsa Maria Tako and Yolanda Ponce), the Franquesten (*sic*) monster (Manuel Leal), a cyclops, a dwarf, the Mummy, a werewolf, a quartet of zombies and a deadly robot double of the Blue Demon! They sure must have loved (Abbott and Costello) *Meet Frankenstein* (1948) in Mexico.

SANTO Y EL TESORO DE DRACULA

(aka EL VAMPIRO Y EL SEXO)
Mexico, 1968. Dir: René Cardona. With: Santo (Rodolfo Guzman Huerta), Aldo Monti, Noelia Noel, Roberto G. Rivera, Carlos Agosti, Alberto Rojas. Cinematografica Calderon. Colour.

Comic strip-style wrestling/horror movie. Scientist Noel uses a time machine and ends up being bitten by Agosti's Count Alucard (Dracula). Santo, the silver masked hero, watches it all from his secret laboratory and follows her back in time to destroy both the vampire and his treasure. An export version, featuring more nudity, was released as *El Vampiro y el Sexo*.

Sequel: LA VENGANZA DE LAS MUJERES VAMPIRO (qv; 1969)

SCREAM AND SCREAM AGAIN

UK, 1969. Dir: Gordon Hessler. With: Vincent Price, Christopher Lee, Peter Cushing, Judy Huxtable, Alfred Marks, Michael Gothard. American International/Amicus. Colour.

A cult classic of the science fiction/horror genre, which benefits from a clever and amusing performance by Marks as harassed police superintendent Bellaver, investigating a series of savage murders where each of the bodies has been sucked dry of blood. Christopher Wicking's confused screenplay, based on Peter Saxon's novel *The Disorientated Man*, finally leads to a plot by scientist Price to create a new race of superbeings. The three horror stars are grievously wasted (particularly Cushing, who shares no scenes with the other two and is killed off early on). "But what of the dream?" asks Price. "There is only nightmare," replies Lee.

BLOOD-GHOULS)
Italy, 1962. Dir: Roberto Mauri. With: Walter Brandy (Brandi), Dieter Eppler, Graziella Granata, Alfredo Rizzo, Paolo Solvay. Pacemaker. B&W.

A young honeymoon couple both take undead lovers in a castle full of vampires. This time Brandi (*The Playgirls and the Vampire; The Vampire and the Ballerina* [both 1960]) plays the hero, Wolfgang.

A TASTE OF BLOOD

(aka THE SECRET OF DR. ALUCARD)
USA, 1967. Dir: Herschell Gordon Lewis. With: Bill Rogers, Elizabeth Wilkinson, Thomas Wood, Otto

TASTE THE BLOOD OF DRACULA

UK, 1969. Dir: Peter Sasdy. With: Christopher Lee, Linda Hayden, Anthony Corlan, Geoffrey Keen, Peter Sallis, John Carson. Hammer Films. Colour.

The fourth in Hammer's Dracula series and one of the best. Salesman Roy Kinnear is travelling through Europe when he witnesses the climax of *Dracula Has Risen from the Grave* (1968). Collecting up the Count's cape, ring and dried blood, he returns to Victorian London where he sells the artifacts to the depraved Lord Courtney (Ralph Bates). Secretly a disciple of Dracula, Courtney calls upon the powers of darkness and revives the Count, who revenges himself on three families through their children. The literate script by John Elder (Anthony Hinds) explores the repressed sexuality of Victorian values, while Lee's suave vampire is used as a catalyst for sex and death. The climax apparently has God destroying Dracula in church! The next entry in Hammer's series, *Scars of Dracula* (1970), wasn't a sequel to anything.

THEATRE OF DEATH

(USA: aka BLOOD FIEND)

UK, 1966. Dir: Samuel Gallu. With: Christopher Lee, Lelia Goldoni, Julian Glover, Evelyn Laye, Jenny Till, Ivor Dean. Pennea. Colour.

Lee stars as Phillipe Darvas, a playwright with hypnotic powers, who is suspected of a series of vampire murders around the Grand Guignol Theatre of Death in Paris. The plot is filled with false clues and red herrings that will keep you guessing the killer's identity until the end. Glover plays the police doctor hero and Ivor Dean is an unlikely French police inspector. Director Gallu has a flair for weird camera angles.

TORE NG DIYABLO

Philippines, 1969. Dir: Lauro Pacheco. With: Jimmy Morato, Pilar Pilapil, Rodolfo Garcia, Lucita Soriano, Ramon D'Salva, Diana Dean. Santiago.

A pregnant woman who sucks the life out of lizards is sought by Dracula-like D'Salva to bear his vampire child. In the end he must battle a werewolf (Garcia) before both are destroyed by a lucky earthquake. Based on the *Lagim Komiks* comic book series by Nelsa Morales, the title translates as *Tower of the Devil*.

THE TORTURE ZONE

(Orig: LA CAMARA DEL TERROR. USA: aka FEAR CHAMBER/THE TORTURE CHAMBER)

Mexico/USA, 1968. Dir: John (Juan) Ibanez. With: Boris Karloff, Julissa, Charles (Carlos) East, Isela Vega, Yerye Beirute, Eva Muller. Filmica Vergara/Columbia/Parasol. Colour.

The third of four Mexican movies Boris Karloff (confined to a wheelchair with only one lung) made just before his death. This one involves the discovery of a stone creature in a volcano which needs human blood to survive. Karloff's obsessed scientist creates a chamber to scare kidnapped women before drawing their blood, but his assistant (Vega) and her mad hunchback feed the creature with more victims until it grows out of control. Eighty-one year-old Karloff's scenes were filmed in Los Angeles by co-writer Jack Hill. Not released in Britain until 1988, it includes some mild scenes of sex and sadism and marks a tragic end to Karloff's career.

[redacted]

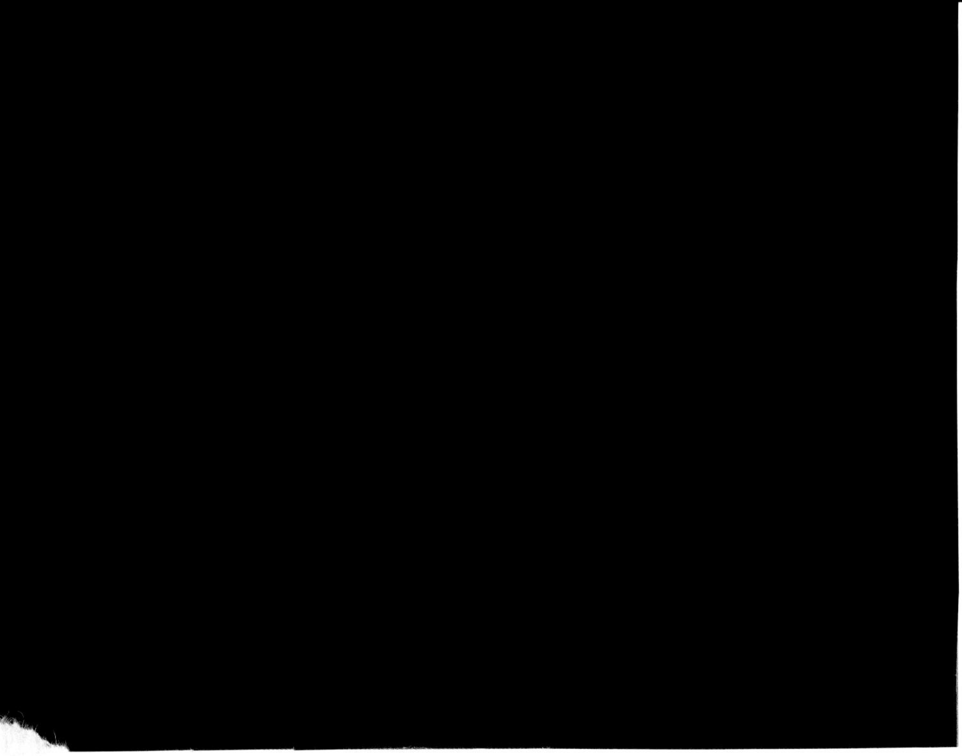

TOWER OF THE SCREAMING VIRGINS

(Orig: DER TURM DER VERBOTENEN LIEBE/LA TOUR DE NESLE. USA: aka THE SWEETNESS OF SIN) Germany/France/Italy, 1968. Dir: Leo Joannon (Francois Legrand). With: Mario-Ange Anies, Jean Piat, Ursula Glass (Uschi Glas), Terry Torday, Dada Galoff, Veronique Vendell. E.G.E./Rapid Films. Colour.

Marquerita, the wife of King Louis X, is suspected of being a vampire-witch when she has her lovers killed by an arrow which leaves the mark of the vampire on their throats. Colourful historical 'adult' feature, based on a play by Alexander Dumas. Includes a hunchback and an incongruous jazz and bongo score.

LA TRAITE DU VAMPIRE

France, 1960. Dir: Pierre Boursons. With: Jean Boullett, Michele Vian.

A short film featuring vampires.

TRANSYLVANIA 6-5000

USA, 1963. Dir: Chuck Jones. Voices: Mel Blanc. Warner Bros. Colour.

Inventive seven minute animated Bugs Bunny short, made towards the end of Warner's original series (1938-63). Bugs enters a spooky Transylvanian castle to use the phone and is menaced by the resident vampire, Count Bloodcount. As usual, he manages to turn the tables on the bloodsucker.

IL TUNNEL SOTTO IL MONDO

Italy, 1968. Dir: Luigi Cozzi. With: Alberto Moro, Bruno Salviero, Anna Mantovani, Lello Maraniello, Gretel Fehr, Isabell Karllson. Idea Film. Colour.

Based on the short science fiction story 'The Tunnel Under the World' by Frederik Pohl. A man discovers an entire town being electronically controlled by a giant corporation. Pietro Rosati appears as an alien vampire. This apparently includes footage from Cozzi's *Isabell, A Dream* featuring Dracula, Frankenstein's monster and the Mummy (actors wearing Don Post masks).

L'URLO DEL VAMPIRO

Italy. Dir: T. Fec. With: Milion Chery, Peppino Spoletini, Gianna Giacchi, Franco Vietri, Angela Cavalli, Antonio D'Agostino. Pao.

A traditional-looking vampire disintegrates at the end. The title translates as *The Cry of the Vampire.*

LAS VAMPIRAS

Mexico, 1968. Dir: Frederico Curiel. With: John Carradine, Mil Mascaras, Maria Duval, Marta Romero, Maura Monti, Pedro Armendariz Jr. Filmica Vergara/Columbia. Colour.

Another entry in Mexico's wrestling/horror movie stakes. Carradine plays the Dracula-like leader of a group of female vampires who are defeated by wrestling heroes Mascaras and Duval. This was the third of four horror movies Carradine made in Mexico for producer Luis Enrique Vergara in 1968.

THE VAMPIRE

Poland, 1968.

Half-hour short with a dance attended by 'vampires'.

THE VAMPIRE AND THE BALLERINA

(Orig: L'AMANTE DEL VAMPIRO) Italy, 1960. Dir: Renato Polselli. With: Helene Remy, Maria Luisa Rolando, Walter Brandi, Tina Gloriani, Isarco Ravaioli, John Turner. CIF Consorzio Italiano Films/United Artists. B&W.

During a storm, two young ballet dancers (Remy and Gloriani) take refuge in an old castle where they are terrorised by a vampire countess (Rolando) and her ugly, undead servant Herman (Brandi). The two villains are finally destroyed by sunlight.

LE VAMPIRE DE DUSSELDORF

(aka EL ASESINO DE DUSSELDORF) France/Italy/Spain, 1964. Dir: Robert Hossein. With: Robert Hossein, Marie-France Pisier, Roger Dutoit, Annie Andersson, Michel Dacquin, Anne Carrere. Georges de Beauregard Productions/Benito Perojo/Mega Films. B&W.

Yet another version of the true-life crimes of child murderer Peter Kürten, the Vampire of Dusseldorf. Previously filmed as *M* in 1931 and 1951.

A VAMPIRE FOR TWO

(Orig: UN VAMPIRO PARA DOS) Spain, 1965. Dir: Pedro Lazanga Sabater. With: Gracita Morales, José Luis Lopez Vazquez, Fernando Fernan Gomez, Trini Alonso, Goyo Lebreros, José Oyas. Belmar. B&W.

The comedy duo of Morales and Lopez Vazquez play Spanish servants menaced by German vampire Baron von Rosenthal (Gomez) and his undead family. Apparently it's not very funny.

THE VAMPIRE OF THE OPERA

(Orig: IL MOSTRO DELL'OPERA/IL

VAMPIRO DELL'OPERA)
Italy, 1964. Dir: Renato Polselli. With: John McDouglas (Giuseppe Addobbati), Vittoria Prada, Marc Marian (Marco Mariani), Barbara Howard (Howerd), Catla Cavelli. Nif. B&W.
Director Polselli started filming *Il Vampiro dell'Opera* the year after he completed *The Vampire and the Ballerina* (1960). It was finally finished in 1964 and released as *Il Mostro dell'Opera*. Loosely based on Gaston Leroux's novel, ravenous vampire Stefano (Addobbati) preys on a troupe of actors who are rehearsing in an old opera house. He falls in love with the star of the show (Prada), who is the reincarnation of his long-lost love, and introduces her to the delights of bloodsucking. Low budget sexploitation.

VAMPIRES D'ALFAMA
France, 1963. Dir: Pierre Kast.
Short animated film.

A VAMPIRE'S DREAM
(Orig: UM SONHO DE VAMPIROS)
Brazil, 1969. Dir: Ibere Cavalcanti. With: Ankito, Irma Alvarez, Janet Chermoni, Sonelia Costa, Augusto Mala Filho, Robson Bob. UCB/Ser-Cine. Colour.
Comedy about a doctor (Ankito) who is given the choice by Death of dying or becoming a vampire. He chooses the latter, and proceeds to put the bite on those in power.

THE VAMPIRE'S RAPE
(Orig: LE VIOL DU VAMPIRE/LA REINE DES VAMPIRES)
France, 1967. Dir: Jean Rollin. With: Solange Pradel, Bernard Letrou, Ursule Pauly, Nicole Romain, Catherine Deville, Jacqueline Sieger. Les Films ABC/ Sam Selsky. B&W.
Originally made as a short, then expanded to feature length, Rollin's first film is about two crazy blood-drinking sisters who think they are cursed by a sword-wielding vampire. This amateurish blend of arty imagery, narrative incoherence and mild eroticism set the tone for many of the director's later movies. Although highly admired by some critics, Rollin's work only occasionally rises to the lyrical heights he so obviously aims for.

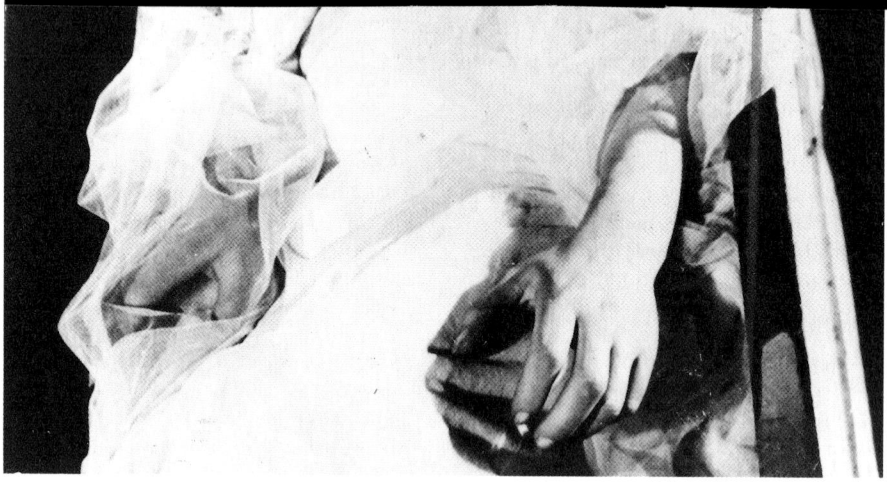

Above: The Vampire and the Ballerina.

VAMPIRE WOMAN
(Orig: XI XUEFU)
Hong Kong, 1962. Dir: Li Tie. With: Bai Yang (Bak Yin), Zhang Huoyou (Cheng Wo-Yau), Huang Manli (Wong Manlee), Rong Xiaoyi, Jiang Zhongping (Keung Chung-ping). Zhong Lian. B&W.
Family melodrama with horror trappings. When a woman (Bai Yang) is seen sucking the blood of her baby, she is accused of vampirism and punished by being buried alive. It turns out that the child had been poisoned by an evil servant (Zhongping) and she was trying to save it.

VAMPIRISME
France, 1967. Dir: Patrice Duvic and Bernard Chaouat. With: Michel Beaune, Guy Mineur, Jean-Pierre Bouyxou, Alain Le Bris, Bernard Chaouat, Bernard Tretton. Films du Cosmos. B&W.
Twelve minute comedy short showing vampires going about their daily business: drinking blood, a baby vampire sucking its mother's blood, advertising for vampires, etc.

EL VAMPIRO AECHECHA
Mexico, 1962. With: Germán Robles, Nestor Zarvade, Blanca del Prado.
The title translates as *The Lurking Vampire*. In a dream sequence, a young boy opposes a vampire-killer who preys on small children. Based on a story by William Irish (aka Cornell Woolrich), this might be a 1959 Argentinian film.

LOS VAMPIROS DEL OESTE
Mexico, 1963. Dir: Juan Oetega.

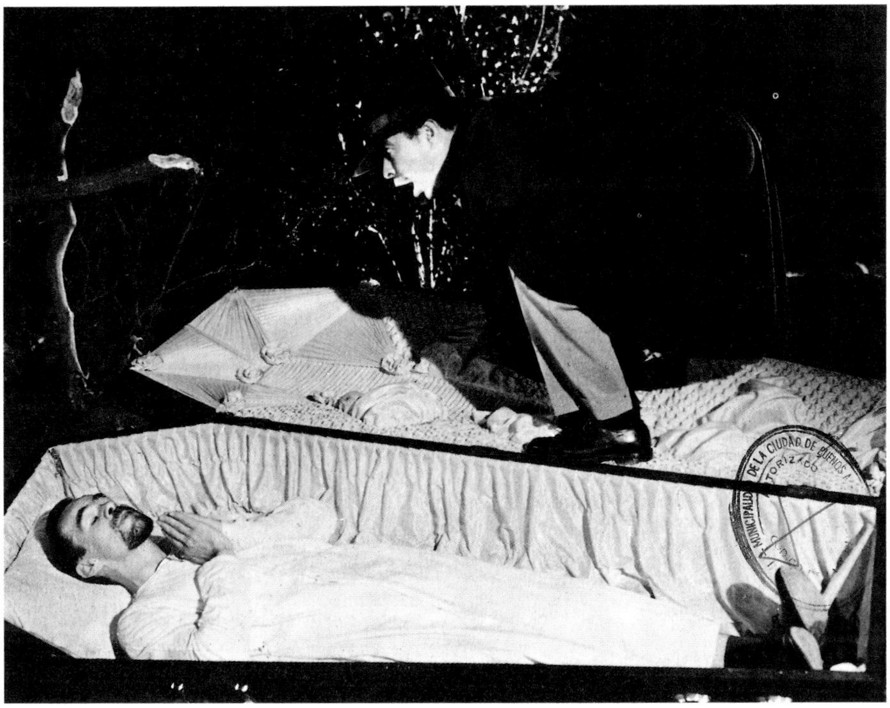

Above: A Vampire's Dream.

With: Joaquin Cordero, Alma Fuentes, William Murray, José Elias Moreno. B&W.
A series of mysterious deaths in a small village are investigated by a government agent.

LA VENGANZA DE LAS MUJERES VAMPIRO

(aka SANTO EN LA VENGANZA DE LAS MUJERES VAMPIRO)
Mexico, 1969. Dir: Federico Curiel.

Above: La Venganza de las Mujeres Vampiro.

With: Santo (Eric del Castillo or Rodolfo Guzmán Huerta), Norma Lazareno, Gina Romand, Aldo Monti, Victor Junco, Patricia Ferrer. Cinematografica Flama/Peliculas Latinoamericanas. Colour.
This is not really a late sequel to *Samson vs. the Vampire Women* (1961), despite the title. Using the blood of a nightclub dancer, mad Dr Brancor (Junco) revives the undead Countess Mayra (Romand) who believes that Santo, the silver masked wrestler, is the descendant of the man who staked her vampire ancestors. The doctor also creates the Frankenstein-like Razos (Nathaniel Leon) from spare cadavers.
Sequel: SANTO Y BLUE DEMON CONTRA DRACULA Y EL HOMBRE LOBO (qv; 1972)

VIJ

(aka VIY)
Russia, 1967. Dir: Konstantin Yershov and Giorgio Kropachyov. With: Natalia Varlei, Leonid Kuravlev, N. Kutuzov. Mosfilm. Colour.
Based on Nikolai Gogol's story 'The Vij' (also the basis for *Black Sunday* [1960] and several other films). For three nights, a student (Kuravlev) is forced to spend the night with the corpse of a possessed woman (Varlei). She returns to life and uses her vampires and demons to attack and kill him. The impressive special effects at the climax were created by Aleksandr Ptushko.

THE WORLD OF ABBOTT AND COSTELLO

USA, 1965. With: Bud Abbott, Lou Costello, Lon Chaney Jr, Marjorie Main, Tom Ewell, Bela Lugosi. Vanguard/Universal. B&W.
Presented by Amicus producers Max J. Rosenberg and Milton Subotsky, this compilation of scenes from Abbott and Costello's movie comedies features mostly routine clips and redundant commentary by Gene Wood and Jack E. Leonard. The most memorable excerpts are from the team's fantasy movies, including *Abbott and Costello Go to Mars* (1953), *Abbott and Costello Meet the Mummy* (1955), an uncredited *Abbott and Costello Meet Dr. Jekyll and Mr. Hyde* (1953), *Hold That Ghost* (1941), *...Meet the Invisible Man* (1951) and, best of all, *Meet Frankenstein* (1948; featuring Chaney Jr's Wolf Man and Lugosi's Count Dracula).

THE WORLD OF THE VAMPIRES

(Orig: EL MUNDO DE LOS VAMPIROS)
Mexico, 1960. Dir: Alfonso Corona Blake. With: Guillermo Murray, Mauricio Garces, Erna Martha Bauman, Silvia Fournier, José Baviera, Mari Carmen Vela. Cinematografica Calderon/ American International Pictures. B&W.
Vampire Sergio Sotubai (Argentinian actor Murray) plays an organ made out of human skulls and bones in his subterranean vault. He is opposed by occultist Rodolfo (Garces), who uses soundwaves to overcome the vampire before pushing him into a pit of stakes. The undead disciples look like werewolves.

YOKAI DAISENSO

Japan, 1968. Dir: Yoshiyuki Kuroda. With: Yoshihiko Aoyama, Akane Kawasaki, Osamu Okawa, Tomoo Uchida, Hajme Kimuru. Daiei. Colour.
A governor of Izu province is possessed by Daimon, a blood-sucking Babylonian demon. The creature is finally defeated by a local water spirit and various other monsters.

the

By the early 1970s, Hammer was looking for something to spice up its vampire movies. That something turned out to be S-E-X. Initially teaming up with American International, the studio produced **The Vampire Lovers (1970)**, *a sexually explicit version of J. Sheridan Le Fanu's 'Carmilla' which brought the lesbian subplot to the fore. They quickly followed it up with two sequels,* **Lust for a Vampire (1970)** *and* **Twins of Evil (1971).**

After the disappointing **Scars of Dracula (1970)**, *Hammer also decided to ring the changes with Christopher Lee's Count, updating his exploits to contemporary London. In* **Dracula A.D. 1972 (1972)** *and* **The Satanic Rites of Dracula (1973)** *they once again added Peter Cushing to the mix, as Van Helsing's grandson. Lee finally had enough of Hammer's series and decided to quit, although he was happy to portray the character in* **One More Time (1970), Bram Stoker's Count Dracula (1970), Dracula and Son (1976)** *and the documentary* **In Search of Dracula (1971).**

John Forbes-Robertson donned the Count's cape and fangs to oppose Cushing's Van Helsing for a final time in **The Legend of the 7 Golden Vampires (1974)**, *and Hammer attempted various vampiric variations with* **Vampire Circus (1971), Captain Kronos Vampire Hunter (1972)**

The House That Dripped Blood.

1970s

and even **Countess Dracula (1970)**, *the latter inspired by the blood-bathing exploits of Elizabeth Bathory, also the basis for Harry Kumel's stylish* **Daughters of Darkness (1971)** *and* **The Legend of Blood Castle (1972)**.

Vampyros Lesbos die Erbin des Dracula (1970) *and* **The Blood Spattered Bride (1972)** *were yet two more variations on 'Carmilla', and other lesbian vampires turned up in* **The Velvet Vampire (1971)**, **Vampyres (1974)** *and the arty excesses of French director Jean Rollin.*

Blacula.

Other memorable movie Draculas of the 1970s included Louis Jordan, Jack Palance, Frank Langella, David Niven, George Hamilton, Peter Cushing, Klaus Kinski, Paul Naschy, Howard Vernon and porno star Jamie Gillis. As if that wasn't enough, there was also **Blacula (1972)**, **Deafula (1975)**, **Count Yorga, Vampire (1970)**, **Mama Dracula (1979)**, **Lady Dracula (1977)**, *singer/songwriter Harry Nilsson as* **Son of Dracula (1973)**, *and even* **Dracula's Dog (1977)**!

Seventy-three year-old veteran John Carradine played the Count one last time in **Nocturna, Granddaughter of Dracula (1979)**, *and he kept the fangs in for two Mexican movies,* **Mary, Mary, Bloody Mary (1975)** *and* **The Vampire Hookers (1979)**.

However, the bubble had to eventually burst, and by the end of the 1970s Hammer, Amicus and American International were all gone. The third and most successful horror cycle was finally over and most of the great horror stars were either dead, semi-retired or had turned their backs on the genre.

It was time to introduce some young blood...

mute bisexual vampire who kills her lovers through fellatio. She eventually drowns herself in a bath of blood to be with the lover (Taylor) she emasculated. Various permutations of this Franco mess exist, ranging from a straight horror film without much sex to a hardcore version. The director also photographed, scripted and edited the film, as well as appearing as Dr Roberts who, along with the blind Dr Orloff (Jean-Pierre Bouyxou), discovers the Countess' secret.

BARRY McKENZIE HOLDS HIS OWN...

UK/France/Australia, 1974. Dir: Bruce Beresford. With: Barry Crocker, Barry Humphries, Donald Pleasence, Ed Devereaux, Dick Bentley, Frank Windsor. Reg Grundy/EMI. Colour.

Left: *Blacula. (FJA).*
Below: *Captain Kronos Vampire Hunter.*

ALABAMA'S GHOST

USA, 1972. Dir: Frederic Hobbs. With: Lani Freeman, Pierre LePage, The Turk Murphy Jazz Band. Ellman/Bremson International. Colour.

Billed as 'A super hip horror movie', a vampire rock group on motorcycles battle a ghost in this regional release written, produced and directed by Hobbs. A blaxploitation rarity.

ANGELES Y QUERUBINES

Mexico, 1972. Dir: Rafael Corkidi. With: Ana Luisa Peluffo, Helena Rojo, Jorge Humberto Robles, David Silva, Roberto Canedo, Cecilia Pezet. Cine Producciones. Colour.

Includes three stories, the middle one about vampire bride Angela (Rojo).

THE BARE BREASTED COUNTESS

(Orig: LA COMTESSE NOIRE/LA COUNTESS AUX SEINS NUS/LES AVALEUSES. USA: aka EROTIKILL/ THE LOVES OF IRINA) France/Belgium/Portugal, 1973. Dir: J.P. Johnson (Jesús Franco). With: Lina Romay, Alice Arno (Marie-France Broquet), Jack Taylor, Monica Swinn, Jess Franck (Jesús Franco), Luis Barboo. General Films/Eurocine. Colour.

The Countess Irina Karlstein (Romay) is a

The second Barry McKenzie film, based on the cartoon strip in *Private Eye* magazine. Barry (Crocker) and his Australian pals uncover a plot by the sinister Erich Count Plasma (Pleasence) to kidnap the Queen of England so that she can be used to promote the Transylvanian tourist industry. A bad taste comedy, with copious vomiting, a bloody kung fu battle, a vampire staked with a sharpened French loaf and a hunchbacked assistant named Dorothy. Humphries plays the dreadful Edna Everage as well as several other characters, and a number of British comedians (Tommy Trinder, Derek Guyler, Arthur English, Roy Kinnear and John Le Mesurier) are totally wasted.

THE BAT PEOPLE

USA, 1974. Dir: Jerry Jameson. With: Stewart Moss, Marianne McAndrew, Michael Pataki, Paul Carr, Arthur Space, Robert Berk. American International. Colour.

Originally announced as *It Lives By Night*. When biologist Moss is bitten by vampire bats, he turns into a briefly seen man-size bat monster created by Stan Winston. Low-key horror movie in which Pataki stands out as a sleazoid cop who blows his own head off when attacked by bats.

BEDTIME WITH ROSIE

UK, 1974. Dir: Wolf Rilla. With: Una Stubbs, Diana Dors, Johnny Briggs. FPD. Colour.

Comedy with a nightmare sequence involving a vampire.

BLACULA

USA, 1972. Dir: William Crain. With: William Marshall, Denise Nicholas, Vonetta McGee, Gordon Pinsent, Thalmus Rasulala, Emily Yancy. American International. Colour.

One of the better blaxploitation movies. Marshall plays African prince Manuwalde, bitten by Count Dracula (Charles Macaulay), who is revived in modern Los Angeles and seeks the reincarnation of his dead wife. Marshall portrays the vampire with dignity, and veteran character actor Elisha Cook Jr has a cameo role as a hook-handed morgue attendant. Music by The Hues Corporation.

Sequel: SCREAM BLACULA SCREAM (qv; 1973)

BLOOD

USA, 1974. Dir: Andy Milligan. With: Allen Berendt, Hope Stansbury, Eve Crosby, Patti Gaul, Michael Fischetti, Pamela Adams. Damiano/Bryanston. Colour.

More nonsense from writer/director Milligan, filmed on Staten Island in ten days for $20,000. Dracula's daughter, Regina (Stansbury), and the Wolf Man's son, Dr Lawrence Orlovski (Berendt), marry and move to America to raise carnivorous plants. Don't bother.

BLOOD FOR DRACULA

(Orig: DRACULA CERCA SANGUE DI VERGINE E...MORI DI SETE. USA: ANDY WARHOL'S DRACULA) Italy/France, 1973. Dir: Paul Morrissey (and Antonio Margheriti). With: Joe Dallesandro, Udo Kier, Arno Juerging, Maxime McKendry, Milena Vucotic, Vittorio De Sica. CC Champion/Yanne-Rassam/ Bryanston. Colour.

Three of the stars from *Flesh for Frankenstein* (1973) are reunited in this companion movie from the same writer/director(s). Dracula (Kier) and his assistant (Juerging) load up their vintage 1930s car with the Count's coffin and head off to Catholic Italy in search of "wirgin's" blood. Unfortunately, the vampire throws up every time he doesn't get the pure stuff. Roman Polanski turns up in a neat cameo as a villager, and in the bloody finale, Dracula has his arms and legs

Above: The Blood Spattered Bride.

hacked off by revolutionary gardener Dallesandro but still manages to move around. Warhol probably wasn't directly involved in this unsubtle horror comedy.

BLOODLUST

(Orig: MOSQUITO DER SCHAENDER) Switzerland, 1976. Dir: Marijan Vajda. With: Werner Pochath, Ellen Umlauf, Peter Hamm, B. Zamula. Monarex. Colour.

An abused young bookkeeper (Pochath) breaks into mortuaries and mutilates the corpses, drinking their blood through a pipette. He also steals the body of a deranged girl (Umlauf) he secretly loved and enshrines it in his apartment.

BLOOD RELATIONS

(Orig: BLOEDVERWANTEN/LES VAMPIRES EN ONT RAS LE BOL) Netherlands/France, 1977. Dir: Wim Lindner. With: Maxim Hamel, Gregoire Aslan, Sophie Deschamps, Robert Dalban, Eddie Constantine, Ralph Arliss. Jaap van Rij Filmproductie/CTIS. Colour.

Horror comedy based on a story by Dutch author Belcampo (Herman P. Schoenfeld Wichers). A young nurse (Deschamps) suspects that the hospital's blood plasma supply is being stolen by vampire doctor Hamel and his undead policeman son (Arliss). She

tries to destroy them by injecting herself with holy water, but ends up becoming another bloodsucker. Eddie (*Alphaville* [1965]) Constantine plays a priest.

THE BLOOD SPATTERED BRIDE

(Orig: LA NOVIA ENSANGRENTADA. USA: aka TILL DEATH DO US PART) Spain, 1972. Dir: Vincent (Vincente) Aranda. With: Alexandra Bastedo, Maribel Martin, Simon Andreu, Dean Selmier, Monserrat Julio, Angel Lombarte. Morgana Films. Colour.

Yet another version of J. Sheridan Le Fanu's 'Carmilla'. Bastedo (first seen buried in the sand with her breasts showing) is an enigmatic vampire who seduces frigid newlywed Martin. In the end, Martin's husband (Andreu) destroys the women when he finds them sleeping together in a coffin made for two. The climax was heavily cut for British and American release prints.

***Above:** Blood for Dracula*

THE BLUE SEXTET

USA, 1971.

Sex film about a man who makes 8mm movies, one of which includes Dracula-like vampires chasing naked women through a dungeon.

THE BODY BENEATH

USA/UK, 1971. Dir: Andy Milligan. With: Gavin Reed, Jackie Skarvellis, Berwick Kaler, Susan Heard, Richmond Ross, Emma Jones. World Video/Cinemedia. Colour.

More trash from Staten Island's writer/producer/director Milligan, who also photographed it in 16mm on location in London's Highgate Cemetery. Reed portrays the Reverend Algernon Ford, the leader of a family of nineteenth century vampires based at Carfax Abbey. He kidnaps a pregnant relative (Skarvellis) to continue the bloodline. Only the creepy Kaler stands out in another Milligan gorefest which is, if possible, even more amateurish than usual.

BONGO WOLF'S REVENGE

USA, 1970. Dir: Tom Baker. With: Bongo Wolf (William Donald Grollman).

Short film in which the drummer-lecturer pays a visit to the Count Dracula Society.

BRAM STOKER'S COUNT DRACULA

(Orig: EL CONDE DRACULA/ NACHTS WENN DRACULA ERWACHT/IL CONTE DRACULA. USA: COUNT DRACULA) Spain/West Germany/Italy, 1970. Dir: Jess (Jesús) Franco. With: Christopher Lee, Herbert Lom, Klaus Kinski, Frederick Williams, Maria Rohm, Soledad Miranda. Fenix/Corona/Filmar/Towers of London. Colour.

Lee plays Dracula the way Bram Stoker described him, and has more to do than in the Hammer sequels. He starts out as an older man with white hair and a moustache who gets younger after drinking blood. When on screen, Lee dominates the film, but there's good support from Lom as Van Helsing and Kinski as a manic Renfield. Unfortunately, it's written (under his usual pseudonym Peter Welbeck) and produced by Harry Alan Towers, and director Franco ruins everything with his relentless zooms and pans.

Remake: DRACULA (qv; 1973)

THE BRIDE'S INITIATION

USA, 1976. Dir: Duncan Stewart. With: Carol Connors, Constance Murray, Ambrosia, Candida Robbins, Mark Brock, Tony Manhall. VCX. Colour.

More hardcore antics, as a semen – drinking Dracula kidnaps and seduces a pair of newlyweds. In the end, the Count turns gay and goes off with the detective investigating the couple's disappearance. Also includes ugly witches, female vampires and the cannibalism of private parts.

THE BRIDES WORE BLOOD

USA. Dir: Robert R. Favorite. With: Dolores Heisel. Regal. Colour.

A vampiric demon plans to impregnate an unsuspecting blonde (Heisel) in this low budget chiller, filmed in Jacksonville, Florida. Director Favorite manages to botch most scenes, including the vampire's death-by-sunlight transformation.

CAPTAIN KRONOS VAMPIRE HUNTER

UK, 1972 (1974). Dir: Brian Clemens. With: Horst Janson, John Carson, Shane Briant, Caroline Munro, John Cater, Ian Hendry. Hammer Films. Colour.

This was the first and, unfortunately, only film in a proposed series created by writer/director Clemens (TV's *The Avengers*). A heady blend of Hammer vampires, comic book violence, spaghetti westerns, heroic fantasy and offbeat comedy. Swashbuckling soldier of fortune Kronos (Janson), hunchback assistant Prof Hieronymous Grost (Cater), and busty gypsy Carla (Munro) must discover the identity of a vampire (a relation to the Karnstein family) who steals youth instead of blood. Could it be guest stars John Carson, Ian Hendry or Wanda Ventham? The direction is sometimes unsure, but there's plenty of new vampire lore and some stunning visuals.

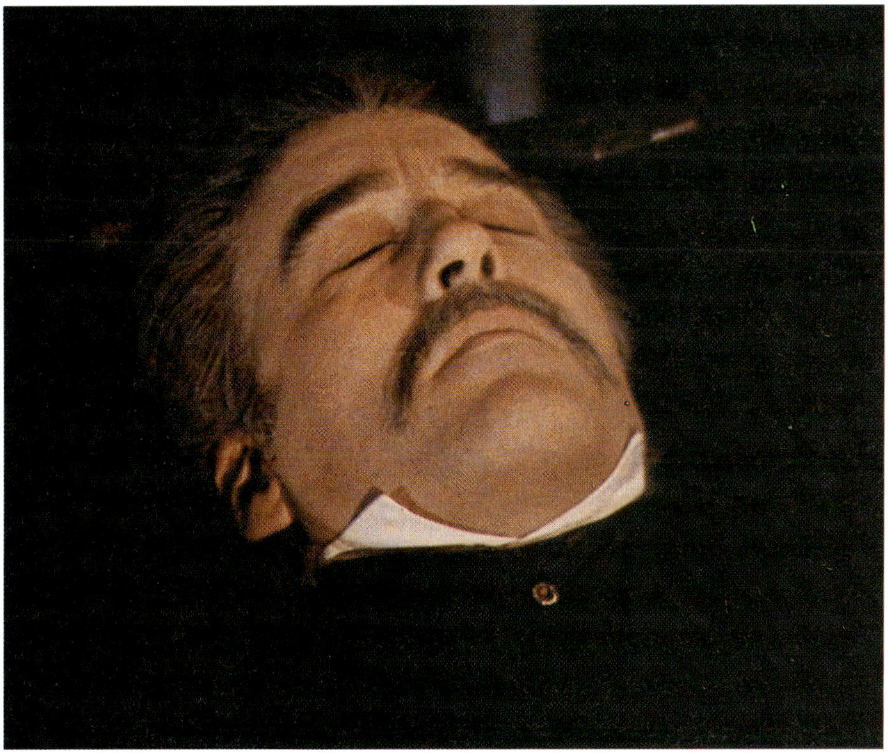

Above: *Bram Stoker's Count Dracula.*

CAPULINA CONTRA LOS MONSTRUOS

Mexico, 1972. Dir: René Cardona. With: Gasper Henaine 'Capulina', Gloriella, Hector Andremar. Estudios America/Panorama Films/Azteca Films. Colour.

More humour from the moustachioed comedian Capulina as he meets a vampire, the Frankenstein monster and a werewolf. Don't they ever get tired of this plot in Mexico?

CAPULINA CONTRA LOS VAMPIROS

Mexico, 1972. Dir: René Cardona. With: Gasper Henaine 'Capulina', Rosy Mendoza, Juan Gallardo, Carlos Agosti, Aurelio Perez (Chori). Producciones Zacarias/Clasa-Mohme. Colour.

Comedy featuring moustachioed comedian Capulina (Henaine), who hides in a suit of armour from the vampires pursuing him. Directed by horror veteran Cardona.

CASE OF THE FULL MOON MURDERS

(aka SEX ON THE GROOVE TUBE. UK: CASE OF THE SMILING STIFFS) USA, 1971. Dir: Sean S. Cunningham. With: Fred Lincoln, Ron Browne, Cathy Walker, Harry Reems, Sheila Stuart. Lobster Enterprises/Dana Films. Colour.

Hardcore/softcore feature from Cunningham, the producer of *The Last House on the Left* (1972) and director of *Friday the 13th* (1980), filmed in Florida. A *Dragnet*-style parody of sex films, with a female vampire (Walker) who kills by fellatio. Reems went on to star in the legendary *Deep Throat* (1972).

CASUAL RELATIONS

USA, 1973. Dir: Mark Rappaport. With: Sis Smith, Mel Austin, Paula Barr, Adrienne Claiborne, Peter Campus, Alan Dahl. Colour/B&W.

Underground feature that includes a spoof film-within-a-film entitled *A Vampire's Love*. Editor/writer/producer/director/distributor Rappaport opens and closes his film with stills and footage from Murnau's *Nosferatu* (1922).

IL CAVALIERE COSTANTE NICOSIA DEMONIACO OVVERO DRACULA IN BRIANZA

Italy, 1975. Dir: Lucio Fulci. With: Lando Buzzanca, Sylva Koscina, Christa Linder, Moira Orfei, Rossano Brazzi, Valentina Cortese. Titanus/Coralta Cinematografica. Colour.

Vampire sex comedy from director Fulci, better known for his zombie movies. While on a trip to Romania, entrepreneur Buzzanca is bitten by Dragulescu (John Steiner). Fearing that he has been 'infected' by homosexuality, Sicilian comic Buzzanca discovers that drinking blood heightens his sexual prowess. Sounds really funny, doesn't it?

A CLOCKWORK ORANGE

UK, 1971. Dir: Stanley Kubrick. With: Malcolm McDowell, Patrick Magee, Adrienne Corri, Miriam Karlin, Michael Bates, Warren Clarke. Polaris/ Warner Bros. Colour.

Based on the novel by Anthony Burgess, Kubrick's disturbing masterpiece follows the violent exploits of malcontent Alex (McDowell) and his gang, the Droogs, in a not-too-distant future when law and society have completely broken down. In one scene, Alex imagines himself as a vampire. The film caused an outcry when first released and has been withdrawn from distribution in Britain for many years.

CHANTOC CONTRA EL TIGRE Y EL VAMPIRO

Mexico, 1971. Dir: Gilberto Martinez Solares. With: Tin-Tan (German Valdes), Gregorio Casal, Aurora Cavel, Lina Marin, Marisa, Carlos Nieto. Cinematografica RA. Colour.

More comic strip vampires from Mexico, as the eponymous hero battles the twin foes of the title.

Top: Count Dracula.
Above: Countess Dracula.

CHOSEN SURVIVORS

USA/Mexico, 1974. Dir: Sutton Roley. With: Jackie Cooper, Bradford Dillman, Richard Jaeckel, Alex Cord, Diana Muldaur, Pedro Armendariz Jr. Metromedia/ Cinerama/Columbia. Colour.

A group of B-movie stars, trapped beneath the desert during a thermonuclear test, battle against a plague of bloodthirsty vampire bats. TV movie-type thrills.

CHRONIQUE DE VOYAGE

France, 1970. Dir: Robert de Laroche. With: Marc Olivier Cayre, Claude Moro, Francine Roussel.

Surreal half-hour short, which includes the heroine in the clutches of a vampire. Narrated by Fabien Roy.

CONFESSIONS OF A MALE ESCORT

(Orig: OBSZONITATEN)
West Germany, 1974. Dir: Alois Brummer. With: Stefan Grey, Sandra Reni, Miriam Moor. Brummer/Farb. Colour.

Softcore comedy set in a spooky house. Includes a vampire, a zombie and a proposed penis transplant!

COUNT DRACULA

UK, 1977. Dir: Philip Saville. With: Louis Jourdan, Frank Finlay, Susan Penhaligon, Judi Bowker, Mark Burns, Jack Shepherd. BBC-TV. Colour.

Billed as 'A gothic romance', this British made-for-TV movie is overlong at two-and-a-half hours (it was shown in three parts in the USA). It's a fairly faithful adaptation of the Bram Stoker novel (and even includes the scene of Dracula crawling head-first down a castle wall), but the mix of film and video gives it an uneven quality. Jourdan is too debonair as the Count, although director Saville manages to include a few Hammer-type shock moments and there's solid support from Finlay's Van Helsing and Shepherd's Renfield.

Remake: DRACULA (qv; 1979)

COUNT EROTICA, VAMPIRE

USA, 1971. Dir: Tony Teresi. With: John Peters, Mary Simon, Paul Robinson. Lobo Productions. Colour

Hardcore vampire movie.

COUNTESS DRACULA

UK, 1970. Dir: Peter Sasdy. With: Ingrid Pitt, Nigel Green, Sandor Eles, Maurice Denham, Lesley-Anne Down, Patience Collier. Hammer Films. Colour.

Despite the title, this is in fact based on the real-life exploits of Elizabeth Bathory. Eighteenth century Hungarian Countess Elisabeth (Pitt) bathes in the blood of virgins to remain youthful. The excellent Nigel Green is her faithful servant who helps her obtain victims. A slow moving historical drama from Hammer, with very little horror (except for a nasty stabbing) and a climactic wedding that is pure melodrama. A good cast overact dreadfully.

COUNT YORGA, VAMPIRE

USA, 1970. Dir: Bob Kelljan (Robert Kelljchian). With: Robert Quarry, Roger Perry, Michael Murphy, Michael Macready, Donna Anders, Judith Lang. Erica/American International. Colour.

Originally planned as a sex film titled *The Loves of Count Iorga*, this low budget vampire chiller is set in modern Los Angeles. Former child star Quarry is effective as Count Yorga, portraying the suave vampire with wit and intelligence. Writer/director Kelljan brings some style to the murky photography, and star/producer Macready got his father, veteran actor George Macready, to narrate the opening and closing scenes. The corpse-white make-up of the vampires looks creepy, there's a nice twist ending and almost everyone ends up dead (or undead!).

Sequel: THE RETURN OF COUNT YORGA (qv; 1971)

Above: *Creatures of Evil.*
Below left: *Count Yorga, Vampire.*

CREATURES OF EVIL

(Orig: DUGO NG VAMPIRA. USA: aka CURSE OF THE VAMPIRES) Philippines/USA, 1970. Dir: Gerardo de Leon. With: Amelia Fuentes, Romeo Vasques, Eddie Garcia, Johnny Monteiro, Rosario del Pilar, Mary Walter. Sceptre Industries/Hemisphere Pictures. Colour.

Director de Leon and star Fuentes are reunited from *The Blood Drinkers* (1966) for this unusual vampire thriller, shot in vibrant colour. A brother and sister return to their father's estate, only to discover that he keeps their dead mother — now a vampire — chained in a basement crypt, where he periodically whips her. When the brother also becomes a vampire, it ends in tragedy for everyone. More a soap opera than a horror film, this family saga also includes a couple of ghosts and a lot of religious symbolism.

CRYPT OF THE LIVING DEAD

(Orig: LA TUMBA DELA ISLA MALDITA. USA: aka HANNAH QUEEN OF THE VAMPIRES. UK: aka VAMPIRE WOMAN) Turkey/USA, 1972. Dir: Ray Danton (and Julio Salvador). With: Andrew Prine, Mark Damon, Teresa Gimpera, Patty Sheppard (Shepard), Ihsan Genik, Mariano Rey. Atalas Films/Coast Industries. Colour.

Atmospheric night sequences and an unusual setting make this an interesting vampire thriller. Actor-turned-director Danton imaginatively uses the Turkish locations to tell the story of 700 year-old undead queen Hannah (Gimpera), the bride of Louis VII, resurrected on Vampire Island. The climax features a vampire, burned to a crisp, still attacking villagers.

CUADECUC (VAMPIR)

Spain, 1970. Dir: Pedro Portabella. With: Christopher Lee, Herbert Lom, Soledad Miranda, Fred Williams, Jack Taylor. Films 59 Barcelona. B&W.

Overlong, experimental short that uses electronic effects instead of natural sound (such as the incongruous noise of a jet plane over scenes of a funeral hearse). The best sequences show cast members joking around behind the scenes on *Bram Stoker's Count Dracula* (1970). The grainy black and white photography doesn't help.

CURSE OF THE DEVIL

(Orig: EL RETORNO DE WALPURGIS) Spain/Mexico, 1973. Dir: Carlos

Aured. With: Paul Naschy (Jacinto Molina), Fay (Fabiola) Falcon, Vidal (Antonio Vidal) Molina, May Oliver (Maritza Olivares), Maria Silva, Ana Farra. Loyus Films/Producciones Escorpion/Atlas International. Colour.

Naschy's seventh outing as El Hombre Lobo (following *Dr. Jekyll and the Werewolf* [1971]). He plays a Hungarian inquisitor cursed by the satanic Countess Elisabeth Bathory (Patty Shepard) as she burns at the stake. Centuries later, his descendant (also Naschy) turns into a werewolf until staked with a silver dagger. **Sequel: NIGHT OF THE HOWLING BEAST (1975)**

DAUGHTERS OF DARKNESS

(Orig: LA ROUGE AUX LEVRES/BLUT AUF DEN LIPPEN. USA: aka CHILDREN OF THE NIGHT)

Belgium/France/West Germany, 1971. Dir: Harry Kumel. With: Delphine Seyrig, Andrea Rau, John Karlen, Danielle Ouimet, Paul Esser, Georges Jamin. Showking/Maya/Roxy/Cine Vog. Colour.

Stylish, sensual, erotic chiller, filmed under the title *Erzebeth*. Newlyweds Ouimet and Karlen stay at an out-of-season seaside hotel in Ostend and are seduced by Seyrig's stunning thirties-looking Countess Bathory and her companion/lover (Rau). Despite several bloody deaths, director Kumel never quite reveals if the Countess is really a centuries-old vampire. The film combines moments of great visual poetry with camp splendour, resulting in an almost dream-like intensity. Original release prints excluded a postscript featuring Ouimet.

THE CURSE OF THE VAMPIRE

(Orig: LA LLAMADA DEL VAMPIRO)

Spain, 1971 (1973). Dir: Joseph de Lacy (José Maria Elorietta). With: Beatriz Lacy, Nicholas Ney, Ines Skorpio, Diana Sorel, Loretta Martin, Loli (Loretta) Tovar. Lacy Films/Sesena/Arco Films. Colour.

Dr Greta Metterlich (Lacy) and her assistant (Sorel) are invited to stay at the sinister mansion of Carl von Rysselbert (Ney). He turns out to be a vampire who puts the bite on Sorel and attacks Lacy before being staked.

DEAD OF NIGHT

USA, 1976. Dir: Dan Curtis. With: Ed Begley Jr, Patrick Macnee, Anjanette Comer, Elisha Cook Jr, Horst Buchholz, Joan Hackett. Dan Curtis Productions. Colour.

Three more scripts by Richard Matheson for a proposed *Dead of Night* series were incorporated into this second made-for-TV movie (following *Trilogy of Terror* [1975]). 'Second Chance' is based on a time travel story by Jack Finney and 'Bobby' is an original reworking of 'The Monkey's Paw'. The middle episode is based on Matheson's own short story, 'No Such Thing as a Vampire': Professor Gheria (Macnee) and his beautiful wife (Comer) live in an old mansion. One night she is attacked by a vampire — or is she? A young doctor (Buchholz) is called, and the denouement is fairly predictable.

DEAFULA

USA, 1975. Dir: Peter Wechsberg. With: Peter Wechsberg, James Randall, Dudley Hemstreet, Lee Darrel, Gary R. Holmstrom, Katherine Wilson. Signscope. B&W.

Writer/director Wechsberg, who is deaf, stars as theology student Steve Adams, infected before birth by Dracula (Holmstrom). He periodically grows fangs, a big nose and turns into Deafula, until finally destroyed by religious symbols while

Left: Dracula (1979).

Left: *Dracula A.D. 1972.*

trapped by the police in a church. What makes this low budget vampire pic unique is that it was filmed entirely in sign language (with a minimal voice-over commentary) for the hearing-impaired. It also includes a hunchbacked assistant with tin-can hands.

THE DEATHMASTER

USA, 1972. Dir: Ray Danton. With: Robert Quarry, Bill Ewing, Brenda Dickson, John Fielder, Betty Anne Rees, William Jordan, Bob Picket. R.F. Productions/World Entertainment/American International Pictures. Colour.

Robert (Count Yorga) Quarry plays Khorda, a long-haired vampire whose coffin is washed ashore in southern California. He becomes a guru to a group of hippies in this dated film directed by ex-actor Danton, also responsible for *Crypt of the Living Dead* (1972). Quarry was associate producer.

A DEUSA DE MARMORE — ESCRAVA DO DIABO

Brazil, 1978. Dir: Rosangela Maldonado. With: Rosangela Maldonado, José Mojica Marins, João Paulo, Luandy Maldonado, Anadir Goe, Anita Nunes. Panorama Do Brazil. Colour.

Maldonado wrote, produced, directed and starred in this sex/horror movie. She plays a 2000 year-old woman whose deal with the Devil means she will always remain young by sucking the lifeforce out of her victims with a fatal kiss during sex. In the end, she reverts to her real age when confronted by a cross.

DEVIL'S NIGHTMARE

(Orig: LA PLUS LONGUE NUIT DU DIABLE/LA NOTTE PIU LUNGA DEL DIAVOLO. USA: aka VAMPIRE PLAYGIRLS/THE DEVIL WALKS AT MIDNIGHT/CASTLE OF DEATH/ SUCCUBUS)

Belgium/Italy, 1971. Dir: Jean Brismée. With Erika Blanc (Enrica Bianchi Colombatto), Jean Servais, Daniel Emilfork, Jacques Monseau, Ivana Novak, Shirley Corrigan. Delfino Film/Cetelci. Colour.

A group of travellers are trapped by a storm in a creepy castle. Co-writer/director Brismée gives the film a dream-like quality by making each of the victims symbolize one of the seven deadly sins, killed off by Blanc's succubus, the servant of a bizarre-looking Satan (Emilfork). Imaginative photography can't overcome the wooden performances.

THE DEVIL'S PLAYTHING

(aka VEIL OF BLOOD)

Switzerland, 1973. Dir: Joe (Joseph W.) Sarno. With: Nadia Senkowa, Untel Syring, Marie Forssa, Ulrike Butz, Flavia Reyt, Nico Wolf. Leisure Time/Monarex. Colour.

A castle full of sexy nuns prepare for the return of Baroness Vaga, a vampire burned at the stake in the Middle Ages.

THE DEVIL'S SKIN

Singapore, 1970. With: Ingrid Hu, Meng Li, Sun Tao. Cathay. Colour.

A fairy vixen duels with a vampire.

THE DEVIL'S WEDDING NIGHT

(Orig: IL PLENILUNIO DELLE VERGINE)

Italy, 1973. Dir: Paul Solvay (Luigi Batzella). With: Sara Bay (Rosalba Neri), Mark Damon, Frances Davis (Francesca Romana Davila), Miriam Barrios (Esmeralda Barros), Stan Papps (Xiro Papas), Sergio Pislar. Virginia Cinematografica/ Dimension Pictures. Colour.

Twin brothers (Damon) search for the legendary ring of the Nibelungen in Transylvania. Every twenty-five years it has the power to evoke a witches' sabbat. Bay takes her clothes off a lot as the vampire Countess del Vries, who bathes in virgin's blood. You've seen it all before.

LA DINASTIA DRACULA

Mexico, 1978. With: Fabian Forte. Colour.

Forte plays another Mexican Dracula.

DOCTOR DRACULA

USA, 1977. Dir: Al Adamson and Paul Aratow. With: John Carradine, Donald Barry, Larry Hankin, Susan McIver, Geoffrey Land, Regina Carrol. Independent-International/ Rafael Film Associates. Colour.

Anatol Gregorio (Land) is really Count Dracula, who thwarts the satanic plans of the occult Society of the Bleeding Rose, or the Evil Ones, headed by Carradine and Hankin (who believes he is the reincarnation of Svengali). The Count is finally blown to pieces. Apparently this is a re-edited version of Aratow's *Lucifer's Women* (1975), with extra footage shot by Adamson. It's still pretty terrible.

DRACULA

UK/USA, 1973. Dir: Dan Curtis. With: Jack Palance, Simon Ward, Nigel Davenport, Pamela Brown, Fiona Lewis, Penelope Horner. Dan Curtis Productions. Colour.

Underrated adaptation of Bram Stoker's novel, originally made for American television but released theatrically (in a cut version) overseas. The script, by Richard Matheson, borrows heavily from Hammer's 1958 version but, probably because of its small screen origins, concentrates on the Count's Byronic qualities instead of his bloodletting. Palance, not the most subtle of actors, gives one of his better performances as a more human Dracula, motivated as much by love as bloodlust. Davenport's Van Helsing is perhaps a little too dynamic and Lewis far too voluptuous as Lucy, but overall this is a particularly effective version of the story thanks to excellent colour photography and stylish period setting.

Remake: COUNT DRACULA (qv; 1977)

DRACULA

UK/USA, 1979. Dir: John Badham. With: Frank Langella, Laurence Olivier, Donald Pleasence, Kate Nelligan, Trevor Eve, Jan Francis. Mirisch/Universal. Colour.

Langella recreates his Broadway hit role in this overblown version of the much-filmed novel. Director John Badham makes it look atmospheric and hauntingly beautiful, helped by a big budget, superb production design and a lush John Williams score, but it's all so *boring*. Pleasence is fine as Dr Seward and Tony Haygarth makes a nicely maniacal Renfield; however, Olivier's performance as Van Helsing sounds more like a homage to Peter Sellers' Inspector Clouseau, Nelligan and Eve fail to bring any spark to their respective roles of Lucy and Jonathan Harker, and the best scene in the movie (and the only one to inspire even a shiver of fear) is when Van Helsing confronts his red-eyed vampiric daughter in an old mine shaft.

Remake: NOSFERATU THE VAMPYRE (qv; 1979)

DRACULA A.D. 1972

UK, 1972. Dir: Alan Gibson. With: Christopher Lee, Peter Cushing, Stephanie Beacham, Christopher Neame, Michael Coles, Marsha Hunt, Caroline Munro. Hammer Films. Colour.

***Top:** Daughters of Darkness.*
***Above:** Devil's Nightmare.*

Originally announced as *Dracula Today*, the sixth in Hammer's Dracula series updates the Count to 1970s swinging Chelsea. It actually works surprisingly well, thanks to Alan Gibson's stylish direction, good production values and the chance, fourteen years after the original, to see Lee and Cushing (as Van Helsing's grandson) once again pitted against each other. The dialogue and life-style of the overage hippies was already dated when the film was released and is simply an embarrassment. However, there's a great pre-credits flashback sequence, solid support by Michael Coles as a police inspector and some nice original touches (such as Neame's vampiric Johnny Alucard

coming to a nasty end in the shower). Music by Stoneground.
Sequel: THE SATANIC RITES OF DRACULA (qv; 1973)

DRACULA AND SON

(Orig: DRACULA, PERE ET FILS) France, 1976. Dir: Edouard Molinaro. With: Christopher Lee, Bernard Menez, Marie-Helene Breillat, Catherine Breillat, Jean-Claude Dauphin, Anna Gael. Quartet Films. Colour.
Three years after he quit playing the Count for Hammer, Lee appeared as a grey-haired Dracula in this comedy which marked the début of the director of *La Cage aux Folles* (1978). Fleeing Transylvania, the Count arrives in present day Paris where he becomes a movie star. Apparently, the original film was a clever inspiration for *Love at First Bite* (1979), but the re-edited and re-dubbed version released in America is a travesty.

DRACULA BLOWS HIS COOL

(Orig: GRAF DRACULA IN OBERBAYERN) West Germany, 1979. Dir: Carlo Ombra. With: Gianni Garko, Betty Verges, Bea Fiedler, Giacoino Rizzo, Ralf Wolter, Linda Grondier. Lisa-Barthonia Film. Colour.
Silly sex comedy in which a group of *Playboy* models turn Castle Dracula into a hotel and disco — until the Count (Garko, who also appears as the photographer hero) and his vampire mistress (Verges) show up. More knockabout humour than horror, although there are a couple of atmospheric moments amongst the nudity. For some reason, all the terrible disco songs are in English. This was originally going to be called *Dracula Sucks* in America until they found out about the porno film with the same title.

DRACULA PRISONER OF FRANKENSTEIN

(Orig: DRACULA CONTRA FRANKENSTEIN/DRACULA LE PRISONNIER DE FRANKENSTEIN. USA: THE SCREAMING DEAD) Spain/France, 1972. Dir: Jess (Jesús) Franco. With: Howard Vernon (Mario Lippert), Dennis Price, Genevieve Deloir, Josiane Gibert, Albert (Alberto) D'Albes, Mary Francis. Interfilme/Fenix Films/ Prodif Ets. Colour.
The first of three films by Franco, loosely connected by many of the same characters and actors. Dr Frankenstein (a sick-looking Price, dubbed by a younger voice) and his mute servant Morpho (Luis Barboo) revive a green-faced Dracula (Vernon), so that together with his vampire brides they can create an undead army to conquer the world. Fernando Bilbao plays a Karloff-like Frankenstein monster, and Dr Seward, a gypsy witch and a mangy werewolf (Brandy) are also involved. This was supposedly a homage to director James Whale! More tedious ineptitude from director Franco and another nail in the coffin of Dennis Price's career.
Sequel: THE EROTIC RITES OF FRANKENSTEIN (1972)

THE DRACULA SAGA

(Orig: LA SAGA DE LOS DRACULA. USA: SAGA OF THE DRACULAS/ DRACULA — THE BLOODLINE CONTINUES) Spain, 1972. Dir: Leon Klimovsky. With: Tina Sainz, Tony Isbert, Narciso Ibañez Menta, Helga Liné, Maria Kosti, J.J. Paladino. Profilmes. Colour.
The Count's granddaughter, Berta (Sainz), returns to the ancestral castle to meet Dracula (Ibañez Menta) and the (undead) family — the unborn child she carries is the last heir to the aristocratic title. An interesting idea, which also features a monstrous cyclopic child and music by J. Sebastian Bach.

DRACULA'S DOG

(UK: ZOLTAN...HOUND OF DRACULA) USA, 1977. Dir: Albert Band. With: Michael Pataki, Reggie Nalder (Alfred Reginald Natzler), José Ferrer, Jan Shutan, Libbie Chase, John Levin. Vic Cinema. Colour.

Below: Dracula (1979).

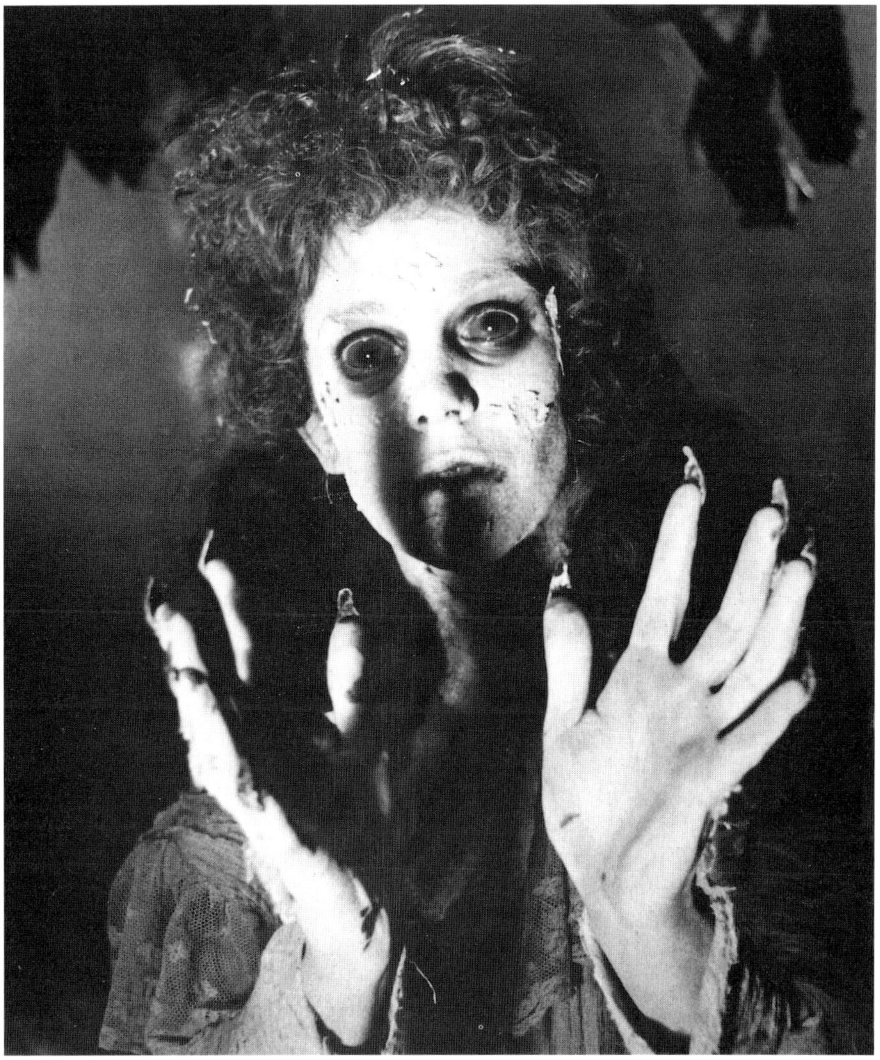

Directed by producer Charles Band's father, Albert (*I Bury the Living* [1958]) Band, this low budget horror film has a wonderfully silly premise: Dracula's vampire dog and his undead servant (the creepy looking Nalder) escape from their Transylvanian tomb and travel to modern Los Angeles to find the Count's last living relative (Pataki). The scenes of a pack of vampire dogs attacking Pataki's all-American family are laughable, much of the photography is too dark and Ferrer's career hits rock-bottom as a Van Helsing-type vampire hunter. An enjoyable time-waster.

DRACULA'S GREAT LOVE

(Orig: EL GRAN AMOR DEL CONDE DRACULA. UK: DRACULA'S VIRGIN LOVERS. USA: aka CEMETERY GIRLS/VAMPIRE PLAYGIRLS). Spain, 1972 (1975). Dir: Javier Aguirre. With: Paul Naschy (Jacinto Molina), Haydée Politoff, Rossana Yanni, Mirta Miller, Ingrid Garbo, Vic Winner. Janus Films/Eva Films. Colour.

Spain's great horror star Naschy co-scripted and stars as Dr Wendell, really Count Dracula, who runs a strange nursing home and turns three unwary travellers into vampires. He falls in love with a fourth (Politoff), and wants to use her in an attempt to bring his dead daughter back to life. This was probably the first Dracula to commit suicide with a stake!

DRACULA'S LUSTERNE SEX-VAMPIRE

Switzerland, 1970. Dir: Mario d'Alcala. With: Des Roberts, Alon d'Armand, Ola (Ula) Copa, Horror-Charlie, Ike Haussler, Claudia Barron. RCS Film/Monarex. Colour.

The title translates as *Dracula's Vampire Lust*. More sex and vampires with Roberts, who also starred in *Guess What Happened to Count Dracula* (1970).

DRACULA SUCKS

(aka LUST AT FIRST BITE/ DRACULA'S BRIDE) USA, 1979. Dir: Philip Marshak. With: Jamie Gillis, Annette Haven, John Leslie, Serena, Detlef Van Berg (Reggie Nalder), Kay Parker. First International Pictures/MR Productions/Kodiak. Colour.

All-star (including John Holmes and Seka) porno adaptation of the story, released in both hard- and softcore versions. A virtual scene-for-scene remake of the 1930 movie, the soundtrack borrows snippets of dialogue (including Bela Lugosi's voice) from old radio shows. A pseudonymous Reggie Nalder (real name, Alfred Reginald Natzler) makes a creepy Van Helsing, Gillis is surprisingly effective as Dracula, and McGoogle Schlepper (Richard Bulik) is the most manic Renfield since Dwight Frye. A photo-magazine was published by Dolphin.

Remake: BRAM STOKER'S DRACULA (qv; 1992)

DRACULA VS. FRANKENSTEIN

(aka BLOOD OF FRANKENSTEIN/ THEY'RE COMING TO GET YOU. UK: aka REVENGE OF DRACULA) USA, 1970. Dir: Al Adamson. With: J. Carrol Naish, Lon Chaney, Zandor Vorkov (Roger Engell), Anthony Eisley, Regina Carrol, Greydon Clark. Independent-International. Colour.

Feeble, seventy year-old, wheelchair-bound veteran Naish came out of retirement to play the last Dr Frankenstein, experimenting with blood in an attempt to cure his crippled legs. He is aided by such side-show horrors as monster axe murderer Groton the Mad Zombie (a pathetic-looking Chaney Jr) and a dwarf (Angelo Rossitto). Russ Tamblyn (as a biker) and Jim Davis are special guest stars. Forrest J Ackerman was the technical consultant and plays Dr Beaumont, who is crushed to death by a puffy Frankenstein monster (John Bloom). Vorkov's hammy Dracula has a ring that zaps people — including ageing hippy hero Eisley. The electronic equipment was originally created by Ken Strickfaden for *Bride of Frankenstein* (1935). This was another mess from director Al Adamson, who shot it over a couple of years (originally as *The Blood Seekers* in 1969). It marked a tragic end to the careers of both Naish and Chaney.

Right: *Dracula vs. Frankenstein. (FJA).*
Below: *Dracula's Dog.*

EVERY HOME SHOULD HAVE ONE

UK, 1970. Dir: Jim Clark. With: Marty Feldman, Judy Cornwall, Shelly Berman, Julie Ege, Patrick Cargill, Dinsdale Landen. British Lion. Colour.

Pop-eyed comedian Feldman's first starring role. He plays an advertising executive whose daydream fantasies include being Pan and a vampire.

THE EVIL OF DRACULA

(Orig: CHI O SUU BARA)
Japan, 1975. Dir: Michio Yamamoto. With: Toshio Kurosawa, Mariko Mochizuki, Shin Kishida, Hunie Tanaka, Katsuhiko Sasaki, Mio Ota. Toho. Colour.

The third and last of Yamamoto's series of vampire films for Toho. Inspired by J. Sheridan Le Fanu's 'Carmilla', the principal (Tanaka) of a girl's school is one of the undead, said to be a descendant of Dracula himself. A teacher finally destroys the vampire with a red-hot poker.

EL FANG-DANGO

USA. Dir: Tony deNonno. With: Tony Travis, Chris Jones, Susan Rockower. Showtime. B&W.

Fourteen minute made-for-TV short. In this silent movie-style comedy, Travis plays Dracula with fang-ache.

FASCINATION

France, 1979. Dir: Jean Rollin. With: Franca Mai, Brigitte Lahaie, Jean-Marie Lemaire, Fanny Magier, Miriam Watteau, Alain Plumey. Les Films ABC/Comex. Colour.

After making a number of hardcore movies, Rollin returned to the horror genre with this story about a cult of blood-drinking women. They meet in a castle and ritually slaughter and devour men. Problems arise when one of the women (Mai) falls in love with their next victim (Lemaire). As usual, the visuals far outstrip the storyline and performances.

LA FILLE DE DRACULA

(aka LA HIJA DE DRACULA)
France/Portugal, 1972. Dir: Jesús Franco. With: Britt Nichols, Anne Libert (Josiane Gibert), Howard Vernon (Mario Lippert), Alberto Dalbes, Luis Baroo, Daniel J. White. Comptoir Francais du Film/ Interfilme. Colour.

Another shoddy sex/horror cheapie from Franco, the last in a loosely connected trilogy featuring many of the same characters and actors. Following the death of Dracula (Vernon), Maria Karnstein (Nichols) learns from her dying mother that she is the daughter of the Count and is given the key to his crypt.

DER FLUCH DER SCHWARZEN SCHWESTERN

Switzerland, 1973. Dir: Joseph W. Sarno. With: Heidrun Hankammer, Nadja Henkova, Maria Forsa, Anke Seyring. Colour.

Obscure sex/horror movie involving vampires

FOOLS

USA, 1970. Dir: Tom Gries. With: Jason Robards, Katherine Ross, Scott Hylands, Roy C. Jenson, Mark Bramhall, Marc Hannibal. Translor/Cinerama. Colour.

Romantic drama in which Robards plays waning horror film star Matthew South, who watches himself as a vampire in one scene.

GANJA & HESS

(aka BLOOD COUPLE/DOUBLE POSSESSION/BLACK EVIL/BLACK OUT: THE MOMENT OF TERROR/ BLACK VAMPIRE)
USA, 1973. Dir: Bill Gunn. With: Duane Jones, Marlene Clark, Leonard Jackson, Mabel King, Bill Gunn, Sam Waymon. Kelly-Jordan Enterprises. Colour.

This arty vampire movie, shot in New York, is a welcome attempt to get away from the blaxploitation cycle of the early seventies. Duane Jones plays Dr Hess Green, who becomes a black vampire when he's stabbed with an ancient Myrthian dagger by his assistant (writer/ director Gunn). He turns his attacker's wife into a vampire before finally committing suicide. This has been reissued in several different versions in America. See the original if you can.

Above: Every Home Should Have One.

GARU, THE MAD MONK

USA, 1970. Dir: Andy Milligan. With: Neil Flanagan, Judith Israel, Jacqueline Webb, Julia Willis, Ron Keith, Paul Lieber. Maipix/Nova International. Colour.

More insanity from writer/producer/director Milligan, filmed in New York. In the name of The Lost Souls Church of Mortavia, mad monk Father Garu (Flanagan) tortures prisoners with the aid of his vampire-witch mistress Olga (Webb) and hunchbacked assistant Igor. At just over an hour it's still too long.

Above: *Dracula (1973).*
Right: *Guess What Happened to Count Dracula. (FJA).*

GIDGET GETS MARRIED

USA, 1971. Dir: E.W. Swackhamer. With: Michael Burns, Monie Ellis, Don Ameche, Joan Bennett, Macdonald Carey, Corrine Camacho. Universal. Colour.

TV movie continuation of the sixties film series, as Burns and Ellis play young newlyweds in Glossop, Maryland. Paul Lynde impersonates various movie characters, including Count Dracula. It's terrible.

GO FOR A TAKE

UK, 1972. Dir: Harry Booth. With: Reg Varney, Norman Rossington, Sue Lloyd, Dennis Price, Julie Ege, Patrick Newell. Century Films International/Rank. Colour.

Not only was Dennis Price reduced to appearing in Jess Franco movies, but he turns up as himself playing a plump Count Dracula in this dire British comedy. Varney and Rossington are two gamblers on the run from gangsters who hide out in a film studio. It's not very funny.

GRAVE OF THE VAMPIRE

USA, 1972. Dir: John Hayes. With: William Smith, Michael Pataki, Lynn Peters, Diane Holden, Jay Adler, Kitty Vallacher. Clover/ Millenium Productions/ Entertainment Pyramid. Colour.

William Smith is the reluctant vampire offspring of the undead Caleb Croft (Pataki), who raped Smith's mother in an open grave. He sets out to find his father and destroy him. An odd vampire movie that tries to do something different with the clichés. Pataki turned up as the Count in *Dracula's Dog* five years later.

GUESS WHAT HAPPENED TO COUNT DRACULA

(aka THE MASTER OF THE DUNGEON)
USA, 1970. Dir: Laurence Merrick. With: Des Roberts, Claudia Barron, John Landon, Robert Branche, Frank Donato, Sharon Beverly. Merrick International. Colour.

Count Yorga imitation with Roberts playing modern vampire Count Adrian, who frequents Sunset Strip and the Dracula's castle discotheque. Includes sequences filmed in Hollywood's famed Magic Castle. Besides a straight horror version, this reputedly exists in both softcore and gay versions. Merrick wrote, directed and executive produced.

HALLOWEEN WITH THE ADDAMS FAMILY

(Orig: HALLOWEEN WITH THE NEW ADDAMS FAMILY)
USA, 1977. Dir: Dennis Steinmetz. With: John Astin, Carolyn Jones, Jackie Coogan, Ted Cassidy, Lisa Loring, Vito Scotti. Charles Fries/ NBC-TV. Colour.

Disappointing revival of the hit 1960s series, based on Charles Addams' cartoons. Original cast members Astin, Jones, Coogan and Cassidy are reunited in a story which also features Suzanne Krazna as Countess Dracula. Shot-on-video, it was reissued as a TV movie in 1980.

HANNO CAMBIATO FACCIA

Italy, 1971. Dir: Corrado Farina. With: Adolfo Celi, Giuliano Disperati, Geraldine Hooper, Francesca Modigliani, Amedeo Tommasi, Rosalba Bongiovanni. Filmsettanta/Garigliano. Colour.

Allegorical fantasy with Celi (*Thunderball* [1965]) as Nosferatu, the undead boss of a business empire who offers Disperati a directorship if he will ruthlessly exploit people. Heavy on the symbolism.

THE HORRIBLE SEXY VAMPIRE

(Orig: EL VAMPIRO DE LA AUTOPISTA)
Spain, 1970. Dir: Jim Delavena and Arthur Davidson (José Luis Madrid). With: Waldemar (Wolfgang) Wohlfahrt, Patricia Loran, Luis Iduni, Adela Tauler, Joe Camroy (Anastasio Campoy), Barta Barry. Cinefilms/Paragon. Colour.

Wohlfahrt stars as Count Oblensky, who must spend the night with his lover (Loran) in the cursed ancestral castle. They are haunted by the vampiric Baron von Winninger, who also likes to attack naked women.

HORROR OF THE BLOOD MONSTERS

(aka CREATURES OF THE PREHISTORIC PLANET/CREATURES OF THE RED PLANET/FLESH CREATURES OF THE RED PLANET/ THE FLESH CREATURES/HORROR CREATURES OF THE PREHISTORIC PLANET/SPACE MISSION OF THE LOST PLANET/VAMPIRE MEN OF THE LOST PLANET)
USA, 1970 (1972). Dir: Al Adamson. With: John Carradine, Robert Dix, Vicki Volante, Joey Benson, Jennifer Bishop, Bruce Powers. Independent-International. Colour.
Another mess from producer/director Adamson. Testy scientist Carradine leads a cheap-looking space mission to a new galaxy where they land on an alien planet poisoned by chromatic radiation. This is just a cheap explanation for Adamson's use of colour-tinted footage from *One Million B.C.* (1940), *Unknown Island* (1948) and a black and white Filipino movie with snake men, bat demons and claw creatures. They even advertised the process as 'Spectrum X'! Theodore Gottlieb narrates some opening nonsense about vampire tribes planning to conquer the Earth. Featuring tacky-looking special effects by David L. Hewitt and camerawork by William (Vilmos) Zsigmond.

HORROR OF THE ZOMBIES

(Orig: EL BUQUE MALDITO)
Spain, 1974. Dir: Armando de Ossorio. With: Maria Perschy, Jack Taylor, Carl Leonard (Carlos Lemos), Blanca Estrada, Barbara Rey, Manuel de Blas. Ancla Century/Belen Films/Independent-International. Colour.
A follow-up to *Return of the Evil Dead* (1973), the third in the Blind Dead series is all at sea. This time a boat full of bikini-clad models is boarded by the mummified, blood-lusting Templarios Knights.
Sequel: NIGHT OF THE SEAGULLS (qv; 1975)

HORRORRITUAL

USA, 1972. With: Barry Atwater. Warner Bros. Colour.
Three minute promotional film made to be shown with the American release of *Dracula A.D. 1972* (1972). Atwater (from *The Night Stalker* [1971]) stars as a vampire in this horror/comedy short.

THE HORROR SHOW

USA, 1979. Dir: Richard Schickel. With: Anthony Perkins, Boris Karloff, Bela Lugosi, Charles Laughton, Claude Rains, Lon Chaney Sr. Universal. Colour/B&W.
Documentary celebrating 'sixty magical years of movie monsters' from Universal studios. Hosted by Perkins, and including clips of all the above plus Lon Chaney Jr, Vincent Price, Christopher Lee, Bette Davis, John Barrymore, Janet Leigh, Lee Remick, Robert Shaw, Charlton Heston and many more from *Dracula* (1930), *Frankenstein* (1931), *Psycho* (1960), *The Phantom of the Opera* (1943), etc. Produced, written and directed by Schickel.

Below: Dracula's Great Love.

HOUSE OF DARK SHADOWS

USA, 1970. Dir: Dan Curtis. With: Jonathan Frid, Grayson Hall, Joan Bennett, Kathryn Leigh Scott, Roger Davis, Nancy Barrett. Metro-Goldwyn-Mayer/Dan Curtis. Colour.
Feature version of the popular *Dark Shadows* (1966-71) daytime TV serial. Many of the original cast repeat their roles although, in this version, Barnabas Collins (Frid) is an evil vampire preying on the Collins family. Accidently freed from his coffin by Willie Loomis (John Karlen), the 150 year-old member of the undead is convinced his long lost love has been reincarnated in Maggie Evans (Scott). Grayson Hall plays Doctor Julia Hoffman who believes vampirism is a curable disease. In the end, Barnabas is dispatched with a crossbow bolt. When he ages, the reason he looks just like Dustin Hoffman in *Little Big Man* (1970) is because Dick Smith was responsible for both make-ups.
Sequel: NIGHT OF DARK SHADOWS (1971)

HOUSE OF DRACULA'S DAUGHTER

USA, 1973. Dir: Gordon Hessler. With: John Carradine, Peter Lorre Jr (Eugene Weingand), David Carradine, Lorraine Day, Broderick Crawford. Universal Entertainment. Colour.
A real rarity — it was either never made or never completed! The interesting cast supposedly includes Weingand, who was not related to Peter Lorre and was apparently taken to court for using the name illegally in a number of films.

THE HOUSE THAT DRIPPED BLOOD

UK, 1970. Dir: Peter Duffell. With: Christopher Lee, Peter Cushing, Nyree Dawn Porter, Denholm Elliott, Jon Pertwee, Ingrid Pitt. Amicus. Colour.
Robert Bloch scripted four of his stories for this episodic horror thriller. After renting an old house in the country, Paul Henderson (Pertwee), one of Britain's foremost horror stars, disappears. Stoker, an estate agent, relates the tragic history

of the house to the investigating police inspector... In the fourth tale, Pertwee's unpleasant movie star buys an old cloak, but when his co-star (Pitt) wears it she becomes a real vampire. He ends up as her victim in this tongue-in-cheek version of 'The Cloak'. The other stories (about a fictional character coming to life, a creepy wax museum and a voodoo doll) are also pretty good.

HYOCHO NO BIJO

Japan, 1977. Dir: Umeji Inoue. Shochiku. Colour.

TV movie based on R. Edogawa's story 'Kyuketsuki' ('Vampire').

IMMORAL TALES

(Orig: CONTES IMMORAUX. USA: THREE IMMORAL WOMEN) France, 1974. Dir: Walerian Borowczyk. With: Lise Danvers, Charlotte Alexandra, Pascale Christophe, Fabrice Luchini, Paloma Picasso, Florence Bellamy. Argos/New Line Cinema. Colour.

A collection of four erotic stories aimed at art house audiences. The third and best sequence stars Picasso's daughter Paloma as a lesbian Countess Erzebet Bathory, bathing in the blood of virgins to stay young. One of the other episodes is about Lucretia Borgia. A fifth segment, based on *Beauty and the Beast*, was expanded by Borowczyk into *The Beast* (1974).

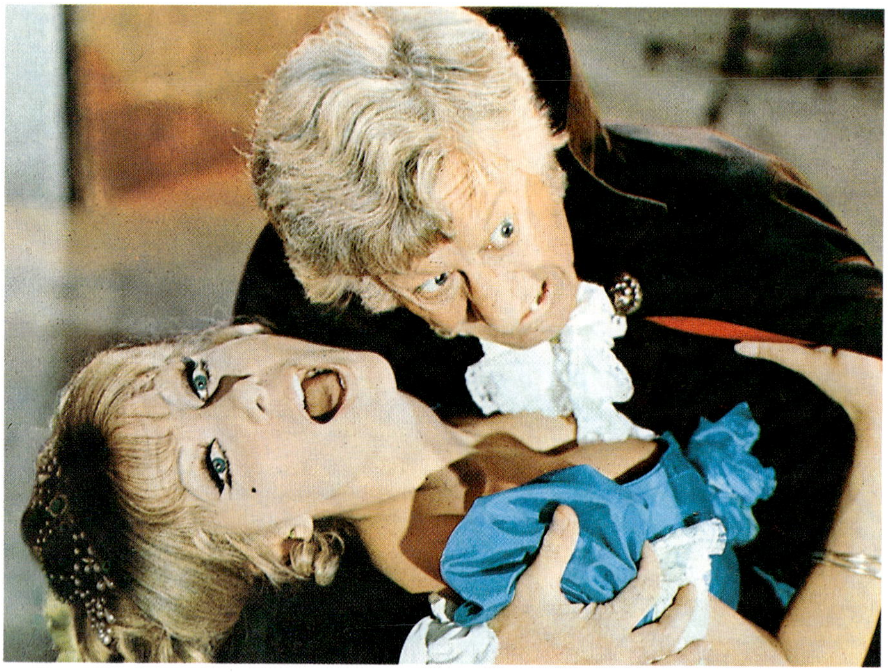

INCENSE FOR THE DAMNED

(USA: BLOODSUCKERS) UK, 1970 (1973). Dir: Michael Burrowes (Robert Hartford-Davis). With: Patrick Macnee, Peter Cushing, Alex Davion, Johnny Sekka, Madeline Hinde, Patrick Mower. Lucinda Films/Titan International/Grand National. Colour.

Based on Simon Raven's novel *Doctors Wear Scarlet*, this muddled horror thriller was finally released after three years, following several lawsuits and with the director's name removed from the credits. What's left attempts to explain vampirism as a sexual perversion (although there is still an inexplicable supernatural element and it takes a stake through the heart to dispatch them). Macnee (star of TV's *The Avengers*) plays a retired Greek general who agrees to help a young woman (Hinde) rescue her fiancé (Mower) from a cult of Greek vampires. It also features Edward Woodward, and Peter Cushing has a brief cameo as the principal of an Oxford university.

THE INCREDIBLE MELTING MAN

USA, 1977. Dir: William Sachs. With: Alex Rebar, Michael Alldredge, Burr DeBenning, Myron Healy, Ann Sweeny, Rainbeaux Smith. Quartet/American International. Colour

This uncredited remake of *First Man Into Space* (1958) features Rebar as an astronaut who returns from orbiting Saturn as a bloodseeking monster. Rick Baker created the disgusting effects. Jonathan Demme (who directed *The Silence of the Lambs* [1991]) turns up in a small role.

IN SEARCH OF DRACULA

(Orig: PA JAKT EFTER DRACULA. UK: aka IN SEARCH OF THE REAL DRACULA) Transylvania/Sweden, 1971. Dir:

Above: *The House That Dripped Blood.*
Left: *House of Dark Shadows.*

Calvin Floyd (and Tony Forsberg). With: Christopher Lee. Aspekt Films. Colour.
Travelogue-type documentary about vampires, made for Swedish TV and based on the book of the same title by Raymond McNally and Radu Florescu. Narrator Christopher Lee looks at the historic facts, the folklore, the literature and finally the films. He also appears as himself, Vlad Tepes and Count Dracula (in scenes shot especially for the film). Includes clips from *Nosferatu* (1922) and Hammer's *Scars of Dracula* (1970).

LA INVASION DE LOS MUERTOS

Mexico, 1972. Dir: René Cardona. With: Blue Demon (Alejandro Cruz), Crista Linder, Zorek, Jorge Mistral, Cesar Silva, Luis Mariscal. Azteca. Colour
This time Mexican wrestler Blue Demon takes on Dracula (Silva), a zombie (Mariscal) and the Frankenstein monster (Tarzan Moreno). Directed by horror veteran Cardona.

INVASION OF THE BLOOD FARMERS

USA, 1972. Dir: Ed Adlum. With: Norman Kelley, Tanna Hunter, Bruce Detrick, Paul Craig Jennings, Jack Neubeck, Richard Erickson. Ed Adlum Productions/NMD. Colour.
Laughable low budget thriller, co-written, produced and directed by Adlum (who also wrote *Shriek of the Mutilated* [1974]). A Druid blood cult kidnap victims from a small town in an attempt to revive their ancient queen. Terrible performances, particularly from the lisping lead villain, and a ludicrous mock-James Mason narration. The gore effects are unconvincing, and the 'songs' were co-written by someone named A.J. Smut! The ads warned: 'Don't eat before you see this show and you'll have nothing to lose!!'

JONATHAN

(aka JONATHAN, VAMPIRE STERBEN NICHT)

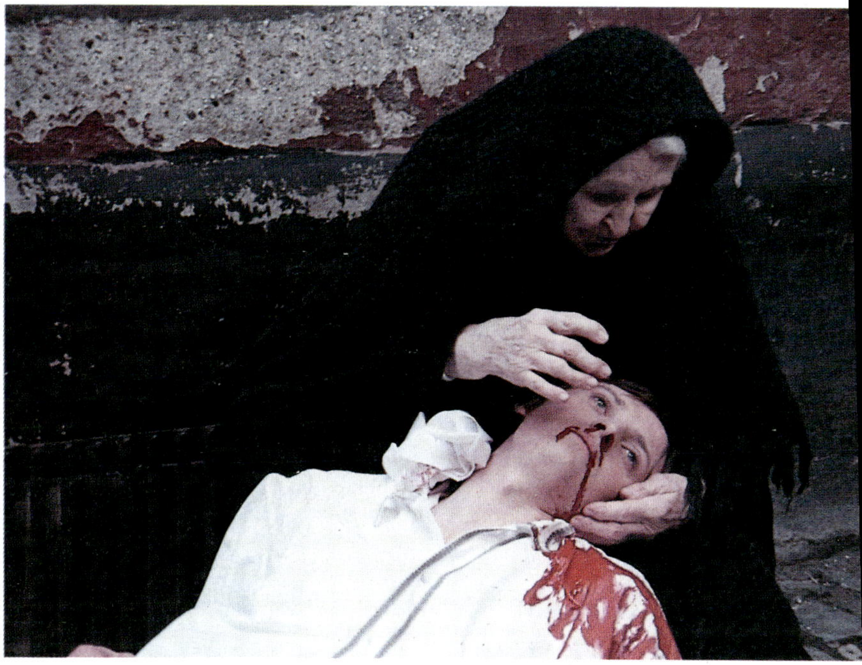

allegory for the rise of fascism. The eponymous hero is, of course, Jonathan Harker (Jung), a member of the peasant resistance movement who is sent by an old professor (von Schab) to destroy Krumm's Führer-like Dracula and his blackshirted thugs. The Count and his undead acolytes are finally driven into the sea and destroyed. Cinematographer Robbi Müeller contributes remarkably fluid camerawork. Scenes of sex and violence were apparently added after release to make the film more commercial.

EL JOVENCITO DRACULA

Spain, 1975. Dir: Carlos Benpar (Carlos Benito Parra). With: Carlos Benpar (Carlos Benito Parra), Susanna Estrada, Victor Israel, Marina Ferri, Veronica Miriel, Norma Kerr. Los Films del Mediterraneo. Colour.
Low budget comedy. Benpar stars as the last descendant of Count Dracula, who travels to Transylvania to claim his inheritance. But the descendant of Van Helsing is the town mayor who wants to turn Castle Dracula into a tourist attraction. Characters are named after those in Bram Stoker's novel.

Top: Jonathan.

KATHAVAI THATTEEYA MOHNI PAYE

India, 1975. Dir: M.A. Rajaraman. With: C.R. Patiban, Sanjivirajan, Desikan, Lisa. Anuradha International. Colour.
The reign of terror of a cursed vampire prince is ended by a private detective in this Tamil horror film, inspired by

bove: The Legend of the 7 Golden ampires.

[redacted] little girl in 1876. When her coffin is exhumed one hundred years later, she is transformed into a beautiful woman (Kraft) who has to drink five litres of blood a day to survive. She eventually falls in love with a policeman (Harris), and they end up together in her coffin. Special effects by Colin Chilvers.

LAKE OF DRACULA

(Orig: CHI O SUU ME)
Japan, 1971. Dir: Michio Yamamoto. With: Mori Kishida, Midori Fujita, Osahide Takahashi, Sanae Emi, Kaku Takashina, Hideji Ohtaki. Toho. Colour.

A young artist, Akiko (Fujita), moves into a house near a lake and starts reliving her childhood nightmares. She discovers a nearby mansion is occupied by a golden-eyed vampire (Kishida), who is eventually impaled on a sword by his zombie grandfather. Yamamoto's improved follow-up to his *The Night of the Vampire* (1970) owes much to Fisher's *Dracula* (1958) and the rest of the Hammer series.

LEGACY OF SATAN

USA, 1973. Dir: Gerard Damiano. With: Lisa Cristian, John Francis, Paul Barry, Christ Helm, Deborah Horlen, Ann Paul. Damiano Films. Colour.

Tedious occult thriller, written, edited and directed by Damiano, best known for his porno classic *The Devil in Miss Jones* (1973). Cristian plays Maya, a New York housewife who is lured into a cult of satanic vampires led by Dr Muldavo (Francis). Nothing much more happens until the end when, disowned by the Devil (Lord Rakish), Muldavo is transformed into a horrible-looking corpse. If this ever included any sex scenes they are definitely missing from most prints, which usually run just under an hour!

THE LEGENDARY CURSE OF LEMORA

(Orig: LEMORA, THE LADY DRACULA. USA: aka LEMORA A CHILD'S TALE OF THE SUPERNATURAL/LADY DRACULA)
USA, 1973. Dir: Richard Blackburn. With: Lesley Gilb, Cheryl (Rainbeaux) Smith, William Whitton, Hy Pike, Maxine Ballantyne, Steve Johnson. Blackburn Productions. Colour.

This low budget supernatural chiller succeeds because of its bizarre atmosphere and Gilb's sensuous vampire. Set in 1920s Georgia, a young church singer (Smith) has a series of disturbing sexual fantasies: her gangster father is used to lure her to an old village dominated by Lemora (Gilb), a beautiful vampire whose followers include a group of strange children. However, the blood-drinking disease has also created many grotesque monstrosities living in the surrounding woods. Director Blackburn turns up as a Reverend. The Catholic Film Board gave the film a condemned rating.

THE LEGEND OF BLOOD CASTLE

(Orig: CEREMONIA SANGRIENTA. USA: aka THE FEMALE BUTCHER/ BLOOD CEREMONY)
Spain/Italy, 1972. Dir: Jorge Grau. With: Lucia Bose, Espartaco Santoni, Ewa Aulin, Ana Farra, Lola Gaos, Franca Grey. X Films/Luis Films. Colour.

Serious version of the Bathory legend, given an exploitation release in America ('Schooled in carnage and blood she butchered 610 nubile young virgins'). Bose portrays the descendant of the original Countess Bathory, who retains her youth by bathing in the blood of virgin victims obtained by her vampire husband. This ponderous, arty movie has the vampires being put on trial for their crimes! Co-writer and director Grau was a former assistant to Michelangelo Antonioni.

THE LEGEND OF THE 7 GOLDEN VAMPIRES

(USA: THE SEVEN BROTHERS MEET DRACULA)
Hong Kong/UK, 1974. Dir: Roy Ward Baker. With: Peter Cushing, Julie Ege, David Chiang, Robin Stewart, Shih Szu, Robert Hanna. Hammer Films/Shaw Brothers. Colour.

Hammer's final Dracula movie to date brings Peter Cushing back for one last time as Van Helsing, but Christopher Lee is replaced by a theatrical John Forbes-Robertson as the Count. This is an enjoyable blend of kung fu and Hammer horror as Van Helsing and companions travel to a Chinese village to protect its inhabitants from a band of masked, marauding vampires. The scenes of the vampires' zombie slaves, rising EC Comics-like from their graves, are effective, but the make-up looks cheap and more care could have been taken with the script. American audiences had to wait six years to see this. The same year, Hammer announced *Kali: Devil Bride of Dracula* with Cushing again to play Van Helsing, but it was never made.

LEONOR

Spain/France/Italy, 1975. Dir: Juan Buñuel. With: Michel Piccoli, Liv Ullmann, Ornella Mutti, Antonio Ferrandis, José Maria Caffarel, Angel del Pozo. Goya Films/Transeuropa Films. Colour.

Co-written and directed by the son of director Luis Buñuel, this fourteenth century fairy tale is based on a story by Ludwig Tieck. Piccoli plays a knight obsessed with his dead wife (Ullmann). He makes a deal with the Devil to bring her back to life, but she returns as a plague-carrying vampire. Music by Ennio Morricone.

LET'S SCARE JESSICA TO DEATH

USA, 1971. Dir: John Hancock. With: Zohra Lampert, Barton Heyman, Kevin O'Connor, Getchen Corbett, Alan Manson, Mariclare Costello. Paramount. Colour.

Recovering from a nervous breakdown, Jessica (Lampert) is taken by her husband Duncan and friend Woody to stay in an old Connecticut farmhouse reputedly haunted by a vampire girl (Corbett). She soon starts seeing and hearing strange things and, from the title, you'd expect that someone's trying to drive her insane. The surprise twist is that it's all really happening — there really is a vampire who drowned in the lake and the local community are all undead (although they walk around in daylight). Débuting director Hancock gives the film a slow, dreamlike quality, but is let down by a confused script, ugly photography and weak performances.

Above: Let's Scare Jessica to Death.

LEVRES DE SANG

France, 1975. Dir: Jean Rollin. With: Jean-Lou Philippe, Anne Briand, Nathalie Perrey, Willy Braque, Paul Biscaglia, Cathy Castel. Off Production/Scorpion 5/Nordia Films. Colour.

Probably one of Rollin's best films. Co-writer Philippe plays a young man obsessed with a woman in white (Briand) he sees in visions. She leads him to a cemetery, where he opens the coffins and releases a horde of female vampires. In the end he discovers that the woman is his sister, buried by his mother for vampirising his father. This complicated Oedipal fantasy includes some wonderfully poetic images.

LINDA LOVELACE FOR PRESIDENT

USA, 1976. Dir: Claudio Guzman. With: Linda Lovelace, Scatman Crothers, Joe E. Ross, Mickey Dolenz, Louis Quinn, Chuck McCann. Selectatape. Colour.

Silly sex comedy, available in various hard- and softcore versions, starring Lovelace, probably the world's most famous porno star. Besides the surprising line-up of guest stars, this also includes a talking chimp, a dwarf, H-bomb footage and a Dracula-like vampire!

LIPS OF BLOOD

(Orig: LE SANG DES AUTRES/LES CHEMINS DE LA VIOLENCE/EL SEGRETTO DE LA MOMIA/PERVERSIONS SEXUELLES)
France/Spain, 1972. Dir: Ken Rudder (Alejandro Parti Gelabert and Pierre Chevalier). With: Michael Flynn, Richard Vitz, Georges Rigaud, Manon Treviere, Catherine Frank, Teresa Gimpera. Les Films de l'Epee/Orbita Films. Colour.

Softcore horror film set in Dartmoor Castle. When the perfectly preserved body of an ancient Egyptian boy is revived by an electrical experiment, it needs fresh blood to survive. To get its female victims' blood circulating faster, the mummy rapes them. Also includes a murderous crawling hand.

LISZTOMANIA

UK, 1975. Dir: Ken Russell. With: Roger Daltrey, Sara Kestelman, Paul Nicholas, Fiona Lewis, Veronica Quilligan, Nell Campbell. Goodtimes Enterprises/Warner Bros. Colour.

Highly fantastic version of the life of composer Franz Liszt (Daltrey). Includes a vampire-like Richard Wagner (Nicholas),

LOVE AT FIRST BITE

USA, 1979. Dir: Stan Dragoti. With: George Hamilton, Susan Saint James, Richard Benjamin, Dick Shawn, Arte Johnson, Sherman Hemsley. Melvin Simon/American International. Colour.

Sophisticated Dracula spoof with Hamilton as a suave Count (complete with mock Lugosi accent), who is forced to leave Transylvania when the authorities convert his castle into a gymnasium, and jet to New York in his casket with devoted manservant Renfield (a lunatic Johnson). Good support from James' unusual heroine, who enjoys the Count's advances; Benjamin as a jealous psychiatrist and descendant of Van Helsing; and Shawn's baffled police lieutenant. Robert Kaufman's script sparkles with witty dialogue and Dragoti directs with style and charm.

a Frankenstein-type monster and cameos by Ringo Starr, Rick Wakeman, Oliver Reed and Georgina Hale.

LOVE — VAMPIRE STYLE

(Orig: BEISS MICH, LIEBLING!) West Germany, 1970. Dir: Helmut Föernbacher. With: Patrick Jordan, Herbert Fuchs, Eva Renzi, Dieter Augustin, Brigitte Skay, Ralf Wolter. New Art Film-UFA/ Cinerama. Colour.

Stupid softcore sex comedy about a postman (Jordan) with an inexhaustable libido. A psychiatrist grows fangs out of frustration.

LUST FOR A VAMPIRE

UK, 1970. Dir: Jimmy Sangster. With: Ralph Bates, Barbara Jefford, Suzanna Leigh, Michael Johnson, Yutte Stensgaard, Helen Christie. Hammer Films/EMI. Colour.

Originally announced as *To Love a Vampire*, this was the second in Hammer's Karnstein trilogy and a follow-up to *The Vampire Lovers* (1970). It has almost nothing to do with J. Sheridan Le Fanu's classic story, but instead involves gratuitous nudity and lesbian relationships in a nineteenth century girls finishing school, where one of the students is the reincarnation of a vampire. Bates gives a strong performance in a role originally intended for Peter Cushing, and Stensgaard is impressive as the vampiric Mircalla (aka Carmilla). Mike Raven (real name, Austin Churton Fairman) plays Count Karnstein (with a dubbed voice) and the vampires seem happy to wander around in broad daylight. Director Sangster brings little style to the film, which utilizes the same sets as *Scars of Dracula* (1970) and even shots of Christopher Lee's bloodshot eyes! In one scene the entire camera crew is plainly visible. Hammer's most sexual movie, it was cut for an 'R' rating in America.

Sequel: TWINS OF EVIL (qv; 1971)

THE LUST OF DRACULA

USA, 1971.

Sex film with vampires.

O MACABRO DR SCIVANO

Brazil, 1971. Dir: Raúl Calhado and Rosalvo Cacador. With: Edmundo Scivano (Raúl Calhado), Luis Leme, Oswaldo de Souza, Henricao (Henrique Filipe), Lauro Sawaya, Genesio Aladim. Natus Producoes Cinematografica. B&W.

A failed politician, Dr Scivano (co-director Calhado), dabbles in voodoo and in return for some gold nuggets he is turned into a vampire. He is finally reduced to dust by a crucifix.

MADHOUSE

UK, 1974. Dir: Jim Clark. With: Vincent Price, Peter Cushing, Robert Quarry, Adrienne Corri, Natasha Pyne, Linda Hayden. American International/Amicus. Colour.

Filmed under the much better title *The Revenge of Dr. Death*. When American International Pictures wanted to use up their horror stars' contracts, they got Amicus to throw together this old fashioned but entertaining horror whodunit, loosely based on Angus Hall's novel *Devilday*. Price plays Hollywood film star Paul Toombes, whose career as Dr Death was cut short by the horrific decapitation of his fiancée. Years later, the actor is convinced by scriptwriter Herbert Flay (Cushing) to travel to England to recreate the character in a television series. But life becomes a nightmare for Toombes when his arrival coincides with a series of brutal murders. Quarry, as an unsympathetic TV producer, recreates his vampiric Count Yorga for a fancy dress party, and Cushing also appears as one of the undead. This includes so many clips from old AIP/Roger Corman movies that both Boris Karloff and Basil Rathbone get a special credit. Price sings the end song.

***Below:** Love at First Bite.*

THE MAD LOVE LIFE OF A HOT VAMPIRE

USA, 1971. With: Jim Parker, Jane Bond, Kim Kim.

Parker stars as Dracula, who has his women draw blood through fellatio in this limp sex film. Also includes a hunchback. The Count is destroyed by sunlight.

MAMA DRACULA

Belgium, 1979. Dir: Boris Szulzinger. With: Louise Fletcher, Maria Schneider, Marc-Henri Wajnberg, Alexander Wajnberg, Jimmy Shuman, Jess Hahn. Valisa Films/Radio Television Belge Francaise. Colour.

Horror comedy based on the Elisabeth Bathory legend. Louise Fletcher stars as the Countess, who bathes in virgins' blood to preserve her beauty. She brings Professor Van Bloed (Shuman) to her Transylvanian castle to develop artificial blood, aided by the Countess' undead twin sons (comedians the Wajnberg Brothers). Schneider plays policewoman Nancy Hawai investigating the vampire's murderous activities.

MARTIN

USA, 1976. Dir: George Romero. With: John Amplas, Lincoln Maazel, Christine Forrest, Elayne Nadeau, Sarah Venable, Tom Savini. Laurel. Colour.

Bleak, downbeat, low budget vampire movie from the director of *Night of the Living Dead* (1969). After moving to Pennsylvania, eighteen year-old Martin (Amplas, making a powerful screen début) is accused of being a nosferatu by elderly relative Maazel. In fact, the disturbed Martin ignores the traditional methods and kills with a razor blade and syringe, although lyrical flashbacks seem to reveal that his claims to be eighty-four years old are true. Make-up artist Tom Savini, producer Richard Rubinstein and writer/director Romero (as a Priest) all appear in cameo roles. The abrupt ending is particularly harrowing.

MARY, MARY, BLOODY MARY

Mexico, 1975. Dir: Juan Lopez Moctezuma. With: Christina Ferrare, David Young, John Carradine, Helena Rojo, Arthur (Arturo) Hansel, Enrique Lucero. Translor/Roala. Colour.

Above: Lust for a Vampire.

Christina Ferrare (Mrs John DeLorean) plays a bisexual vampire artist pursued by the police and haunted by a mysterious figure in black. It turns out to be her father (Carradine), rotting away as a blood-drinker, out to destroy her and so save her from the family curse. Carradine doesn't have many lines and remains masked (to hide a double) until almost the end.

McCLOUD: McCLOUD MEETS DRACULA

USA, 1977. Dir: Bruce Kessler. With: Dennis Weaver, J.D. Cannon, Terry Carter, Diana Muldaur, John Carradine, Reggie Nalder. Glen A. Larson/Universal/NBC-TV. Colour.

Made-for-TV movie in the long-running series based on *Coogan's Bluff* (1968), originally shown as part of the *NBC Mystery Movie* slot. While the New York police force searches for a sniper (Joe Stone) terrorising the city, veteran horror film star Loren Belasco (Carradine) is a suspect when Marshall Sam McCloud (Weaver) is called in to investigate a series of apparent vampire attacks.

MESSIAH OF EVIL

(USA: aka DEAD PEOPLE/RETURN OF THE LIVING DEAD/REVENGE OF THE SCREAMING DEAD)

USA, 1973. Dir: Willard Huyck. With: Michael Greer, Mariana Hill, Royal Dano, Elisha Cook, Joy Bang, Anitra Ford. A V/M Production. Colour.

A low budget variation on *Night of the Living Dead* (1969), co-scripted by director Willard Huyck and producer Gloria Katz (the team behind *American Graffiti* [1973]). Hill is looking for her father in a Californian coastal town, where a 'Dark Stranger' returns after one hundred years to spread a mysterious sickness which turns the inhabitants into vampiric zombies. Crude editing and weak performances are offset by some poetic horrors. Veterans Elisha Cook Jr and Royal Dano have cameos as a drunken bum and the missing artist-father respectively. Director Walter Hill is also featured down the cast.

MIDI MINUIT

France, 1970. Dir: Pierre Philippe. With: Sylvie Fennec, Beatrice Arnac, Daniel Emilfork, Jacques Portet, Laurent Vergez, Patrick Jouanne. Albertine Films/Plan-Film. Colour.

Psychological horror thriller set in southern France, where a vampire-like killer (Vergez) rips his victims apart with an iron-clawed glove.

MRS. AMWORTH

UK/Canada, 1975. Dir: Alvin Rakoff. With: Glynis Johns, Derek Francis, John Phillips, Pip Miller, Ronald Russell, Betty Tucker. Highgate Associates/HTV/OECA. Colour.

Colour.
Juvenile TV movie, originally shown in two parts on the *World of Disney* series. Whitaker plays a fan of Dracula films who, along with his brother (Kolden), decides to transform an old lighthouse into the location for an amateur horror movie. However, it also turns out to be a hideout for jewel thieves.

NECROPOLIS

Italy, 1970. Dir: Franco Borcani. With: Viva Auder, Tina Aumont, Carmelo Bene, Pierre Clementi, B. Corazzari, Paul Jabara. Cosmoseion/Q Productions. Colour.
Art movie which purports to be a 'state-

Left: *Madhouse.*
Below: *Martin.*

Beautifully photographed half-hour TV movie, based on the classic vampire story by E.F. Benson. Johns plays Mrs Amworth, a 300 year-old vampire spreading a mysterious sickness through an English village at the height of summer. Only Francis Urcombe (Phillips) isn't taken in by her image of the perfect hostess and he seeks to prove she is one of the undead with the help of Benson (Francis). The scenes of Johns running in slow motion through an old churchyard with the sound of giant wings beating on the sountrack are particularly effective. This was the pilot for a series to have been called *Classics Dark and Dangerous*.

THE MURDER MANSION

(Orig: LA MANSION DE LA NIEBLA/QUANDO MARTA URLO DALLA TOMBA)
Spain/Italy, 1970. Dir: Francisco Lara Polop. With: Analia Gade, Andres Resino, Anna Lisa Nardi, Evelyn Stewart (Ida Galli), Franco Fantasia, Eduardo Fajardo. Mundial Film/Tritone Filmindustria/Avco-Embassy. Colour.
Lost in the fog, a couple spend the night in an old mansion haunted by ghosts and vampires. It turns out to be a plot to drive the wife insane.

THE MYSTERY IN DRACULA'S CASTLE

USA, 1972. Dir: Robert Totten. With: Johnny Whitaker, Scott Kolden, Clu Gulager, Mariette Hartley. Buena Vista/NBC-TV.

ment about life'. Includes Countess Elizabeth Bathory (here called Marthory), the Frankenstein monster, Satan, King Kong, Attila the Hun, Montezuma, the Minotaur and other characters.

🦇

THE NIGHT STALKER

USA, 1971 (1972). Dir: John Llewellyn Moxey. With: Darren McGavin, Carol Lynley, Simon Oakland, Ralph Meeker, Claude Akins, Charles McGraw. American Broadcasting Companies. Colour.

McGavin stars as investigative journalist Carl Kolchak in the first of two made-for-TV pilot movies for *Kolchak: The Night Stalker* series. Richard Matheson's tight script (based on a then unpublished novel by Jeff Rice) has Kolchak hunting a night-time killer in Las Vegas who turns out to be real vampire Janos Skorzeny (Barry Atwater). However, nobody wants to publish the story, the police refuse to help and the super-human killer is prepared to silence him — permanently. Includes cameos by veterans Kent Smith and Elisha Cook Jr. When first shown, this stylish horror thriller was the highest rated TV movie ever in America.

Sequel: THE NIGHT STRANGLER (1972)

🦇🦇🦇🦇

NIGHTMARE IN BLOOD

(UK: HORROR CONVENTION)
USA, 1978. Dir: John Stanley. With: Jerry Walter, Dan Caldwell, Barrie Youngfellow, John H. Cochran, Ray K. Goman, Kerwin Mathews, Xeromega. Colour.

Low budget chiller set during a horror movie convention. Malekai (Walter), the star of a number of vampire movies, turns out to be the real thing. And the revived corpses of Burke and Hare are his psychotic assistants! Amateurish nonsense aimed at film buffs and comic fans, co-written, co-produced and directed by the San Francisco TV horror host and author. Special guest star Mathews (*The 7th Voyage of Sinbad* [1958]) turns up briefly in one of Malekai's movies and Kathy (Kathleen) Quinlan is also in there somewhere.

🦇

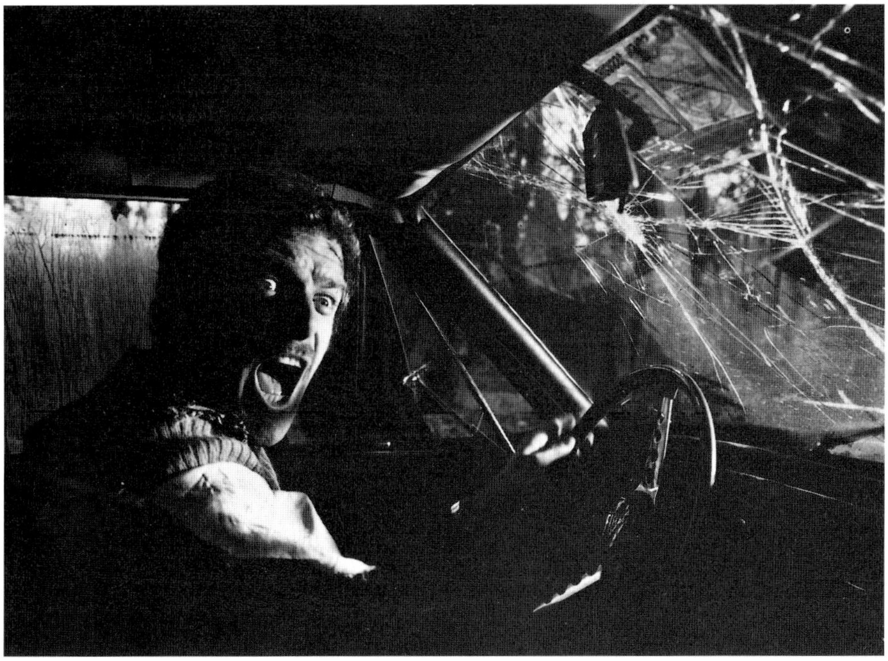

THE NIGHT OF THE DEVILS

(Orig: LA NOTTE DEI DIAVOLI/LA NOCHE DE LOS DIABLOS)
Italy/Spain, 1972. Dir: Giorgio Ferroni. With: John (Gianni) Garko, Agostina Belli, Mark Roberts, Cinzia de Carolis, Teresa Gimpera, Umberto Raho. Filmes Cinematografica/Due Cinematografica/ Copernices. Colour.

Another reworking of Alexei Tolstoy's story 'The Wurdalak', previously adapted by Mario Bava in *Black Sabbath* (1963). A crazed young man, Nicola (Garko), believes that the peasant family of his girlfriend (Belli) has been possessed by vampires. From the director of *Mill of the Stone Women* (1960). Check out the Bava version instead.

🦇½

NIGHT OF THE SEAGULLS

(Orig: LA NOCHE DE LAS GAVIOTAS. USA: aka TERROR BEACH/ NIGHT OF THE DEATH CULT)
Spain, 1975. Dir: Amando de Ossorio. With: Victor Petit, Mary (Maria) Kosti, Sandra Mozarosky,

Above left: *The Night of the Devils.*
Below left: *Nocturna, Granddaughter of Dracula.*

Julie James, Julia Saly, José Antonio Calvo. Ancla Century Films/ Profilmes. Colour.
Follow-up to *Horror of the Zombies* (1974), and the fourth and last in the Blind Dead series. When a young doctor and his wife move to a small fishing village, they discover that the taciturn locals sacrifice white-robed virgins to the blind undead Templarios Knights who offer up their hearts to a hideous sea-monster idol. In the end, the blood-drinking zombies turn to dust when the idol is destroyed. As usual, de Ossorio was responsible for the special make-up effects. An unofficial sequel, *La Cruz del Diablo*, also appeared in 1975 and was directed by John Gilling, and the Templars even resurfaced in Jesús Franco's *La Mansion de los Muertos Vivientes* (1981).

NIGHT OF THE SORCERERS

(Orig: LA NOCHE DE LOS BRUJOS) Spain/Portugal, 1973. Dir: Armando de Ossorio. With: Simon Andreu, Kali Hansa, Jack Taylor, Maria Kosti, Lorena Tower (Loretta Tovar), Joseph (José) Thelman. Profilmes/Hesperia/Avco-Embassy. Colour.
In the African jungle, an expedition discovers a voodoo tribe of beautiful vampire women in leopard skins. Includes zombies, screaming severed heads and cannibalism-in-negative. A disappointment from the director of the Blind Dead movies.

THE NIGHT OF THE VAMPIRE

(Orig: CHI O SUU NINGYO) Japan, 1970. Dir: Michio Yamamoto. With: Kayo Matsuo, Akira Nakao, Yukiko Kobayashi, Yoko Minazake, Atsuo Nakamura, Junya Usami. Toho. Colour.
Kobayashi portrays Yuko, a ghostly vampire who revenges herself on the world she believes treated her unkindly. In the end she kills her father (Usami), which results in her body turning to dust. Sold under the title *The Vampire Doll*.

NIGHTWING

USA, 1979. Dir: Arthur Hiller. With: Nick Mancuso, David Warner, Kathryn Harrold, Stephen Macht, Strother Martin, George Clutesi. Columbia. Colour.
Based on the novel by Martin Cruz Smith. When an old native American medicine man calls on his gods to destroy the world, a plague of deadly vampire bats invades the desert. This interesting blend of Red Indian mysticism and modern science is stylishly directed and beautifully photographed. Henry Mancini supplies an evocative score, and Carlo Rambaldi's mechanical bats look better than the dodgy optical work. Mancuso plays a policeman with an attitude, ably supported by Warner's obsessive bat hunter (his long soliloquy really imbues the creatures with supernatural menace) and Strother Martin in his last role.

NOCTURNA, GRANDDAUGHTER OF DRACULA

USA, 1979. Dir: Harry Tampa (Hurwitz). With: Yvonne De Carlo, John Carradine, Nai Bonet, Tony Hamilton, Brother Theodore (Gottlieb), Sy Richardson. Compass International/Nai Bonet Enterprises. Colour.
Along with *Love at First Bite*, this was the other disco Dracula movie of 1979. It makes *Billy the Kid versus Dracula* (1965) look like a classic as poor seventy-three year-old John Carradine portrays the Count for the last time (he keeps his fangs in a glass of water and shares a double coffin with De Carlo!). Ex-belly dancer (and executive producer) Bonet plays Drac's granddaughter, who runs off to New York with a musician. Songs by Gloria Gaynor, Vicki Sue Robinson and Moment of Truth.

LE NOSFERAT OU LES EAUX GLACEES DU CALCUL EGOISTE

Belgium, 1974. Dir: Maurice Rabinowicz. With: Veronique Peynet, Maïté Nahyr, Martine Bertrand, Guy Pion, Quentin Milo. Les Films du Groupe de Chambre. Colour.
Political satire, based on the director's own play. A bourgeois killer drinks the blood of prostitutes in this mixture of songs and newsreel clips. Blown up from 16mm.

NOSFERATU THE VAMPYRE

(Orig: NOSFERATU: PHANTOM DER NACHT) West Germany/France, 1979. Dir: Werner Herzog. With: Klaus Kinski, Isabelle Adjani, Bruno Ganz, Roland Topor, Walter Ladengast, Paul Monette. Werner Herzog Filmproduktion/Gaumont/ Twentieth Century Fox. Colour.
Produced, written and directed by Werner Herzog, this remake of F.W. Murnau's 1922 movie is, if anything, even more lethargic than the original. Kinski looks very effective in the Max Schreck-style make-up, but his apathetic vampire just shuffles around the decaying streets, wearily stealing blood from victims. The supporting cast is equally lifeless (excuse the pun), and author Roland Topor (*The Tenant*) gives a bizarre performance as Renfield. This was filmed in both English and German language versions.
Sequel: VAMPIRE IN VENICE

Emilio Martinez Lázaro, Francisco Bellmunt and Jaime Chávarri. With: Marta May, Charo López, Marisa Paredes, Romy, Julián Ugarte, Carlos Otero. PC Teide. Colour.

The title translates as *Blood Pie*. Four part horror movie with episodes about medieval witchcraft ('Tarota'), the Frankenstein legend ('Victor Frankenstein'), Romans versus Celtic vampires ('Terror Entre Cristianos') and a ghostly chiller ('The Dance').

PEOPLE

USA, 1979. Dir: Gerard Damiano. With: Eric Edwards, Kasey Rodgers, Serena, Jamie Gillis, Susan McBain, Kelly Green. Damiano. Colour.

Six hardcore sex stories from the director of *Legacy of Satan* (1973). The third episode is titled 'Vampires'.

PEPITO Y CHABELO VS. LOS MONSTRUOS

Mexico, 1973. Dir: José Estrada. Pepito Romay, Chabelo. Alameda. Colour.

The comedy team confront various creatures, including a vampire and Frankenstein's monster.

EL POBRECITO DRACULIN

Spain, 1976. Dir: Juan Fortuny. With: Joe Rigoli, Lo-sele Roman,

(qv; 1988)
Remake: DRACULA SUCKS (qv; 1979)

ONE MORE TIME

UK, 1970. Dir: Jerry Lewis. With: Peter Lawford, Sammy Davis Jr, Esther Anderson, Maggie Wright, Leslie Sands, John Wood. Chrislaw/Tracemark/United Artists. Colour.

Unfunny comedy sequel to *Salt and Pepper* (1968), which also starred executive producers Lawford and Davis Jr as Soho nightclub owners who can't stay out of trouble. An unbilled Christopher Lee and Peter Cushing turn up very briefly as Dracula and Baron Frankenstein.

PASTEL DE SANGRE

Spain, 1971. Dir: José Maria Vallés,

Victor Israel. Mezquiriz. Colour.
A Spanish vampire comedy featuring Dracula.

QUEM TEM MEDO DE LOBISOMEM

Brazil, 1974. Dir: Reginaldo Faria. With: Reginaldo Faria, Stepan Nercessian, Camila Amado, Carlos Kroeber, Christina Aché, Fatima Freire. Ipanema/Circus/Faria. Colour.
A Brazilian comedy about two men and a woman who fall foul of a bizarre family which includes a vampire and a werewolf.

RABID

Canada, 1976. Dir: David Cronenberg. With: Marilyn Chambers, Frank Moore, Joe Silver, Howard Ryshpan, Patricia Gage, Susan Roman. Dibar Syndicate. Colour.
Porno star Chambers is surprisingly good as the victim of a skin graft experiment that results in the growth of a phallus-shaped blood-drinking organ. She infects her victims with a rabies-like epidemic that quickly spreads throughout the city of Montreal. Writer/director Cronenberg basically reworks themes from his first feature, *Shivers* (1974), but with more confidence. An effective low budget thriller with a downbeat ending, this won the awards for Best Screenplay and Best Special Effects at the 1977 Sitges Horror Film Festival.

REINCARNATION OF ISABEL

(Orig: RITI MAGIE NERE E SEGRETE ORGE DEL TRECENTO. USA: aka THE GHASTLY ORGIES OF COUNT DRACULA)
Italy, 1973. Dir: Ralph Brown (Renato Polselli). With: Mickey Hargitay, Rita Calderoni, Max Dorian, Moschera Consolata, Marcello Bonini, W. Darni. GRP. Colour.
Hargitay, a former Mr Universe and husband of Jayne Mansfield, stars in this witchcraft thriller. A group of satantists, trying to revive a 400 year-old witch in the vaults beneath a castle, turn into vampires before being destroyed by the local villagers. Heavy on the sex and violence.

RENDEZVOUS

USA, 1973. Dir: Cortlandt B. Hull. B&W.
Underground film which uses clips from *Nosferatu* (1922), Lugosi's *Dracula* (1930), *Son of Dracula* (1943), *House of Dracula* (1945) and Hammer's *Dracula* (1958), set to the music of Frank Sinatra's 'Strangers in the Night'.

REQUIEM FOR A VAMPIRE

(Orig: REQUIEM POUR UN VAMPIRE/VIERGES ET VAMPIRES. USA: aka VIRGINS AND THE VAMPIRES/CAGED VIRGINS/ CRAZED VAMPIRE)
France, 1971. Dir: Jean Rollin. With: Marie Pirre Castel, Mireille D'Argent, Philippe Gaste, Louise Dhour, Dominique Toussaint, Michel Delesalle. Les Films ABC. Colour.
The fourth in a series of sex/vampire films by Rollin. After escaping from a reformatory, two girls seek shelter in an old château and are trapped by a sadistic vampire (Delesalle) and her sect of the undead. In the end the vampires commit suicide by sealing themselves up forever. More arty tedium from the overrated Rollin.

Below: Rabid.

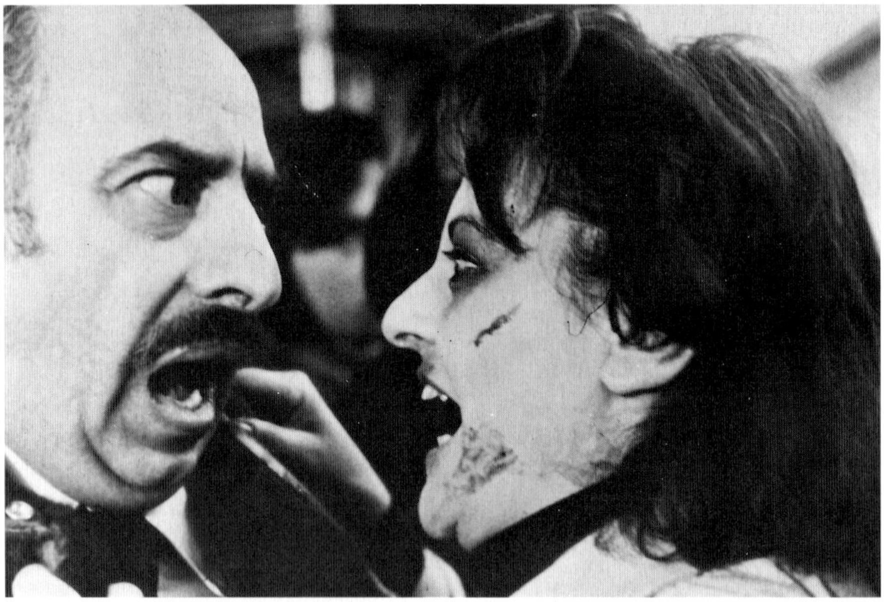

EL RETORNO DE LOS VAMPIROS

Spain, 1971. Dir: José Maria Zabalza. With: Simon Andreu, Marta Monterrey. Uranzu Films. Colour.

The title probably says it all.

THE RETURN OF COUNT YORGA

USA, 1971. Dir: Bob Kelljan (Robert Kelljchian). With: Robert Quarry, Mariette Hartley, Roger Perry, Yvonne Wilder, Edward Walsh, George Macready. Peppertree/ American International. Colour.

Improved sequel/remake of *Count Yorga, Vampire* (1970), co-written by star Wilder and director Kelljan. Quarry gives a splendidly aloof performance as the vampire (no explanation of how he is revived) preying on an isolated Californian orphanage and falling in love with Hartley. The direction is more assured, the vampire attacks have greater impact and there's even some amusing comedy relief. Producer Michael Macready found a cameo role for his veteran father, George (who does a great impersonation of Margaret Rutherford), as a batty vampire hunter in his last film. Also includes a clip from *The Vampire Lovers* (1970).

RETURN OF THE EVIL DEAD

(Orig: EL ATAQUE DE LOS MUERTOS SIN OJOS. USA: aka ATTACK OF THE BLIND DEAD)

Spain, 1973. Dir: Armando de Ossorio. With: Tony Kendall (Luciano Stella), Fernando Sancho, Esther Ray (Esperanza Roy), Frank Blake (Frank Braña), Lone Fleming, Loretta Tovar. Profilm/Ancla Century Films/Atlas International. Colour.

The first of three sequels to *Tombs of the Blind Dead* (1971). During the annual celebration of the massacre of the Knights Templar, the blind mummified zombies attack a village, seeking the blood of their victims by sound. A group of fairly unpleasant people take refuge in a church. The slow motion shots of the Templars on horseback (often taken from the first film) are still quite eerie. As with the original, director de Ossorio was also in charge of the special effects make-up.

Sequel: HORROR OF THE ZOMBIES (qv; 1974)

LE ROUGE DE CHINE

France, 1977. Dir: Jacques Richard. With: Jacques Richard, Agathe Vannier, Bernard Dubois. Les Films Elementaires. Colour/B&W.

Written, directed, edited by and featuring Richard, this minimalist art movie is supposedly a homage to vampires.

LE SADIQUE AUX DENTS ROUGES

Belgium, 1970. Dir: Jean-Louis van Belle. With: Jane Clayton, Albert Simono, Daniel Moosmann. Cinevision Productions. Colour.

Billed as 'Un film de sex horreur' and inspired by AIP's monster movies of the 1950s. A scientist transforms an obsessed teenager into a toothy vampire, who then runs amok at a fancy dress party.

SALEM'S LOT

USA, 1979. Dir: Tobe Hooper. With: David Soul, James Mason, Lance Kerwin, Bonnie Bedelia, Lew Ayres,

Above left: *Santo y Blue Demon Contra Dracula y el Hombre Lobo. (FJA).*
Below: *The Satanic Rites of Dracula.*

Elisha Cook. Warner Bros. Colour.
Three hour TV mini-series, based on Stephen King's sprawling vampire novel. Paul Monash's script remains surprisingly faithful to the book while condensing the plot and characters. When writer Ben Mears (Soul) returns to his home town of Salem's Lot he relives his childhood fears of the Marsten House, now occupied by vampire Kurt Barlow (Reggie Nalder in impressive Nosferatu-type make-up) and his human agent Mr Straker (the excellent Mason). Pretty soon the whole town is infected by the undead. Although director Hooper handles the vampire attacks effectively, he has trouble with the more intimate scenes. The film's major change/flaw has Straker as the chief villain while reducing Barlow to only a supporting role. Veterans Ayres, Cook Jr and Marie Windsor are wasted. The shorter theatrical version includes more gore.
Sequel: A RETURN TO SALEM'S LOT (qv; 1987)

SANTO CONTRA LOS CAZADORES DE CABEZAS

Mexico, 1970. Dir: René Cardona. With: Santo (Eric del Castillo or Rodolfo Guzman Huerta), Nadia Milton, F. Fernandez. Zacarias. Colour.
Santo, the silver masked wrestler, sets out to stop the mad Dr Mathus using the blood of the living to revive the dead.

SANTO Y BLUE DEMON CONTRA DRACULA Y EL HOMBRE LOBO

Mexico, 1972. Dir: Miguel M. Delgado. With: Santo (Eric del Castillo), Blue Demon (Alejandro Cruz), Nubia Marti, Aldo Monti, Augustin Martinez Solares, Eugina San Martin. Cinematografica Calderon/Azteca Films. Colour.
Revived by his hunchbacked assistant, Dracula (Monti) returns the Wolf Man to life. Wrestling heroes Santo and the Blue Demon battle numerous vampires and werewolves before the two lead monsters fall into a pit of stakes. This could be a sequel to *Santo en el Tesoro de Dracula* (1968).

THE SATANIC RITES OF DRACULA

(USA: COUNT DRACULA AND HIS VAMPIRE BRIDE)
UK, 1973. Dir: Alan Gibson. With: Christopher Lee, Peter Cushing, Michael Coles, William Franklyn, Freddie Jones, Joanna Lumley.

***Above:** Requiem for a Vampire.*
***Left:** The Return of Count Yorga.*

Hammer Films/Warner Bros. Colour.
Originally announced as *Dracula is Dead and Well and Living in London*. This enjoyable sequel to *Dracula A.D. 1972* (1972) was the last in Hammer's series to feature Lee as the Count. A fast-paced blend of sci-spy and horror, Dracula is now a Howard Hughes-type tycoon in contemporary London, planning to release a deadly new plague virus to hasten Armageddon. The Dracula/Van Helsing confrontation recalls the earlier films, and the Count's destruction in a hawthorn bush adds a twist to the mythology. Lee even gets to do a mock-Lugosi accent! It wasn't released in America for five years.

SCARS OF DRACULA

UK, 1970. Dir: Roy Ward Baker. With: Christopher Lee, Dennis

Waterman, Jenny Hanley, Christopher Matthews, Patrick Troughton, Michael Gwynn. Hammer Films. Colour.
Hammer's fifth Dracula movie has no connection with any other entry in the series. The script by John Elder (Anthony Hinds) returns Lee's Count to his Transylvanian castle, where he is revived by a rubber bat vomiting blood. When young rake Matthews spends the night at the castle, his brother and girlfriend (Waterman and Hanley) go looking for him. It's all been done before, and despite using a number of ideas from Bram Stoker's original novel (Dracula crawling up the castle wall), this is just an attempt by Hammer to introduce more nudity (Anoushka Hempel's sensuous vampire) and some mild S&M (the Count whipping his servant, Klove [Troughton]) into the series. This time Dracula is impaled on a metal spike and fried by a lightning bolt.

SCREAM BLACULA SCREAM

USA, 1973. Dir: Bob Kelljan (Robert Kelljchian). With: William Marshall, Don Mitchell, Pam Grier, Michael Conrad, Richard Lawson, Janee Michelle. American International Pictures. Colour.
Disappointing sequel to *Blacula* (1972), made towards the end of AIP's blaxploitation period by Count Yorga director Kelljan. Marshall's dignified vampire Prince Manuwalde is resurrected through black magic and tries to use the powers of voodoo queen Grier to cure his blood-drinking affliction. This is surprisingly wordy and slow-moving, however it does include some nice man-into-bat transformations and a few shock vampire attacks.

SEX EXPRESS

UK, 1975. Dir: Derek Ford. With: Heather Deeley, James Lister, Derek Martin, Jack Rigby, Terry Walsh, Tim Burr. Blackwater. Colour.
Four erotic fantasies, one featuring Lister as a vampire, another involving ghosts.

SISTERS OF SATAN

(Orig: ALUCARDA. USA: aka INNOCENTS FROM HELL)
Mexico, 1975. Dir: Juan Lopez Moctezuma. With: Tina Romero, Susana Kamini, Claudio Brook, David Silva, Lily Garza, Martin Lasalle. Films 75/Yuma Films. Colour.

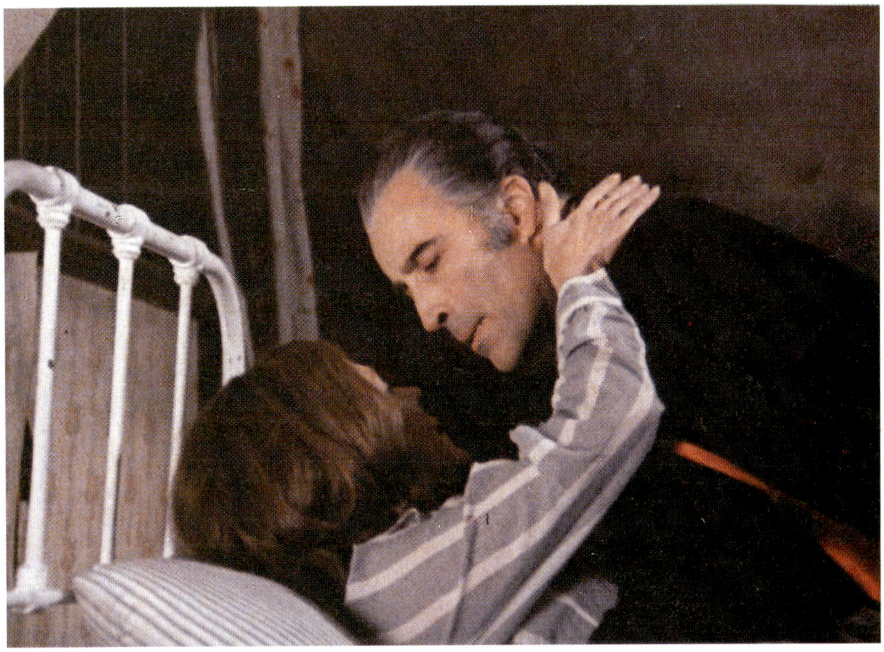

Despite the almost anagrammatic original title, this mix of sex and gore from the director of *Mary, Mary, Bloody Mary* (1975) is about nineteenth century possessed nuns. Justine (Kamini) is sent to a monastery and quickly succumbs to the evil influence of Alucarda (Romero). This leads to them drinking each other's blood, biting other nuns on the neck, participating in a black magic orgy with a goat-headed demon and Justine rising naked from a blood-filled coffin.

SON OF DRACULA

(aka YOUNG DRACULA)
UK, 1973. Dir: Freddie Francis.

Top: The Satanic Rites of Dracula.
Above: Scars of Dracula.

With: Harry Nilsson, Ringo Starr, Rosanna Lee, Freddie Jones, Dennis Price, Skip Martin. Apple/ Cinemation. Colour.
Filmed under the title *Count Downe*, this is a musical horror film in which Harry Nilsson plays the son of Dracula. Producer Ringo is Merlin the Magician and Dennis Price (who died the same year) turns up as Van Helsing. No wonder director Francis went back to being a cinematographer on such movies as *The Elephant Man* (1980) and *Dune* (1984).

(FJA).

SONS OF SATAN

USA, 1973. Dir: Lancer Brooks. With: Robert McKay, Tom Payne, Ned Burke, Carl Ford, Bill North, Tex Neeley. Blue & Brooks. Colour.

Gay pastiche of 1940s horror films, featuring black magic rituals and McKay as a vampire.

SPERMULA

France, 1975. Dir: Charles Matton. With: Dayle Haddon, Udo Kier, Susannah Djian, Georges Géret, Ginette Leclerc, Jocelyne Boisseau. PPFC. Colour.

Superior softcore science fiction film. On another planet, Haddon is the leader of a society of beautiful vampire virgins who live in an art deco castle and drink you-know-what instead of blood. Once on Earth, she falls in love with Kier.

STAR VIRGIN

USA, 1979. Dir: Linus Gator. With: Kari Klark, Tracy Walton, Jeanette Harlow, Maureen O'Hara, Trisha Cole, Brenda Leggs. Gail/VCX. Colour.

Hardcore science fiction sex film in which a penial robot (Kevin Thompson) shows a test tube-created woman (*Hustler* centrefold Klark) various sex scenes involving the now defunct human race. These include a 1950s Garden of Eden sequence with a human-headed snake (J.C. Phillips), and a silent black and white Dracula spoof, with an Igor character wearing a Richard Nixon mask and the Count (Johnny Harden) sinking more than his teeth into his victim. It's not anywhere near as interesting as it sounds.

STRANGE LOVE OF THE VAMPIRES

(Orig: EL EXTRANO AMOR DE LOS VAMPIROS. USA: aka NIGHT OF THE WALKING DEAD)
Spain, 1974. Dir: Leon Klimovsky. With: Emma Cohen, Carlos Ballesteros, Vicky Lusson, Rafael Hernandez, Barta Barry, Mari Paz Pondal. Richard Films. Colour.

A young woman (Cohen) falls in love with an undead aristocrat (Ballesteros) and they sleep together for a night. Afterwards, she finds herself called to a sinister castle populated by his vampire followers. Angry villagers finally kill her along with the rest of the undead.

STURMTRUPPEN

Italy, 1977. Dir: Salvatore Samperi. With: Renato Pozzetto, Lino Toffolo, Cochi Ponzoni, Teo Teocoli, Jean Pierre Marielle, Corinne Clery. Achille Manzotti. Colour.

Based on the Italian anti-war comic strip by Bonvi. It includes a sequence in a hospital room with a vampire and the Frankenstein monster.

SUCK ME, VAMPIRE

France, 1975. Dir: Maxime Debest. Off. Colour.

Porno horror movie with vampires.

TAME RE CHAMPO NE AME KEL

India, 1978. Dir: Chandrakant Sangani. With: Naresh Kumar, Snehalata, A. Joshi, Rajanibala. Kanodia. Colour.

Below: Scars of Dracula.

A vampire woman marries a man on the condition that they never sleep together.

TENDER DRACULA

(Orig: LA GRANDE TROUILLE/ TENDRE DRACULA)
France, 1974. Dir: Pierre Grunstein. With: Peter Cushing, Alida Valli, Miou-Miou, Nathalie Courval, Bernard Menez, Stephanie Shandor. Renne Productions/Les Filmes Ch Fechner/VM Productions/AMLF/ Scotia. Colour.
Comedy in which Cushing plays a vampire movie actor named MacGregor who wants to abandon horror films for more romantic roles. His producer sets up a series of fake murders in the actor's castle home to convince MacGregor to return to the genre. In French prints, Cushing's voice was dubbed by Jean Rochefort.

TENDERNESS OF WOLVES

(Orig: DIE ZARTLICHKEIT DER WOLFE)
West Germany, 1973. Dir: Ulli Lommel. With: Kurt Raab, Jeff Roden, Margit Carstensen, Wolfgang Schenk, Rainer Werner Fassbinder, Ingrid Caven. Tango Film. Colour.
Arty but disturbing version of the true-life case of Fritz Haarman, a homosexual murderer and blood-drinker, who murdered around twenty-five young boys in pre-Nazi Germany. Producer Rainer Werner Fassbinder turns up in a supporting role. Director Lommel's career went downhill after this.

THIRST

Australia, 1979. Dir: Rod Hardy. With: David Hemmings, Chantal Contouri, Shirley Cameron, Max Phipps, Henry Silva, Rod Mullinar. F G Film Productions/New South Wales Film Corporation. Colour.
Hemmings plays Dr Fraser, the head of the Hyma Brotherhood, who kidnap Contouri (they believe her to be a descendant of their founder, Countess Bathory) and try to convince her to join their vampiric cult of blood-drinkers. An unusual variation on the theme, made with style.

THE THIRSTY DEAD

(aka BLOOD CULT OF SHANGRI-LA)
Philippines, 1974. Dir: Terry Becker. With: John Considine, Jennifer Billingsley, Judith McConnell, Fredricka Meyers, Tani Gutherie. Rochelle/International Amusement. Colour.
The slaves of jungle cult leader Considine kidnap beautiful women for blood sacrifices to keep him eternally young. Low budget Filipino movie that has to be seen to be believed.

THOSE CRUEL AND BLOODY VAMPIRES

(Orig: LAS ALEGRES VAMPIRAS DE VOGEL)
Spain, 1974. Dir: Julio Pérez Tabernero. With: Agata Lys, Maria José Cantudo, Germán Cobos, Rafael Conesa. Titanic. Colour.
Two beautiful women visit a European village in search of vampires.

TIEMPOS DUROS PARA DRACULA

Spain/Argentina, 1976. Dir: Jorge M. Darnell. With: José Ruiz Lifante, Miguel Ligero, Maria Noel, Adolfo Linvel, Alfonso de Grazia. Aitor/ Espacio. Colour.
The Count's grandson returns to Transylvania.

THE TIME OF VAMPIRES

(Orig: VRIJEME VAMPIRA)
Yugoslavia, 1971. Dir: Nikola Majdak. Dunav/Zagreb. Colour.
Nine minute animated comedy about vampires' midnight visits to a haunted graveyard.

TOMBS OF THE BLIND DEAD

(Orig: LA NOCHE DEL TERROR CIEGO. USA: aka THE BLIND DEAD)
Spain/Portugal, 1971. Dir: Armando de Ossorio. With: Oscar Burner, Lone Fleming, Maria Silva, José Telman, Helen Hay (Maria Elena Arpon), Juan Cortes. Plata Films/Inerfilme/Hallmark. Colour.
Popular horror film that spawned three sequels. A thirteenth century religious sect known as The Templarios Knights are blinded by crows and executed for killing women as part of their blood rituals. They return in modern times as bloodseeking mummified skeletons, who locate their victims by sound. The opening torture scenes are cut from some prints. Director de Ossorio was also in charge of the special effects make-up.
Sequel: RETURN OF THE EVIL DEAD (qv; 1973)

Above: Vampire Circus.

TRAIN RIDE TO HOLLYWOOD

USA, 1975. Dir: Charles Rondeau. With: Guy Marks, Phyllis Davis, 'Bloodstone', Jay Lawrence, Roberta Collins, Jay Robinson. Arista Films/ CJFC. Colour.
Features doubles of many famous Hollywood film stars and a funeral with Count Dracula dancing in a deserted western street.

A TRIP WITH DRACULA

USA, 1970.
Underground film.

TWILIGHT PEOPLE

(aka BEASTS)
Philippines/USA, 1972. Dir: Eddie Romero. With: John Ashley, Pat Woodell, Jan Merlin, Pam Grier, Charles Macaulay, Ken Metcalfe. New World Pictures. Colour.
Uncredited version of H.G. Wells' novel *The Island of Doctor Moreau* from co-writer/co-producer/director Romero (who had already executive produced a version

back in 1959, titled *Terror is a Man*). Co-producer Ashley stars as an ex-Nazi scientist creating manimals on a remote island — these include a flying bat man, an ape man, a tree woman and the prerequisite panther woman (Grier). Roger Corman was co-executive producer.

TWINS OF EVIL

UK, 1971. Dir: John Hough. With: Peter Cushing, Dennis Price, Madeleine Collinson, Mary Collinson, Isobel Black, Kathleen Byron. Hammer Films. Colour.

Third and probably best of Hammer's Karnstein trilogy, based on characters created by J. Sheridan Le Fanu. Damien Thomas is the pleasure-seeking Count Karnstein who is transformed into a vampire (who can walk around in daylight) by his ancestor, Countess Mircalla (Katya Wyeth). He is opposed by Cushing's Gustav Weil, the fanatical leader of a group of sadistic Puritan witchhunters. The Collinson sisters were *Playboy*'s first twin playmates (October 1970) and, despite some mild sex scenes and some serious gore, John Hough's careful direction makes this one of Hammer's better later efforts.

VAARWHEL

(UK: THE ROMANTIC AGONY)
Holland, 1973. Dir: Guido Peters. With: Pieke Dassen, Nettie Blanken, Rik Bravenboer. Cinema Film. Colour.

A near-immortal man travels through time from the Stone Age to the twenty-ninth century. In one episode, Blanken plays a vampire who steals plasma from the local blood bank. Music by Ennio Morricone.

VALERIE AND HER WEEK OF WONDERS

(Orig: VALERIE A TYDEN DIVU)
Czechoslovakia, 1970. Dir: Jaromil Jires. With: Jaroslava Schallerova, Helena Anyskova, Petr Kopriva, Jiri Prymek, Jan Klusak. Barrandov. Colour.

The thirteen year-old Valerie lives in a dream world that includes her incestuous eagle-brother, a lecherous priest who tries to burn her at the stake and a grandmother who turns into a vampire ancestor to regain her youth.

VAMPIRA

(USA: OLD DRACULA)
UK, 1974. Dir: Clive Donner. With: David Niven, Teresa Graves, Jennie Linden, Nicky Henson, Peter Bayliss, Bernard Bresslaw. Columbia/World Film Services. Colour.

Even David Niven's urbane Dracula can't save this terrible vampire spoof. The Count reads *Playboy* and shows tourists around his castle. But when his lost love, Vampira, Countess Dracula, is revived as a jive-talking black woman (Graves), he is appalled and sets out for swinging London to 'cure' her. In the end, he turns black as well! Jeremy Lloyd's screenplay might have been funnier if it didn't rely so heavily on crude slapstick humour and tired old vampire jokes. Bayliss gets all the best scenes as Maltravers, Dracula's faithful servant, and the cast includes horror veterans Linda Hayden, Veronica Carlson and Freddie Jones.

THE VAMPIRE

Austria, 1976. Dir: Karin Brandaner.

Short satire on horror movies.

VAMPIRE

USA, 1979. Dir: E.W. Swackhamer. With: Jason Miller, Richard Lynch, E.G. Marshall, Kathryn Harrold, Jessica Walter, Barrie Youngfellow. Company Four/MTM. Colour.

Modern day vampire thriller with no blood in sight. That's because it was made by Mary Tyler Moore's company for TV. When work begins on converting an old San Francisco family estate into a church and park, police are soon confronted with several gruesome killings, reminiscent of a thirty year-old series of unsolved murders. Former policeman Harry Kilcoyne (Marshall) believes a vampire has been released and teams up with architect John Rawlins (Miller) to destroy the monster. Lynch is marvellously evil as the undead Anton Voytek, and the imaginative script by Steven Bochco and Michael Kozoll ends with the vampire vowing to return. Unfortunately, no TV series followed.

VAMPIRE CIRCUS

UK, 1971. Dir: Robert Young. With: Adrienne Corri, Laurence Payne, Thorley Walters, John Moulder-Brown, Anthony Corlan, Lynne Frederick. Hammer Films. Colour.

Unusual vampire chiller from Hammer. Director Young was apparently given a very tight production schedule and, when he ran over, shooting simply stopped and he had to assemble what he had. This probably explains the film's tight editing, occasional dream-like atmosphere and abrupt storyline. When the Circus of Nights sets up camp in the small Serbian village of Schtettel, plague breaks out and the villagers blame the curse of vampire Count Mitterhouse (Robert Tayman), staked in his castle years before. In fact,

Left: *Twins of Evil.*

the Count's cousin Emil (Corlan) is the leader of the troupe and he plans to revive Mitterhouse, who has vowed to revenge himself on those who destroyed him. The film includes a panther woman, twin acrobats who turn into bats, a magical hall of mirrors and Dave Prowse as a strongman. It ends with almost the entire cast being slaughtered.

THE VAMPIRE HAPPENING

(Orig: GEBISSEN WIRD NUR NACHTS)
West Germany, 1971. Dir: Freddie Francis. With: Pia Dagermark, Thomas Hunter, Ingrid van Bergen, Ferdy (Ferdinand) Mayne, Lyvia Bauer, Joachim Kemmer. Acquila Films. Colour.
Francis' uneven career as a director hits rock-bottom with this horror comedy, which features Ferdy Mayne, parodying his role as a vampire in *Dance of the Vampires* (1967). This time he holds orgies in an old castle and flies around in a helicopter full of beautiful women! Dagermark (also the producer's wife) stars as Hollywood actress Betty Williams, who resembles her vampire ancestor with predictable results. It's not very funny.

THE VAMPIRE HOOKERS

(USA: aka SENSUOUS VAMPIRES)
Philippines, 1979. Dir: Cirio H. Santiago. With: Lenka Novak, Karen Stride, Katie Dolan, John Carradine, Bruce Fairbairn, Trey Wilson. Cosa Nueva Productions/ Caprican Three/Saturn International. Colour.
Seventy-three year-old Carradine (dressed in a white suit) plays the leader of a group of sexy vampires who lure victims back to his crypt. Despite Vic Diaz's farting vampire, some reviewers couldn't decide if this was meant to be a comedy or not.

VAMPIRE KUNG-FU

Hong Kong, 1972. Dir: Li Fai Mon.
Martial arts meets the undead.

THE VAMPIRE LOVERS

UK, 1970. Dir: Roy Ward Baker. With: Ingrid Pitt, George Cole, Kate O'Mara, Peter Cushing, Ferdy (Ferdinand) Mayne, Douglas Wilmer, Dawn Addams. Hammer Films/ American International. Colour.
The first of three Hammer films based on J. Sheridan Le Fanu's 'Carmilla'. Tudor Gates' screenplay remains fairly faithful to the original story, but with greater emphasis on vampire Carmilla/Mircalla/ Marcilla's lesbian seductions. Polish-born Ingrid Pitt is too old for the role, but veterans Cushing and Wilmer know that decapitation will destroy the undead. This had a higher budget than most Hammer vampire films, reflected in the excellent production values.
Sequel: LUST FOR A VAMPIRE (qv; 1970)
Remake: THE BLOOD SPATTERED BRIDE (qv; 1972)

VAMPIRE LUST

USA. Dir: Vladimir. With: John Leslie, Alexandra, Luda Diva. Pacific Coast/Roger Wald. Colour.
Hardcore vampires, scripted by 'Al Hazrad'!

THE VAMPIRE'S BITE

USA, 1972.
Hardcore vampire movie.

THE VAMPIRE'S NIGHT ORGY

(Orig: LA ORGIA NOCTURNA DE LOS VAMPIROS/LA NOCHE DE LOS VAMPIROS. USA: aka ORGY OF THE VAMPIRES)
Spain, 1972. Dir: Leon Klimovsky. With: Jack Taylor, Dianik

Zurakowska, Charo Soriano, Helga Liné, Manuel de Blas, Emma Cohen, Carlos Ballesteros. International Amusement/Atlantida. Colour.
When their minibus breaks down, a group of six tourists spend the night in the Transylvanian town of Tonia. They soon discover that it is populated entirely by vampires, who don't mind a bit of cannibalism on the side.

THE VAMPIRE'S THRILL

(Orig: LE FRISSON DES VAMPIRES. USA: aka SEX AND THE VAMPIRE) France, 1970. Dir: Jean Rollin. With: Sandra Julien, Dominique, Nicole Nancel, Michel Delahaye, Jacques Robiolles, Marie-Pierre Tricot. Films ABC/Les Films Modernes. Colour.
One of Rollin's more imaginative films, with some moments of striking imagery. Honeymooning couple Sandra Julien and Jean-Marie Durand spend the night in an old castle and are both seduced by beautiful vampire Isolde (Dominique). Some of the most memorable sequences include the vampire emerging from a grandfather clock on the stroke of midnight and the blood of a dove splashed across a coffin.

LOS VAMPIROS DE COYOACAN

Mexico, 1973. Dir: Arturo Martinez. With: Germán Robles, Sasha Montenegro, Mil Maschras, Superzan, Carlos Lopez Moctezuma. Mario Cid/Azteca Films. Colour.
Mexican wrestling movie which marks the return of star Robles (*The Vampire* [1957], etc) as a bloodsucker.

VAMPIRO 2000

Italy, 1972. Dir: Riccardo Ghione. With: Nino Castelnuevo, Dominique Boschero, Lucio Dalla, Carlo de Leyo, Rada Rassimov, Francisco Rabal. Canguro. Colour.
There is some doubt that this was ever completed or released.

VAMPYRES

(USA: VAMPYRES DAUGHTERS OF DRACULA/BLOOD HUNGER/ SATAN'S DAUGHTERS) UK, 1974 (1976). Dir: Joseph (José) Larraz. With: Marianne Morris, Anulka, Murray Brown, Brian Deacon, Sally Faulkner, Michael Byrne. Essay/Rank Films. Colour.
Despite the title, Marianne Morris and *Playboy* foldout (May 1973) Anulka are not really vampires but a pair of bisexual ghosts who seduce visitors to their old mansion and drink their blood. They have no fangs, can move around in daylight and don't sleep in coffins. Despite the sex and gore, director Larraz manages to reduce the plot to a lethargic exercise. When released on video in the USA as *Satan's Daughters*, a new title sequence included footage from Hammer's *The Vampire Lovers* (1970)!

Above: The Vampire Lovers.

VAMPYROS LESBOS DIE ERBIN DES DRACULA

(aka EL SIGNO DEL VAMPIRO/LAS VAMPIRAS) West Germany/Spain, 1970. Dir: Franco Manera (Jesús Franco). With: Susan Korda (Soledad Miranda), Dennis Price, Ewa Ströemberg, Paul Mueller, Hiedrum Kussin, Victor Feldman. CCC Telecine/Fenix Films. Colour.
Filmed in Turkey, this combines elements of the Countess Elizabeth Bathory legend with J. Sheridan Le Fanu's 'Carmilla' and Bram Stoker's 'Dracula's Guest'. Soledad Miranda plays Count Dracula's descendant, Nadina, who entices young women to her isolated island, then seduces and kills them to remain young. The German version (released in 1971) apparently includes a great deal more sex and violence than the version which finally appeared in Spain in 1974. Franco (who also appears in the film) continues to irritate with his camera zooms, and the career of English actor Dennis Price reaches a new low. Supposedly based on Bram Stoker's 'The Strange Adventure of Jonathan Harker' ('La Extrana Aventura de Jonathan Harkei')!

VAULT OF HORROR

(USA: aka TALES FROM THE CRYPT II) UK, 1973. Dir: Roy Ward Baker. With: Dawn Addams, Tom Baker, Michael Craig, Denholm Elliott, Glynis Johns, Edward Judd. Amicus/Metromedia. Colour.
After the success of *Tales from the Crypt* (1972), Amicus followed it up with this second all-star anthology of horror stories adapted by producer Milton Subotsky from the EC Comics of the 1950s. Unfortunately, the film aims more for laughs than chills, which ruins 'Midnight Mess', in which Daniel Massey (after murdering real-life sister Anna) stumbles upon a very special restaurant for vampires, where he ends up on the menu. The other stories involve an insufferably neat husband, a macabre double-cross, a stolen Indian rope trick and an artist's voodoo revenge. In the framing story, five people trapped in an underground vault recount their recurring dreams to each other while waiting for the elevator to be repaired. Of course, it turns out that they are already dead.

THE VELVET VAMPIRE

(UK: aka THE WAKING HOUR)
USA, 1971. Dir: Stephanie Rothman. With: Michael Blodgett, Sherry Miles, Celeste Yarnall, Paul Prokop, Gene Shane, Bob Tessier. New World Pictures. Colour.

From the co-director of *Blood Bath* (1966) comes this slow moving vampire movie, featuring Yarnall as centuries-old Diana LeFanu who moves around in sunlight and sleeps with her dead husband in his coffin. She invites young married couple Blodgett and Miles to her desert home and seduces both of them, until she is finally destroyed by hippies with crosses.

VLAD TEPES

Romania, 1978. Dir: Doru Nastase. With: Stefan Sileanu, George Constantin, Teofil Vilcu. Romaniafilm. Colour.

The story behind the real Dracula, Vlad Tepes, the fifteenth century Romanian prince who impaled his enemies.

VOODOO HEARTBEAT

USA, 1972. Dir: Charles Nizet. With: Ray Molina, Philip Ahn, Ern Dugo, Forrest Duke, Ebby Rhodes, Mike Zapata. Ray Molina/TWI. Colour.

The ads warned that you had to be 'mature enough to witness the shocking detail' of this low budget horror movie shot in Las Vegas. Producer Molina stars as an Elvis lookalike who is turned into a blood-drinking monster by a stolen voodoo serum.

WEB OF THE SPIDER

(Orig: NELLA STRETTA MORSA DEL RAGNO/DRACULA IM SCHLOSS DES SCHRECKENS/PRISONNIER DE L'ARAIGNEE)
Italy/West Germany/France, 1970. Dir: Anthony M. Dawson (Antonio Margheriti). With: Anthony Franciosa, Michèle Mercier, Klaus Kinsky (Kinski), Peter Carsten, Karen Field, Silvano Tranquilli. DC7/Paris Cannes/Terra. Colour.

Director Margheriti's colour remake of his own *Castle of Blood* (1964). Sceptical American reporter Franciosa accepts a bet by Edgar Allan Poe (an uneven cameo by Kinski, whose name is misspelled on the credits) that he can't survive the night in a deserted old mansion haunted by vampiric ghosts. The muddled script trots out all the old supernatural clichés. Supposedly based on Edgar Allan Poe's *Night of the Living Dead* — huh?

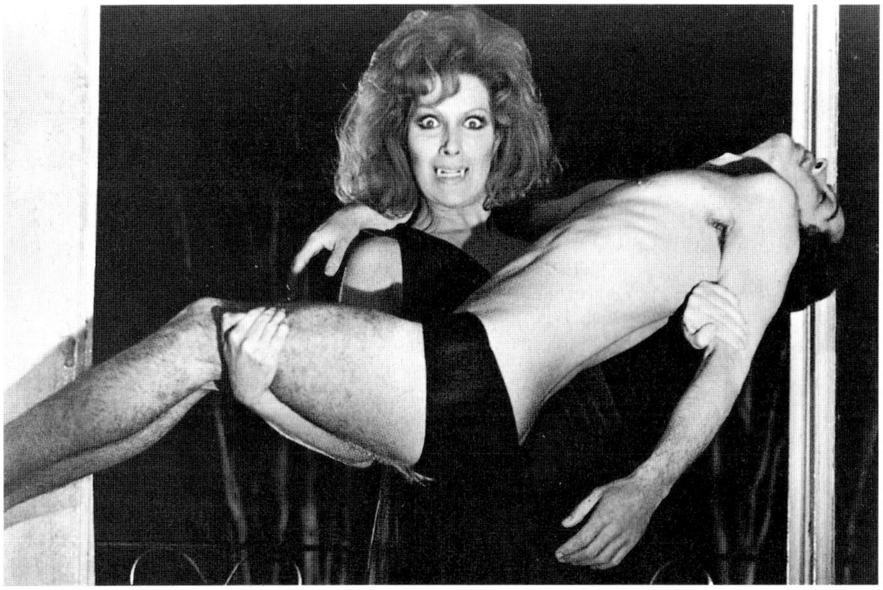

Top: *The Vampire's Night Orgy.*
Above: *The Velvet Vampire.*

THE WEREWOLF VS. THE VAMPIRE WOMAN

(Orig: LA NOCHE DE WALPURGIS/ NACHT DER VAMPIRE. USA: aka BLOOD MOON. UK: SHADOW OF THE WEREWOLF)
Spain/West Germany, 1970 (1972). Dir: Leon Klim (Klimovsky). With: Paul Naschy (Jacinto Molina), Patty Shepard, Gaby Fuchs, Barbara Capell (Kapel), Andrew Reese (Andres Resino), Julio Peña. Plata Films/Ellman Enterprises. Colour.

Fifth in the series, and a sequel to *Fury of the Wolfman* (1970). When a silver bullet is removed from the body of werewolf Count Waldemar Daninsky (Naschy, who also scripted), he returns to life and goes in search of vampire/witch Countess Waldessa (Shepard) and her silver cross.

Sequel: DR. JEKYLL AND THE WEREWOLF (1971)

WINTER WITH DRACULA

Romania/UK, 1971. Border. Colour.

Despite the title, this tedious half-hour travelogue only makes a passing reference to Vlad Tepes, the inspiration for Bram Stoker's *Dracula*.

the

teen monsters had been around since the rebellious 1950s, when American International dealt with adolescent angst in **I Was a Teenage Werewolf (1957), I Was a Teenage Frankenstein (1957), Blood of Dracula (1957)** and their ilk.

With the end of the old studio system and the growth of the video industry, a new breed of independent producer began churning out product aimed specifically at the youth market. One of the most successful entries in this vampiric sub-genre was **The Lost Boys (1987)**, with its gang of hip, leather-jacketed undead, but there were plenty of other teenage bloodsuckers ready to put the bite on the box office in **Fright Night (1985), Once Bitten (1985), Vamp (1986), My Best Friend is a Vampire (1987), Near Dark (1987), Fright Night Part 2 (1988), Beverly Hills Vamp (1988)** and the appositely titled **Teen Vamp (1988)**.

Television was also not slow to capitalize upon the vampire's new found popularity amongst younger generations, and TV movies such as **I, Desire (1982), The Midnight Hour (1985), Nightlife (1989), Daughter of Darkness (1989)** and **Nick Knight (1989)** invited the undead across the threshold and into the home.

The Monster Squad

The vampire was soon being

1980s

Vampire's Kiss.

Jitters (1988).

Despite making a few nominal appearances under his own name and others, or lending his appellation to several misleading titles, Dracula himself was perhaps most noticeable during the 1980s by his big screen absence.

It was therefore all the more surprising that Bram Stoker's immortal Count would once again come to the rescue of the moribund vampire genre...

spoofed in a glut of horror comedies, although apparently serious attempts to adapt modern vampire fiction — from the stylistic vacuum of Whitley Strieber's **The Hunger (1983)** *and outer space excesses of Colin Wilson's* **Lifeforce (1985)**, *through to the technical inadequacies of the Stephen King sequel* **A Return to Salem's Lot (1987)** *— probably raised significantly more laughs.*

The Hong Kong cinema added its own distinctive variation to the mythology with the hugely popular 'hopping vampires' of the **Mr. Vampire** *series and its numerous imitations, and the undulating undead were even exported to Canada for a curious hybrid,* **The**

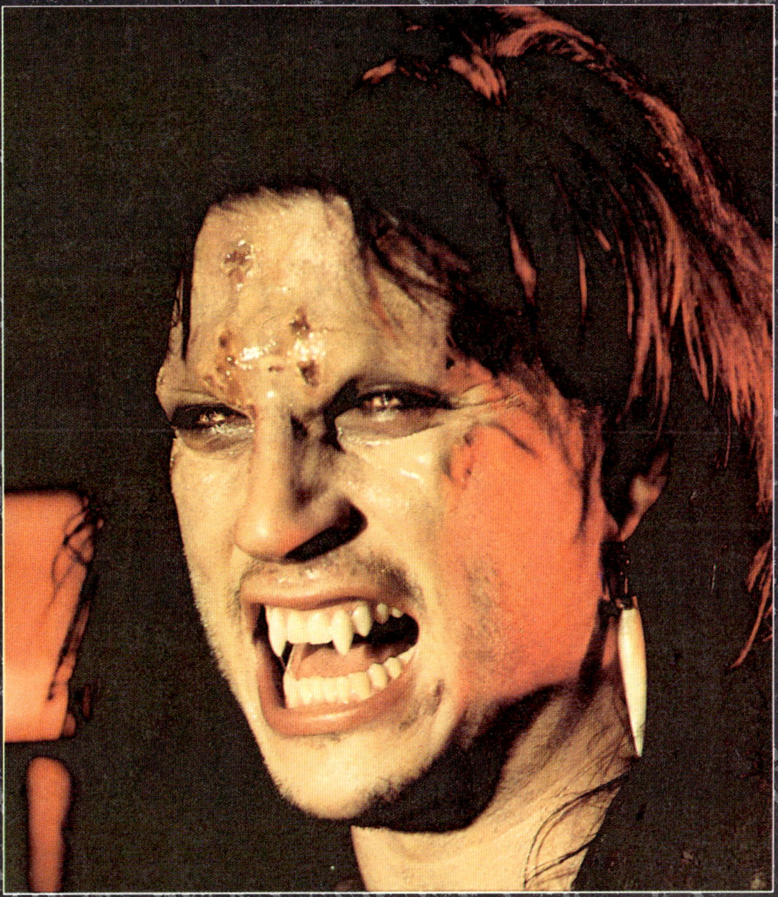

The Lost Boys.

ANEMIA

Italy, 1986. Dir: Alberto Abruzzese and Achille Pisanti. With: Hans Zischler, Gioia Maria Scola, Gérard Landry. RAI. Colour.

Political satire in which Umberto, the forty year-old leader of Italy's Communist Party (German actor Zischler), becomes a bloodsucker after reading the morbid memoirs of his mysterious grandfather.

THE BAD SISTER

UK, 1983. Dir: Laura Mulvey and Peter Wollen. With: Dawn Archibald, Isabel Dean, Kevin McNally, Matyelock Gibbs, Hugh Millais, Neil Cunningham. Moving Picture Company/Channel 4/ Modelmark. Colour.

Made-for-TV movie, shot entirely on videotape. Archibald plays a Scottish girl living in London, who sets out on a dream-like journey to discover her secret past and the cause of her mother's mysterious death. Based on a novel by Emma Tennant, this is arty for art's sake. Slow-moving, confusing and pretentious, only the recurring vampire motif holds any interest.

THE BEASTMASTER

USA, 1982. Dir: Don Coscarelli. With: Marc Singer, Tanya Roberts, Rip Torn, John Amos, Josh Milrad, Rod Loomis. Leisure Investment. Colour.

Juvenile sword and sorcery adventure, co-written and directed by twenty-eight year-old Coscarelli (*Phantasm* [1979]). Overlong at nearly two hours, but Singer makes a likeable barbarian hero, Dar, who can talk with the animals. His quest brings him into contact with busty ex-*Charlie's Angels* star Roberts, Torn's evil priest Maax, zombie guards in bondage gear, a trio of witches, a 'seeing' ring and, best of all, a race of giant vampire creatures (led by Daniel Zormeier). An odd mixture of violence and cuteness.

Sequel: BEASTMASTER 2: THROUGH THE PORTAL OF TIME (1991)

BECAUSE THE DAWN

USA, 1988. Dir: Amy Goldstein. With: Edwige Sandy Gray, Gregory St John. Colour.

Rambling, arty, forty-five minute short about modern New York girl Marie who also happens to be a centuries-old lesbian vampire. Her jaded existence leads her to sing the blues, pose for a photographer, and ride in a mystical horse and carriage through Times Square. Music by Sting.

Above: Because the Dawn.

LA BELLE CAPTIVE

France, 1983. Dir: Alain Robbe-Grillet. With: Daniel Mesguich, Gabrielle Lazure, Cyrielle Claire, Daniel Emilfork, François Chaumette. Argos. Colour.

Inspired by Rene Magritte's famous painting, from which it takes its title. Lazure stars as a mysterious vampire-woman who hires a private detective.

BEVERLY HILLS VAMP

USA, 1988. Dir: Fred Olen Ray. With: Britt Ekland, Eddie Deezen, Tim Conway Jr, Jay Richardson, Michelle Bauer, Robert Quarry. American-Independent/Austin Enterprises. Colour.

Awful, low budget horror comedy from prolific co-producer/director Fred Olen Ray. A trio of nerdy would-be filmmakers arrive in Hollywood and visit a Beverly Hills bordello run by vampire Madam Cassandra (Ekland) and her three undead hookers. It's just another excuse for the director to include a succession of naked breasts. Deezen's impersonation of Jerry Lewis continues to be as irritating as the original, while guest star Robert Quarry (playing a priest in a wheelchair) is a long way from the relative sophistication of the Count Yorga films.

BILLY THE KID AND THE GREEN BAIZE VAMPIRE

UK, 1985. Dir: Alan Clarke. With: Phil Daniels, Alun Armstrong, Bruce Payne, Louise Gold, Eve Ferret, Richard Ridings. ITC/Zenith. Colour.

Borderline fantasy/musical about snooker! Daniels plays a dislikeable working class hero who challenges middle class champion Armstrong (who likes to live and dress as a vampire for no apparent reason) to a final, deciding match. The songs are terrible, the characters unsympathetic and the direction reflects all the worse excesses of music videos. Even the climactic revelation that Armstrong's character possesses real supernatural powers can't save this from being a disaster.

THE BLACK ROOM

USA, 1981 (1984). Dir: Elly Kenner and Norman Thaddeus Vane. With: Stephen Knight, Cassandra Gaviola, Jimmy Stathis, Clara Perryman, Charlie Young, Linnea Quigley. Lancer Productions. Colour.

Low budget story about an incestuous brother and sister (Knight and Gaviola) who rent out a room in their Beverly Hills mansion to a couple cheating on each other. The voyeuristic brother is a contemporary vampire, who suffers from a rare form of anaemia and needs fresh blood to survive. Too timid to touch his victims, he relies on medical transfusions to control his hereditary illness.

BLOOD LUST

UK, 1980. Dir: Russell Gay. Harrison Marks Company. Colour.

Hardcore Dracula movie, released in 8mm as part of the Mystra series.

BLOODSUCKERS FROM OUTER SPACE

USA, 1984. Dir: Glen Coburn. With: Thom Meyers, Laura Ellis, Dennis Letts, Big John Brigham, Pat Paulsen, Chris Heldman. One-of-Those Productions. Colour.

Low budget science fiction spoof, filmed in Texas. A strange alien wind turns members of the local farming community into blood-drinking zombies. This results in the creatures retaining their original personalities after they're undead. The outbreak of blood-spewing is not helped by a group of incompetent scientists, an ineffectual President of the United States (comedian Paulsen) and a nuclear-mad US General.

BLUE LAMP IN A WINTER NIGHT

Hong Kong, 1985. Dir: Yao Funa. Colour.

Turn-of-the-century story about a love triangle, involving ghosts and vampires.

BODY DOUBLE

USA, 1984. Dir: Brian De Palma. With: Craig Wasson, Gregg Henry, Melanie Griffith, Deborah Shelton, Guy Boyd, Dennis Franz. Columbia. Colour.

De Palma's complex thriller borrows plot elements from Hitchcock's *Rear Window* (1954) and *Vertigo* (1958), as voyeuristic out-of-work actor (Wasson) is duped into witnessing a murder. The film opens with him being fired from a low budget porno vampire movie called *Vampire's Kiss*.

BUENAS NOCHES, SENOR MONSTRUO

Spain, 1982. Dir: Antonio Mercero. With: Regaliz, Paul Naschy (Jacinto Molina), Luis Escobar, Fernando Bilbao. Frade. Colour.

Musical/comedy for children, with Naschy as a werewolf (not Waldemar Daninsky), plus Count Dracula, the Frankenstein monster and Quasimodo. The title translates as *Good Evening, Mr Monster*.

CAFE FLESH

USA, 1982. Dir: Rinse Dream (Stephen Sayadian). With: Andrew Nichols, Paul McGibboney, Pia Snow (Michelle Bauer), Marie Sharp, Robert Dennis, Becky Savage. Caribbean. Colour.

Flashy, erotic science fiction film, set in a post-holocaust 'mutant universe'. The few remaining Sex Positives are forced to perform for the Sex Negatives in the Café Flesh. Includes Nichols as a vampiric emcee (with a mock-Lugosi accent) and a performer with fangs. Released in both hard– and softcore versions. From the director of *Dr. Caligari* (1989).

CARNE DE TU CARNE

Colombia, 1984. Dir: Carlos Mayolo. With: Adriana Herran, David Guerrero, José Angel. Producciones Visuales. Colour.

Muddled political satire from Colombia, about a wealthy family involved in incest and vampirism. The film is dedicated to Roman Polanski and Roger Corman.

LES CHARLOTS CONTRE DRACULA

France, 1980. Dir: Jean-Pierre Desagnat. With: Les Charlots, Amelie Prevost, Andreas Voutsinas, Gerard Jugnot, Vincent Martin, Dora Doll. Planfilm/Belstar Productions/Stephan Films/Films de la Tour. Colour.

French vampire spoof in which Dracounet, the son of Dracula, dreams of becoming a vampire just like his dear dad. However, he can't become one of the undead until he can find a woman, who is the double of his late mother, to give him a cursed potion to drink. The three-member Les Charlots (Charlot being the nickname of Charlie Chaplin in France) were a sixties group famous for their parodies of well-known songs.

CHILLERS

USA, 1988. Dir: Daniel Boyd. Raedon. Colour.

Independent horror anthology movie, made in West Virginia by college professor Boyd. Five people miss their bus and pass the time by telling scary stories. A girl's boyfriend turns out to be a white-eyed ghost; an adult camp leader is really a crazy killer; a woman meets a TV newsman who is a vampire; a young man can wish people from the obituary columns back to life; and a female student is possessed by an Indian spirit. When the next bus turns up it takes them all to Hell. Better than you'd expect.

THE CLOSE ENCOUNTER OF THE VAMPIRE

Hong Kong, 1986. Dir: Yuen Ping. Colour.

Horror comedy set in medieval China. Three cowardly exorcists take on a hopping vampire, while a group of orphans are menaced by a kiddie spook.

Below: *Billy the Kid and the Green Baize Vampire.*

THE CRAVING

(Orig: EL RETORNO DEL HOMBRE LOBO)
Spain, 1980. Dir: Jack (Jacinto) Molina. With: Paul Naschy (Jacinto Molina), Julia Saly, Silvia Aguilar, Narciso Ibañez Menta, Azucena Hernández, Beatriz Elorietta. Dalmata Films. Colour.

Naschy's ninth movie as El Hombre Lobo Waldemar Daninsky and a follow-up to *Night of the Howling Beast* (1975). The Wolf Man is revived when two graverobbers remove a silver cross from his heart, and he is soon settling an old score with the undead Elizabeth Bathory and her female vampires. Naschy also wrote and directed the movie, which was a major flop in Spain. The scenes of the vampire women have an imaginative, dream-like quality that is missing from the rest of the film.

Sequel: THE BEAST AND THE MAGIC SWORD (1983)

CURSE OF THE WICKED WIFE

(aka WICKED WIFE)
Hong Kong, 1984. Dir: Wong King-Fang. Colour.

When twins are separated at birth, one goes to live with a rich family, the other with a poor family. There are subplots involving a vampire and an evil landowner who kills his victims with 'death bugs'. The climax has the heroine spewing up all kinds of insects!

DANCE OF THE DAMNED

USA, 1988. Dir: Katt Shea Ruben. With: Starr Andreef, Cyril O'Reilly, Tom Ruben, Deborah Ann Nassar, Marla Ford. Concorde/Virgin Vision. Colour.

When suicidal stripper Jodie (Andreef) goes home with a tall dark stranger (O'Reilly), she discovers he's a vampire who wants her to describe to him all the pleasures he misses, like the feel of sunlight. A low budget attempt to do something different with the genre, directed by ex-actress and Corman protégé Katt Shea Ruben.

Remake: TO SLEEP WITH A VAMPIRE (qv; 1992)

DAUGHTER OF DARKNESS

USA/Hungary, 1989. Dir: Stuart Gordon. With: Anthony Perkins, Mia Sara, Robert Reynolds, Dezsu Garas, Jack Coleman, Erika Bodnar. King Phoenix Entertainment/ Accent. Colour.

The first TV movie from director Stuart (*Re-Animator* [1985]) Gordon is something of a disappointment. Plagued by recurring nightmares, a young American girl (Sara) travels to Ceausescu's Romania to discover the father she's never known. He turns out to be Anton Crainic (Perkins), a 200 year-old vampire who helps her escape from the undead survivors of his ancient family. This unfortunately lacks much of the style and humour Gordon has brought to his other projects.

DEADLINE

(USA: aka ANATOMY OF A HORROR)
Canada, 1980. Dir: Mario Azzopardi. With: Stephen Young, Sharon Masters, Marvin Goldhar, Jeannie Elias, Cindy Hinds, Phillip Leonard. Horror Picture Films/ACFC. Colour.

Young portrays horror novelist and screenwriter Steven Lessey (based on you-know-who), who is driven insane by his success and family problems. He eventually writes this film and then kills himself! Co-writer/director Azzopardi visualises a number of extracts of Lessey's work, including a mutant baby, a mad Nazi scientist using the sound of a punk band to make people explode and, best of all,

Left: *Dracula's Widow.*

vampire nuns. Stephen King could probably sue!

DEVIL'S VINDATA

Thailand/Hong Kong, 1986. Dir: L. Chang-Xu. Colour.

The title is supposed to be *Devil's Vendetta*! When the Devil devours the pulsating heart of a Buddhist priest, he is transformed into a beautiful demoness. He/she then decides to return from the afterlife as a vampire.

DINNER WITH THE VAMPIRE

Italy, 1988. Dir: Lamberto Bava. With: George Hilton, Patrizia Pellegrino, Riccardo Rossi, Valeria Milillo, Yvonne Scio, Isabel Russinova. Dania-Devon/Reteit Alia/Surf Film. Colour.

Unimaginative comedy/horror thriller from co-writer/director Bava, filmed in English. Three girls and a boy are invited by famous horror film director Yurek (Hilton) to visit his eerie castle. However, their host is revealed to be a vampire and he challenges the teenagers to find a way to kill him and finally end his boring, centuries-old existence. There's a hunchbacked servant and a *Dorian Gray* plot-twist involving an old black and white horror film.

DRACULA

Japan, 1980. Dir: Minori Okazaki. Toei Animation Co. Colour.

Full-length animated feature, based on Marvel Comics' *The Tomb of Dracula* series. Quincy Harker, the son of Jonathan, and his band of vampire hunters pursue a moustachioed Dracula, whose baby son is killed by Satan. Colourful, if static, animation and a complicated plot for kids.

DRACULA EXOTICA

(UK: LOVE AT FIRST GULP)
USA, 1981. Dir: Warren Evans. With: Jamie Gillis, Samantha Fox, Vanessa Del Rio, Marlene Willoughby, Christine Deshaffer, Randy West. Entertainment Ventures/VCA. Colour.

Gillis repeats his role as Count Dracula from *Dracula Sucks* (1979) in this vampire movie available in both hard- and softcore versions. This time, cursed by God to become one of the undead, he pursues a female CIA agent (Fox) who is the reincarnation of the virgin he raped 500 years ago. In the end, Dracula turns from a bat into a dove of peace!

DRACULA RISES FROM THE COFFIN

Republic of Korea, 1982. Dir: Lee Hyoung Pyo. With: Kang Yong Suk, Park Yang Rae. Tai Chang Inc. Colour.

Dracula is obsessed with a young student and follows her back to Korea, where he appears at the girl's wedding. However, her husband and a Buddhist monk defeat the Count with some spiritual kung fu.

DRACULA'S LAST RITES

(USA: aka LAST RITES)
France/USA 1980. Dir: Domonic Paris. With: Patricia Lee Hammond, Gerald Fielding, Victor Jorge, Michael Lally, Mimi Weddell. New Empire Features/Cannon. Colour.

Lucard, a small town mortician, the sheriff and a local doctor are all vampires who drink the blood of accident cases, then drive a stake through their hearts to avoid unwanted competition. This low budget horror film, shot in upstate New York, is most notable for its technical incompetence.

DRACULA'S WIDOW

USA, 1988. Dir: Christopher Coppola. With: Sylvia Kristel, Josef Sommer, Lenny Von Dohlen, Marc Coppola, Stefan Schnabel, Rachel Jones. De Laurentiis Entertainment. Colour.

Any promise of an erotic twist on the legend with the casting of ex-Emmanuelle Kristel is quickly forgotten in this dire vampire movie, which remained on the shelf for a few years following the collapse of De Laurentiis' movie empire. Kristel plays Dracula's widow, transported to America in a crate for a vampire exhibition being mounted by a strange young man (Sommer) in his rundown wax museum. Not very much happens, although Kristel gets to wear some sexy outfits while the film runs its tedious course. Co-writer/director Coppola (twenty-five year-old nephew of Francis Ford) can't seem to decide if this is meant to be a horror film or a comedy. Instead, it's simply a bore.

DRACULA TAN EXARCHIA

Greece, 1983. Dir: Nikos Zervos. With: Kostas Soumas, Yannis Panousis, Vangelis Contronis. Allagi Films. Colour.

Set in Athens, Dracula and his servant dig up the bodies of famous musicians to construct, Frankenstein-like, a superhuman rock star. The last half of the film consists of the creature's performance.

DRAGON AGAINST VAMPIRE

(aka DRAGON VS VAMPIRE)
Hong Kong, 1985. Dir: Lionel Leung. Colour.

Three comic graverobbers meet a vampire

and the lone survivor teams up with an old Shaolin wizard who lives in an underground cave. A restaurant owner is decapitated and his daughter possessed, while the vampire has his secrets tattooed on his back. An incoherent mess with music by Tangerine Dream!

ELUSIVE SONG OF THE VAMPIRE

Taiwan, 1987. Dir: Takako Shira. Colour.

Confused story about a man in ancient China whose home is haunted by a quartet of hopping vampires. While he enlists the aid of a kung fu sorcerer to defeat them, the transvestite king steals the soul of a princess and refuses to return it until she can replace it with the soul of a male virgin. Then things get even more complicated!

ELVIRA MISTRESS OF THE DARK

USA, 1988. Dir: James Signorelli. With: Elvira (Cassandra Peterson), W. Morgan Sheppard, Daniel Greene, Susan Kellermann, Jeff Conaway, Edie McClurg. New World Pictures/NBC Productions. Colour.

Totally unfunny horror comedy based around vampiric TV movie hostess Elvira, who learns that she has inherited a spooky old house. What might have been a fun variation on the old dark house plot is ruined by the lowbrow humour (numerous breast jokes) and Peterson's minimal talents as an actress. Only Sheppard, as her evil great uncle who turns into a spell-casting demon to gain a recipe book of spells, makes any effort.

EVILS OF THE NIGHT

(aka SPACE MONSTERS)

USA, 1984. Dir: Mardi Rustam. With: Karrie Emerson, Neville Brand, Aldo Ray, Tina Louise, John Carradine, Julie Newmar. Lightning. Colour.

Brand and Ray play two crazies who abduct young girls to keep evil alien vampires Carradine and Newmar supplied with fresh blood. Low budget thrills, but just look at that cast!

FADE TO BLACK

USA, 1980. Dir: Vernon Zimmerman. With: Dennis Christopher, Tim Thomerson, Gwynne Gilford, Normann Burton, Linda Kerridge, Morgan Paull. Leisure Investment/Movie Ventures/American Cinema. Colour.

Nerdy Dennis Christopher plays a crazy film buff who kills off those people he doesn't like by taking on the persona of his favourite movie characters. These include Richard Widmark, Hopalong Cassidy, the Mummy and Count Dracula. Features Marilyn Monroe look-alike Kerridge, Mickey Rourke as a young punk and a climax set on the roof of Mann's Chinese Theater in Hollywood.

FERAT VAMPIRE

(Orig: UPIR Z FERATU)

Czechoslovakia, 1982. Dir: Juraj Herz. With: Jiri Menzel, Dagmar Veskrnova, Jana Brezkova, Jan Schmid, Petr Cepek. Barrandov. Colour.

Director Herz parodies the horror genre with this story about a car which runs on the blood of its driver. Loosely based on a story by Roald Dahl.

FRIGHT NIGHT

USA, 1985. Dir: Tom Holland. With: Chris Sarandon, William Ragsdale, Amanda Bearse, Stephen Geoffreys, Roddy McDowall, Jonathan Stark. Vistar/Columbia. Colour.

Screenwriter Tom Holland (*Psycho II* [1983], etc) makes his directorial début with this horror comedy. When young Charlie Brewster suspects his suave nextdoor neighbour (a likeable Sarandon) is a vampire, the only person to believe him is ham horror actor Peter Vincent (a fun cameo by veteran McDowall). Featuring excellent make-up effects and an exciting climax. However, some sequences seem a bit extreme when compared to the jokiness of the first half. Forrest J Ackerman supplied the movie props.

Sequel: FRIGHT NIGHT PART 2 (qv; 1988)

Above: *Elvira Mistress of the Dark.*
Below: *Fright Night.*

FRIGHT NIGHT PART 2

USA, 1988. Dir: Tommy Lee Wallace. With: Roddy McDowall, William Ragsdale, Traci Lin, Julie Carmen, Jonathan Gries, Russell Clark. Columbia. Colour.

Okay sequel to *Fright Night* (1985). Three years after destroying the undead next door, Charlie Brewster (Ragsdale) is just getting over the experience when Regine (Carmen), the seductive sister of the original vampire, turns up for revenge. With the help of failed TV horror host Peter Vincent (McDowall) and his new girlfriend (Lin), Charlie has to learn to believe in the undead again before he can destroy them. Another uneven mixture of horror and humour, but likeable characters and impressive special effects make this an entertaining follow-up.

THE GAMES OF THE COUNTESS DOLINGEN OF GRATZ

(Orig: LES JEUX DE LA COMTESSE DOLINGEN DE GRATZ)

France, 1980. Dir: Catherine Binet. With: Michel Lonsdale, Carol Kane, Katia Wastchenko, Robert Stephens, Marina Vlady, Marilu Marini. Les Films du Nautile/ Prospectacle/Perec/Zajdermann. Colour.

Based on a book by Unica Zurn and a chapter from Bram Stoker's *Dracula*. A young woman, Louise (Kane), suspects a family friend of being a vampire.

GAYRACULA

USA, 1983. Dir: Roger Earl. With: Tim Kramer, Douglas Poston, Steve Collins, Ray Medina, Max Cooper. Marathon. Colour.

The title says it all: a homosexual Dracula in Transylvania.

GEEK MAGGOT BINGO

USA, 1983. Dir: Nick Zedd. With: Robert Andrews, Brenda Bergman, Richard Hell, Donna Death, (John) Zacherle, Bob Martin. Weirdo Films/Penetration. Colour.

Zedd follows up his directing début on *They Eat Scum* (1979) with this horror spoof featuring a female vampire (Death), a mad doctor Frankenstein (Andrews), Bruno Zeus as a hunchback, some nudity and a two-headed Formaldehyde Man (created by Ed French). Shot in 16mm on obviously cardboard sets. TV horror host Zacherle is shown sleeping during the breaks.

Above: Fright Night Part 2.

THE GONG SHOW MOVIE

USA, 1980. Dir: Chuck Barris. With: Chuck Barris, Robin Altman, Mabel King, Jaye P. Morgan, Buddy Didio, Murray Langston. Chuck Barris Productions. Colour.

Fictionalised behind-the-scenes look at the cult TV show which presented the often bizarre talents of people searching for fame. One of the contestants in this dire comedy is Count Banjola, who dresses like Dracula and hangs upside-down while playing the banjo!

GRAVEYARD DISTURBANCE

(Orig: DENTRO IL CIMITRIO)

Italy, 1987. Dir: Lamberto Bava. With: Gregory Lech Thaddeus, Lea Martino, Beatrice Ring, Gianmarço Tognazzi, Karl Zinny, Lino Salemme. Reteitalia/Dania/Devon. Colour.

Made-for-TV movie about a group of teenagers who find themselves in a ghostly old graveyard inn. For a bet, they descend into the tunnels of Hell and meet a variety of vampires, zombies and other creatures (mostly played for laughs) until they return to confront the Grim Reaper himself. Co-writer/director Bava makes a cameo appearance as a shopkeeper, and he even includes a nod to his father's far superior *Black Sunday* (1960).

GRAVEYARD SHIFT

Canada, 1986. Dir: Gerard Ciccoritti. With: Silvio Olivierio, Helen Papas, Cliff Stoker, Don

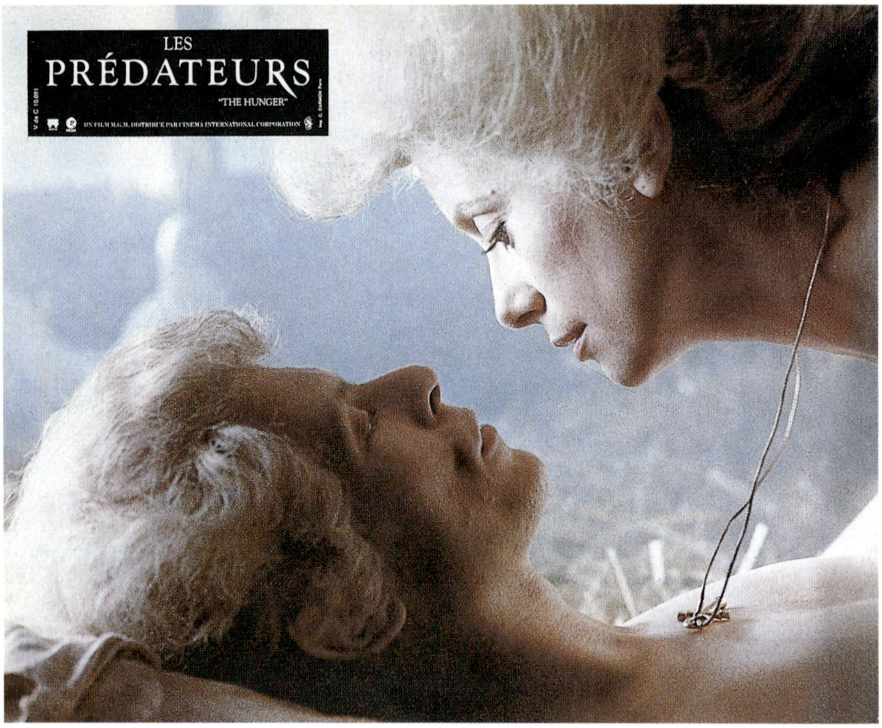

Jones, Dorin Ferber, Lesley Kelly. Cinema Ventures/Lightshow Communications. Colour.
Olivierio plays a 350 year-old all-night cab driver who is also an urban vampire. He wants to give up his undead harem to live with a suicidal female director (Papas) of mock-Gothic rock videos. In this movie, vampirism apparently cures cancer.
Sequel: THE UNDERSTUDY: GRAVEYARD SHIFT II (qv; 1988)

HAUNTED COP SHOP 1

Hong Kong, 1984. Dir: Jeff Lau. Colour.
When vampires infest a meat-packing plant, the special Monster Police Squad are called in to stop them. Unfortunately they fail, and the Police Commissioner relegates them to menial jobs until the undead invade the county hospital. Impressive special effects.
Sequel: HAUNTED COP SHOP 2 (qv; 1986)

HAUNTED COP SHOP 2

Hong Kong, 1986. Dir: Jeff Lau. Colour.
This improved sequel to the 1984 original features non-stop action. The vampire-creature is destroyed by the hero urinating into a pool and completing an electrical circuit!

HELLO DRACULA

Hong Kong, 1985. Dir: Henry Wu-Leung. Colour.
A dead body, reanimated by a child-vampire, becomes Dracula. The local officials recruit three vampire hunters from Europe and a magician creates a gang of bug-children to battle the undead. Includes a musical dance number with some friendly vampires, a vampire baseball game and the Count being blown up by a child wearing a belt of dynamite. Pretty unbelievable!

HORRIBLE HORROR

USA, 1986. Dir: David Bergman. With: Zacherley (John Zacherle). Movietime/Goodtimes Home Video. Colour/B&W.
Video collection of random genre clips, with fifties TV horror host Zacherley. Includes excerpts from *The Brainiac* (1961), *Bride of the Monster* (1955), *She Demons* (1958), etc, plus, most interesting of all, out-takes from (Abbott and Costello) *Meet Frankenstein* (1948).

HOWL OF THE DEVIL

(Orig: EL AULLIDO DEL DIABLO) Spain, 1988. Dir: Paul Naschy (Jacinto Molina). With: Paul Naschy (Jacinto Molina), Caroline Munro, Howard Vernon (Mario Lippert), Sergio Molina. Lorion. Colour.
Naschy not only writes and directs, but he also plays ten classic horror roles as a crazy actor. These include a vampire, the Frankenstein monster, Fu Manchu, Mr Hyde, the Phantom of the Opera, Quasimodo, the Devil, his zombie twin and, of course, a werewolf. A blend of horror nostalgia and explicit gore, Vernon turns up as a sinister manservant. This was Naschy's first film shot in English. The ad art depicts Mexican star Germán Robles as the vampire!

THE HUNGER

UK/USA, 1983. Dir: Tony Scott. With: Catherine Deneuve, David Bowie, Susan Sarandon, Cliff De Young, Beth Ehlers, Dan Hedaya. Metro-Goldwyn-Mayer. Colour.
Based on Whitley Strieber's novel, Tony Scott's movie suffers from an emphasis on style over content. Deneuve is impressive as the centuries-old vampire queen who seduces scientific researcher Sarandon when her previous companion (rock star Bowie) begins to age rapidly. Her undead lovers — who continue to survive, no matter how decayed their bodies are — eventually revenge themselves in the horrific climax. The sex scenes between Deneuve and Sarandon are pretty steamy.

HYSTERICAL

USA, 1982. Dir: Chris Bearde. With: William Hudson, Brett Hudson, Mark Hudson, Cindy Pickett, Clint Walker, Richard Kiel. H&W Film Works/Cinema Works/New World. Colour.
Unfunny horror spoof written by and starring American TV comedy trio the Hudson Brothers. It's about a haunted lighthouse with Kiel as a one hundred year-old zombie brought back to life by the ghost of his mistress (Julie Newmar). Includes cameos by Murray Hamilton, Bud Cort, John Larroquette, Keenan Wynn and Gary Owens, amongst others, and a prologue featuring Charlie Callas as a manic Count Dracula.

I, DESIRE

USA, 1982. Dir: John Llewellyn Moxey. With: David Naughton, Dorian Harewood, Brad Dourif, Marilyn Jones, Barbara Stock, Arthur Rosenberg. Columbia/ Green-Epstein/ABC-TV. Colour.
Surprisingly downbeat TV movie about an undead Hollywood hooker. Naughton (*An*

American Werewolf in London [1981]) plays a law student obsessed by the knowledge that there is a vampire (Stock) loose in modern day Los Angeles. When no-one will believe him, except for Dourif's odd street character, he sets about tracking the creature down — even if it means him losing everything. Director Moxey did it better with *The Night Stalker* (1971), but he still handles the vampire attacks with style and flair.

I LIKE BATS

(Orig: LUBIE NIETOPERZE)
Poland, 1985. Dir: Grzegorz Warchol. With: Katarzyna Walter, Marek Barbasiewicz, Malgorzata Lorentowicz, Jonasz Kofta, Edwin Petrykat, Jan Prochyra. The Polish Corporation for Film Production/ Film Polski. Colour.

Walter plays a busty vampire feeding off bats in her attic. Unable to get along with humans, she eventually visits a psychiatrist who first locks her up and then falls in love with her. Finally they marry and that ends her curse! Heavy-going allegory.

I MARRIED A VAMPIRE

USA, 1984. Dir: Jay Raskin. With: Rachel Golden, Brendan Hickey, Ted Zalewski, Deborah Carroll, Temple Aaron, David Dunton. Troma. Colour.

A young woman discovers that her husband, Robespierre, is a vampire having one-night stands with other women. A very unfunny, low budget comedy.

THE INN OF THE FLYING DRAGON

(aka ONDSKANS VARDSHUS)
Sweden/Ireland, 1981. Dir: Calvin Floyd. With: Per Oscarsson, Patrick Magee, Marilu Tolo, Curt Jurgens, Brendan Price, Niall Toibin. Aspekt Film/Dragon Co/National Film School of Ireland. Colour.

Loosely based on J. Sheridan Le Fanu's story 'The Room in the Dragon Volant'. A young nobleman becomes obsessed with a beautiful countess (Tolo), who is accompanied by a sinister old man. A series of strange deaths and the sight of an old crone dressed in the same clothes as the young woman suggest that the undead might be at work.

THE JITTERS

Canada/USA/Japan, 1988. Dir: John M. Fasano. With: Sal Viviano, Marilyn Tokuda, James Hong, Frank Diets, Doug Silberstein, Handy Atmadja. Gaga Communications/Fascination/ Prism. Colour.

For fans of Hong Kong hopping vampires comes this westernised version, filmed in Toronto and set in LA's Chinatown district. It's an enjoyable, if silly, horror comedy in which murder victims are revived by Hong and his son as the pointy-eared undead, to seek vengeance against a violent street gang.

JONATHAN OF THE NIGHT

USA, 1987. Dir: Buddy Giovinazzo. With: Don Striano, Mitch Maglio, Melissa Tait, Eric Collica, Ricky G. 2000 AD. Colour.

Ten minute short written, produced and directed by Giovinazzo (*Combat Shock* [1984]), designed to interest backers in a full length feature. Unfortunately, the amateurish performances and grainy photography hardly enhance this tale of a modern day vampire at a New York party. Music by Ricky G., who has a brief cameo as a drunken slob.

THE KISS

USA/Canada, 1988. Dir: Pen Densham. With: Joanna Pacula, Meredith Salenger, Nicholas Kilbertus, Mimi Kuzyk, Jan Rubes, Shawn Levy. Columbia/Tri-Star. Colour.

Originally announced as *The Host*. Pacula stars as forever-young model Felice, who also happens to be a shape-changing vampire who passes the family curse down through the female line with a kiss.

Co-written by Stephen (*Gothic* [1986]) Volk, this includes a wonderfully tacky zombie-cat and a chainsaw-in-the-swimming pool climax, both created by make-up effects supremo Chris Walas.

KRVAVA PANI

Czechoslovakia, 1981. Dir: Viktor Kubal. CFP/Koliba. Colour.

Full length animated version of the Countess Elizabeth Bathory legend.

KUNG FU FROM BEYOND THE GRAVE

Hong Kong. Orchids International Video. Colour.

A kung fu hero sets out to avenge his father's murder by an evil magician. During a martial arts battle, the villain calls on Dracula to aid him, and the Count promptly flies in. Also includes wizards, occult rays, flying ghosts, zombie ghosts and a headless ghost!

KUNG FU VAMPIRE BUSTER

(Orig: NEW MR. VAMPIRE)
Hong Kong, 1986. Dir: Xen Lung Ting. With: Ricky Hui (Xu Guanying). Colour.

The first of a rival series of films attempting to duplicate the success of Golden Harvest's popular 'hopping vampire' series. Hui, who starred in *Mr. Vampire* (1985), finds his soul fused with that of the ghost of a woman who committed suicide. A vampire also eventually turns up in this action comedy.

THE LAST HORROR FILM

USA, 1982 (1984). Dir: David Winters. With: Caroline Munro, Joe Spinell, Glenn Jacobson, Mary Spinell, Sean Casey. Shere Productions. Colour.

The two stars of *Maniac* (1980) are reunited in another low budget splatter movie. Filmed on location at the Cannes Film Festival (Marcello Mastroianni and Karen Black have 'walk ons'), Spinell plays crazy would-be director Vinny Durand who wants horror movie queen Jana Bates (Munro) to star in his project, *The Loves of Dracula*. When she turns him down, he goes on a murder spree, filming his victims until the 'surprise' ending. This even includes Spinell's real-life mother (who won the best actress award for her role at the Sitges Film Festival!).

LEGEND OF EIGHT SAMURAI

Japan, 1984. Dir: Kinji Fukasaku. With: Hiroko Yakushimaru, Henry Sanada, Sue Shiomi, Sonny Chiba, Mickey Narita. Toei Company. Colour.

Spectacular martial arts fantasy/adventure, which includes an evil princess who bathes in blood to stay young.

LIFEFORCE

UK/USA, 1985. Dir: Tobe Hooper. With: Steve Railsback, Peter Firth, Frank Finlay, Nicholas Ball, Mathilda May, Patrick Stewart. Cannon/Tri-Star. Colour.

Loosely based on Colin Wilson's novel *The Space Vampires*, Tobe Hooper's lively blend of science fiction and horror begins like *Alien* (1979), turns into a remake of *Quatermass and the Pit* (1967) and ends up looking like a Hammer Gothic! When a gigantic alien spaceship is dicovered in the cone of Halley's comet, three humanoid bodies are returned to Earth. Pretty soon an alien/vampire woman (May) has turned most of London into rampaging bloodsucking zombies. A wooden cast (Firth's ludicrous SAS officer, Finlay's sub-Van Helsing), laughable script (Dan O'Bannon and Don Jakoby) and unconvincing make-ups are saved by John Dykstra's impressive optical effects. This cost $25,000,000 and looks like a 1950s British B-movie!

LITTLE SHOP OF HORRORS

UK/USA, 1986. Dir: Frank Oz. With: Rick Moranis, Ellen Greene, Vincent Gardenia, Steve Martin, James Belushi, John Candy. Geffen/ Warner Bros. Colour.

Big budget remake of Roger Corman's 1960 cult classic, based on the 1982 off-Broadway hit musical (original screenwriter Charles B. Griffith had to sue for credit). Corman may have filmed his version in two days, but this took over a year to shoot (including a new, happy ending after disastrous previews) at a cost of around $30,000,000! Moranis plays Seymour Krelborn, who works in a skid row florists and grows Audrey II, a talking plant (voiced by Levi Stubbs of The Four Tops) that needs human blood to survive. Martin is great as a sadistic dentist, but the cameos by Belushi, Candy and Bill Murray (in the original Jack Nicholson role) are just thrown away. Directed by the voice of Miss Piggy.

THE LOST BOYS

USA, 1987. Dir: Joel Schumacher. With: Corey Feldman, Corey Haim, Bernard Hughes, Jason Patric, Kiefer Sutherland, Dianne Wiest. Warner Bros. Colour.

***Below:** Lifeforce.*

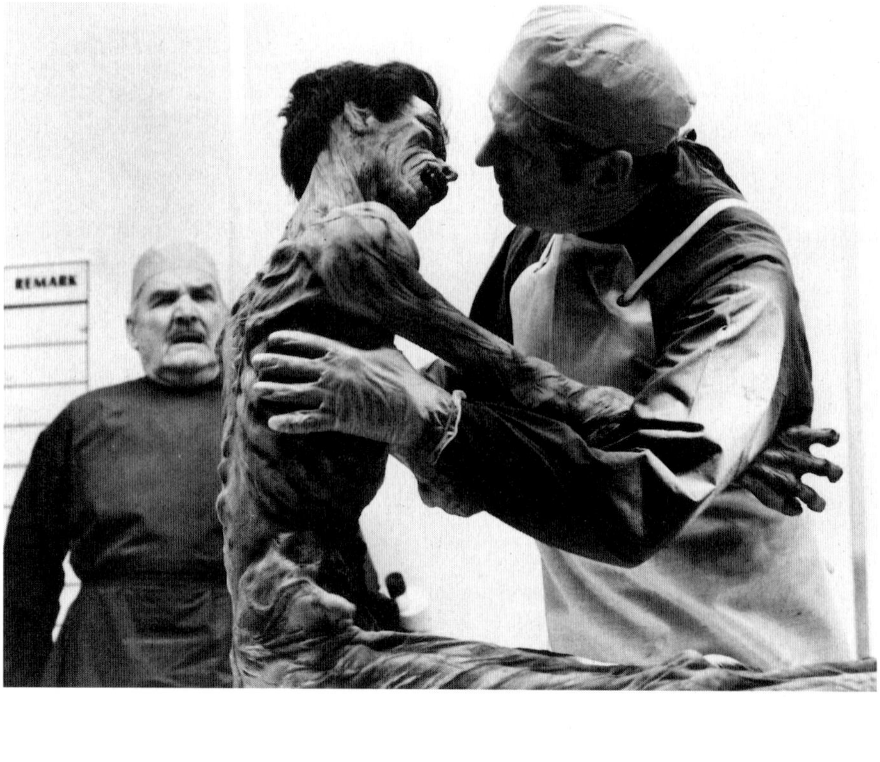

Predictable teen horror comedy from *The Omen* (1976) producers Richard Donner and Harvey Bernhard. When brothers Sam (Haim) and Michael (Patric) move to the west coastal town of Santa Clara, they soon discover its dark secret — a gang of teenage vampires (led by Donald Sutherland's son, Kiefer) are preying on the transient crowds. When Michael is infected and begins to turn into one of the undead, it is up to Sam and the bizarre Frog brothers (who run a local comic book store) to confront and destroy the vampires. Some interesting ideas are wasted in this flashy blend of nerds and rock music.

THE LOST PLATOON

USA, 1989. Dir: David A. Prior. With: William Knight, David Parry, Stephen Quadros, Lew Pipes, Roger Bayless, Jack Vogel. Action International Pictures. Colour.

War correspondent Knight discovers four vampire soldiers — one of whom (Parry) could even be Count Dracula — who have fought in successive conflicts down through the centuries. A clever idea, but not helped by the low budget. Filmed in Alabama.

LOVE ME VAMPIRE

Hong Kong, 1987. Dir: Irene Wang. Colour.

Teenage horror comedy which appears to have been inspired by *Fright Night* (1985).

LOVES OF THE LIVING DEAD

(aka HEAVEN WIFE, HELL WIFE)
Hong Kong, 1984. Dir: Ho Menga. Colour.

Includes plenty of blood, zombies and a beautiful vampire queen in a short red dress.

LUGOSI THE FORGOTTEN KING

USA, 1985. Dir: Mark S. Gilman and Dave Stuckey. With: Forrest J Ackerman, Carroll (Carol) Borland, Ralph Bellamy, Alex Gordon, John Carradine. Operator 13 Productions. Colour/B&W.

45 minute video compilation of rare newsclips and interviews, hosted by Ackerman. Includes trailers for *Dracula* (1930), *Mark of the Vampire* (1935) and *Plan 9 from Outer Space* (1958), amongst many others.

LUST IN THE FAST LANE

USA, 1984. Dir: Adam. With: Ginger Lynn, Tom Byron, Eric Edwards, Crystal Breeze, Traci Lords. Paradise Visuals. Colour.

Bored and restless, Byron and a pudgy underage Lords decide to leave town for the weekend. After the inevitable flat tyre on a lonely road, they make their way to the eerie-looking house of swinging couple Lynn and Edwards. After various combinations of hardcore sex, the two hosts are revealed to be vampires, and over the course of the weekend the unsuspecting couple have also been turned into the undead — doomed to stay and have sex for eternity.

MAGIC COP

(aka MR. VAMPIRE V)
Hong Kong, 1989. Dir: H. Ching. With: Lam Ching Ying. Movie Impact/Millifame Productions. Colour.

Fifth entry in the popular series. Ying plays Uncle Fung, a regional police detective, who travels to the big city and teams up with his nephew to investigate a vampire-witch who uses reanimated corpses for drug trafficking.

THE MARK OF LILITH

UK, 1986. Dir: Bruna Fionda, Polly Gladwin and Islling Mack-Nataf. With: Pamela Lofton, Susan Franklyn, Jeremy Peters, Patricia St. Hilaire, Michael Cudlip, Faye Chang. Rc-Vamp Productions/ London College of Printing/Circles.

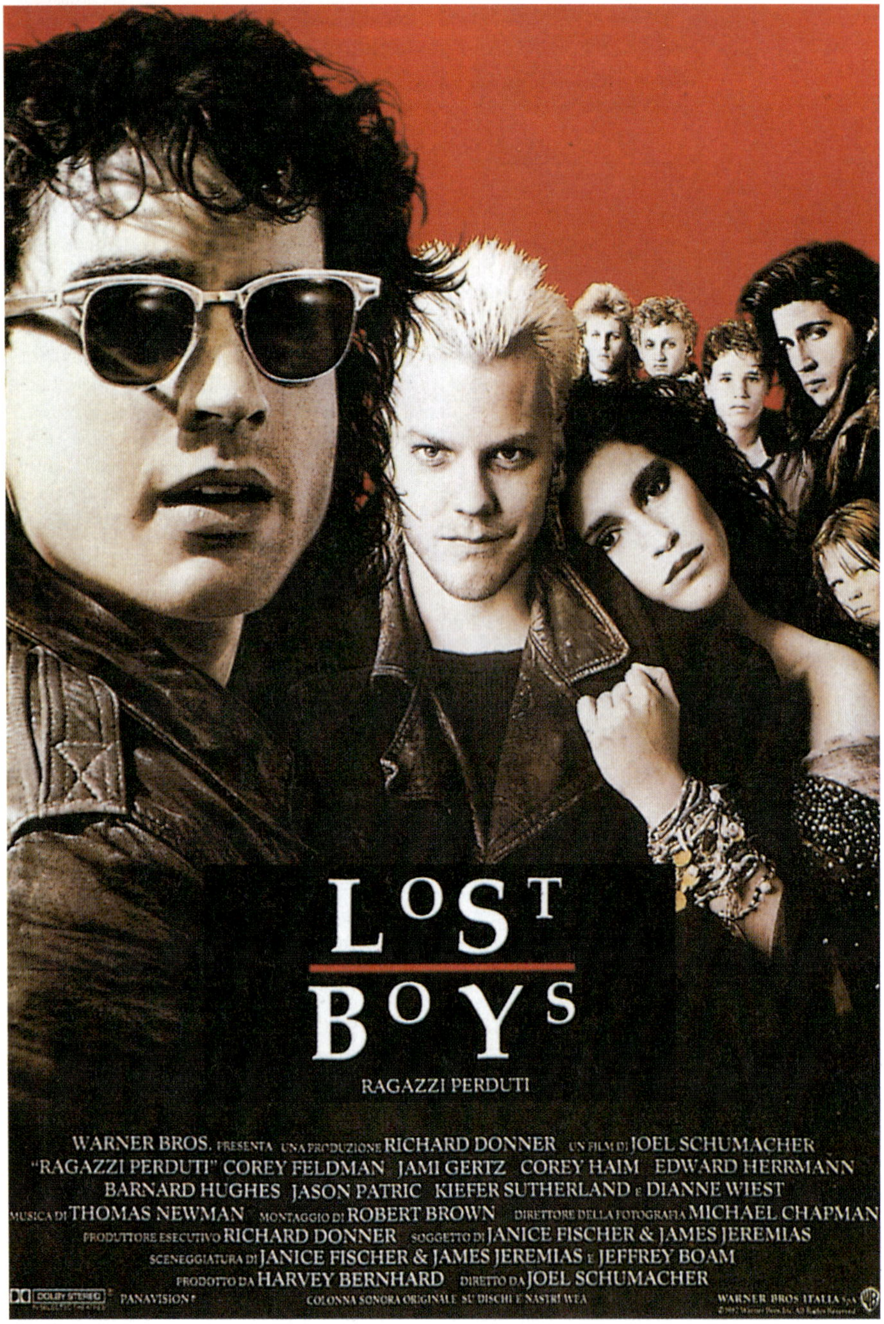

Colour.
Half-hour 16mm experimental short about a black lesbian filmmaker (Lofton), researching mythic images of monstrous women. She meets immortal bisexual female vampire Lillia (Franklyn), who wants to escape from her undead male companion. They discuss politics, patriarchy and horror films.

MIDNIGHT

USA, 1988. Dir: Norman Thaddeus Vane. With: Lynn Redgrave, Tony Curtis, Steve Parrish, Rita Gam, Frank Gorshin, Wolfman Jack. SVS Films/Midnight Inc. Colour.
Comedy murder-mystery in which Redgrave plays the titular vampiric TV horror hostess. Her unscrupulous boss (Curtis) will do anything to get the copyright to her hit chat show, and soon the bodies begin piling up.

THE MIDNIGHT HOUR

USA, 1985. Dir: Jack Bender. With: Shari Belafonte-Harper, Levar Burton, Kevin McCarthy, Dick Van Patten, Wolfman Jack, Dedee Pfeiffer. ABC-TV/Vidmark Entertainment. Colour.
Made-for-TV comedy/thriller, in which Belafonte-Harper plays Lucinda, an eighteenth century vampire-witch accidentally resurrected on Halloween by a group of teens. Pretty soon the small Massachusetts town is filled with ghouls, demons, the walking dead, a werewolf and a midget zombie. Wolfman Jack is heard as a disc jockey.

MIXED UP

Hong Kong, 1985. Dir: Henry S. Chen. Colour.
A teens-in-peril horror comedy featuring a vampire and a Frankenstein-like creature. During the climax, the two monsters battle it out on a yacht.

MOM

USA, 1989. Dir: Patrick Rand. With: Jeanne Bates, Mark Thomas Miller, Art Evans, Mary McDonough, Stella Stevens, Brion James. TWE. Colour.
Low budget comedy chiller with screen psycho James as a blind cannibal/vampire who bites grey-haired Bates and turns her into a shades-wearing member of the undead. Her TV newsman son (Miller) is embarrassed by her behaviour and tries to keep her locked up. Stevens has a fun cameo as a drunken hooker.

LA MOMIA NACIONAL

Spain, 1981. Dir: José Ramón Larraz. With: Francisco Algora, Azucena Hernández, Quique Camoiras, José Jaime Espinosa, Lili Murati, Paloma Hurtado. José Frade Productions. Colour.
A mummy comedy from the director of *Vampyres* (1974)! When the wrappings from a 1,000 year-old Egyptian princess (Hernández) are removed, she is revived as a beautiful nymphomaniac. Also includes a vampire doctor and a happy ending.

THE MONSTER CLUB

UK, 1980. Dir: Roy Ward Baker. With: Vincent Price, Donald Pleasence, John Carradine, Stuart Whitman, Richard Johnson, Barbara Kellerman. Sword & Sorcery/ITC. Colour.
All-star horror vehicle aimed at children by ex-Amicus producer Milton Subotsky. Based on three stories by R. Chetwynd-Hayes, who is played in the film by Carradine. When he is bitten by the desperate Eramus (Price), the author is taken by the grateful vampire back to meet his

friends at The Monster Club. The first two stories are about a Shadmock with a lethal whistle and a village full of ghouls. However, the third story, introduced by film producer Lintom Busotsky (Anthony Steel), is about a small boy who must protect his mother (Britt Ekland) and vampire father (Johnson) from the Bleeny — the Special Branch concerned with blood crimes, led by an evil Donald Pleasence. Terrible music and a silly script, but good to see the stars having fun with the material.

THE MONSTER SQUAD

USA, 1987. Dir: Fred Dekker. With: Andre Gower, Robby Kiger, Stephen Macht, Duncan Regehr, Tom Noonan, Brent Chalem. Taft Entertainment/Keith Barrish. Colour.

From writer/director Dekker (*Night of the Creeps* [1986]) and co-writer Shane Black comes a delightful horror comedy for children that echoes the Universal series of the 1940s. Dracula (an impressive Regehr) is in a small American town to recover an amulet of evil and only a group of kids, known as the Monster Squad, recognise the danger. Despite the intervention of Van Helsing (Jack Gwillim), the Count teams up with the Frankenstein monster (Noonan), a wolf man, gill man and mummy to create havoc. Great special effects, non-stop action and a nice sense of reverence make this a minor gem. Kids should love it.

LA MORTE VIVANTE

France, 1982. Dir: Jean Rollin. With: Marina Pierro, Françoise Blanchard, Mike Marshall, Carina Barone, Fanny Magieri, Patricia Besnard-Rousseau. Les Films ABC/Films Aleriaz/Films Du Yaka/Sam Selsky. Colour.

A chemical waste spillage revives a beautiful dead woman (Blanchard). With the help of a devoted childhood friend (Pierro), she sticks her fingers into victims' bodies and drinks their blood. As her memories return, the vampiric zombie needs more and more blood until she destroys her companion. Not as visually imaginative as some of his other films, co-writer/director Rollin still manages to give the film a nicely surreal atmosphere.

MR. VAMPIRE

Hong Kong, 1985. Dir: Lau Kun Wai. With: Ricky Hui (Xu Guanying), Moon Lee, Lam Ching Ying, Pauline Lau, Anthony Chan, Wu Ma. Golden Harvest/Paragon Films. Colour.

Wonderfully inventive horror comedy involving an evil reanimated vampire, a group of hopping zombies, the hideous ghost of a sexy young woman and plenty of kung fu action. When the time comes for Mr Yan (Wong Ha) to reinter his father's corpse, it suddenly rises from the dead and Mr Yan becomes the first victim of the vampire (Yuen Wah). Director Lau Kun Wai ensures there's never a slow moment, and a likeable cast, good production values and some marvellous effects makes this a minor classic of Hong Kong fantasy cinema.

MR. VAMPIRE IV

Hong Kong, 1988. Dir: Law Lit. With: Ricky Hui (Xu Guanying). Colour.

Hui, the star of the first *Mr. Vampire* (1985), returns in this fourth entry in the popular comedy horror series. While two priests battle each other with magic, a gay vampire wreaks havoc amongst a travelling group of Chinese nobles.

MR. VAMPIRE III

Hong Kong, 1987. Dir: Wong Kee Hung. With: Lam Ching Ying, Richard Ng, Lui Fong, Billy Lau. Colour.

Lam Ching Ying plays a Taoist priest in turn-of-the-century China battling a demoness and her undead army. Comedy actor Ng, playing a conman caught between the combatants, is aided by two friendly vampires. Darker and gorier than previous entries in the popular series.

MR. VAMPIRE II

Hong Kong, 1986. Dir: Sung Kan Shing. Colour.

This follow-up to *Mr. Vampire* (1985) features many of the same cast members in new roles. An undead child, searching for its vampire parents in modern Hong Kong, is helped by a widower and his children. This was apparently such a big hit in Japan that it spawned a TV series!

THE MUNSTERS' REVENGE

USA, 1981. Dir: Don Weis. With: Fred Gwynne, Al Lewis, Yvonne De Carlo, K.C. Martel, Jo McDonnell, Bob Hastings. Universal. Colour.

Terrible made-for-TV movie that revives the characters fifteen years after the regular series finished. Herman (Gwynne) and the vampiric Grandpa (Lewis) have to prove their innocence when the villainous Dr Dustin Diablo (an over-the-top Sid Caesar) uses robot doubles of the pair to go on a crime spree. Gwynne and Lewis don't look like they've aged at all and do their best to carry the movie. But Weis' lacklustre direction, an insipid supporting cast (particularly Hastings' aggravating Phantom of the Opera) and the awful

Below: The Lost Boys.

dubbed laughter make this reunion a sad mistake. Amongst the waxwork robots is the Creature from the Black Lagoon and another wearing a Tor Johnson mask.

NEAR DARK

USA, 1987. Dir: Kathryn Bigelow. With: Adrian Pasdar, Jenny Wright, Lance Henriksen, Bill Paxton, Jenette Goldstein, Tim Thomerson. F/M Entertainment. Colour.

An impressive solo directing début for co-writer Bigelow. Oklahoma farm boy Pasdar becomes involved with sultry Wright and is 'adopted' by her travelling companions — a gang of sleazy, psychopathic, nomad vampires led by Henriksen. Despite the low budget, this is beautifully photographed, with an intelligent script and great performances. Two action sequences — a massacre in a bar and a motel shoot-out — are particularly outstanding. Only the weak ending (a simple blood transfusion cures the vampire virus) lets it down.

MUTANT

(aka NIGHT SHADOWS)
USA, 1984. Dir: John 'Bud' Cardos. With: Wings Hauser, Bo Hopkins, Lee Montgomery, Jody Medford, Jennifer Warren, Marc Clement. Film Ventures International. Colour.

Surprisingly effective low budget SF/horror thriller in which the inhabitants of a mid-western town are turned into zombies through chemical pollution. Director Cardos builds the tension carefully before releasing an army of blood-drinking ghouls on the few survivors. The shock moments work well, thanks to the effective zombie make-up (which owes much to *Invisible Invaders* [1959]). Good production values, a Richard Band score, exciting script and solid performances combine with some genuine chills.

MY BEST FRIEND IS A VAMPIRE

USA, 1987.Dir: Jimmy Huston. With: Robert Sean Leonard, Cheryl Pollak, René Auberjonois, Evan Mirand, Fannie Flagg, David Warner. Kings Road Entertainment. Colour.

Better than usual teen horror comedy. When Leonard is bitten by a vampire, it causes problems with his home and school life. Luckily he has suave vampire Auberjonois to teach him how to survive

Above: Near Dark.

NATIONAL LAMPOON'S CLASS REUNION

USA, 1982. Dir: Michael Miller. With: Gerrit Graham, Fred McCarren, Miriam Flynn, Stephen Furst, Shelley Smith, Michael Lerner. ABC Motion Pictures/PSO. Colour.

During a class reunion at the Lizzie Borden High School, a maniacal killer stalks the corridors and confronts nymphomaniacs, drug addicts, a case of Devil possession and even a vampire (Jim Staahl). With a hit-and-miss script by John Hughes, director Miller has trouble keeping all the elements under control, but there are some laughs to be found. Chuck Berry and Misty Rowe are also caught up in the chaos.

NICK KNIGHT

(UK: aka MIDNIGHT COP)
USA, 1989. Dir: Farhad Mann. With: Rick Springfield, John Kapelos, Robert Harper, Richard Fancy, Michael Nader. Colour.

Enjoyable TV movie pilot for the series *Forever Knight* (1992). Ex-teenage heart-throb Springfield plays a vampire cop who lives in an abandoned movie theatre and, naturally enough, covers the night shift. While investigating a break-in at an archaeological museum, he is forced to confront Lacroix (an evil-looking Nader), the age-old vampire who originally turned him into one of the undead. Mann directs like it's a rock video, and Springfield makes a likeable, if unusual, hero.

and use his new-found talents to outwit rabid vampire hunter Warner (who pulls out all the stops). Director Huston scores with likeable characters, an entertaining script (by Tab Murphy) and some fun with the clichés.

THE MYSTERIOUS DEATH OF NINA CHEREAU

1988. Dir: Dennis Berry. With: Maud Adams, Scott Renderer, Alexandra Stewart. Colour.

A ten year-old murder mystery is resurrected when the alleged killer escapes from a mental asylum. It turns out to be another variation on the Countess Elizabeth Bathory legend.

Above: *The Monster Squad.*
Right: *The Monster Club.*

NIGHTLIFE

Mexico/USA, 1989. Dir: Daniel Taplitz. With: Ben Cross, Maryam D'Abo, Keith Szarabajka, Camille Saviola, Jesse Corti, Glenn Shadix. MCA/Cine Enterprises/MTE. Colour.
Made-for-cable TV vampire comedy. D'Abo looks great as a hundred year-old member of the undead, being chased around Mexico City by her vampiric ex-lover Vlad (Cross, overacting) and being wooed by Szarabajka as the doctor who is trying to find a cure for her blood 'disease'. Taplitz's direction is not light enough to carry the black humour, but it still has its moments.

NOT OF THIS EARTH

USA, 1988. Dir: Jim Wynorski. With: Traci Lords, Arthur Roberts, Lenny Juliano, Rebecca Perle, Ace Mask, Roger Lodge. New Horizons/ Concorde. Colour.
Exact, if inferior, remake of Roger Corman's 1957 cult classic. This time Roberts plays the blood-seeking alien who is transporting suitcases full of the stuff back to his parched planet. Ex-underage porno queen Lords turns up as a nurse who discovers what he is up to. Cheap laughs, cheap production.

ONCE BITTEN

USA, 1985. Dir: Howard Storm. With: Lauren Hutton, Jimmy Carrey, Karen Kopins, Cleavon Little, Thomas Ballatore, Skip Lackey. The Samuel Goldwyn Company. Colour.
Embarrassing horror comedy. Teen nerd Carrey is seduced by centuries-old vampire Hutton because he's still a virgin. Director Storm includes all the gags you would expect.

ONE DARK NIGHT

(UK: aka ENTITY FORCE)
USA, 1982. Dir: Thomas McLoughlin. With: Meg Tilly, Melissa Newman, Robin Evans, Leslie Speights, Donald Hotton, Adam West. The Picture Company Inc. Colour.
Filmed under the title *Night in the Crypt*, this low budget horror thriller was written and directed by mime actor McLoughlin for just $800,000. Tilly spends the night in a mausoleum and is menaced by a psychic vampire. The reanimated corpses (created by the Burman Studio) are not nearly as realistic as they should be, but the electrical effects (filmed live on the set) are quite impressive.

Above: Sundown The Vampire in Retreat.

ONE EYE-BROW PRIEST

(Orig: NEW MR. VAMPIRE II)
Hong Kong, 1987. Dir: Mason Ching. Colour.
Once again, this involves a wizened priest battling the hopping undead. There's a crazy kung fu climax and some mild nudity, but otherwise it's more of the same.

OUTBACK VAMPIRES

(USA: aka THE WICKED)
Australia, 1987. With: Brett Climo, Richard Morgan, Angela Kennedy. Guild/Select. Colour.
Vampire Sir Alfred Terminus and his undead family rule the outback community of Yarralumala. When their car breaks down, Lucy, Bronco and Nick stumble into town and soon find themselves invited to dinner — as the main course on the menu!

PALE BLOOD

USA, 1989 (1991). Dir: V.V. Dachin Hsu. With: George Chakiris, Wings Hauser, Pamela Ludwig, Diana Frank, Darcy DeMoos. Noble Entertainment Group. Colour.
After hearing about a series of vampire-like killings in Los Angeles, Michael Fury, a real vampire (*West Side Story*'s Chakiris), teams up with obsessed researcher Ludwig to solve the murders, hoping to find another of his own kind. Instead, they discover a manic sword-wielding Hauser,

who wants to capture the undead on videotape. Includes music by Agent Orange and a clip from Murnau's *Nosferatu* (1922).

PANDEMONIUM

Australia, 1988. Dir: Haydn Keenan. With: David Argue, Amanda Dole, Esben Storm, Arna-Maria Winchester, Rainee Skinner, Kery Mack. KFM/Smart Street/Tra La La. Colour.

An attempt to produce an instant weirdo cult horror movie along the lines of *The Rocky Horror Picture Show* (1975). An escaped lunatic (Argue) and a buxom girl (Dole) raised by dingoes stumble into a deserted movie studio and a collection of vampires, lesbian Nazis, drag queens, crippled movie stars, mad scientists, a Hitler clone and a witch. Pretentious and crude comedy.

POLISH VAMPIRE

(aka A POLISH VAMPIRE IN BURBANK)

USA, 1983. Dir: Mark Pirro. With: Mark Pirro, Lori Sutton, Bobbi Dorsch, Brad Waisbren, Hugh O. Fields, Eddie Deezen. Pirromount/ Peacock Films. Colour.

Writer, producer and director Pirro stars as Dupah, a Polish vampire who has never bitten anyone before. Kicked out of his castle in the Burbank hills by his father, he sets off to find his own victim and ends up with the girl of his dreams. This comedy was the first film shot in Super-8mm format to be shown on a national cable network, and it ended up grossing over $500,000 on video! From the Sacramento-based creator of *Curse of the Queerwolf* (1987).

PURA SANGRE

Colombia, 1983. Dir: Luis Ospina. With: Florina Lemaitre, Carlos Mayolo, Humberto Arango, Luis Alberto Garcia, Gilberto 'Fly' Forero, Franky Linero. Luis Ospina Productions/Castano. Colour.

When a Howard Hughes-type ailing business tycoon requires fresh blood to survive, a trio of assistants supply victims from the country's youngsters in this political allegory.

RED AND BLACK

China, 1986. Dir: Andrew Kam Yuen Wah. Colour.

This political allegory opens in 1941 during the Japanese occupation of the Chinese mainland. A man is infected by a Japanese vampire but manages to impale himself in an underground cavern. Twenty-five years later he is accidentally revived and infects the People's Leader of the Communist Revolution.

A RETURN TO SALEM'S LOT

USA, 1987. Dir: Larry Cohen. With: Michael Moriarty, Samuel Fuller, Andrew Duggan, Ricky Addison Reed, June Havoc, Evelyn Keyes. Larco Productions/Warner Bros. Colour.

A sequel to Stephen King's novel and the 1979 TV mini-series in name only. After a ludicrous native sacrifice (which looks as if it was filmed in the director's back yard), anthropologist Moriarty and his disturbed son (Reed) move to the town of Salem's Lot where head vampire Duggan tries to convince them to stay and chronicle the history of the ancient community. However, the intervention of a testy Nazi hunter (a great performance by veteran director Fuller) convinces them to destroy the undead townsfolk. One of Cohen's most technically incompetent films, it appears to have been cobbled together from outtakes.

SATURDAY THE 14TH

USA, 1981. Dir: Howard R. Cohen. With: Richard Benjamin, Paula Prentiss, Jeffrey Tambor, Severn

Darden, Kari Michaelsen, Stacy Keach Sr. New World/Embassy. Colour.
Despite the misleading title, this is not a spoof on slasher films but a parody of old dark house/monster movies. Real-life married couple Benjamin and Prentiss move into a spooky old house which a pair of vampires (Tambor and Nancy Lee) also want to own. When their son (Kevin Brando) uses a book of evil to conjure up a number of creatures (left over from *Galaxina* [1980]), strange things start to happen... Severn Darden is great as a Van Helsing-type character who turns out to be the real villain when the vampires save the day. Despite the low budget, this often silly comedy includes some imaginative gags (such as the television that can only get *The Twilight Zone*). Produced by Julie Corman.
Sequel: SATURDAY THE 14TH STRIKES BACK (qv; 1988)

Above: *A Return to Salem's Lot.*
Left: *Vamp.*

SATURDAY THE 14TH STRIKES BACK

USA, 1988. Dir: Howard R. Cohen. With: Jason Presson, Ray Walston, Avery Schreiber, Patty McCormick, Leo V. Gordon, Michael Berryman. Concorde. Colour.
Semi-sequel to the 1981 original. A group of monsters invade a birthday party. Pamela Stonebrook plays a vampire.

SCOOBY-DOO AND THE RELUCTANT WEREWOLF

USA, 1988. Dir: Ray Patterson. Voices: Don Messick, Casey Kasem, Hamilton Camp, Jim Cummings, Joanie Gerber, Ed Gilbert. Hanna-Barbera Productions/Worldvision Enterprises. Colour
Made-for-TV animated feature based on the *Scooby-Doo* series. A green-faced Dracula turns Scooby's friend Shaggy into a werewolf so that he can take part in the Transylvania monster road race. Also includes the Frankenstein monster, the Mummy, Dr Jekyll and Mr Snyde, and Genghis Kong.

SESAME STREET PRESENTS: FOLLOW THAT BIRD

USA, 1985. Dir: Ken Kwapis. With: Carroll Spinney, Paul Bartel,

Sandra Bernhard, John Candy, Chevy Chase, Waylon Jennings. Colour.
Cute mix of puppets and live action, based on the characters created by Jim Henson and Frank Oz for TV's *Sesame Street* and *The Muppets*. Big Bird is placed in a foster home but decides to hitchhike back to Sesame Street, encountering various guest stars who should know better along the way. Includes the Count, a vampiric puppet from the TV series.

THE SEVEN VAMPIRES

(Orig: AS SETE VAMPIROS)
Brazil, 1986. Dir: Ivan Cardoso. With: Alvamar Tadei, Andrea Beltrao, Ariel Coelho, Bene Nunes, Cole Carlo Mossi, Danielle Daumerri. Embrafilme/Superoito Productions. Colour.
Low budget horror/comedy/musical. When a carnivorous plant is imported into 1950s Rio de Janiero, it eats the face off a dedicated botanist and infects his wife with a mysterious malady. Pretty soon she is staging a cabaret act titled The Dance of the Seven Female Vampires, while a masked killer terrorises the city, draining the blood from victims. A mixture of bad comedy and gratuitous nudity.

SEXANDROIDE

France, 1987. Dir: Michel Ricaud. With: Daniel Dubois, Petit Pascal Company. Colour.
Science fiction and vampires both feature in this blend of hardcore and horror.

SHADOWS IN THE DARK

USA, 1989. Dir: Bruce Seven. With: Tianna, Bionca, Victoria Paris, Cheri Bush, Samuna Ray, Linn Schee. 4-Play. Colour.
The plot of this hardcore vampire movie sounds similar to *Dance of the Damned* (1988). Randy Spears plays an alien vampire who watches various sex acts performed in a moody nightclub. Afterwards, he asks the participants some personal questions before being destroyed by sunlight.

SPIRIT VS. ZOMBI

Taiwan/Hong Kong, 1989. Dir: Yao Fenpan. Colour.
Maudlin tale about a vampire father and his young son resurrected in modern Taiwan. Despite the title, there are no spirits or zombies. At the climax, the undead father is blown to pieces.

SPOOKY FAMILY

Hong Kong, 1989. Dir: Law Lit. Colour.
From the creators of the popular *Mr. Vampire* series, this horror comedy is filled with non-stop action and impressive special effects. A group of evil magicians revive the Copper Vampire, the most evil being in the world, by mixing their tainted blood with the creature's own. Ghost hunter Master Chu Kar, his strange family, and a couple of friendly ghosts are hired to destroy the undead monster.
Sequel: SPOOKY FAMILY 2 (qv; 1991)

SUNDOWN THE VAMPIRE IN RETREAT

USA, 1988. Dir: Anthony Hickox. With: David Carradine, Maxwell Caulfield, Morgan Brittany, Bruce Campbell, Jim Metzler, John Ireland. Vestron Pictures. Colour.
Inventive horror comedy co-written and stylishly directed by Anthony Hickox, who dedicated it to his late father, director Douglas. Carradine plays Mardulak (really Count Dracula), the leader of a group of vampires living peacefully in the community of Purgatory, somewhere in the American west. When a human family led by Metzler arrive in town, followed by a manic descendant of Van Helsing (Campbell, mugging outrageously), villains Caulfield and Ireland lead a vampire revolt. Great fun, and a chance to see Carradine recreate one of his father's most famous roles. Not released in America until 1991.

THE SUPERGRASS

UK, 1985. Dir: Peter Richardson. With: Adrian Edmondson, Peter Richardson, Jennifer Saunders, Alexei Sayle, Keith Allen, Nigel Planer. The Comic Strip/Recorded Releasing. Colour.
Comedy feature inspired by *The Comic Strip Presents...* TV series. Ronald Allen turns up as Robertson, a vampiric police inspector.

Below: Vampire in Venice.

Above: Waxwork.

TEEN VAMP

USA, 1988. Dir: Samuel Bradford. With: Clu Gulager, Karen Carlson, Angie Brown, Beau Bishop, Mick Lane, Evans Dietz. Jim McCullough Productions/New World International. Colour.

Filmed on a shoestring budget in Tennessee, this predictable horror comedy features Beau Bishop as another teen nerd whose life is changed when he is bitten by a vampire hooker. It's the usual plot, helped here by a good script from writer/director Bradford. Unfortunately, the film suffers from dark, ugly photography and amateurish performances. Star Gulager is obviously slumming in a cameo as a vampire-hunting priest.

TO DIE FOR

USA, 1988. Dir: Deran Sarafian. With: Brendan Hughes, Sydney Walsh, Amanda Wyss, Scott Jacoby, Micah Grant, Steve Bond. Arrowhead Entertainment/Lee Caplin/Skouras. Colour.

Undead Vlad Tepish (Hughes) tries to put the bite on beautiful estate agent Walsh, but he's opposed by his arch-enemy, Tom (Bond), who is another vampire. *Night of the Living Dead* (1969) star Duane Jones turns up briefly in his last role, and the movie is dedicated to his memory.

Sequel: SON OF DARKNESS: TO DIE FOR II (qv; 1991)

THE TOMB

USA, 1985. Dir: Fred Olen Ray. With: Cameron Mitchell, John Carradine, Susan Stokey, Richard Alan Hench, Michelle Bauer, Sybil Danning (Sybelle Denninger). Trans World Entertainment. Colour.

Low budget homage to the Universal Mummy series from Olen Ray, the king of the Z's. A pair of fortune hunters break into an Egyptian tomb and release ancient vampire witch-queen Nefratis (Bauer). She follows her stolen treasure to America, where she zaps her victims with magic powers and feeds a lesbian (Dawn Wildsmith) to a bed full of snakes. Carradine turns up in one scene as Egyptian expert Mr Andoheb. Great cast, low concept.

TOOTHLESS VAMPIRES

Hong Kong, 1987. Dir: Lee Hun Yu. Colour.

Gore-filled horror/black comedy about a family of vampires who, due to a genetic fault, do not have fangs. They are therefore forced to try various ludicrous schemes for getting blood.

THE TRAIL

(Orig: PAO DAN FEI CHE) Hong Kong, 1983. Dir: Ronny Yu. With: Ricky Hui (Xu Guanying), Zhang Zeshi, Cheung Fat, Miao Tian, Tin Liang, Hsu Siu. Golden Harvest. Colour.

Atmospheric horror movie in which a vampire uses zombie slaves to smuggle opium.

TRAMPIRE

USA, 1987. Dir: C.C. Williams. With: Angela Baron, Jodi (Nikki Knights), Angel Kelly, Carol Hall, Titian, Randy West. Fantasy Home Video. Colour.

Hardcore comedy/sex movie in which Angela Baron plays a night-hunting vampire who lives off semen instead of blood. Nikki Knights, Angel Kelly and Titian are her slaves. West plays a scientist who has vowed to defeat them and uses Tom Byon as his 'secret weapon' to 'stake' the vampire and her minions.

TRANSYLVANIA 6-5000

USA/Yugoslavia, 1985. Dir: Rudy De Luca. With: Jeff Goldblum, Ed Begley Jr, Joseph Bologna, Carol Kane, John Byner, Pat Harrington Jr. New World Pictures. Colour.

Goldblum and Begley Jr play two reporters for a sleazy tabloid newspaper sent to Transylvania to get a scoop on the monsters. It turns out that Frankenstein's creature is just an accident victim, the Mummy has had plastic surgery, the Wolf Man has a hair condition and the seductive vampire (Geena Davis) wants more attention. Unfunny comedy which steals its title from (a much better) 1963 Bugs Bunny cartoon.

TRANSYLVANIA TWIST

USA, 1989. Dir: Jim Wynorski. With: Robert Vaughn, Teri Copley, Steve Altman, Ace Mask, Angus Scrimm,

Steve Franken. Concorde/New Horizons. Colour.
Silly but inventive horror comedy, with numerous in-jokes for film buffs and H.P. Lovecraft fans. Altman plays Dexter Ward, who must recover the ancient *Book of Ulthar*, stolen from Arkham Library and hidden in the castle of vampire Byron Orlok (Vaughn). He's aided by Orlok's niece (Copley) and a descendant of Van Helsing (Mask). Includes fun pastiches of Fisher's *Dracula* (1958), *Phantasm* (1979) and the AIP Poe films, plus cameo appearances by Pinhead (make-up designer Dean Jones), Freddy Krueger, Leatherface, Jason, Kelli Maroney, Brinke Stevens and an uncredited Forrest J Ackerman. Twenty years after his death, Boris Karloff makes a special appearance as himself (courtesy of unused footage from *The Terror* [1963]). Shot in nineteen days on a $1,000,000 budget. Roger Corman was executive producer.

THE UNDERSTUDY: GRAVEYARD SHIFT II

Canada, 1988. Dir: Gerard Ciccoritti. With: Wendy Gazelle, Mark Soper, Silvio Oliviero, Ilse Von Glatz, Timothy Kelleher, Lesley Kelly. Cinema Ventures. Colour.
This odd sequel to *Graveyard Shift* (1986) has real vampire Oliviero resurrected on the set of a low budget horror movie about a snooker-playing(!) vampire. There's not much in the way of scares in this arty and pretentious Canadian production, as the often confusing plot meanders its way through to the inevitable ending where fiction and reality merge. The film-within-a-film scenario might have worked in better hands, but the cast of unknowns and director Ciccoritti's reliance on style over content doom this to failure.

VAMPIRE AT MIDNIGHT

USA, 1987. Dir: Gregory McClatchy. With: Jason Williams, Gustav Vintas, Lesley Milne, Esther Alise, Jeanie Moore, Ted Hamaguchi. Key Video/Skouras International. Colour.
Stylish-looking thriller let down by a pointless script. Williams (the star of *Flesh Gordon* [1974]) is an LA cop investigating a series of murders in which all the victims are drained of blood. Could new-age hypnotist Dr Radcoff (Vintas) be a vampire? Actually, despite the title, he isn't.

VAMP

USA, 1986. Dir: Richard Wenk. With: Chris Makepeace, Sandy Baron, Robert Rusler, Dedee Pfeiffer, Gedde Watanabe, Grace Jones. Baker Films/New World Pictures. Colour.
A teen horror comedy which is actually stylish, witty and scary. Three college kids, looking to find a stripper for an upcoming fraternity house party, stumble across the After Dark club run by Grace Jones' mute Egyptian Queen, Katrina, and her undead slaves. Co-written by first-time director Wenk, the humour is often grim (comedy relief Watanabe is burned to death as a vampire) and the bloodsucker make-ups are excellent. Great support from Sandy Baron as a vampire emcee who dreams of moving to Las Vegas, Dedee Pfeiffer as the scatty young heroine and Billy Drago as a punk.

VAMPIRE HUNTER D

Japan, 1985. Dir: Tayoo Ashida. Epic/Sony/Streamline Pictures. Colour.
Billed as 'the first animated horror film for adults!', this futuristic adventure is set in 12,090 AD on an Earth which has been overrun with vampires. When his girlfriend Doris is kidnapped, an enigmatic bounty hunter known only as 'D' sets out to destroy the undead Count Magus Lee. The English language version was produced by Carl Macek.

VAMPIRE IN VENICE

(Orig: NOSFERATU A VENEZIA. UK/USA: aka VAMPIRES IN VENICE) Italy, 1988. Dir: Augusto Caminito. With: Klaus Kinski, Barbara de Rossi, Yorgo Voyagis, Anne Knecht, Donald Pleasence, Christopher Plummer. Scena/Reteitalia/ Vestron. Colour.

Visually striking sequel to *Nosferatu the Vampyre* (1979). Kinski returns as the weary vampire (with hair this time) to modern day Venice to find love and death during the Carnival. Plummer plays the Van Helsing-type who tries to destroy him. Like the original, this plods along and, with Caminito's dull direction and confusing script, it has only the evocative photography to recommend it. Kinski apparently refused to wear the vampire make-up from the earlier film and ended up directing much of the film himself. Luigi Cozzi was brought in to try and make some sense of it all.

VAMPIRE KNIGHTS

USA, 1987. Dir: Daniel M. Peterson. With: Ken Abraham, Billy Frank, Daniel M. Peterson, Robin Rochelle, Thomas Kingsley, Ann Michaels. Mezcal Films/Filmtrust. Colour.

Yet another low budget vampire comedy. Tazar, Zanetet and Elissa are a trio of beautiful vampire women in modern Transylvania who are hunted by a TV horror host (director Peterson) and the single member of his club, the Vampire Knights, committed to the destruction of the undead.

VAMPIRE PRINCESS MIYU

Japan, 1988. Dir: Hirano Toshihiro. Voices: Watanabe Naoko, Koyama Mami, Kobayashi Kiyoko, Toriumi Katsumi, Nakamura Hidetoshi, Matsuoka Yooka. Sooeishinsha/ Pony Canyon/AnimEigo. Colour.

Animated feature which includes episodes one ('Unearthly Kyoyo') and two ('A Banquet of Marionettes') of a multipart series. Female spiritualist Himiko suspects that Miyu and her mysterious companion are responsible for a series of vampire attacks. Together they oppose the diabolical forces of the Shinma. Michael House directed the English language version.

VAMPIRE RAIDERS — NINJA QUEEN

1989. Dir: Bruce Lambert. With: Agnes Chan, Chris Peterson. Colour.

White ninjas versus black ninjas in the hotel business.

VAMPIRES

(aka ABADON/FRIGHT HOUSE) USA, 1988. Dir: Len Anthony. With: Duane Jones, Jackie James, Robin Michaels, Orly Benyair, Kit Jones. Colour.

Okay, pay attention because this is going to be confusing. Originally released in 1988, this stars Duane Jones (from *Night of the Living Dead* [1969] and *Ganja and Hess* [1973]) in a muddled occult chiller about a machine that keeps the owner looking young and beautiful. The title was then changed from *Vampires* to *Abadon*, and the film combined with *Fright House* (1989), also produced and directed by Anthony, which has Al Lewis (Grandpa from *The Munsters*) investigating mysterious suicides in an old house on campus. You probably won't care.

VAMPIRE'S BREAKFAST

Hong Kong, 1986. Dir: Wong Chun. Colour.

Comedy/horror thiller in which a Hong Kong newspaper reporter uncovers a community of vampires. When the police don't believe him, he sets out to prove his story.

VAMPIRES IN HAVANA

(Orig: ¡VAMPIROS EN LA HABANA!) Cuba/Spain/West Germany, 1985. Dir: Juan Padron. Voices: Frank Gonzalez, Manuel Marin, Irela Bravo, Carlos Gonzalez, Mirella Guillot, Carmen Solar. Icaic/TE/ Durniok. Colour.

Full-length animated comedy set in 1933, when two rival vampire groups arrive in Havana to squabble over Professor Von Dracula's cream, Vampisol, which enables the undead to survive in daylight. The hero is Dracula's nephew, Pepe, who doesn't even know he's a vampire thanks to his uncle's invention. This also includes a werewolf and some good-natured politics.

VAMPIRE'S KISS

USA, 1988. Dir: Robert Bierman. With: Nicolas Cage, Maria Conchita Alonso, Jennifer Beals, Elisabeth Ashley, Kasi Lemmons, Bob Lujan. Hemdale. Colour.

A typically bizarre performance by Cage as Peter Lowe, a young literary agent who believes that he has been bitten by a beautiful vampire (Beals) while making love. He becomes a different person, shunning the sunlight, fearing the cross and eating beetles until, wearing plastic fangs and impersonating Max Schreck, he begins attacking women. This doesn't make a whole lot of sense. See Romero's *Martin* (1976) instead.

VAMPIRES LIVE AGAIN

Hong Kong, 1987. Dir: Kam Yoo Tu. Colour.

Shot-on-video blend of bad comedy and lame horror.

Below: The Supergrass.

VAMPIRES ON BIKINI BEACH

USA, 1988. With: Jennifer Badham. Colour.

Californians save their beach from a group of vampires.

VAMPIRES STRIKE BACK

Hong Kong, 1988. Dir: Kam Yoo Tu. Colour.

Another shot-on-video mess from Tu.

VENGEFUL VAMPIRE GIRL

(Orig: HUPHYOKWI YANYO)
Korea, 1981. Dir: Kim In Soo. With: Choi Bong, Chong Hi Jung. Han Jin Enterprises. Colour.

When a woman is raped by a wealthy governor, she bites her own tongue off and bleeds to death. Ten years later a pair of graverobbers dig her up and she returns as a ghostly vampire seeking revenge. She is finally dispatched by a martial arts expert. This was a gory remake of one of the (non-vampire) stories in *Myonuriui Han* (1971).

VINCENT PRICE'S DRACULA

(USA: DRACULA — THE GREAT UNDEAD)
UK, 1982. Dir: John Muller. With:

Above: Vampire's Kiss.

Vincent Price. M&M Film Productions/Atlantis. Colour.

Hour-long drama/documentary in which Price sends himself up as the sinister host and narrator explaining the legend of Count Dracula and real Vlad the Impaler. Similar to *In Search of Dracula* (1971) with Christopher Lee, this includes footage from a Transylvanian epic about Vlad Tepes' exploits, as well as clips from *Mark of the Vampire* (1935), *The Return of the Vampire* (1943) and *The Return of Dracula* (1957). Price makes the most of the tedious script.

WAXWORK

USA, 1988. Dir: Anthony Hickox. With: Zach Galligan, Deborah Foreman, Michelle Johnson, Dana Ashbrook, Miles O'Keefe, John Rhys-Davies. Vestron. Colour.

Six teens take a midnight tour of David Warner's mysterious wax museum and are drawn into the exhibits to confront a werewolf, the Mummy, the Marquis De Sade and ex-Tarzan Miles O'Keefe (with long blond hair and designer stubble) as Count Dracula. The ludicrous Keystone Cops-type climax has a wheelchair-bound Patrick Macnee leading an attack on all the above monsters, plus Mr Hyde, the Golem, the Phantom of the Opera, etc. The special effects by Bob Keen's Image Animation (*Hellraiser* [1987]) are the best thing in this shoddy horror comedy.

Sequel: WAXWORK II: LOST IN TIME (qv; 1991)

WHO IS AFRAID OF DRACULA

(Orig: FRACCHIA CONTRO DRACULA/FRACCHIA VS DRACULA)
Italy, 1985. Dir: Neri Parenti. With: Paolo Villaggio, Gigi Reder, Edmund Purdom, Ania Pieroni, Isabella Fearrare (Ferrari). Faso Film/Titanus/Maura International. Colour.

Horror spoof in which star and co-writer Villaggio recreates his comic character Fantozzi as Fracchia, an unsuccessful estate agent who tries to sell a cheap Transylvanian castle to a myopic client (Reder). Purdom plays a Lugosi-like Dracula and Pieroni turns up as his undead sister, Countess Oniria. The knockabout climax also throws in the Frankenstein monster and a group of zombies.

WOLNYOUI HAN

Republic of Korea, 1980. Dir: Kim In Soo. With: Chin Bong Chin, Huh Chin. Han Jin Enterprises. Colour.

Folk tale fantasy set in a medieval Korean village. A young girl takes refuge in a swamp and is possessed by an evil spirit in the form of a white cat. She returns as a vampire to revenge herself on those who betrayed her.

the

It was Francis Ford Coppola's $40,000,000 version of **Bram Stoker's Dracula (1992)** that sparked off the vampire movie boom of the early 1990s.

"There has never been an adaptation of Stoker's novel that has done justice to the brilliance of his literary work," claimed screenwriter Jim Hart (**Hook [1991]**). "There's enough action, romance, eroticism and blood to make all three Indiana Jones movies with a couple left over. Dracula can make people commit sexual acts beyond their own imaginations — and well beyond what society would permit. This **Dracula** is the untold story of a true love that never dies."

Coppola (b 1939) assembled an all-star cast for what was loudly touted as the first faithful screen adaptation of Bram Stoker's book, and he insisted: "Certainly this is a new production of **Dracula**, and most certainly, it is a horror film. We've tried to take a fresh look at this story. Usually Dracula is just a reptilian creature in horror films. I want people to understand the historical and literary traditions behind the story. To see that underneath this vampire myth is really fundamental human stuff that everyone feels and knows."

The acclaimed director of the **Godfather** trilogy and **Apocalypse Now (1979)** had started out working for producer Roger Corman (b 1926), and early in his career he was involved with the Yugoslavian film **Operacija Ticijan**, which finally metamorphosised into the cult vampire movie **Blood Bath (1966)**.

Always quick to exploit a new trend, Corman himself rushed two vampire pictures into production, **Dracula Rising (1992)** and **To Sleep With a Vampire (1992)**, the

1990s

latter a remake of a 1988 film. Director John Landis (b 1950) spent considerably more time and money on his vampire thriller **Innocent Blood (1992)**, *but the undead continued to thrive amongst the low budget chills of* **Sorority House Vampires (1992)** *and the British-made* **Tale of a Vampire (1992)**.

There were rock 'n' roll bloodsuckers in both **The Reluctant Vampire (1992)** *and* **In the Midnight Hour (1992)**, **Project Vampire (1992)** *featured scientifically created undead, and even the new Independent States of Eastern Europe jumped on the bandwagon with* **Dracula's Hair (1992)** *and* **The Vampire's Rope (1992)**. *However, the offbeat horror comedy* **Buffy the Vampire Slayer (1992)** *beat them all into movie theatres. Although it hardly set the box office alight, that did not deter other producers from announcing a glut of vampire projects such as* **The Lost Boys 2**, **Red Sleep**, **Subspecies II** *and* **III**, **Forever Young**, **99 Days**, **Soul Survivor**, **Nightland** *and the long-awaited* **Interview With a Vampire**, *based on the bestselling novel by Anne Rice.*

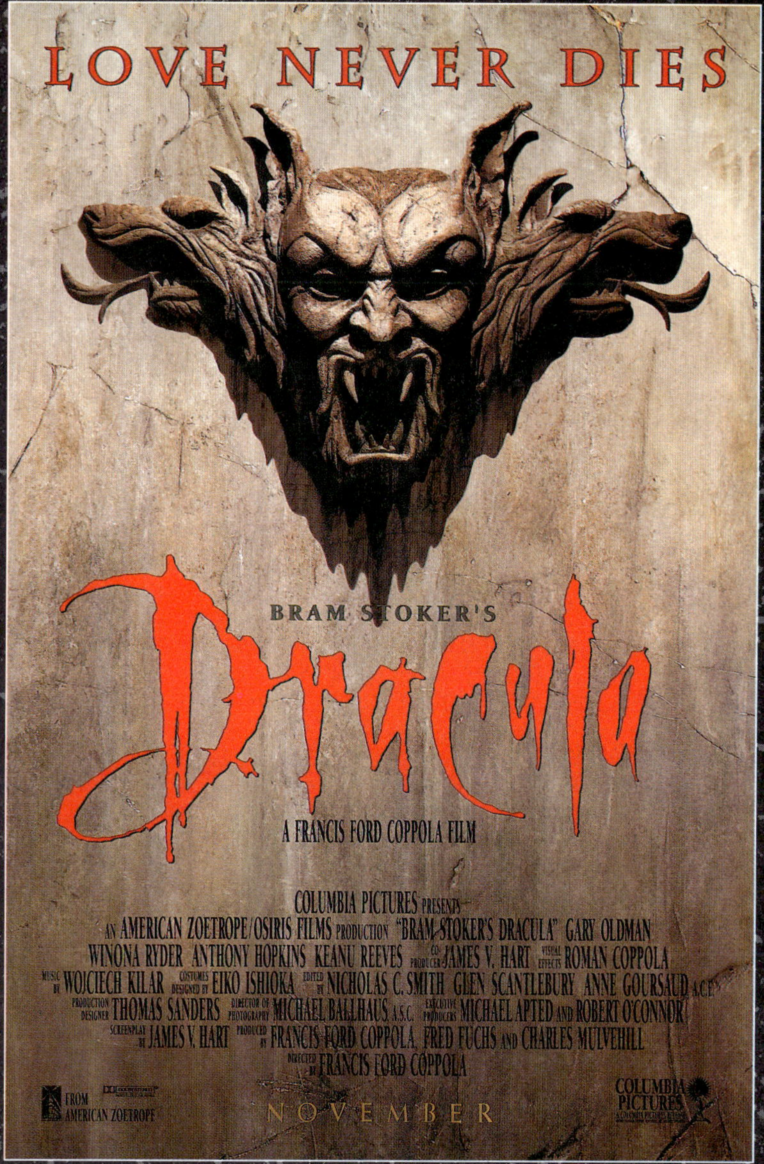

It was exactly seventy years since **Nosferatu**, *F.W. Murnau's first, unauthorised, adaptation of Bram Stoker's book. Vampires were more popular than they had ever been, and the undead once again had a stake in the box office...*

THE ADDAMS FAMILY

USA, 1991. Dir: Barry Sonnenfeld. With: Anjelica Huston, Raul Julia, Christopher Lloyd, Elizabeth Wilson, Christina Ricci, Judith Malina. Paramount. Colour.

Enjoyable big budget feature based on Charles Addams' wonderfully macabre cartoons, which also inspired the popular TV series (1964-1966). As the vampiric Morticia Addams, Anjelica Huston stars in the role she was born to play. The minor story involves the return of Uncle Fester (Lloyd), who could be an impostor after the Addams' family fortune. Ignore the plot, sit back and enjoy the constant barrage of black humour.

THE ARRIVAL

USA, 1990. Dir: David Schmoeller. With: John Saxon, Joseph Culp, Robin Frates, Robert Sampson, Geoff Mansen, Michael J. Pollard. Del Mar Entertainment. Colour.

Predictable science fiction/horror thriller from the creator of the *Puppet Master* series. An old man (Sampson) is possessed by an unseen alien from a crashed meteor. It turns him into a vampire serial killer (Culp) who grows younger with each victim. Genre veteran Saxon plays an FBI investigator, there's another oddball cameo by Pollard, and appearances by Schmoeller as a doctor, fellow director Stuart Gordon as a biker and his wife Carolyn Purdy-Gordon as a complaining wino. See *The Hidden* (1987) instead.

BABY BLOOD

France, 1990. Dir: Alain Robak. With: Emmanuelle Escourrou, Jean-Francois Gallotte, Christian Sininger, Roselyn Geslot, Francois Frapier, Thierry LePortier. Partners Productions/EXO7 Productions. Colour.

A monstrous amoeba forms itself into a phallus and penetrates the womb of a gap-toothed circus girl (Escourrou). It demands to be born, but needs male blood to survive. A group of rugby hooligans supply all it needs. Offbeat black comedy.

BACK TO THE USSR

Finland, 1992. Dir: Jari Halonen. Colour.

Low budget political black comedy about the meeting between a failed drunken worker, Reima, and vampiric communist icon Lenin. The film apparently explores the bloodsucking tendencies between the suicidal Reima's capitalist homeland and his communist ideal.

BANDH DARWAZA

India, 1990. Dir: Tulsi Ramsay and Shyam Ramsay. With: Hashmat Khan, Manjeet Kular, Kunika, Satish Kaul, Anita Sareen, Vijayendra. Ramsay Films/GVi/ Gurpreej Video International. Colour.

Epic two-and-a-half hour Indian vampire musical with totally inappropriate songs. A group of evil acolytes resurrect a demonic red-eyed vampire so that he can revenge himself on the family that originally destroyed him. The film owes much to the Hammer style, and after a superbly atmospheric opening sequence there are some very effective horror scenes, impressive gore and several martial arts battles.

BANGLOW 666

India, 1990. Priwa International. Colour.

More Indian vampires.

BITE!

USA, 1991. Dir: Scotty Fox. With: Alicyn Sterling, Buck Adams, P.J. Sparx, Randy West, Alexandra Quinn, Mike Horner. Legend. Colour.

Triple-X hardcore version of the Count Dracula story with very good production values.

BLOODLUST

Australia, 1992. Dir: Richard Wolstencroft and Jon Hewitt. With: Jane Stuart Wallace, Kelly Chapman, Robert James O'Neill, Phil Motherwell, Paul Moder, James Young. Windhover Productions. Colour.

This crude black comedy claims to be 'the sickest movie ever made'. Three psychotic killers who think they are vampires (Wallace, Chapman and O'Neill) are pursued by religious fanatics, the cops and the mob. Includes multiple stakings, necrophilia, castration, coke-sniffing and softcore sex. Bet you can't wait. Prints were apparently seized by British customs. Music by Revolting Cocks, Pailhead, Lead Into Gold and 1000 Homo DJs.

BLOODTHIRSTY

USA, 1992. Dir: Robert Guy Barrows. With: Ascello Charles, Winston McDaniel, Lia Marino, Stefanie Roumeliotes, Nicole Zafrano, Josh Barrows. Barrows Productions. Colour.

Low budget thriller in which an accident in a virologist's laboratory turns people into crazy blood-drinkers.

Below: *Children of the Night.*

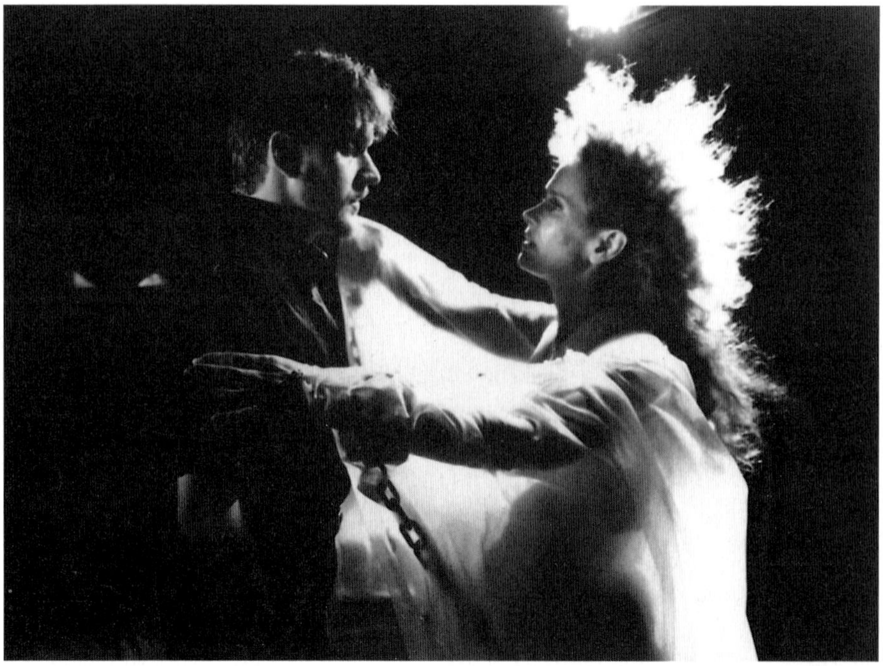

Above: Def by Temptation.

BRAM STOKER'S DRACULA

(aka DRACULA, THE UNTOLD STORY)
USA, 1992. Dir: Francis Ford Coppola. With: Gary Oldman, Winona Ryder, Anthony Hopkins, Keanu Reeves, Richard E. Grant, Tom Waits. Columbia/American Zoetrope/Osiris Films. Colour.
Coppola's overblown $40,000,000 movie was touted as the first faithful screen adaptation of Stoker's novel and the most erotic interpretation to date. 1462: Oldman plays a long-haired Dracula, whose wife drowns herself after being falsely told that her husband was killed driving invaders from his land. Cursing God, the Prince drinks blood and vows that he will never rest in his grave until he has had his revenge. In the 1890s, he travels to London to seduce Mina Harker (Ryder), who he believes to be the reincarnation of his eternal love. However, an enigmatic Van Helsing (Hopkins), Jonathan Harker (Reeves), Dr Seward (Grant), Arthur Holmwood (Cary Elwes) and the Texan Quincy Morris (William Campbell) are around to try and stop him.

BUFFY THE VAMPIRE SLAYER

USA, 1992. Dir: Fran Rubel Kuzui. With: Kristy Swanson, Donald Sutherland, Paul Reubens, Rutger Hauer, Luke Perry, David Arquette. Sandollar/Kuzui Enterprises/Twentieth Century Fox. Colour.
Swanson plays the eponymous heroine, a Valley Girl high school cheerleader, who is told by vampire hunter Merrick (Sutherland) that she is the Chosen One, the descendant of a long line of young women whose destiny is to track down and destroy the King of the Undead, Lothos (Hauer). An unrecognisable Reubens (aka Pee-Wee Herman) plays Amilyn, the vampire's undead henchman, in this comedy/thriller.

CHILDREN OF THE NIGHT

USA, 1990. Dir: Tony Randel. With: Karen Black, Peter DeLuise, Ami Dolenz, Maya McLaughlin, Evan Mackenzie, Garrett Morris. Fangoria Films. Colour.
Black plays the undead mother of McLaughlin, who together plan to infest the small town of Allburg with their blood-drinking habits. David Sawyer is a vampire high priest who keeps the town's children suspended in an underwater crypt as emergency rations. Despite a confusing storyline, director Randel makes the slimy special effects watchable.

CRAZY SAFARI

Hong Kong, 1990. Dir: Lo Weng-Tung. With: Lam Ching Ying, Sam Christopher Chan, NiXau. Colour.
Wild horror comedy variation on *The Gods Must Be Crazy* (1980). A magical priest, HiSing (Ying), and his young ward (Chan) are returning to Hong Kong with the body of a mummified vampire purchased at an auction in England. However, the plane runs out of fuel and is forced to land in the African jungle. While the two heroes are trying to escape the wild animals, the vampire falls from the sky and is immediately hailed as a god by the local natives. The climax involves a battle between the hopping vampire and a superhuman zombie, while the spirit of Bruce Lee(!) is transferred into the native chief (NiXau).

DARKNESS

USA, 1992. Dir: Leif Jonker. Colour.
Very low budget vampire movie, filmed in Wichita, Kansas, by writer/director/producer Jonker for just $100,000. The climactic meltdown sequence apparently sets a world record for exploding heads!

DARK SHADOWS

USA, 1990. Dir: Dan Curtis. With: Ben Cross, Jean Simmons, Roy Thinnes, Barbara Steele, Joanna Going, Jim Fyfe. Dan Curtis Productions/MGM-UA Television/NBC-TV. Colour.
TV movie pilot for the briefly revived series. Horror scream queen Barbara Steele plays Dr Julia Hoffman, a medical researcher trying to cure vampire Barnabas Collins (Cross). Originally shown in two one-hour episodes over two nights on American television.

DAWN

UK, 1990. Dir: Niall Johnson. With: Elizabeth Rees, Geoff Sloan, Craig Johnson, Kate Jones Davies, David Steadman, Louise Murray. Shooting Gallery Productions. Colour.
Low budget horror film, shot on video in Bristol with all the style and sophistication of the worst TV soap opera. Sloan plays Louis, a 200 year-old fangless vampire who seduces and impregnates Rees before she stakes him at sunrise. Too much talk and clumsy action scenes can be blamed on director Johnson, who also produced, scripted and co-edited. Songs by Mesh.

DEF BY TEMPTATION

USA, 1990. Dir: James Bond III. With: James Bond III, Kadeem Hardison, Bill Nunn, Samuel L. Jackson, Minnie Gentry, Cynthia Bond. Bonded Enterprises/Orpheus Pictures/Troma. Colour.
Uneven horror comedy, billed as 'The black rap chiller thriller of the decade'. A young country preacher (Bond III) visits

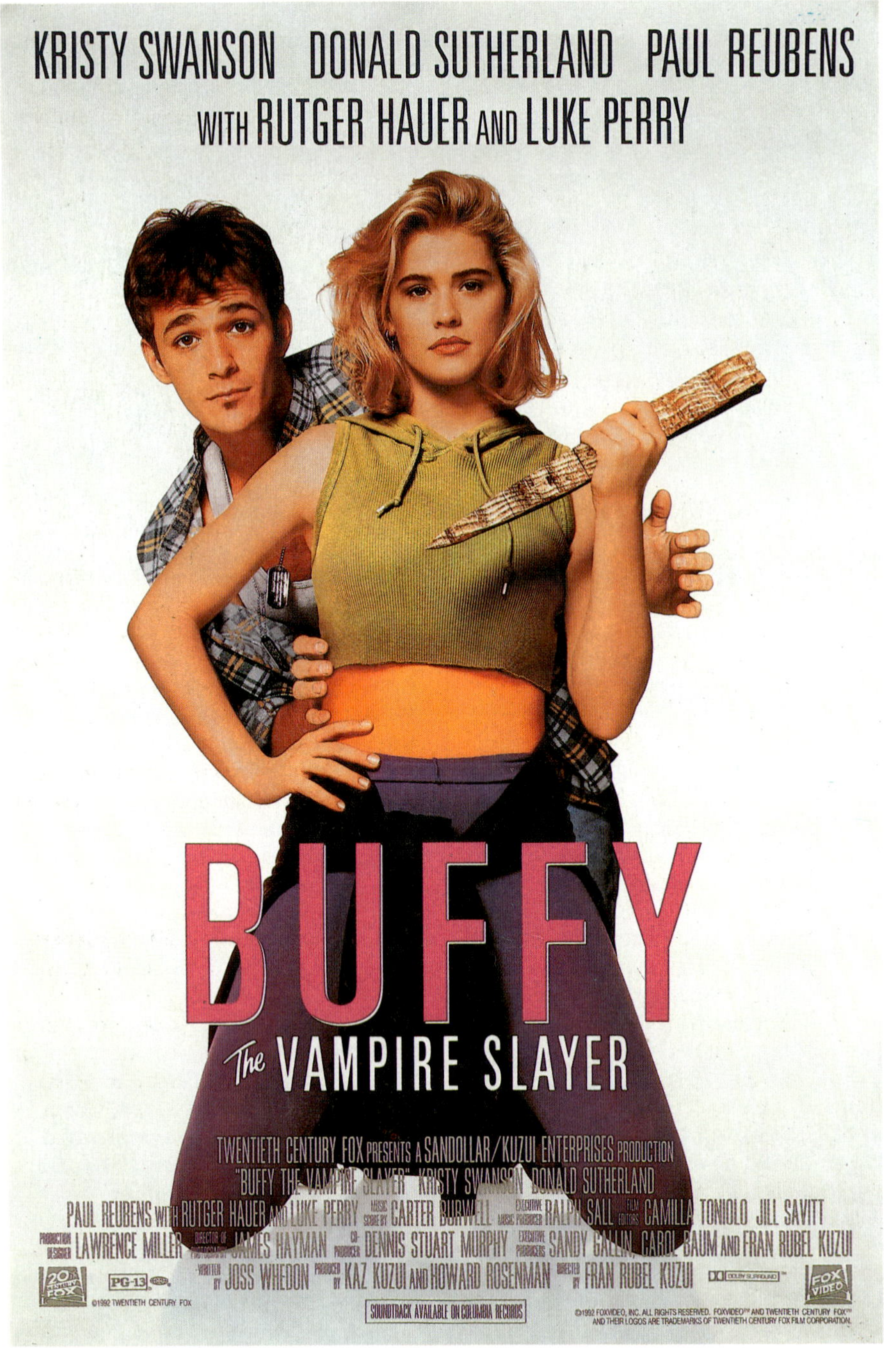

New York and is tempted by a sexy vampiric demon (an excellent début by Cynthia Bond). The humour sits uneasily with the gore and some of the performances leave much to be desired, however this remains an enjoyable chiller written, produced, co-executive produced, music supervised, directed and starring the obviously multi-talented Bond III. Includes special guest appearances by singers Freddie Jackson, Najee and Melba Moore.

DEMON COP

USA, 1991. Dir: Rocco Karega. With: Theresa Fenneaux, Ray Klein, Julia Westland, Tony Zotta, Rocco Karega, Cameron Mitchell. American-Independent Productions. Colour.

Writer/director Karega plays Edward Thurman, a police officer in Colorado Springs, who contracts a rare blood disease that periodically transforms him into a demonic beast with an insatiable urge to kill. Low budget chills, with sleaze veteran Cameron Mitchell as 'special guest star'.

DOCTOR VAMPIRE

Hong Kong, 1991. Dir: Q. Xen Lee. Colour.

Stranded when his car breaks down, a doctor stumbles across a brothel run by vampires and is subsequently bitten by one of the undead girls. However, the couple fall in love and are pursued by the girl's evil bloodsucking pimp. These vampires are the traditional kind, not the hopping variety.

DRACULA CINEMATIC SCRAPBOOK

USA, 1991. Dir: Ted Newson. Rhino Video. Colour/B&W.

Hour long video compilation that includes all the Universal and Hammer vampire trailers, plus scenes from the original *Nosferatu* (1922) and *Uncle Was a Vampire* (1959). Other trailers include *Mark of the Vampire* (1935; in which Lugosi speaks to the audience), *Blacula* (1972), *Billy the Kid versus Dracula* (1965) and *One More Time* (1970; with Christopher Lee). Rhino has also produced equally fascinating tapes based on Frankenstein and the Wolf Man.

DRACULA RISING

USA, 1992. Dir: Fred Gallo. With: Stacey Travis, Christopher Atkins, Doug Wert. Concorde Pictures. Colour.

Filmed in Russia, Bulgaria and Romania. A medical researcher looking for a cure time-travels to nineteenth century Transylvania and becomes a patient of the Count. Produced by Roger Corman.

DRACULA'S HAIR

Commonwealth of Independent States, 1992. Dir: Vadim Prodan. Arto Studio/Rosfilmexport. Colour.

An attempt by the Russians to cash-in on the late 1992 Dracula boom.

EDWARD II

UK, 1991. Dir: Derek Jarman. With: Steven Waddington, Kevin Collins, Andrew Tiernana, John Lynch, Tilda Swinton, Nigel Terry. Working Title/British Screen/BBC-TV. Colour.

Jarman's typically overblown adaptation of the play by Christopher Marlowe. In one scene, the Queen (Swinton) turns into a vampire and bites out Jerome Flynn's throat.

ENCOUNTERS OF THE SPOOKY KIND II

Hong Kong, 1990. Dir: Sammo Hung. With: Sammo Hung. Long Shong Pictures. Colour.

This belated horror comedy sequel to the 1982 hit features vampires, soul stealing and some incredible stunts.

FANGS!

USA, 1992. Dir: Bruce G. Hallenbeck With: Veronica Carlson. Pagan Video. Colour.

Ex-Hammer scream queen Carlson (*Dracula Has Risen from the Grave* [1968], etc) hosts this one hour documentary on vampire movies from Murnau's *Nosferatu* (1922) to the present.

FATHER, SANTA CLAUS HAS DIED

Russia, 1992. Dir: Ugeny Yufit. Anatoly Egorov, Evan Ganzha, Ljudmila Kozlovskava, Valery Krishtapenco, Maxim Gribov. Lenfilm. B&W.

Poetic, almost silent art film which marks the début of director Yufit. Loosely based on Alexei Tolstoy's story 'The Vampire Family' ('The Wurdalak'), it includes elements of horror, science fiction, bondage and humour.

FIRST VAMPIRE IN CHINA

Hong Kong, 1990. Dir: Yam Chun-Lu. Colour.

A great opening sequence and climax (featuring a nasty looking vampire), but let down by a tedious middle section. Includes a mass attack by vampire bats *á la The Birds* (1963).

GRAVEYARD SHIFT

USA, 1990. Dir: Ralph S. Singleton. With: David Andrews, Kelly Wolf, Stephen Macht, Brad Dourif, Vic Polizos, Jonathan Emerson. Columbia/Tri-Star. Colour.

Based on the Stephen King story of the same name. A group of exterminators in a run-down textile factory (the Bachman Mill!) battle a horde of deadly rats from an adjoining cemetery, which are led by a giant mutant bat-rat monster.

GREMLINS 2 THE NEW BATCH

USA, 1990. Dir: Joe Dante. With: Zach Galligan, Phoebe Cates, John Glover, Robert Prosky, Christopher Lee, Dick Miller. Amblin/Warner Bros. Colour.

Executive producer Steven Spielberg and director Dante leave behind the atmospheric chills of *Gremlins* (1984) for a knockabout sequel which is a live-action homage to the classic Warner Bros cartoons (with cameos by Bugs Bunny, Daffy Duck and Porky Pig!). This time the gremlins run riot through the high-tech skyscraper of millionaire Glover. Prosky plays vampiric TV horror host Grandpa Fred, Lee appears as a wacky mad doctor, and watch out for cameos by Dick Miller, Keye Luke, Jerry Goldsmith, Belinda Balaski, Paul Bartel, Kenneth Tobey, John Astin, Henry Gibson, Leonard Maltin, Hulk Hogan, and Tony Randall as the voice of the 'Brain' Gremlin. Special effects by Rick Baker.

HOWLING VI THE FREAKS

USA/UK, 1990. Dir: Hope Perello. With: Brendan Hughes, Michele Matheson, Sean Gregory Sullivan, Antonio Fargas, Carol Lynley, Bruce Martyn Payne. Allied Lane Pringle Productions. Colour.

Sixth in the direct-to-video series, loosely inspired by a trio of books by Gary Brandner. Urbane vampire Harker (Payne) kidnaps a reluctant werewolf (Hughes) and puts the creature on show in his travelling carnival of freaks. Although nowhere near the standard of Joe Dante's first film in the series, *The Howling* (1980), this is still a huge improvement over all the previous sequels, thanks to a strong storyline, the atmospheric desert setting and stylish direction by Perello. At the end, Harker transforms into a man-size bat-monster (impressive make-up, similar to that in *The Bat People* [1974]) to fight the werewolf. Also includes an alligator boy.

I BOUGHT A VAMPIRE MOTORCYCLE

UK, 1990. Dir: Dirk Campbell. With: Neil Morrissey, Amanda Noar, Michael Elphick, Anthony Daniels, Andrew Powell, George Rossi. Dirk Productions. Colour.

Crass, low budget horror comedy, with more gore than wit. Morrissey plays a dispatch rider who buys a demonically possessed motorcycle that runs on blood. As it rides around Birmingham decapitating victims, only sunlight and the sign of the cross have the power to stop it. Elphick is Inspector Cleaver, with terminal garlic breath; Daniels (C3PO in the *Star Wars* series) plays a priest; and Burt Kwouk (from the *Pink Panther* films) has a pointless cameo as 'Fu King Owner' (ha-ha). The special effects were created by Bob Keen's Image Animation.

Above: *I Bought a Vampire Motorcycle.*

INNOCENT BLOOD

USA, 1992. Dir: John Landis. With: Anne Parillaud, Robert Loggia, Anthony LaPaglia, Don Rickles, Linnea Quigley. Lee Rich Productions/Warner Bros. Colour.

A blend of comedy, romance and thriller as Parillaud (*Le Femme Nikita* [1990]) plays Marie, a female vampire with a conscience. She teams up with undercover cop LaPaglia to go after Mafia mobster Sal 'The Shark' Macelli (Loggia). Forrest J Ackerman makes another cameo appearance, along with directors Sam Raimi, Frank Oz and Dario Argento, and special effects wizard Tom Savini.

IN THE MIDNIGHT HOUR

USA, 1992. Dir: Joel Bender. With: Michelle Owens, Dennis McMillen, Greg Greer. Midnight Hour Productions. Colour.

Low budget chiller in which a feisty lady cop is bitten by a young schizophrenic vampire, who presents himself as a sexy rock'n'roll star, an innocent milkman and a pious priest.

LOVE BITES

USA. Campfire Video Productions. Colour.

Gay-oriented (non-porn) vampire horror comedy. After 347 years of one-night stands, the Count is finally ready to settle down. The only problem is that his new *amour* is West Hollywood's top vampire hunter...

THE MALIBU BEACH VAMPIRES

USA, 1991. Dir: Francis Creighton. With: Angelyne, Becky LeBeau, Joan Rudelstein, Marcus A. Frishman, Rod Sweitzer, Francis Creighton. Peacock Films. Colour.

Colonel Ollie West, Congressman Teri Upstart and Rev Timmy Fakker all have secret girlfriends in a Malibu beach house who turn out to be vampires. But instead of drinking blood, these girls inject their victims with a truth serum. This awful sounding horror comedy stars Angelyne of Hollywood Blvd billboard fame. The music is by Paul McCarty (*sic*).

LA MASCHERA DEL DEMONIO

Italy, 1990. Dir: Lamberto Bava. With: Debora Kinski, Eva Grimaldi, Michele Soavi, Piero Nomi, Stanko Molnar, Giovanni Guidelli. Reitalia-Anfri. Colour.

Director Lamberto Bava's remake of Mario Bava's classic *Black Sunday* (1960), based in turn on Nikolai Gogol's story 'The Vij'. This time a group of young friends (including Italian director Soavi) discover the frozen body of vampire/witch Anibas during a skiing trip. Debora Kinski (in a dual role) is no match for Barbara Steele in the original, and Lamberto proves (as if we didn't know) that he has none of his father's talent.

MOON LEGEND

Hong Kong, 1991. Dir: Joey Wang. Colour.

A young swordsman is haunted by recurring dreams of a beautiful vampire, Moon-Cher. Convinced that she is in danger, he sets out on a quest to rescue her. Includes great special effects and a female vampire who sucks her victim's blood through a hollow reed.

MY GRANDPA IS A VAMPIRE

(Orig: MOONRISE/GRAMPIRE) New Zealand, 1991. Dir: David Blyth. With: Al Lewis, Justin Gocke, Milan Borich, Noel Appleby, Pat Evison. Tucker Production Co/ Moonrise Productions. Colour.

Likeable children's adventure, starring eighty-one year-old Al Lewis (*The Munsters*) as friendly vampire Vernon T. Cooger. Twelve year-old Lonny (Gocke) arrives in New Zealand from Los Angeles to spend a holiday with his grandfather Cooger, Aunt Leah (Evison), and his friend, Kanziora (Borich). But the boys stumble across an ancient family secret — Cooger is really a 300 year-old member of the undead, and he pleads with them to protect him from Aunt Leah's unpleasant boyfriend, Ernie, who wants to drive a stake through his heart. Family fun from the director of *Death Warmed Up* (1984) and *Red Blooded American Girl* (1990).

MY LOVELY MONSTER

Germany, 1991. Dir: Michel Bergmann. With: Silvio Francesco, Forrest J Ackerman, Nicole Fischer, Matthias Fuchs, Marlen Diekhoff, Peter Voss. Xenon Films/WDR/SFB. Colour.

Charming spoof on horror films, featuring additional (pun-filled) dialogue and a cameo appearance by Forrest J Ackerman. Francesco plays silent film vampire Maximilian (made up to look like Lon Chaney Sr in *London After Midnight* [1927]) who is freed from a burning piece of nitrate film and suddenly finds himself in a German cinema. It's filled with horror movie references, and also includes appearances by Ferdinand Mayne, Bobbie Bresee and Boris Karloff's daughter, Sara.

NIGHTBREED

UK/USA/Canada, 1990. Dir: Clive Barker. With: Craig Sheffer, Anne Bobby, David Cronenberg, Charles Haid, Hugh Quarshie, Hugh Ross. Morgan Creek/J&M/Braveworld/ Twentieth Century Fox. Colour.

Author Clive Barker's ambitious second outing as a writer/director (after *Hellraiser* [1987]), based on his own novel *Cabal*. Moody hero Sheffer discovers (after he's dead!) that he is the new messiah for a subterranean city of mythical shape-changers, including Catherine Chevalier as a vampiric woman who can transform into smoke. Masked psycho Cronenberg wants them all dead. The jumpy storyline is due to studio interference, but there's some great action scenes and impressive (if underused) Image Animation make-up effects. Veteran John Agar turns up in a neat cameo.

OUT FOR BLOOD

USA, 1990. Dir: Paul Thomas. With: Tori Wells, Raquel Darian, Randy Spears, Kelly Royce, Sherry Taylor, Eric Price. Vivid Video. Colour.

X-rated horror/private eye sex comedy, shot on video. Tori Wells plays a woman named Tori who is unaware that she is the offspring of two members of the undead. However, after dark she transforms into a sex-hungry vampire (in a cut-away tuxedo!) who sucks her victims just where you'd expect. Tantala plays her mother, and there's a hunchback named Igor. This is available in both hard– and softcore versions.

PROJECT VAMPIRE

USA, 1992. Dir: Peter Flynn. With: Myron Natwick, Brian Knudson, Mary-Louis Gemmill, Paula Randoi-Smith, Christopher Wolf, Kelvin Tsao. NBV Productions. Colour.

Three young interns oppose the plans of evil vampire Dr Fredrick Klaus (Natwick) to create a world of vampires with his high-tech superserum. An antidote allows the scientifically created undead to withstand sunlight, thereby enabling them to infiltrate the higher echelons of business and politics. The directing début of ex-Corman art director Flynn.

RED BLOODED AMERICAN GIRL

Canada, 1990. Dir: David Blyth. With: Andrew Stevens, Heather Thomas, Christopher Plummer, Kim Coates, Lydie Denier, Andrew Jackson. SC Entertainment International. Colour.

Dr John Alcore (Plummer) and the staff at his Life Research Foundation are infected with an age-prolonging virus that turns them into blood-drinkers. Research volunteer Paula (Thomas) is infected with the disease and transformed into a super-human killer, while erratic young scientist Owen Urban (Stevens) is employed to find a cure before the virus destroys Alcore and the rest of the scientifically created vampires. Despite Blyth's flashy direction, Allan Moyle's uneven script owes much to the early films of fellow Canadian David Cronenberg.

***Below:** Nightbreed.*

THE REFLECTING SKIN

UK/Canada, 1990. Dir: Philip Ridley. With: Viggo Mortensen, Lindsay Duncan, Jeremy Cooper, Shelia Moore, Duncan Fraser, David Longworth. Fugitive Films/Virgin/ Live Entertainment. Colour.

Atmospheric early fifties drama in which eight year-old Seth Dove (Cooper) sets out to kill reclusive young widow Dolphin Blue (Duncan) because he believes she's a vampire after the blood of his elder brother. A stylish and disturbing début by director Ridley, who scripted *Prick Up Your Ears* (1987) and *The Krays* (1990).

THE RELUCTANT VAMPIRE

USA, 1992. Dir: Malcolm Marmorstein. With: Adam Ant, Kimberly Foster, Roger Rose, Michelle Forbe, Philip Bruns, Judy Tenuta. Waymar Productions. Colour.

Zachary Simms (Adam Ant), a vampiric rock musician, tries to please the woman he loves by reforming and becoming a yuppie. Based on the writer/director's off-Broadway comedy of the late 1970s.

ROCKULA

USA, 1990. Dir: Luca Bercovici. With: Dean Cameron, Tawny Fere, Susan Tyrell, Bo Diddley, Thomas Dolby, Toni Basil. Cannon Pictures. Colour.

Would you believe a vampire musical from the director of *Ghoulies* (1984)? Actually, it's not as bad as it sounds, thanks to stylish production values and likeable performances. 400 year-old teen vampire Ralph (Cameron) is cursed to fall in love with the reincarnation of the same girl (Fere) every twenty-two years. He must save her before she is killed by a pirate with a peg-leg wielding a gigantic ham-bone! The musical numbers may be uneven, but you can't help liking a film that includes a vampire who argues with his wise-cracking mirror(!) image and ends with an Elvis impersonation.

SHERLOCK HOLMES IN CARACAS

Venezuela, 1992. Dir: Juan E. Fresan. With: Jean Manuel Montesinos, Gilbert Dacournan, Carolina Luzardo, Maria Eugenia Cruz, Giles Bickford, Richard Cumming. Big Ben Productions/Tiuna Films/ Foncine. Colour.

Low budget slapstick comedy, loosely based on Arthur Conan Doyle's story 'The Sussex Vampyre'. Montesinos stars as Sherlock Holmes, who merely travels through Caracas on his way to Maracaibo to help an old friend married to an ex-Miss Venezuela (Cruz). Late in the plot, she turns out to be a vampire who threatens the lives of her children. Includes numerous hit-or-miss gags, silly subtitles, a pagan-worshipping governess and Watson (Dacournan) filming everything with a video camera.

SHERLOCK HOLMES: THE LAST VAMPYRE

UK, 1992. Dir: Tim Sullivan. With: Jeremy Brett, Edward Hardwicke, Roy Marsden, Keith Barron, Elizabeth Spriggs, Maurice Denham. Granada Television. Colour.

Made-for-TV movie, based on 'The Sussex Vampyre' by Sir Arthur Conan Doyle. Sherlock Holmes and Dr Watson (Brett and Hardwicke) investigate an apparent vampire in a quiet English village.

SLEEPWALKERS

USA, 1992. Dir: Mick Garris. With: Brian Krause, Mädchen Amick, Alice Krige, Jim Haynie, Cindy Pickett, Ron Perlman. Columbia/ Ion Pictures. Colour.

After an intriguing opening (set in Hitchcock's Bodega Bay and featuring an uncredited Mark Hamill), it's all downhill as incestuous mother and son, Mary and Charles Brady (Krige and Krause), move to Travis, Indiana, and stir up the local cat population. It turns out that they are ancient feline shape-changers, who need

Below: Tale of a Vampire.

to suck the lifeforce from a local popcorn sales girl (*Twin Peaks*' Amick) to survive. Only the town's cats can see through the human disguise of the creatures who inspired the vampire legends. Despite good performances, competent direction and clever special effects, this is one of the dumbest movies ever made. It's based on an original screenplay by Stephen King, who makes a pointless cameo appearance along with horror directors John Landis, Joe Dante, Clive Barker and Tobe Hooper.

SON OF DARKNESS: TO DIE FOR II

USA, 1991. Dir: David F. Price. With: Rosalind Allen, Steve Bond, Scott Jacoby, Michael Praed, Jay Underwood, Amanda Wyss. Arrowhead/Lee Caplin. Colour.

A sequel to the 1988 original, this low budget chiller stars Praed (replacing Brendan Hughes) as Max Schreck(!), a vampire doctor working in a small town casualty unit. While he tries to curb his blood-drinking habits with plasma bags and protect his half-vampire child (Devin Corrie Sims), his equally undead brother Tom (Bond) is happy to tear living victims apart for the red stuff. Hero Jacoby returns from the first film, and Wyss makes an interesting female vampire. Surprisingly effective rift on the myth.

SORORITY HOUSE VAMPIRES

USA, 1992. Dir: Geoffrey de Valois. With: Natalia Bondurant, Eugenie Bondurant, Rachel Wolkow, Shay More, Kenny Gibbs, Robert Bucholz. Digital Vision Entertainment. Colour.

Bucholz plays Count Vlad in this 'environmental vampire story' about the undead attacking a sorority initiation at a cabin in the woods.

SPOOKY FAMILY 2

Hong Kong, 1991. Dir: Law Lit. With: Lam Ching Ying. Colour.

Slightly disappointing sequel to the 1989 original, from the creators of the popular *Mr. Vampire* series. Lam Ching Ying (who plays One Eyebrow Priest from that series) joins the cast of this horror comedy special effects extravaganza.

Left: *Sleepwalkers.*
Below: *Project Vampire.*

STREETS

USA, 1990. Dir: Katt Shea Ruben. With: Christina Applegate, David Mendenhall, Eb Lottimer, Starr Andreeff, Patrick Richwood, Kady Tran. Colour.

Los Angeles junkie hooker Applegate is stalked by crazed vampire cop Lottimer in this low budget thriller directed by Ruben (*Dance of the Damned* [1988]), who also co-scripted with her husband. Shot in nineteen days.

SUBSPECIES

Romania/USA, 1990. Dir: Ted Nicolaou. With: Michael Watson, Laura Tate, Anders Hove, Michelle McBride, Irina Movila, Angus Scrimm. Full Moon Entertainment/ Paramount Home Video. Colour.

Despite being executive produced by Charles Band, this is a pretty good vampire thriller, shot on location in Romania. Two female American college students (Tate and McBride) studying folklore become involved in a struggle between brothers Hove (the evil vampire) and Watson (the hero vampire) for the powers of a Transylvanian blood-stone. David Allen supplied the stop-motion demons.

TALE OF A VAMPIRE

(aka A TALE OF VAMPIRE)
UK/Japan, 1992. Dir: Shimako Sato. With: Julian Sands, Suzanna Hamilton, Kenneth Cranham, Marian Diamond, Michael Kenton, Catherine Blake. State Screen

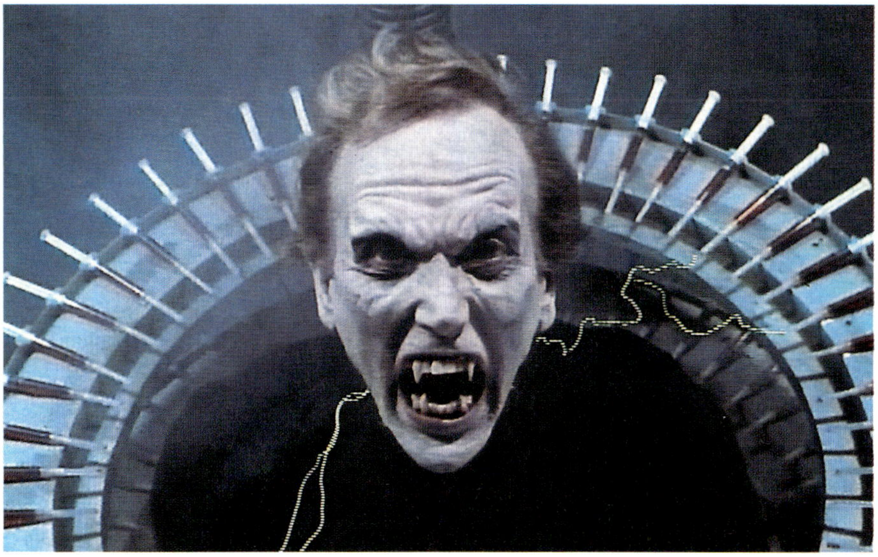

Productions. Colour.
Slow but good-looking début feature by Japanese filmmaker Sato. This was shot on a very low budget in London, and is loosely based on Edgar Allan Poe's poem 'Annabel Lee'. Sands stars as Alex, a melancholic blood-drinker attracted to Anne (Hamilton), a librarian who is the image of Virginia, the lover he lost more than a century ago. Cranham's mysterious immortal vampire hunter turns out to be Poe himself!

THOSE FEEDY ON BLOOD

(aka BLOOD-SUCKERS)
Russia, 1991. Dir: E. Tatarskiy (Eugeny Tatarsky). With: Marina Vladi (Vlady), Andrey Sokolov, Marina Maiko, Donatas Banionis. Lenfilm/Printex. Colour.
Another adaptation of Alexei Tolstoy's story 'The Wurdalak', which suffers from some terrible subtitling (the title is as it is translated on the print!). Rather than confuse you more, I'll quote from the plot synopsis: 'At a high society party of a young officer, Runevsky, meets Dashenka, who is the company of her grandmother Sugrobina. Runevsky falls in love with Dashenka at first glance. A strange young man, Rybarenko, tells him that Sugrobina is a vampire, and reveals the mystery of the ever-lasting monster Sugrobina. A preposterous duel between Runevsky and Dashenka's cousin delays the outcome. However, Runevsky is not aware that Sugrobina had managed to prolong her life by merging it in Dashenka.' Whew, I'm glad that's clear. Includes a particularly eerie sequence where a portrait of Dashenka's dead mother comes to life.

3 MEN AND A LITTLE LADY

USA/UK, 1990. Dir: Emile Ardolino. With: Tom Selleck, Steve Guttenberg, Ted Danson, Nancy Travis, Christopher Cazenove, Fiona Shaw. Touchstone Pictures/Jean Francois Lepetit/Interscope Communications. Colour.
Improved sequel to the hit comedy *3 Men and a Baby* (1987). The unorthodox three-father family is thrown into turmoil when mother Sylvia (Travis) announces she is marrying English lover Edward (Cazenove), taking five year-old Mary (Robin Wiseman) with her. Danson's hammy actor turns up dressed as the vampiric Count Cholesterol for a TV commercial.

TO SLEEP WITH A VAMPIRE

USA, 1992. Dir: Adam Friedman. With: Scott Valentine, Charlie Spradling. Concorde Pictures. Colour.
Low budget remake of the 1988 movie *Dance of the Damned*. A tortured, lonely, 1,000 year-old vampire (Valentine) spends the evening with suicidal Los Angeles stripper Nina (Spradling). Roger Corman was executive producer.

TRILOGY OF FEAR

USA, 1991. Dir: Richard L. Fox Jr, Steve Maier and Kevin Nunan. With: Claude Akins, Louise Le Tourneau, James Coffey, Larry Silver, Frank Cummings, Peter Zaff. Trilogy Group. Colour.
Anthology of three half-hour supernatural tales about a mass murderer ('Saved by the Spell'), a vampire ('Hubert's Homecoming') and a modern day witch who helps the police stop a demented doctor ('Midnight Date').

ULTIMATE VAMPIRE

Hong Kong, 1991. Dir: Andrew Lau. With: Lam Ching Ying, Chin Siu Ho. Colour.
Vampire hunter extraordinaire Lam Ching Ying once again portrays the One Eyebrow Priest in this unofficial sequel to the *Mr. Vampire* series. This time he must save his loyal student (Ho) from the love of an undead beauty.

UNDYING LOVE

USA, 1991. Dir: Greg Lamberson. With: Lee Kayman. Colour.
When a man is seduced by Carmilla, a New York City vampire who has been around since the French Revolution, he becomes one of the undead. Unfortunately, her vampire boyfriend gets jealous.

VALERIE

USA, 1991. Dir: Jay Lind. With:

Left: *Red Blooded American Girl.*

Austin Pendleton, Maria Pechukas, Debbie Rochon. Colour.
Pechukas plays the titular character who, suffering from a mysterious illness, slowly transforms into a vampire. Director Lind combines elements of *The Legendary Curse of Lemora* (1973) with the lesbianism of J. Sheridan Le Fanu's story 'Carmilla'.

UN VAMPIRE AU PARADIS

France, 1992. Dir: Abdelkrim Bahloul. With: Bruno Cremer, Brigitte Fossey, Farid Chopel, Laure Marsac, Helene Sugere, Abdel Kechicho. Les Films Auramax/Canal Plus/CNC/MC-4. Colour.
Comedy about the friendship between a bourgeois French businessman (Cremer) and Nosfer Arbi (Chopel), an escaped lunatic who thinks he's a vampire. Winner of the Chamrousse Comedy Film Festival and the Grand Prix at the annual Paris Festival of Films for Children and Young People, which also voted Laure Marsac best actress. A deft blend of everyday life and the supernatural, the title translates as *A Vampire in Paradise*. Algerian born director Bahloul has a bit part as a grocer.

VAMPIRE BUSTER

Hong Kong, 1990. Dir: Norman Law and Stanley Siu. With: Nick Chan, Simon Cheng, Stanley Fung, Jacky Cheung, May Law, Vivian Leung. In-Gear Film Production. Colour.
Violent horror comedy. Despite the title, there are no real vampires, just a green-faced body-hopping demon accidentally released from an ancient urn and pursued by an exorcist. Plenty of action and slapstick humour. The title on the video box is *Ninja Vampire Buster*.

VAMPIRE COP

USA, 1990. Dir: Donald Farmer. With: William Lucas, Melissa Moore, Ed Cannon, Mal Arnold. Panorama Entertainment. Colour.
Cannon is big blond vampire cop Officer Lucas who sleeps upside-down like a bat, and Moore the TV reporter trying to stop him from vampirising the local drug dealers. Mal Arnold (who starred in *Blood Feast* [1963]) plays a cop sliced up with a chainsaw. Lots of nudity, slow motion action and close-ups of fangs. Filmed on a low budget in Atlanta and Florida.

VAMPIRE'S EMBRACE

USA, 1991. Dir: Glen Andreiev. Colour.
When a man marries a blonde he meets at a horror movie, she turns out to be a 200 year-old vampire. He decides to accept her as she is. Low budget thrills from Westport, Long Island.

THE VAMPIRE'S ROPE

Commonwealth of Independent States, 1992. Dir: Nikolai Gibu. The Nord Company. Colour.
More Russian vampires, scripted by Clara Luchko and Zinaida Chirkova.

VAMPIRES SETTLE ON POLICE CAMP

Hong Kong, 1991. Dir: Lo Wei Lang. Colour.
Behind the unwieldy title is another comedy/horror film, inspired by the popular *Haunted Cop Shop* series. A group of teenagers, studying to join the police force, save the day when they are attacked by vampires.

VAMPIRE TRAILER PARK

USA, 1991. Dir: Steve Latshaw. With: Robert Shurtz, Patrick Moran, Blake Pickett, Bentley Little, Michael Street, Ethel Miller. Cinemondo. Colour.
Low budget vampire comedy filmed in Florida. An undead eighteenth century plantation owner (scriptwriter Moran) and his creepy Aunt Hattie move into a trailer park and invite guests over for dinner. Unfortunately, the bulimic vampire spends most of his time puking up blood all over the walls. Meanwhile, a drunken private eye (Shurtz) and an epileptic psychic (Pickett) cruise the topless bars looking for the vampire who drained her grandmother.

VAMPYRE

USA, 1990. Dir: Bruce G. Hallenbeck. With: Randy Scott Rozler, Cathy Seyler, John Brent, Greg Boggia, Marilyn Semerad, John L. Gilson. Panorama Entertainment/Raedon. Colour.
Despite the title, this is a long, long way from Dreyer's thirties 'classic'. A topless, leather-clad vampiress and her nubile disciples are out to suck blood in this amateurish movie, written, edited, co-produced and directed by Hallenbeck. Only worth catching to see the self-styled 'King of Splatter', author John McCarty, as a victim of the undead. Shot on video in New Jersey for just $20,000.

WANDA DOES TRANSYLVANIA

USA.
Hardcore vampires.

WAXWORK II: LOST IN TIME

(UK: LOST IN TIME)
USA, 1991 (1992). Dir: Anthony Hickox. With: Zach Galligan, Alexander Godunov, Monika Schnarre, Martin Kemp, Sophie Ward, Bruce Campbell. Electric Pictures. Colour.
Great-looking comedy sequel to *Waxwork* (1988), in which the surviving severed hand from the first film frames Sarah (Schnarre) for a murder it commits. To prove her innocence, Mark (Galligan) takes her through the looking-glass time doors into various alternate worlds where Good fights Evil using characters and situations from horror films and fiction. These include clever pastiches of *Frankenstein*, *The Haunting* (1963; in black and white) and *Alien* (1979), plus an original story inspired by Edgar Allan Poe. During their travels, the time-travelling teens also meet Nosferatu (Steve Painter), Mr Hyde, Jack the Ripper, Godzilla, the zombies from *Dawn of the Dead* (1979), and such guest stars as Juliet Mills, David Carradine, John Ireland (his last role), Joe Baker, Patrick Macnee (as a raven!), Maxwell Caulfield, Drew Barrymore and director Hickox. Special effects by Bob Keen's Image Animation.

WITCHCRAFT III: THE KISS OF DEATH

USA, 1991. Dir: R.L. Tillmann. With: Charles Solomon, Lisa Toothman, Dominic Luciano, Leana Hall, Nicole Lauren, William L. Baker. Academy Entertainment. Colour.
Solomon returns from *Witchcraft II: The Temptress* (1989) as Will Spanner, a young lawyer who is the reluctant son of a warlock. This time he confronts a psychic vampire stud (Luciano) who threatens Solomon's girlfriend with a kiss of death. Better than expected.

Appendix 1:

Vampires on TV

This is a selected guide to some of the more interesting television appearances of the vampire over the years. It doesn't pretend to be complete, but once you've seen all the movies listed in this book, you can start tracking down some of the following...

THE ABC COMEDY HOUR: *THE KOPYKATS*

USA, 1972.

A musical episode of this comedy sketch show featured Count Dracula (Tony Curtis) meeting Frankenstein (Frank Gorshin).

THE ADDAMS FAMILY

USA, 1964-66. With: Carolyn Jones, John Astin, Jackie Coogan, Ted Cassidy, Blossom Rock, Lisa Loring, Ken Weatherwax. Filmways/ABC-TV. B&W.

Based on Charles Addams' macabre *New Yorker* cartoons. The oddball family includes the vampiric Morticia (Jones), her husband Gomez (Astin), Uncle Fester (Coogan), the family butler Lurch (Cassidy), Grandmama (Rock), the diabolical children Wednesday (Loring) and Pugsley (Weatherwax), and Thing (who, of course, plays itself). The similar series *The Munsters* débuted the same year.

Sequel: THE ADDAMS FAMILY (qv; 1973)

THE ADDAMS FAMILY

USA/UK, 1973. Voices: Jackie Coogan, Ted Cassidy, Janet Waldo, Lennie Weinrib, Cindy Henderson, Jodie Foster. Hanna-Barbera/NBC-TV. Colour.

Almost forgotten children's series, which ran for sixteen half-hour episodes. Based on the look of Charles Addams' cartoons (animated in Britain by Halas and Batchelor), each week the oddball family travelled in their haunted trailer to a different American city. Only Coogan and Cassidy returned from the original TV series, and Pugsley was voiced by a young Jodie Foster. A new TV cartoon series débuted in 1992.

ALFRED HITCHCOCK PRESENTS: *NIGHT CREATURES*

Canada/USA, 1988. Dir: Richard J. Lewis. With: Brett Cullen, Louise Vallance, Michael Rhoades, Jason Blicker, Ray James. A.H.F./Paragon/Michael Sloan Productions/MCA-TV. Colour.

Half-hour horror pilot, written by executive producer Michael Sloan and introduced by a colourised Hitchcock. Female reporter Vallance suffers from a recurring dream of a demonic horseman. When she meets heavy metal vampire singer Adam Lust/Martin Lecross (Rhoades), her nightmares come true. Music by Disaster Area. The ending was left open for a never-continued series.

THE ALL-NEW POPEYE HOUR: *THE TERRIFYING TRANSYLVANIAN TREK*

USA, 1978. Dir: Alex Lovy. Voices: Jack Mercer, Marilyn Schreffer, Allan Melvin, Daws Butler. CBS-TV. Colour.

Inferior cartoon in which Popeye and Olive meet Dracula (Melvin), Vampetta (Schreffer) and the Frankenstein monster.

BJ AND THE BEAR: *A COFFIN WITH A VIEW*

USA, 1978 (1979). With: Greg Evigan, Sam, Claude Akins, Pamela Helmsley, John Carradine, George Lazenby. Glen A. Larson/Universal. Colour.

Short-lived series about an independent trucker, Billy Joe McKay (Evigan), and his travelling companion, a chimp (Sam). In this episode, they get involved with transporting the coffin of the vampire-like Paul Desmond (Lazenby) and his creepy caretaker (Carradine).

BLAKE'S 7: *DUEL*

UK, 1978. Dir: Douglas Camfield. With: Gareth Thomas, Sally Knyvette, Paul Darrow, Jan Chappell, Michael Keating. BBC-TV. Colour.

The first and second seasons of this sub-*Star Wars* series featured the Mutoids — humans adapted to live on an artificial blood-serum or the blood of enemies of the evil Federation. They are first introduced in this episode, which portrays their feeding habits in graphic detail. All three episodes are scripted by Terry Nation.

PRESSURE POINT

UK, 1979. Dir: George Spenton Foster. With: Gareth Thomas, Sally Knyvette, Paul Darrow, Jan Chappell, Michael Keating, Sue Bishop. BBC-TV. Colour.

The outer-space outlaws once again confront the Federation's blood-drinking Mutoids.

PROJECT AVALON

UK, 1978. Dir: Michael Briant. With: Gareth Thomas, Sally Knyvette, Paul Darrow, Jan Chappell, Michael Keating, Glynis Barber. BBC-TV. Colour.

Barber plays the principal blood-drinking Mutoid.

THE BOOK TOWER: *VAMPIRE MASTER*

UK, 1979. Dir: Richard Callanan. With: Mark Miwurdz, Gerry Cowan, Dean Manning, Helen Stockdale. Yorkshire Television. Colour.

Magazine show, hosted by Miwurdz, which dramatises extracts from children's books. The first programme included a scene from Virginia Ironside's titular volume.

BUCK ROGERS IN THE 25TH CENTURY: *SPACE VAMPIRE*

USA, 1979. Dir: David Wise. With: Gil Gerard, Erin Gray, Tim O'Connor, Felix Silla, Mel Blanc. Glen A. Larson/Universal. Colour.

In one of the better episodes, Buck (Gerard) must save Wilma Deering (Gray) from becoming the next victim of The Vorvon, an alien soul-stealing nosferatu that wants to turn her into one of the living dead.

CARMILLA

Spain. Dir: Jaime Picas. With: Marisa Paredes, Maria Enriquetta Caballeira.

Spanish TV adaptation of J. Sheridan Le Fanu's novella, with Paredes as Carmilla.

Remake: LE COEUR PETRIFIE CARMILLA (qv; 1987)

CIRCLE OF FEAR: *COUNT VAMPIRE*

USA, 1972. NBC-TV. Colour.

The title and format of *Ghost Story* were dropped after thirteen episodes, but the series continued under this title for the balance of the season. This episode includes clips from Hammer's *Dracula Has Risen from the Grave* (1968).

CLIFFHANGERS: *THE CURSE OF DRACULA*

USA, 1979. With: Michael Nouri, Stephen Johnson, Carol Baxter, Antionette Stella. NBC-TV. Colour.

One-third of a weekly series celebrating the old movie serials. Nouri portrays Count Dracula battling Johnson's Kurt Van Helsing. The first four episodes were later edited into *Dracula 79* and all ten episodes were compiled into a two hour TV movie, *World of Dracula*.

LE COEUR PETRIFIE: *CARMILLA*

France, 1987. Dir: Paul Planchon. With: Aurelle Doazan, Emmanuelle Meysignac, Marc Michel, Yvette Stahl, Paulette Schlegel, Roland Kieffer. FR3 Alsace. Colour.

French TV version of the story by J. Sheridan Le Fanu, with Meysignac as Carmilla.
Remake: NIGHTMARE CLASSICS: CARMILLA (qv; 1989)

COLGATE COMEDY HOUR

USA, 1950. With: Bud Abbott, Lou Costello, Lon Chaney, Bela Lugosi, Glenn Strange. NBC-TV. B&W.
Hosts Bud and Lou team up with their co-stars of (Abbott and Costello) *Meet Frankenstein* (1948) for this comedy skit, which features Lugosi as Count Dracula, Chaney Jr playing the Wolf Man and Strange as the Frankenstein monster.

COUNT DUCKULA

(USA: DARKWING DUCK)
UK, 1988. Voices: David Jason, Jack May, Brian Trueman, Jimmy Hibbert, Ruby Wax. Cosgrove Hall Productions. Colour.
The animated adventures of a vegetarian vampire duck, his manservant Igor, housekeeper Nanny and Dr Van Goosewing.

DARKROOM: *THE BOGEYMAN WILL GET YOU*

Canada/USA, 1981. Dir: Rick Rosenthal. With: Helen Hunt, Randolph Powell, Quinn Cummings, Gloria DeHaven, R.G. Armstrong. Universal/ ABC-TV. Colour.
Thirteen part anthology series hosted by James Coburn. This episode, based on a story by Robert Bloch, involves a girl (Cummings) who thinks the mystery man (Powell) pursuing her sister (Hunt) is a vampire. In fact, he's something much worse...

DARK SHADOWS

USA, 1966-71. With: Jonathan Frid, Joan Bennett, Alexandra Moltke, Grayson Hall, Lara Parker. Dan Curtis Productions/ABC-TV. Colour.
Five-days-a-week video soap opera with Frid as 175 year-old vampire Barnabas Collins (in episodes 210-821). This also includes Parker as a vampire-witch, David Selby as a werewolf and a lot of time-travelling into the past. It clocked up an incredible 1,225 episodes and two movie spin-offs during its five year run.
Remake: DARK SHADOWS (qv; 1990)

DARK SHADOWS

USA, 1990 (1991). With: Ben Cross, Jean Simmons, Barbara Steele, Roy Thinnes, Lysette Anthony. Dan Curtis Productions/MGM-UA Television/ NBC-TV. Colour.
Short-lived (nine episodes) revival of the popular day-time Gothic soap opera. Cross replaces Jonathan Frid as reluctant vampire Barnabas Collins, veteran Simmons is Collinwood matriach Elizabeth Collins Stoddard and cult horror star Steele plays Dr Julia Hoffman, the only person who can save Barnabas from his 'curse'.

DOCTOR WHO: *A JOURNEY INTO TERROR*

UK, 1964. Dir: Richard Martin. With: William Hartnell, William Russell, Jacqueline Hill, Peter Purves, Hywel Bennett. BBC-TV. B&W.
The Daleks pursue the TARDIS across time and space, and in the fourth episode ('The Chase') the time-travelling Doctor (Hartnell) and his companions land in a Gothic mansion where they are menaced by Count Dracula (Malcolm Rogers) and the Frankenstein monster (John Maxim), who turn out to be amusement park robots.

THE CLAWS OF AXOS

UK, 1971. Dir: Michael Ferguson. With: Jon Pertwee, Katy Manning, Nicholas Courtney, Bernard Holley. BBC-TV. Colour.
Produced under the title *The Vampire from Space.* The Earth is visited by an organic spacecraft containing beautiful golden aliens, the Axons. Although the visitors offer mineral wealth, the Doctor (Pertwee) discovers that they are in fact hideous tentacled parasites intent on draining the planet of all its energy.

THE CURSE OF FENRIC

UK, 1989. Dir: Nicholas Mallet. With: Sylvester McCoy, Sophie Aldred, Dinsdale Landen, Nicholas Parsons, Anne Reid, Alfred Lynch. BBC-TV. Colour.
The Doctor (McCoy) returns to World War Two Whitby (shades of Stoker's *Dracula*!), where he encounters the vampiric Haemovores and cursed Vikings in this four part espisode. The video release includes extra footage cut from the TV version.

STATE OF DECAY

UK, 1980. Dir: Peter Moffatt. With: Tom Baker, Lalla Ward, Matthew Waterhouse, William Lindsay, Rachel Davies. BBC-TV. Colour.
The TARDIS lands on an unnamed medieval planet in E-Space ruled by vampires Zargo (Lindsay), Camilla (Davies) and Aukon (Emrys James). They await the arising of a giant buried entity, the Great Vampire, banished there by the Time Lords. But when the Doctor (Baker) drives a spaceship through the heart of the creature, the vampires are reduced to dust.

THE STONES OF BLOOD

UK, 1978. Dir: Darrol Blake. With: Tom Baker, Mary Tamm, Susan Engel, Beatrix Lehmann, Nicholas McArdle. BBC-TV. Colour.
While searching for the third segment of the Key of Time on Earth, the Doctor (Baker) encounters a blood-drinking circle of stones, the Orgi, controlled by Celtic aliens.

THE DRACK PACK

(UK: THE DRAK PACK)
USA, 1980. Dir: Chris Cuddington and Steve Lumley. Voices: Jerry Dexter, Bill Callaway, Hans Conreid, Chuck McCann, Julie McWhirter. Hanna-Barbera/CBS-TV. Colour.
Cartoon series in which Drack Jr (Dexter), Frankie Frankenstein and Howler, the teenage sons of famous monsters, become heroes and foil Dr Dred and the Organisation of Generally Rotten Endeavours. Also includes a character named Vampira (McWhirter).

DRACULA

USA, 1982. With: Frank Langella. HBO. Colour.
Langella recreates his role as the Count for this cable TV restaging of the hit 1979 Broadway play.

DRACULA THE SERIES

Luxembourg/USA, 1990-91. With: Geordi Johnson, Bernard Behrens, Jacob Tierney, Joe Roncetti. Blair Entertainment/Universal. Colour.
Short-lived, half-hour syndicated series, with Johnson as Alexander Lucard, a yuppie business tycoon who is really a blond Count Dracula. He is opposed by three typical teens and their uncle Gustav (Behrens), the great-grandson of Professor Van Helsing. About as good as it sounds.

THE EVIL TOUCH: *THE FANS*

Australia/Canada, 1973. Dir: Vic Morrow. With: Vic Morrow, Alfred Sandor, Enid Lorimer, Queenie Ashton. Amalgamated Pictures/OLOLA Productions/Allied Artists. Colour.
Half-hour syndicated horror/fantasy series, hosted by Anthony Quayle. Morrow stars as horror actor Purvis Green, famous for his Dracula-type roles. He is kidnapped by two old women who impale him on a sword.

FANTASY ISLAND: *VAMPIRE/ WIDOW*

USA, 1978. With: Ricardo Montalban, Herve Villechaize, Robert Reed, Eva Gabor, Jack Elam, Lloyd Bochner, Julie Sommars. Aaron Spelling Productions. Colour.
Long-running series in which visitors spend $50,000 to live out their wildest fantasies on the secluded island of the mysterious Mr Roarke (Montalban) and the diminutive Tatoo (Villechaize). In this episode, a man wants to become a vampire to impress the woman he loves.

THE FLINTSTONES: *THE FLINTSTONES MEET ROCKULA AND FRANKENSTONE*

USA, 1980. Dir: Ray Patterson and Chris Cuddington. Voices: Henry Corden, Jean Vander Pyl, Mel Blanc, Gay Vatterson, Ted Cassidy, Casey Kasem. Hanna-Barbera/NBC-TV. Colour.
Hour-long special in which the modern stone age family meet the two title characters.

FOREVER KNIGHT

Canada, 1992. With: Geraint Wyn Davies, Gary Farmer, Catherine Disher, Nigel Bennett. Paragon Entertainment/Tele-Munchen/Tri-Star Television/CBS-TV. Colour.
Belated series spin-off from the TV movie *Nick Knight* (1989). Davies replaces Rick Springfield as the angst-ridden 760 year-old vampire cop who lives in a steel-shuttered loft and works the night shift. Disher is the medical examiner who knows his secret and Bennett plays his undead nemesis, Lacroix.

FRIDAY THE 13TH THE SERIES: *THE BARON'S BRIDE*

Canada, 1987 (1988). Dir: Bradford May. With: John D. LeMay, Robey, Chris Wiggins, Tom McCamus, Kevin Bundy, Susannah Hoffman. Variety Artists/Lexico/Hometown Films/ Paramount Television. Colour/B&W.
While tracking down another cursed object from the antique shop, Micki (Robey) falls under the spell of a vampire (McCamus) as she and Ryan (LeMay) travel back to nineteenth century London (in black and white) and team up with an unlikely Bram Stoker. No prizes for guessing which book the adventure inspires him to write. One of the series' best episodes, beautifully photographed, atmospherically directed and with some pretty explicit gore for a syndicated TV show.

BOTTLE OF DREAMS

Canada, 1988. Dir: Neill Fearnley. With: John D. LeMay, Robey, Chris Wiggins, R.G. Armstrong,

Elias Zarou. Variety Artists/Lexico/Hometown Films/Paramount Television. Colour/B&W.
In this end of season framing episode, Micki (Robey) and Ryan (LeMay) are trapped inside a vault and re-experience some of their worst moments (including scenes from 'The Baron's Bride', with new sequences that change the ending of that episode).

NIGHT PREY

Canada, 1989. Dir: Armand Mastroioanni. With: John D. LeMay, Robey, Chris Wiggins, Michael Burgess, Genevieve Langlois, Eric Murphy. Variety Artists/Lexico/Hometown Films/Paramount Television. Colour.
A man hunting the vampire (Murphy) who killed his wife, steals the Cross of Fire, a cursed silver crucifix which needs a human sacrifice before it can destroy the undead.

THE SWEETEST STING

Canada, 1988 (1989). Dir: David Winning. With: John D. LeMay, Robey, Chris Wiggins, Art Hindle, Tim Webber, Victor Sutton. Variety Artists/Lexico/Hometown Films/Paramount Television. Colour.
Micki (Robey) and Ryan (LeMay) discover a honey from vampire bees which gives eternal youth.

F TROOP: *V IS FOR VAMPIRE*

USA, 1966. With: Forrest Tucker, Larry Storch, Ken Berry, Melody Patterson, Frank de Kova, Vincent Price. Warner Bros. Colour.
Amusing spoof in which Price plays European actor Count Sforza (with a Bela Lugosi accent!) on a theatrical tour of the American West, who arrives at Fort Courage driving a hearse. He is soon mistaken for a Transylvanian vampire by the members of F Troop.

GET SMART: *THE WAX MAN*

USA, 1967 (1968). Dir: James Komack. With: Don Adams, Barbara Feldon, Edward Platt, Richard Devon, Robert Ridgely, Robert Lussier. Talent Associates/Paramount/NBC-TV. Colour.
In this episode of the sci-spy spoof, Devon plays the sinister owner of a wax museum, who plans to turn Maxwell Smart (Adams) into one of his wax exhibits. Robert Ridgely appears as Dracula.

WEEKEND VAMPIRE

USA, 1965. Dir: Bruce Bilson. With: Don Adams, Barbara Feldon, Edward Platt, Martin Kosleck, Ford Rainey, Roger Price. Talent Associates/Paramount/NBC-TV. Colour.
Smart (Adams) and Agent 99 (Feldon) investigate a series of vampire-like killings of CONTROL agents. They turn out to be the work of the diabolical Dr Drago (horror veteran Kosleck) and his double-barrelled flute, which shoots poisoned ice-pellets into the jugular.

GHOST STORY: *ALTER EGO*

USA, 1972. With: Helen Hayes, Gene Andrusco, Michael James Wixted, Colin Wilcox, Charles Aidman. NBC-TV Colour.
When a lonely young boy, Davey (Andrusco), conjures up an imaginary playmate across his chessboard, he creates an evil counterpart — a psychic vampire that is more than a match for a mere human. Part of a short-lived series (the title was later changed to *Circle of Fear*) developed by Richard Matheson, produced by William Castle and introduced by Sebastian Cabot.

ELEGY FOR A VAMPIRE

USA, 1972. Dir: Don McDougall. With: Marilyn Mason, Hal Linden, Mike Farell, John Milford, Arthur O'Connell. NBC-TV. Colour.
University campus girls are found dead with all the blood drained from their bodies.

THE GROOVIE GOOLIES

USA, 1970. Dir: Rudy Larriva, Don Towsley and Anatole Kursanoff. Voices: Larry Storch, Don Messick, Howard Morris, Jane Webb. Filmation/CBS-TV. Colour.
Hour-long musical cartoon series set in Horrible Hall, with Frankie, Cousin Drac, Wolfie, Mummy, Bella La Ghostly, etc.
Sequel: SABRINA, THE TEENAGE WITCH (qv; 1971)

THE HALLOWEEN THAT ALMOST WASN'T

USA, 1979. Dir: Bruce Bilson. With: Judd Hirsch, Mariette Hartley, Henry Gibson, John Schuck. Concepts Unlimited/ABC-TV. Colour.
Emmy Award-winning special for children. There will be no more Hallowe'en unless Count Dracula (Hirsch), the Frankenstein monster (Schuck), the Wolf Man (Jack Riley), the Mummy (Robert Fitch), the Zombie and Igor can convince the Witch (Hartley) to fly over the moon.

HAPPY DAYS

USA, 1980. Dir: Jerry Paris. With: Henry Winkler, Marion Ross, Anson Williams, Erin Moran, Al Molinaro. Miller-Milkis/Henderson/Paramount/ABC-TV. Colour.
Comedy show set in 1950s surburbia. In this episode, Fonzie (Winkler) dreams he meets a Count Dracula lookalike and a scientist who transfers his coolness into a monster.

THE HARDY BOYS/NANCY DREW MYSTERIES: *THE HARDY BOYS AND NANCY DREW MEET DRACULA*

USA, 1977. Dir: Joseph Pevney. With: Parker Stevenson, Shaun Cassidy, Pamela Sue Martin, Lorne Greene, Paul Williams, Richard Kiel, Lisa Eilbacher. Glen A. Larson Productions. Colour.
Two part juvenile mystery set in a nightclub with a horror motif. Kiel plays a Frankenstein-like monster.

THE HILARIOUS HOUSE OF FRIGHTENSTEIN

USA, 1974. Dir: Rife Markowitz. With: Billy Van, Rais Fiska, Vincent Price. Colour.
Syndicated special in which Count Frightenstein (Van) is a vampire exiled from Transylvania when he fails to bring a monster (named Bruce!) to life. This became a repetitive five-day-a-week series from 1974-75.

KOLCHAK: THE NIGHT STALKER: *THE VAMPIRE*

USA, 1974. Dir: Don Weiss. With: Darren McGavin, Simon Oakland, Jack Grinnage, Suzanne Charney, William Daniels. Universal/Francy Productions/ABC-TV. Colour.
Sequel to the TV movie *The Night Stalker* (1971). Catherine Rawlins (Charney), a female victim of Las Vegas vampire Janos Skorzeny, rises from the grave, seeking blood. As usual, no-one believes newspaper reporter Carl Kolchak (McGavin).

LATE NIGHT HORROR: *NO SUCH THING AS A VAMPIRE*

UK, 1968. Dir: Paddy Russell. With: Andrew Keir, Meg Wynn Owen, Thomas Gallagher, Peter Blythe. BBC-TV. Colour.
Scripted by Richard Matheson and based on his own story. This half-hour episode features Owen as Alexis, the wife of Dr Gheria (Keir), who appears to be the victim of a vampire. The young Dr Vares (Blythe) decides to stand guard outside her room...

THE LITTLE VAMPIRE

West Germany/UK, 1985 . Dir: Rene Bonniere. With: Joel Dacks, Christopher Stanton, Marsha Moreau, Gert Frobe, Michael Gough, Lynn Seymour. Norflicks Productions. Colour.
Children's serial based on the books by Angela Sommer-Bodenburg. A young boy, Anton (Stanton), befriends Rudiger (Dacks), who is the youngest member of an undead family. Horror veteran Gough turns up as an elder vampire.

LOVE, AMERICAN STYLE: *LOVE AND THE VAMPIRE*

USA, 1971. Dir: Charles Rondeau. With: Judy Carne, Robert Reed, Tiny Tim. Paramount. Colour.
Carne and Reed play a couple spending the night in a sinister mansion, where they encounter a vampire played by soprano-voiced singer Tiny Tim.

LOVE AND CURSES: *HABEAS CORPSES*

USA, 1991. With: Kate Hodge, Neil Dickson, Barry Van Dyke, Marta DuBois, Sandra Kerns. The Hollywood Premier Network. Colour.
This originally started out as *She-Wolf of London* (fourteen episodes) before changing its title and location for a further six episodes. In this story, werewolf student Randi Wallace (Hodge) and Prof Ian Matheson (Dickson) investigate a law firm supposedly run by vampires.

MADAME'S PLACE

USA, 1982. Dir: Paul Miller. With: Wayland Flowers, Susan Tolsky, Johnny Haymer, Judy Landers, Bill Kirchenbauer. Brad Lachman/Paramount. Colour.
Adult comedy series which combines puppets with live actors. In this episode, Kirchenbauer plays vampire Baron von Leer.

THE MAN FROM U.N.C.L.E.: *THE BAT CAVE AFFAIR*

USA, 1965 (1966). Dir: Alf Kjellin. With: Robert Vaughn, David McCallum, Leo G. Carroll, Martin Landau, Joan Freeman, Whit Bissell. Arena/NBC-TV. Colour.
UNCLE agents Napoleon Solo (Vaughn) and Illya Kuryakin (McCallum) and hillbilly clairvoyant Clemency McGill (Freeman) travel to Europe to stop vampiric THRUSH agent Count Zark (Landau, doing a

great Bela Lugosi impression) from using his radioactive bats to jam the world's radar systems.

MATINEE THEATER: *DRACULA*

USA, 1956. With: John Carradine. NBC-TV.

Who else but John Carradine could have portrayed the first television Dracula (with a moustache)? Originally broadcast live on 23 November 1956.

Remake: MYSTERY AND IMAGINATION: DRACULA (qv; 1969)

THE MONKEES: *THE MONSTROUS MONKEE MASH*

USA, 1967. Dir: James Frawley. With: David Jones, Micky Dolenz, Michael Nesmith, Peter Tork, Ron Masak, Arlene Martel. Raybert/ Columbia/NBC-TV. Colour.

In this episode of the popular musical comedy series, Count Dracula (Masak, with a Lugosi accent) and his vampiric daughter (Martel) want to turn Davy into one of the undead. Also includes a werewolf (David Pearl), a Frankenstein-like monster (Dick Karp) and a mummy (Bruce Barbour).

THE MONSTER SQUAD

USA, 1976. Dir: Jim Sheldon, Wes Kenney, Herman Hoffman and William P. D'Angelo. With: Fred Gandy, Mike Lane, Buck Kartalian, Henry Polic II. NBC-TV. Colour.

Thirteen episode series in which the monsters — Frankenstein, the Wolf Man (Kartalian, the star of *Please Don't Eat My Mother!* [1972]) and Dracula (Polic II) — pose as wax dummies in a museum by day and spend their nights fighting crime! The guest cast includes Billy Curtis, Marty Allen, Edward Andrews, Jonathan Harris, Julie Newmar and Geoffrey Lewis.

MONSTERS: *SHAVE AND A HAIRCUT, TWO BITES*

USA, 1990. Dir: John Strysik. With: Wil Wheaton, Matt LeBlanc, John O'Leary, Al Mancini. Laurel Entertainment. Colour.

Low budget shot-on-video horror series. Two kids think the town's barbers are vampires in this episode scripted by Dan Simmons and based on his own story.

THE VAMPIRE HUNTER

USA, 1988. With: Robert Lansing, John Bolger, Page Hannah. Laurel Entertainment. Colour.

The nephew of a vampire hunter bites off more than he can chew when trying to impress a lady.

THE WAITING GAME

USA, 1990. Dir: John Fox. With: Doug McKeon, Stephen Burleigh, Carrington Garland, Leo Garcia. Laurel Entertainment. Colour.

Following World War Three, vampires invade a deep-level fallout shelter and confront the surviving humans.

MR & MRS DRACULA

USA, 1980. Dir: Doug Rogers. With: Dick Shawn, Carol Lawrence, Anthony Battaglia, Gail Mayron, Barry Gordon, Ken Olfson. ABC-TV. Colour.

Shawn and Lawrence play the title characters, driven out of Transylvania, who relocate in the Bronx. Inspired by *Love at First Bite* (1979), this was the twenty-five minute pilot for a never-made sitcom series.

THE MUNSTERS

USA, 1964-66. With: Fred Gwynne, Yvonne De Carlo, Al Lewis, Butch Patrick, Beverly Owen, Pat Priest. Kayro-Vue Productions/Universal/ CBS-TV. B&W.

CBS's answer to ABC's slightly better *The Addams Family* features another group of friendly monsters: the Frankenstein monster-like Herman (Gwynne, who could wear the Karloff-style make-up because Universal studios owned the copyright), the vampiric Lily (De Carlo), Grandpa (Lewis, who is revealed to be Count Dracula himself), wolf boy Eddie (Patrick) and the 'horribly' normal Marilyn (played by both Owen and Priest). John Carradine originally turned down the role of Herman, but did appear in several episodes as Mr Gateman, the owner of the mortuary where Herman worked. It ran for seventy episodes and spawned two movies.

Sequel: SATURDAY SUPERSTAR MOVIE: MINI-MUNSTERS (qv; 1973)

THE MUNSTERS TODAY

USA, 1988-91. With: John Shuck, Lee Meriwether, Howard Morton, Hilary Van Dyke, Jason Marsden. MCA-TV. Colour.

Ill-conceived attempt to revive the popular 1960s series with an all-new cast. Morton plays the vampiric Grandpa in this shot-on-video disaster. Incredibly, it survived for seventy-two episodes — two more than the original series!

MYSTERY AND IMAGINATION: *CARMILLA*

UK, 1966. Dir: Bill Bain. With: Natasha Payne, Joseph O'Connor, Roy Marsden, Laurel Mather, Sonia Dresdel, Terence Bayler. ABC-TV. B&W.

Hour-long version of the classic story by Le Fanu.

Remake: CARMILLA (qv)

DRACULA

UK, 1969. Dir: Patrick Dromgoole. With: Denholm Elliott, Corin Redgrave, Suzanne Neve, Bernard Archard, Susan George, Joan Hickson. ABC-TV. Colour.

Faithful adaptation of Bram Stoker's novel, with Elliott as a bearded Count Dracula opposed by Archard's Professor Van Helsing. Also includes a trio of vampire women.

Remake: PURPLE PLAYHOUSE: DRACULA (qv; 1973)

FEET FOREMOST

UK, 1968. Dir: Toby Robertson. With: Neil Stacy, Fiona Hartford, Clive Morton, Timothy West, Fiona Walker. ABC-TV.

An old country manor is haunted by vampire/ghost Lady Eleanor (Walker). Based on a story by L.P. Hartley.

Remake: SHADES OF DARKNESS: FEET FOREMOST (qv; 1983)

NIGHTMARE CLASSICS: *CARMILLA*

USA, 1989. Dir: Gabrielle Beaumont. With: Meg Tilly, Ione Skye, Roy Dotrice, Roddy McDowall, Armelia McQueen, John Doolittle. Colour.

The setting for J. Sheridan Le Fanu's classic story is moved to a Southern plantation just after the American Civil War. Tilly stars as the young woman whose mysterious illness soon becomes apparent when a child is found sucked dry of blood.

LES NOUVELLES BRIGADES DU TIGRE: *LE VAMPIRE DES KARPATES*

France, 1982. Dir: Victor Vicas. With: Pinkas Braun, Arthur Brauss, Feodor Atkine, Jacques Buchelier, Claude Carvin, Gerard Couderc. A2/ TELEcip. Colour.

With the advent of talking pictures in 1929, many silent stars found themselves unable to adapt to the new technology. One such actor is Lucien Desormes (Brauss), who portrayed the Vampire of the Karpates. Rather than be forgotten by his public, Desormes hangs himself in his apartment. However, after his burial, a frightening silhouette — which looks like the undead monster he played on the screen — prowls the streets of Paris at night. After each sighting, a body is found...

OBAKE NO SAMBA, MON MON MONSTER

Japan, 1980. Dir: Yukito Aizawa. With: Hitoshi Omeae, Minorv Sado, Takeshi Sasano, Midori Fukuhara, Jiro Sakagami. Watanabe Kikaku/ Tokyo Hoso 12. Colour.

Musical sitcom featuring Dracula (Sado), the Wolf Man (Sasano) and the Frankenstein monster (Omeae). Whenever the latter drinks wine he turns gay!

THE PHIL SILVERS SHOW: *BILKO'S VAMPIRE*

USA, 1958. Dir: Al DeCaprio. With: Phil Silvers, Harvey Lembeck, Maurice Gosfield, Allen Melvin, Joe E. Ross. CBS-TV. B&W.

Made at the time when Universal's package of 'Shock Theater' movies first appeared on American television. When his regular poker game is repeatedly called off because of 'Shriek Theater' on TV, Sgt Ernest Bilko (Silvers) convinces Ritzik (Ross) that he is turning into a vampire and could be the next star of a Dracula series in Hollywood.

PLAY FOR TODAY: *VAMPIRES*

UK, 1970s. Dir: John Goldschmidt. With: Peter Moran, Paul Moran, Tommy White, Linda Beckett, Jimmy Coleman, Bert Edgar. BBC-TV. Colour.

An obsessed young man, Stu (Peter Moran), searches all over Liverpool for a traditional vampire. John G. Heller plays the object of his quest. Written by Dixie Williams.

PURPLE PLAYHOUSE: *DRACULA*

Canada, 1973. Dir: Jack Nixon Browne. With: Norman Welsh, Nehemiah Persoff, Blair Brown. Canadian Broadcasting Co. Colour.

Shot-on-video production which closely follows the Bram Stoker novel. Canadian actor Welsh plays a white-haired Count Dracula, thwarted by Persoff's Dr Van Helsing. Charlotte Hunt portrays the vampiric Lucy.

Remake: DRACULA (qv; 1982)

THE REAL GHOSTBUSTERS: *NO ONE COMES TO LUPUSVILLE*

Japan/USA, 1986. Voices: Arsenio Hall, Maurice La Marche, Lorenzo Music, Laura Summer, Frank Welker. Columbia Pictures Television. Colour.

Vampire episode of the popular children's cartoon series, based on the *Ghostbusters* movies.

ROD SERLING'S NIGHT GALLERY: *THE BIG SURPRISE*

USA, 1971. Dir: Jeannot Szwarc. With: Vincent Van Patten, Marc Vehanian, Eric Chase, John Carradine. Universal/NBC-TV. Colour.

An old eccentric farmer (Carradine) summons three boys and tells them where to dig for a big surprise. Scripted by Richard Matheson and based on his own story. Each of the episodes is introduced by Rod Serling.

DEATH ON A BARGE

USA, 1972 (1973). Dir: Leonard Nimoy. With: Robert Pratt, Lesley Ann Warren, Brooke Bundy, Lou Antonio, Jim Boles. Universal/NBC-TV. Colour.

Ron (Pratt) falls in love with a mysterious beauty, Hyacinth (Warren), who lives on a barge but will not allow the young man aboard. She is in fact a vampire, unable to cross the running water. Ron's jilted girlfriend, Phyllis (Bundy), decides to confront her rival...

THE DEVIL IS NOT MOCKED

USA, 1971. Dir: Gene Kearney. With: Helmut Dantine, Francis Lederer, Hank Brandt, Martin Kosleck. Universal/NBC-TV. Colour

During World War Two, Nazi General von Grunn (Dantine) invades an old Transylvanian castle which he suspects houses the leader of the local resistance movement. Instead, he discovers it belongs to Dracula (Lederer). Based on the story by Manly Wade Wellman.

THE FUNERAL

USA, 1972. Dir: John Meredyth Lucas. With: Werner Klemperer, Joe Flynn, Charles Macauley, Diana Hale, Leonidas Ossetynski. Universal/NBC-TV. Colour.

Vampire Ludwig Asper (Klemperer) returns from the dead for a more lavish burial. But funeral director Morton Silkline (Flynn) didn't count on the mourners being a witch, a hunchbacked assistant, a werewolf, a homicidal killer (with a Peter Lorre voice!), vampires and ghouls. Amusing episode, scripted by Richard Matheson and based on his own short story.

THE GIRL WITH HUNGRY EYES

USA, 1972. Dir: John Badham. With: James Farentino, Joanna Pettet, John Astin. Universal/NBC-TV. Colour.

The career of struggling photographer David Faulkner (Farentino) quickly takes off when the perfect model (Pettet) walks into his life. All she demands is that he must never follow her, but he soon suspects that she is involved in a series of mysterious deaths committed by a succubus. Based on the story by Fritz Leiber.

HOW TO CURE THE COMMON VAMPIRE

USA, 1972 (1973). Dir: Jack Laird. With: Richard Deacon, Johnny Brown, George Carlin, Rod Serling. Universal/NBC-TV. Colour.

Four men enter a crypt and prepare to dispatch a vampire. A tale with a great deal at stake.

A MATTER OF SEMANTICS

USA, 1971. Dir: Jack Laird. With: Cesar Romero, E.J. Parker. Universal/NBC-TV. Colour.

Count Dracula (Romero) visits the local blood bank and requests a withdrawal.

A MIDNIGHT VISIT TO THE NEIGHBORHOOD BLOOD BANK

USA, 1971. Dir: William Hale. With: Victor Buono. Universal/NBC-TV. Colour.

A vampire (Buono) visits the bedside of a young girl, only to be told that she gave earlier at the office...

MISS LOVECRAFT SENT ME

USA, 1971. Dir: Gene Kearney. With: Sue Lyon, Joseph Campanella. Universal/NBC-TV. Colour

When a vampire (Campanella) hires a blonde babysitter (Lyon), she ends up fleeing in terror.

SMILE PLEASE

USA, 1971 (1972). Dir: Jack Laird. With: Cesare Danova, Lindsay Wagner. Universal/NBC-TV. Colour.

Wagner plays a woman who visits an underground crypt to photograph a vampire (Danova).

SABRINA, THE TEENAGE WITCH

USA, 1971. Filmation/CBS-TV. Colour.

Half-hour animated series, based on the Archie comic book. Includes Cousin Drac and the rest of the monsters from *The Groovie Goolies* in supporting roles.

Sequel: SATURDAY SUPERSTAR MOVIE: PORKY PIG AND DAFFY DUCK MEET THE GROOVIE GOOLIES (qv; 1972)

SATURDAY SUPERSTAR MOVIE: *THE MAD, MAD MONSTERS*

USA, 1972. Dir: Steve Nakagawa. Rankin-Bass/ABC-TV. Colour.

Hour-long animated special. Baron von Frankenstein creates a bride for his monster and hires the ballroom of the Transylvania-Astoria for the wedding on Friday the 13th. Among the guests are his assistant Igor, the Invisible Man and his invisible wife, the Creature, the Mummy, the Wolf Man, Count Dracula and his vampiric offspring Boobula. This was a semi-sequel to the same producers' 1966 movie *Mad Monster Party?*.

MINI-MUNSTERS

USA, 1973. Voices: Al Lewis, Richard Long, Bob Diamond. ABC-TV. Colour.

Hour-long animated special, with Lewis recreating his role as Grandpa, and Long as the voice of Herman. A Dracula-type relative sends his two teenagers, the Frankenstein monster-like Igor and the vampiric Lucretia, to stay with the Munsters. The plot involves a hearse that runs on music, thereby eliminating the pollution caused by exhaust fumes.

Sequel: THE MUNSTERS TODAY (qv; 1988-91)

PORKY PIG AND DAFFY DUCK MEET THE GROOVIE GOOLIES

USA, 1972. Filmation/Warner Bros/ABC-TV. Colour.

Hour-long animated special in which Cousin Drac, Frankie and Wolfie from *The Groovie Goolies* TV series save a number of classic Warner Bros characters from a Phantom of the Opera-type villain. During the climax, the monsters appear in live action.

SHADES OF DARKNESS: *FEET FOREMOST*

UK, 1983. With: Carol Royle, Jeremy Kemp. Granada Television. Colour.

The ghost haunting an old country manor turns out to be a vampire. Scriptwriter Alan Plater updates L.P. Hartley's story to a contemporary setting.

SLEDGE HAMMER!: *THE LAST OF THE RED HOT VAMPIRES*

USA, 1987. Dir: Bill Bixby. With: David Rasche, Anne-Marie Martin, Harrison Page, Bud Cort, Bernie Kopell, Deborah Wakeham. New World Television/Alan Spencer Productions. Colour.

A legendary film star who portrayed vampires returns from the grave in this cop comedy.

THE SONNY AND CHER COMEDY HOUR

USA, 1972. With: Sonny, Cher, Jerry Lewis, Ted Ziegler. Colour.

This Hallowe'en episode includes Dracula as a guest.

STARSKY & HUTCH: *THE VAMPIRE*

USA, 1976. Dir: Bob Kelljan (Robert Kelljchian). With: David Soul, Paul Michael Glaser, Antonio Fargas, Bernie Hamilton, John Saxon, Coleen Camp. Spelling-Goldberg/ABC-TV. Colour.

In a break from the usual car chases, the two undercover buddy-cops confront Saxon's inexplicable vampire, Rene Nadasy. From the director of the Count Yorga films and the *Blacula* sequel.

STRUCK BY LIGHTNING

USA, 1979. Dir: Joel Zwicke. With: Jack Elam, Jeffrey Kramer, Millie Slavin, Jonathan Goldsmith. The Fellows-Keegan Company/Paramount. Colour.

The third episode of this short-lived sitcom features the aging Frankenstein monster (veteran Elam) mixed up in the making of a horror movie. He thinks Dracula (Goldsmith) is real and tries to stake him.

***Above:** Purple Playhouse: Dracula. (FJA).*

SUPERBOY: *RUN DRACULA, RUN*

USA, 1990. Dir: Richard Lewis. With: Gerard Christopher, Stacy Haiduk, Kevin Bernhardt, Louise Seeger Crune. Cantharus Productions/ Alexander & Ilya Salkind. Colour.

Syndicated (1988-91) half-hour adventures of the Boy of Steel (Christopher, who replaced John Haymes Newton for the second and third seasons), from the producers of the *Superman* movies. When a young intern (Bernhardt) has his anti-vampire serum stolen, he reverts into a bloodsucker and turns Lana Lang (Haiduk) into a vampire. She then trys to put the bite on Superboy. Shot on video

YOUNG DRACULA

USA, 1989. Dir: David Nutter. With: Gerard Christopher, Stacy Haiduk, Kevin Bernhardt, Lloyd Bochner, Dennis Neal. Cantharus Productions/Alexander & Ilya Salkind. Colour.

Bernhardt (*Hellraiser III: Hell on Earth* [1992]) plays a young visiting intern seeking a cure for his vampirism by modern medicine. However, he is pursued by an older vampire (Bochner) who doesn't want him cured.

SUPERNATURAL: *DORABELLA*

UK, 1977. Dir: Simon Langton. With: Jeremy Clyde, David Robb, Ania Marson, John Justin, Esmond Knight, Jonathan Hyde. BBC-TV. Colour.

Short-lived series set in Victorian times. Each guest star has to recount a tale of the supernatural to gain entrance to the Club of the Damned. This story involves two young men who fall in love with Dorabella (Marson), a beautiful vampire woman who lures them to the castle of her undead father (veteran Justin).

SUSPENSE: *VAMP TIL DEAD*

USA, 1951. With: Mary Sinclair. B&W.

Vampire episode of this early TV fantasy series.

TALES FROM THE CRYPT: *THE RELUCTANT VAMPIRE*

USA, 1991. Dir: Elliot Silverstein. With: Malcolm McDowell, Sandra Searles Dickinson, George Wendt, Michael Berryman, Paul Gleason, Gloria Dawson. Home Box Office. Colour.

Cable TV series based on the EC comic books of the 1950s. Longtooth (McDowell) is a queasy vampire who gets a job in a blood bank. However, he has to replace the blood he steals when his boss (Wendt) notices the shortage. Berryman turns up as Van Helsing.

THE SECRET

USA, 1990. Dir: Michael Riva. With: Larry Drake, Grace Zabriskie, Mike Simmrin, Georgann Johnson, Stella Hall, William Frankfather. Home Box Office. Colour.

A young orphan boy is adopted by a wealthy, reclusive couple who turn out to be vampires fattening him up for dinner. In the 'twist' ending, the potential victim turns out to be a werewolf.

WEREWOLF CONCERTO

USA, 1992. Dir: Steve Perry. With: Timothy Dalton, Dennis Farina, Walter Gotell, Charles Fleischer, Reginald Veljohnson, Beverly D'Angelo. Home Box Office. Colour.

It's the old vampire versus werewolf plot as a number of suspicious guests in a remote hotel are killed off by a murderous shape-changer.

TALES FROM THE DARKSIDE: *THE CIRCUS*

USA, 1986. Dir: Michael Gornick. With: William Hickey, Kevin O'Connor, Jacques Sandulescu, David Thorton, Ed French. Laurel Entertainment. Colour.

George A. Romero wrote this episode of the low budget, shot-on-video horror series, based on a story by Sydney J. Bounds. A showman (Hickey) keeps a Nosferatu-like vampire, a werewolf and a mummy amongst his attractions.

MY GHOSTWRITER, THE VAMPIRE

USA, 1987. Dir: Frank de Palma. With: Jeff Conaway, Roy Dotrice, Jillie Mack, Chi Chi Navarro. Laurel Entertainment. Colour.

A hack horror writer (Conaway) gets a best-selling book out of the life of a 900 year-old Dracula-type (Dotrice) who wants a safe place to hide his coffin. Based on a story by Scott Edelman.

STRANGE LOVE

USA, 1986. Dir: Ted Gershuny. With: Harsh Nayyar, Patrick Kilpatrick, Marcia Cross. Laurel Entertainment. Colour.

A doctor in the 1930s helps a married couple who turn out to be vampires. However, the undead wife falls in love with him.

THRILLER: *MASQUERADE*

(UK: BORIS KARLOFF PRESENTS)

USA, 1961. Dir: Herschel Daugherty. With: Elizabeth Montgomery, Tom Poston, John Carradine, Jack Lambert, Dorothy Neumann. Hubbell Robinson Productions/Universal/ NBC-TV. B&W.

Ghoulishly funny chiller, based on a short story by Henry Kuttner. Modern honeymooners Montgomery and Poston take refuge for the night in a run down old dark house belonging to a trio of creepy hillbillies, led by Carradine. He scares his guests with tales of local vampire attacks, but in the twist ending it is the young couple who turn out to be undead. Filmed on the *Psycho* sets, and introduced by Boris Karloff.

TREMPLIN

France, 1969. Dir: Henri Dassa and Bernard Soulie. With: Bernard Soulie.

Soulie portrays Count Dracula in this French TV production.

THE TWILIGHT ZONE: *MONSTERS!*

USA, 1986. Dir: B.W.L. Norton. With: Ralph Bellamy, Oliver Robins, Kathleen Lloyd, Bruce Solomon, Lewis Dauber. CBS Entertainment Productions/Persistence of Vision. Colour.

During a lonely summer, Toby (Robins), a young horror film fan, befriends a strange old man, Emile Francis Bendictson (Bellamy), who claims to be a 147 year-old vampire. Tired of his undead existence, he tells the boy he has returned home to die, but warns that midnight holds monsters much worse than vampires... A nicely sentimental horror story, with a wonderful performance by veteran Bellamy.

RED SNOW

USA, 1986. Dir: Jeannot Szwarc. With: George Dzundza, Barry Miller, Vladimir Skomarovsky, Victoria Tennant, Rod Colbin. CBS Entertainment Productions/Persistence of Vision. Colour.

Ordered to investigate the unusual deaths of two Party members near the Arctic circle, a sympathetic KGB Colonel (Dzundza) travels to a Siberian village where it remains dark for most of the year. His investigations uncover a community of vampires dating back to Stalin's rule who live in symbiosis with the exiled dissidents. A clever script (by Michael Cassutt), strong performances and good special effects help make this one of the better new *Twilight Zone* episodes.

TWIST IN THE TALE: *THE NOMADS*

USA, 1977. With: David Birney. A Quinn Martin Production. Colour.

A Vietnam veteran (Birney), recovering from a mental breakdown, discovers that space-roving vampires are about to take over the Earth. The problem is that no-one will believe him.

UPIOR

Poland, 1967. Dir: Stanislaw Lenartowicz. With: Jan Machulski, Aleksandra Zawieruszanka, Jadwiga Chojnacka, Zdzislaw Marczewski, Ryszard Ronczewski, W. Pyrkosz. KADR Film Unit. Colour.

Half-hour short film about a young man (Machulski) at a ball, who rescues the heroine from other guests who are vampires. It apparently has a rational explanation with a twist ending. The title translates as *Vampire*.

VIRTUAL MURDER: *A DREAM OF DRACULA*

UK, 1992. Dir: Philip Draycott. With: Nicholas Clay, Kim Thomson, Ronald Fraser, Jill Gascoine, Alfred Marks, Peggy Mount. BBC Pebble Mill. Colour.

Is Dracula really kidnapping young women and draining their blood? Or are criminal psychologist Dr John Cornelius (Clay) and Samantha Valentine (Thomson) hunting someone with a vampire fixation? Julian Clary plays a flamboyant coffin-maker and Fraser turns up as Van Helsing in this episode of the shot-on-video comedy/thriller series.

WIDE WORLD OF ENTERTAINMENT: *HORROR HALL OF FAME — A MONSTER SALUTE*

USA, 1974. With: Vincent Price. ABC-TV. Colour.

Documentary in which Price performs a brief scene from *Dracula* and vampire expert/author Raymond T. McNally appears wearing a Dracula cape. Also includes clips from *Mark of the Vampire* (1935), *Dracula Has Risen from the Grave* (1968) and *Blacula* (1972).

YOU ASKED FOR IT

USA, 1954. With: Art Baker, Bela Lugosi. ABC-TV. B&W.

At a viewer's request, Lugosi plays Dracula, summoned by his servant to rise from his coffin. He then performs his 'Vampire Bat Illusion'. Out of character, he tells emcee Baker that he will soon star in a TV series called *Dr. Acula*. It was never made.

Appendix 2:

Index of Film Reviews

Index

Bibliography

I am indebted to the authors and editors of the following books and magazines which were consulted in the compilation of this work:

Asian Trash Cinema
The Aurum Film Encyclopedia: Horror (Aurum Press, 1985) edited by Phil Hardy
The Aurum Film Encyclopedia: Science Fiction (Aurum Press, 1991) edited by Phil Hardy
Castle of Frankenstein
Cinefantastique
The Dracula Book (The Scarecrow Press, 1975) by Donald F. Glut
L'Ecran Fantastique
Fangoria
Femme Fatales
Focus on Film No15
Hoffman's Guide to SF, Horror and Fantasy Movies 1991-92 (Corgi Books, 1991)
Hollywood Gothic (W. W. Norton & Company, 1990) by David J. Skal
Horror and Science Fiction Films (The Scarecrow Press, 1972, 1982, 1984; three volumes) by Donald C. Willis
Horror Film Stars (McFarland, 1981) by Michael R. Pitts
Horror in the Cinema (A. Zwemmer/A. S. Barnes, 1970) by Ivan Butler
Horror Movies: An Illustrated Survey (Secker & Warburg, 1967) by Carlos Clarens
Impact
John McCarty's Official Splatter Movie Guide Volume 2 (St. Martin's Press, 1992)
Karloff the Man, the Monster, the Movies (Curtis Books, 1973) by Denis Gifford
Leonard Maltin's TV Movies and Video Guide (Signet/New American Library)
Mad Movies
Midnight Marquee No30
Movie Monsters (Studio Vista/Dutton, 1969) by Denis Gifford
Nightmare Movies (Harmony Books, 1989) by Kim Newman
Photon No18, No19 and No21
Psychotronic
The Psychotronic Encyclopedia of Film (Ballantine Books, 1983) by Michael Weldon
Reference Guide to Fantastic Films (Chelsea-Lee Books, 1972, 1973, 1974; three volumes) compiled by Walt Lee
The Seal of Dracula (Lorrimer Publishing, 1975/Minoustchine, 1976) by Barrie Pattison
Shock Xpress
Shock Xpress 1 (Titan Books, 1991) edited by Stefan Jaworzyn
Starburst
Video Watchdog
Video Watchdog Book (Video Watchdog, 1992) by Tim Lucas
We Are the Weird

and, of course, Forry Ackerman's *Famous Monsters of Filmland*, which began it all for me twenty-eight years ago.

Above: *Dracula (1958).*